CHILDREN OF GODS & MONSTERS

Book Two of the Aurorian Trilogy

Lacie M. Lou

Overcaffeinated Author Publishing LLC

Identifiers: ISBN 978-1-963955-02-6 (paperback) | ISBN 978-1-963955-03-3 (e-book) | LCCN 2024918641

Book Cover by David Gardias

Chapter Illustrations by Lacie M. Lou

First edition 2024

*Never dim your light to make those who sit
in the dark more comfortable.
Burn so brightly that they can't ignore you.*

Content Warnings

Discussion of Past Trauma

Allusion to Sexual Assault

Child Abuse
(via memory flashback)

Blood / Gore

Torture
(on page)

Motherhood
(secondary character, no depiction of birth)

Prologue

HANDS REACH FOR ME. They stretch from the inky darkness, pawing at my arms that I've drawn close to protect my face. Nails claw across my skin.

I scream. It's a guttural screech, akin to that of a trapped animal. My arms are useless in blocking the clawed fingers from reaching me.

My cries go unheard.

Behind the outstretched, shadowy hands lie dozens of glowing red eyes. Eyes that hold ravenous, predatory hunger–for me.

I gasp and shoot upright, my panicked eyes taking in the quiet room around me. My breath comes in short pants. The soft fabric of my shirt sticks to my soaked, sweaty skin.

The calm dark of the night settles around me, the clawed hands no longer reaching from the shadows to steal me away.

It was only a dream. I try to convince myself with a sigh of relief.

From the corner of the room one pair of unblinking, red eyes watches me. I stare back, daring them to blink first.

Eliana

"**S**TAY WITH ME ELIANA," a scared voice whispers over me.

Worried voices in hushed tones argue with one another from somewhere near me. I want to know what they're talking about. I lift my hand, and a blinding pain radiates from my gut. My hand falls back limply to my side. At least I think it does. Every part of me is burning with pain.

A dagger stabbed into my gut. My dagger.

Who stabbed me? Cire. No, not Cire–Vaiccar.

I freed Vaiccar.

I moan from the pain. A cool, damp cloth dabs at my forehead, the motion so achingly familiar. If I open my eyes it won't be my mother, and so I keep them closed, content to pretend she's caring for me as I die.

Am I dying? I think to myself. *Is this what dying feels like?*

"What do we do?"

"My *Amorei*, we must return to the Burroughs with the others. Eliana needs more care than we can provide."

"But–"

"I know, my *Amorei*. I know. There's nothing we can do for him now."

A sob is choked down, and the hand dabbing my forehead trembles. I want to comfort them, but my body is on fire.

Strong arms fold around me, cradling my body and lifting me up. A cool breeze caresses my skin, and I sigh with relief. The searing pain temporarily subsides.

"Almost there, Eliana," a deep voice murmurs over me.

"Mythica, there's no time to explain."

"Oh my stars, what happened?" A soft, wrinkled hand brushes over my forehead. "She's burning up. Take her to Pyria."

The strong arms holding me jostle. A soft "sorry" is whispered to me, I think. I leave the warmth of their embrace for the soft comfort of a blanket.

"Pyria, can you help her? She was stabbed ..." The voices grow quieter as they move away from me. I strain my ears to listen. "... something else wrong ... poison perhaps."

Six weeks have passed since I was rescued from the Aceolevia, the Haematitian Council's stronghold. Six weeks since I was stabbed by a monster wearing Cire's face and Kai was left behind at the mercy of that monster. Since I first connected to my magic.

I was brought back to the Burroughs, my people's name for the hideout they've carved for themselves in the very mountains our ancestors turned to for protection when they fled after the Great War. The camp is always bustling with energy as my people carry out the daily chores of maintaining our makeshift home. There's the work of tending to the crops we have managed to coax into growing in the near darkness of the mountain cavern, the business of foraging the mountains and surrounding forest for food, and the dangerous task of scouting for and hunting dark beasts.

Every day there are reports of a sighting, and at least once a week someone successfully hunts a monster down, putting the poor animal, or person, out of its misery. More and more the beasts are warped people, twisted by the darkness and malevolent magic of the plague that's spread further into our valley, bringing with it blight and monsters. No one has been lost, yet, but it's only a matter of time before Vaiccar's dark influence claims one of our own.

If the mundane day to day responsibilities were not enough for our small group to manage, there's now the added work of beginning lessons to master the elemental magic that's begun to resurface randomly amongst the young and old of our clan. With the resurgence of elemental gifts comes a lot of complications. It's been one hundred years since anyone in Hevastia's harnessed natural magic, and all knowledge of the skills has since died out. My hope lies in the written accounts of those who lived before magic disappeared.

When Kai shattered the siphon stones surrounding Hevastia's Heart, Lady Hevastia's magic was released, no longer confined by the crystal prisons. During the same fight where Kai restored magic, my blood was shed over the Heart, triggering the Aurorian Prophecy and releasing Vaiccar from the spiritual prison he's been trapped in for several millennia, allowing him to take permanent residence in Cire's body.

I don't remember much after Vaiccar plunged my dagger into my gut and shed my blood, fulfilling the prophecy's conditions of his release. Alana claims I became possessed by Lady Hevastia's spirit, burning white with unfathomably hot fire, and announced the prophecy before her spirit disappeared. I haven't been able to reconnect with my magic, Lady Hevastia, or Princess Atrya since then.

I set down my quill, unsure of where to begin writing. The ink splotch soaks into my parchment, a dark blot on an otherwise clean page. I sit fully up, fluffing the pillow behind me. I have been on strict bed rest since I was brought home, constantly being doted on by Hama, and even Alana. I think they both choose to busy themselves worrying over me rather than confronting the brutal truth of Cire and Kai's fates. I swallow a lump in my throat. They're not the only ones trying to distract themselves from painful thoughts.

Lady Hevastia please protect him. For the third time today, I plead with the stars to protect Kai. I don't know whether my cries for aid go unheard, or what Kai's fate is.

Hama told me when I first awoke that my wound had become infected. Vaiccar must have poisoned the blade before stabbing me. My fingers gingerly run across the ragged stitches on my stomach, a now constant reminder of what I'm up against. And how woefully unprepared for it I am.

I set my journal aside and grab my mother's journal from her early days as chieftess. With strict orders to rest and recover, I have been using the time to learn more about our history and magic, about my role as the auror, and about my mother. When I first opened her journal, I hadn't realized it was hers. My mother had neat, orderly handwriting, every word deliberate. This journal is filled with hastily scrawled thoughts in sloppy, looping handwriting.

My fingers trail along the latest page I've marked, careful not to tear the parchment as I fold the corner. Mythica will kill me if she catches me committing such *crimes* against her books, as she claims, but it is the simplest way to track the small breadcrumbs of information this journal has provided about one of the greatest mysteries of my life. *Who is my father?*

As a small girl, I begged my mother for any information about my father, desperate for some connection to a faceless ghost that haunted me in my dreams. Her responses were so vague, the only proof he ever lived was in the truth of my own existence. Was she haunted by his ghost too? I'm still desperate to know.

Sometimes she would surprise me and tell me he was kind-hearted, gentle-natured, strong, and capable. She claimed I got my wild spirit from her, but my gentle and nurturing nature from him. At six years old, I easily accepted these little nuggets, tucking them close to my heart. As a rebellious teen, I would push her to tell me more, still searching for my features in a man's face in our village, on every merchant that passed through–to no avail. Finally, when I was fourteen, she admitted that he had been a traveling merchant, and that he had never returned to our village. The truth somehow hurt worse than longing to know, and I secretly wished to go back to ignorance and young, childish hope.

If it pained my mother to admit that he left and never came back, she never let on. I mostly saw her strength, her undying love for our people, and her sense of duty above all else. Around me stands the reminder of how much my people have rebuilt without her guidance, and I know that despite the hardship and mistakes, she would be proud of our resilience. Her eyes would glisten with pride for my dedication to righting the wrongs committed against all of Hevastia–that I had risen from the ashes to bear the burden of being the auror willingly.

I flip the page to the next entry.

Entry 257

The Elders met with me again this evening. No matter how many times I assure them, they continue to press me to maintain the line of succession. Elder Sebastian dared to give me one month to make my choice. One month! The audacity of men to tell a woman what to do with her body.

I stormed out of the council hall, choosing to pace the fence line north of the village, where the fields lead to the base of the mountains and the sky opens up to show the gods and all their stars. I admit that my outburst was not very chieftess-like, but they make me so mad!

A note is scratched into the margins of the entry. I squint, the words are in the same handwriting, but cramped along the edge of the page. I read them aloud.

"I pray to Lady Hevastia to guide me." The words dissipate into the air of my empty tent, held close like a secret kept.

My eyes return to the page, eagerly scanning for the next note, hope, and gut-clenching anxiety, a storm raging in my gut.

Entry 258

Two weeks have passed. I have not spoken with the Elders of the choice I must make. It's hardly a choice if one is being forced to choose between duty to the prophecy and duty to one's own self.

A travel caravan arrived this morning, the last of this season. It was led by Ryder, now a young man of twenty. He is an orphan of our village, adopted by a young merchant

couple fifteen years ago on their last trip through the mountains. It's been a long time since our people have seen him. I watched from the sidelines as the merchants traded with our trappers for pelts, our farmers for grain, and our craftspeople for homemade goods. It was as Gurdiele and a merchant were haggling over the worth of a spool of fresh spun wool that Ryder approached me.

We had been friends as children, many, many years ago. Tonight, Ryder and his fellow merchants joined us for a harvest feast as we ate, drank, and danced around the fire. They told stories of their harrowing travels across the land, and of the people they met in each village. All the time, Ryder sat close to me and his presence was not unwelcome.

My finger traces the deep groove where the quill pressed too hard on the parchment, the words "duty to one's self" underlined so harshly the paper is almost torn.

Entry 259

The caravan has stayed with us for two weeks, far longer than anyone expected. This morning I invited Ryder to join me on a trip into the forest, up into the mountains—claiming that he deserved the opportunity to connect with his "ancestral land." The council whispers of the prophecy less these days, content to watch and wait.

Entry 260

The Council of Elders called a meeting for tonight. I'm expected to announce that I've made my choice in Ryder. I haven't told him yet of what's expected of me, of what would be asked of him if he were to accept my proposal. I plan to tell him everything tonight, to ask him to stay here with me. Oh stars, I hope he says yes.

The ink smudges, wiped away with a wet cloth and a patient, diligent hand. The writing over the dark stain is more restrained, and neat rather than the fast scrawl of the previous sentence. Unease settles into my gut.

I was found several yards into the treeline, tangled in a bramble. Barely conscious and beaten.

Someone carried me back to the village, calling for a healer. It's been two days and I am still not ready to talk to anyone. I've been told the merchant caravan left to return down the mountain, and as it rolled out I think I took a breath for the first time in days.

There was a witness, or so I've been told. I told Ryder how I felt, and he was elated. Perhaps the responsibility of ensuring a female heir frightened him. I don't understand what went wrong.

Upon hearing the witness's account, several of our strongest hunters took to the mountain path, and when they came upon the caravan, they took revenge upon them all, bringing Ryder back alive to face trial for his crimes.

Entry 261

Two weeks have passed. Ryder stood trial for his actions yesterday. The Council of Elders sentenced him to death by 100 cuts. He was carried to the depths of the forest, far from the village borders, and left for dead.

Entry 262

Two months since. This morning, I couldn't hold down my breakfast. Pyria thinks I am pregnant. Lady Hevastia, help me.

A note in my mother's handwriting is neatly written in the margin.

The Council of Elders never discussed the prophecy with me again.

A single tear splatters against the parchment as the words begin to blur before my watery eyes. I close the journal, and begin to sob.

The burden my mother wrote of in her letter to me, it wasn't about being an auror at all. She had no idea I was gifted. It was about being forced to perpetuate the blood line, the prophecy line.

Another large sob racks my body.

My mother had that choice taken from her.

I tuck my knees close, my stitches straining with the movement, but I grit my teeth and continue to cry. I shed tears for my mother, finally releasing all the sadness and emotions I have tried to keep buried for these past six weeks and in the months since I lost her.

There's a soft whoosh as the tent flap is drawn aside. The crunch of boots on stone stops in front of me. My cot bounces with the weight of someone sitting next to me. I breathe in slowly and exhale. Strong arms fold around me, pulling me close, and I lean into them, pretending with eyes closed that this person is my mother, even for only a moment. When I finally calm enough to open my bloodshot eyes, Alana's concerned face watches mine.

"Is everything okay, Eliana?" Her voice rings with concern that pulls down her fierce features.

I sniffle loudly, wiping my snotty nose on the back of my grubby sleeve. "Yes, I'm fine."

Alana squeezes my hand, a knowing expression crossing her face as she gently wipes my tears, waiting for me to say more.

I sigh heavily. "Alana, have you ever wanted to know something so badly, but when you find out the truth it's worse than anything you ever feared? This truth ... cuts deeper than any sword. It changes everything."

"You don't have to tell me what you've learned in that book of yours," she says as she taps my mother's journal, "but, whatever it is, the past simply cannot be rewritten. Though it may hurt, the truth of the past does not define the course of the future, you choose what to do with this information and how it affects you."

I sniffled more softly this time. My hands are in my lap, my fingers knotting together and falling apart as I fidget to help with my nerves.

"It's ... made me view my life differently. I always knew there was so much of my mother's life that I would never learn about, that I secretly hoped someday she would share with me. But what I learned ... it's so horrible. To have found out in this way, it's almost a betrayal of her trust. She must have been hurting so much, and I never knew."

"Does it make you think differently of her?"

"No, I still think of her as the same strong, caring, and loving mother she was to me and our people my whole life. I appreciate her resiliency and strength more. I wish it had not been born of such horrific circumstances." My voice falls quiet.

Alana's strong hand grips my shoulder, giving it a soft shake. "She will always be your mother, a complex woman forged by her own life's experiences—as you are. Her identity's not changed, despite your shift in perception or understanding of her experiences."

"I wish she had told me."

"Perhaps she was trying to spare you this pain." In Alana's eyes is understanding and compassion. A shared pain.

"Still," I sigh, wiping my eyes. "All those times I asked, how that must have felt like a fresh wound to remind her of the worst day of her life."

"That's one one to look at it. From everything I've heard about your mother, her life was filled with her love for you. It doesn't completely erase that ache, but I choose to think your mother felt gratitude for her beautiful life with you."

Kai

THE MOSS GROWING ALONG the aged stones of the ceiling is a browning green color, barely holding on to life as it climbs from the outer wall of the cell into the rank depths of the dungeon. My jaw clenches, a groan of pain escaping as I turn my body toward the *solari,* their light barely shining into my cell through the sliver cut out of the stone.

My last memory before waking in this dank cell was of Cire's warm breath on my neck as the imposter possessing his body threatened me with all varieties of torture. His eyes were void of life, so cold and merciless. The memory of his smile–all teeth and no joy–sends a chill down my arms.

If I had to guess, I have been trapped in this gods-forsaken cell for approximately two weeks. In that time, Not-Cire hasn't made an appearance, but the same boy I scared last time I resided in this cell, Larsus, brings down stale bread crusts and dirty water twice a day. My body grows weak from malnourishment and unclean water. If I don't succumb to the torture, the food is sure to take me eventually.

I close my eyes and lean my head against the stone, letting my imagination take me away from the dank cell, awful food, and the suffocating aloneness.

The temple's outdoor garden comes into view in my mind's eye. It's an early spring day, and the ground is dotted with fresh growth. Buds are just beginning to form on the large tree in the far corner. The soft gurgling of the fountain breaks the silence of the serene garden. I breathe deeply, enjoying the smell of the ground after a rain shower, the feel of the solari warming my skin.

I open my eyes to small, chubby fingers extended into the air as I wiggle them, casting shadows over my face from staring into the solari. The giggle of another child pulls my attention away from the sky and back to the garden I stand in. Their laughter echoes across the stone walkway and I follow it, sneaking along the path, hiding behind tall, overgrown plants not yet trimmed for the fresh season.

There! A shoe sticks out from behind the base of one of the statues scattered throughout the garden. This one in particular shows a woman with outstretched arms holding a ball of light, represented by a yellow crystal nested in the palm of her hands.

I creep forward and pounce on the young boy hiding behind the statue, Cire. He kicks at me, trying to escape, but I'm stronger, and I pin him in place, declaring victory with a whoop and holler. We both laugh riotously, enjoying the game and each other's company on this rare occasion to play and miss classes. The other boys and Sefrina, the only girl in our class, chose to go to the swimming pond for the day, but Cire and I asked to stay back and spend our free day in the garden.

"Kai, do you think someday we will have a statue in a garden somewhere?" Cire asks, laying down so that our heads are next to each other, lying opposite directions, facing the sky. He sighs contentedly.

"I'm not sure. We would probably have to do something incredibly powerful to get a statue," I reply logically. "High Priestess Tallulah is more powerful than us. Surely she will get a statue someday."

A shadow blocks the solari, casting me and Cire into the shade.

"Only those who wish to live in infamy seek to have their likeness cast in stone. I seek a humble life in grand service to the True Faith," a voice coming from the tall shadow replies. I pull myself onto my elbows and squint into the solari. High Priestess Tallulah smiles kindly down at me and Cire.

"High Priestess," I squeak, jumping to attention. Cire grunts as he pulls himself up from the ground to stand beside me. "We didn't hear you enter the garden."

"Kai, Cire," she says, her hands extended to each of us. I place my hand in her own, and she begins to lead us out of the garden. "Have you been enjoying your day free of studies?"

"Most definitely!" Cire declares, smiling ear to ear. "Kai and I were playing hide and seek in the garden. We're going to run foot races in the grand entrance hall next."

High Priestess Tallulah laughs, and it's a beautiful sound. "Is that so?" she asks, the laughter now spreading to her eyes that twinkle in the light. "Well, if you're too busy, then perhaps I won't invite you to join me for an afternoon meal."

"We can join you," I reply before Cire can respond. He glares at me behind High Priestess Tallulah's back, sticking out his tongue. I scrunch my nose at him in response, daring him to say something about it.

"Ah, you're too kind," High Priestess Tallulah says, winking at me. I blush, realizing she caught Cire and I making faces behind her back. We continue following her deeper into the temple to her private study. It's one of my favorite rooms in the Aceolevia. It smells like the old books the High Priestess collects and the flowers she propagates to plant in the garden.

She motions for us to sit down, and Cire and I race to reach the bigger chair across from her desk. Cire cheats, tripping me. As I fall, my hand accidentally catches a large vase, and it lands on the floor next to me, shattering into a hundred fragments. Tears well in my eyes, and Cire gasps. High Priestess Tallulah clucks her tongue, tutting over Cire's behavior. I clutch my hand in my lap, blood already dripping onto my shoes from where the vase cut me.

"Kai, go visit Miss Agnus and Healer Truily." High Priestess Tallulah has her back to me, her attention on Cire who now cowers from her in the large chair. "I need to have a word with Cire over his behavior."

"High–" I whimper, trying to draw her attention to me. "I'm sorry."

She glances back at me and gives me a brief smile despite the anger flaring in her eyes. "It's not your fault, Kai. Now run along."

"Yes, High Priestess." I step carefully over the broken vase pieces and to the door, opening and shutting it quickly. My throbbing hand demands I leave immediately to visit the healers, but I stop and press my ear against the door, listening. The voices are muffled on the other side.

"Cire, you disappoint me again. Have I not been explicitly clear with you?" High Priestess Tallulah's voice is sharp. "Kai is not to bleed. His blood is sacred, special." The soft echo of the smack of

a hand on a soft cheek carries through the door. "You are nothing without him. Do not ever let this happen again." Another smack. "Have I been clear?"

"Yes, High Priestess," Cire mumbles.

"Give me your hand," High Priestess Tallulah snarls, snapping her fingers with impatience. "Three cuts this time in tithe for your actions. One for being childish, the second for injuring Kai, and the third for breaking my favorite vase."

I press my ear closer to the door and gasp quietly when High Priestess Tallulah pulls her dagger from its metal sheath on her hip. Cire whimpers as the dagger is drawn across his palm. A hot tear slides down my cheek, and I swipe it away with my non-bloodied hand before turning away to hurry to the healers. A man with red eyes stands in the shadows, staring at me. My face heats with a deep blush at being caught while eavesdropping. I run. High Priestess Tallulah will be upset if she finds out I allowed more of my blood to be spilled.

A sharp pain in my side pulls me from the childhood memory. I wipe the sleep from my eyes and open them to Cire's face directly in front of my own. I yell out, swinging at him, but my body is so weak that my arm barely moves from my side before falling back into my lap. He laughs deeply, a noise unlike Cire's true laugh, despite coming from his mouth. Another testament to the otherness lurking under his skin.

"Pleasant nap, I hope," Not-Cire says, smiling cruelly. "I didn't mean to interrupt." He snaps his fingers and two Morei guardians, men I don't recognize, come into the cell.

There's a quick shuffle of bare feet on wet stone as Larsus scurries in after them, bending down to unchain my ankle. The weight of the manacle falls off, and I roll my ankle, flexing my left foot for the first time since being brought back here. Rough hands grab me by the shoulders, hauling me out of the cell. I don't recognize these men in Morei uniforms as they drag me by the armpits. I try feebly to shake them off, but my efforts are met with gruff laughs and a lot more jostling as they carry me further into the dungeon, back to the room that reeks of stale blood.

I remember the last time I was strapped to this table, when High Priest Marius drugged me with that unknown dark liquid.

Is that liquid responsible for Cire acting differently?

I struggle against the restraints as the guardians clamp large, heavy manacles around my arms and legs, leaving me to lie prone on the table. The sound of boots on stone echoes down the hallway and into this high-ceilinged chamber. Hooks and other gruesome tools hang from the ceiling on blood crusted chains. A cold sweat begins to crawl over my body, my heart beating faster with fear.

Not-Cire brings his face close to mine again and smiles. "Hello, Kai. We haven't been properly introduced. My name is Vaiccar."

I grunt as I pull against the restraints, leaning closer to spit in his face. He growls with disgust and raises the back of his hand as if to hit me, but thinks better of it.

"I don't give a shit who you are, asshole," I growl at him.

"You're going to regret doing that," Vaiccar hisses. "I have the means of hurting you in ways you cannot yet fathom." He leans in so close that the heat of his breath brushes against my ear as he whispers, "So, if I were you, I would work to stay on my good side."

He picks up a rather nasty saw from the table, turning it in the torchlight. I swallow, trying to hide my fear. He sets the saw down, grabbing a shiny handle with a tiny, thin blade attached on the end.

"This one is new, but I heard it cuts skin like an oar through still water." His teeth flash, twisting Cire's handsome face into a gruesome visage. "Let's see if the rumor is true."

Vaiccar leans over me, sliding the thin blade across my left bicep, slowly drawing it across the muscle, bearing down on it harder as he cuts me. I cry out in pain, my throat sore from lack of water these past weeks.

He lifts the blade and proceeds to draw two more lines. All the while I scream, thrashing my body against the table, unable to escape. When he's satisfied, Vaiccar sits down on a high stool next to me, wiping the thin blade on a white cloth before tucking it back into his pocket.

"Now that I have your attention, I'm going to tell you a story." He sighs. The blade clatters on the tray of instruments. Vaiccar sits tall, his arms crossed in his lap.

"It's a tragedy about a man who had it all. A pretty girl, prominence in his village, riches, and endless comfort." Vaiccar counts off each item on his fingers. "This man, he loved her. She was said to be the bright star of their humble village. But the girl did not love the man back. She was *dishonest*." He hisses the word.

"She chose to trick him and run off with a different man. He was heartbroken by her betrayal. Who is she to court a worldly god? How dare she think she could leave the hero?" Vaiccar's voice is laced with hatred.

He smiles. "Well, it didn't matter. It could be dealt with. The hero sought revenge against the wicked, unfaithful girl and the god she dared to love." He spits the word love, face turning down into a scowl. After a breath he smiles, showing all his teeth.

"The hero got his revenge. The unfaithful girl had to be reminded that he was powerful, how he was the right choice that she neglected to see. So he killed her lover and generously offered to take her back.

"After all, no one would want her now that she had lain with a worldly god. When she rejected him, his heart shattered. She banished him from her sight using the power she stole.

"Now, after thousands of years, that same man is back, and he's ready to make her and everything she loves pay." He wipes the sweat from my brow using the bloodied cloth. "And you, Kai, will have a starring role in how this story unfolds."

He smiles, picking up the thin blade once more. The blade slices across my forehead, my vision running red with my own blood as it pools in my eyes. I scream until my throat is raw.

Eliana

Hama pokes their head in right as I stand up to put on a robe. "Did I hear someone say they're up for a short jaunt?" They smile, taking three large strides across the tent before pulling me into a tight hug.

"Hama, dear, Eliana is not feeling quite that good, please be gentler," Alana chides, a smile in her voice. They both laugh and I chuckle softly along with them.

"It's alright Hama, I appreciate the enthusiasm. I'm excited to leave this dusty tent as well. I'm glad Mythica finally cleared me to begin exercising again."

"Sit, sit," they order me. Hama ushers Alana from the tent with a dismissive flick of their wrist. I sit on the stool, and Hama steps up behind me, a hairbrush in hand. They lovingly brush my hair, mindful of the knots and tangles. I'm swatted once for squirming as Hama drags my brush through an especially nasty snarl in my hair.

I'm released from the stool with a satisfied smack of Hama's lips. They pull my arms up, and I wince. Hama doesn't notice. They're busy slipping a simple dress over my arms and dropping it to cascade down to the floor.

Now that I am dressed and my hair's braided back, Hama takes one of my arms in theirs and begins escorting me into the hustle and bustle of the Burroughs.

"Eliana, there is so much to show you. First, we can take you to the gardens. I think you will be most impressed with how your people have devised ingenious ways to make plants grow in near darkness. Then, we can go to the makeshift school they've built. The children have all been asking about you. If you want, we can get a sweet from the *tehendra* along the way, and of course you have to visit my new shop!"

Alana places a sturdy hand on Hama's shoulder, stopping them from continuing. "I think a walk to the *tehendra* for something to eat and to see your new shop will be more than enough exercise for the first day." Hama blushes, patting my hand, and with a deep huff of discontentment they reply, "Very well, Alana." I giggle. "Come, princess," Hama beckons with a wink, " we have a *single* errand to attend to."

Hama walks arm in arm with me to the *tehendra*. Nearly all of the Burroughs is visible from the high risers built to help ease the flow of traffic as my people carry about their chores. Several pull carts take up the entire width of the cavern paths. It's breathtaking to behold how in such a short time they have built a truly marvelous new home.

My gut pinches at the thought of our old village, now buried under ashes, haunted by the dark beasts and other monsters from distant parts of Hevastia.

"What has your eyes staring off in the distance, Eliana?" Hama's soft voice cuts through my thoughts, bringing me back to our scenic walk.

"It's nothing."

The shouts of the villagers grow louder as we descend from the risers. Names of goods are shouted, mixed with friendly greetings and children squealing as they run wildly through the small crowd. Hama continues to guide me through the chaos. As we wind our way through, people call out my name, and lots of hands reach out with quick prayers of thanks and healing murmured over me. In the swirl of color illuminated by the torches and the intoxicating blend of familiar noises, I lose all sense of worry and let the familiar tune of life carry me through the crowd.

"What do you think?" Hama asks, a glowing smile alight on their face.

Past Hama sits a brightly colored tent modeled similarly to the one they left behind in Wildewell. There are no gemstones sewn into the cloth. Instead it's decorated with silver threads marking the lines of constellations, the tapestry of the gods.

"It's beautiful, Hama!"

Their smile widens.

"Do you miss Wildewell?" I ask.

Hama waves a hand, dismissing me. "No, this is where my heart and my work belong. Did you know other refugees from Wildewell joined us here?"

"They did?" A small jolt of surprise runs down my spine. "Why would they do that?"

"Why don't you ask them yourself?" At that, Hama pulls me into the tent and I find myself shoulder to shoulder with vaguely familiar faces, twelve in total.

"Hello," I greet them nervously.

"Princess Eliana, it's a pleasure," responds an older man with graying hair and deep brown, kind eyes. He bows his head, and everyone follows, murmuring their own greetings and well wishes.

"I'm Daneth," says the old man, his hand outstretched between us. "Mythica heard of our plight after the *craicabra* attacked Wildewell and destroyed the village. She offered us asylum in exchange for our agreement to help tend to the Burroughs. On the condition, of course, that we acknowledge you as the rightful leader of Hevastia and denounce all affiliations with the Haematitian Council and the Aceolevia."

"I-I don't know what to say," I stammer.

Rightful ruler of Hevastia? I never signed up for that!

"It's an honor to serve the auror." A middle-aged woman steps forward, smiling.

A vast pit forms in my stomach, threatening to spill out of my gut and swallow me whole in one gulp. In six short months I have gone from being the irresponsible daughter of the Chieftess, to the avenger of my people's slaughter, and now the savior of a long-forgotten prophecy, the Auror of Hevastia.

"Chieftess?" Daneth's use of my mother's title is a hot knife into my gut.

"Eliana, please." I swallow. "My mother is–was–Chieftess."

"Of course," he nods, "my apologies. We desire nothing more than to live here, and humbly serve you and the greater good of Hevastia."

"Thank you for your willingness to contribute to our survival here in the mountains and your faith in me. I'm truly humbled." The words tumble from my mouth. All twelve refugees smile kindly, whispering prayers over me as Hama leads me from the tent.

"They can be so intense," Hama jokes, laughing to themself.

Our walk back from the *tehendra* is a comfortable silence.

Back in my tent, I collapse on the pile of blankets and pillows on my small bed. The aches and pains of walking after six weeks bedridden are catching up to me. I fall asleep some time later, fitful dreams of my mother, Kai, and Cire haunting me throughout the night.

Several days pass in a similar blur. Hama, Alana, and Tenya have all taken it upon themselves to be my designated aunts and caretakers. They each escort me through the Burroughs, distracting themselves and myself from the worries and threats that lie beyond our makeshift home. I'll never tell Alana or Hama, but I've come to prefer Tenya's company.

My walks with Tenya are often filled with the sound of the Burroughs. There are no questions or endless chatter, and it allows me time to think and observe. With Tenya there are no expectations or pretenses. After a lifetime on the fringe of our clan, she's perfected the art of moving through a crowd without attracting attention, somehow being both a part of the fluid, changing dynamics of the group and yet apart from it all, slicing through it with grace.

Everyone is eager to greet me and express their support and their thanks. But, I haven't done anything to earn their unwavering trust. Their love is almost suffocating at times. So, being able to slip through busy corners undetected has been invaluable.

As the auror I'm as equally isolated from everyone as when I was simply "the chieftess's daughter." I've been placed on a pedestal without any say in the matter, and I worry over what will happen when I inevitably fail them.

There's a soft tap on my shoulder.

What's on your mind? You look troubled? Tenya signs to me.

I'm okay. Grateful for a chance to escape the expectations of everyone else. They all think I will bear them on my shoulders and lift us and all of Hevastia from the darkness ... but I don't know what my magic can do yet. I'm still weak from my injuries.

Absentmindedly my hand drifts to my shoulder, then my gut.

If I can't even manage to walk the entire Burroughs before collapsing. What hope do I have for saving everyone, let alone just one person?

There's no need for me to say their names. Kai and Cire are on my mind–on all of my friend's minds—every waking minute.

I will find a way to get you both back. I swear it. I won't leave you there at the mercy of that monster.

Vaiccar's cruel smile haunts me every time I close my eyes, his vile touch lingering on my skin–a stain no amount of soap can scrub away. Trust me, I've tried.

Tenya signs for me to take a few calming breaths, exaggerating her own breathing to carry her point. I breathe in, holding for three counts before exhaling.

It's going to be okay, Eliana. No one expects you to stop Vaiccar in a day.

I take another calming breath.

I wish I knew where to begin.

She motions for me to follow her, and we duck off of the risers, passing through a small gathering of neighbors before taking a tunnel I have not explored yet. I follow her deeper into the cavern as she stops to take a torch from the wall and beckons me to keep up. I walk right into Tenya's back, distracted by the soft glow of the minerals reflecting in the firelight.

Tenya, where have you brought us?

She smiles at me, ushering me in front of her. We turn the corner and I suck in a breath. The tunnel falls away, revealing a small, hidden lake. The walls of the cavern glisten with the same minerals of the tunnel, large crystals jutting from the rock.

"This is incredible ..." my voice trails off. I walk further into the cavern. Stalactites of crystal reach toward the calm surface of the lake. "Amazing," I whisper, breathless. Torchlight dances off the crystals, illuminating the pool and casting a soft glow in the cavern.

Tenya waves her hand, pulling my attention to her. *I found this last week. I thought maybe you could train here? It's secluded and serene, perfect for performing soul magic–don't you think?*

I smile ear to ear. *This place is perfect.* I sign to her, and a smile lights up her face.

I'll tell Mythica. She will be pleased to hear we found somewhere. Tenya signs to me. *Do you think you're ready to train?*

"I'm ready to try." I say out loud, and sign, trying to convince myself as much as Tenya.

I follow Tenya away from the hidden lake, and the boisterous echo of the *tehendra* reaches us before we reach it. I hadn't even realized we took a different turn in the tunnels than when we walked in. Everyone is bustling around me, shouts echoing across this part of the Burroughs as my people barter, trade, and experience life together. Some of the Wildewell refugees help Tyr and Maendril with loading chopped wood into a cart.

"Tyr, Maendril!" I wave to them, and Maendril drops his log, almost upsetting the whole stack as he strides to greet me and Tenya. Tyr sets his log down with more care before rushing to his *Amorei*, Tenya.

I am pulled into a crushing hug as Maendril lifts me off the ground, squeezing me tightly. "It's good to see you up and about, Eliana." The rumble of his laughter rattles in my bones, a thunderous echo in the cavern.

Tenya places a hand on Maendril's arm, pulling his attention to her. She quickly signs to tell him to put me down. *She's not healed enough for one of your hugs,* Tenya scolds.

He chuckles, jostling me a little as he sets me down. "Sorry about that, Princess. Hope I didn't rough you up too much." He leans in and whispers comically, "your friend Hama will have my head."

Tyr laughs. "Alana and Hama have been a huge help getting the refugees settled, but," Tyr whistles, "Alana is demanding. Still don't understand how she nabbed sweet Hama's heart, but they're a cute pair." Tyr pulls Tenya close, hugging her.

I make a gagging motion at Maendril and he laughs deeply, clapping me on the back and almost sending me sprawling to the ground.

"Maendril, friend, watch yourself," Tyr shouts, catching me as I stumble.

I laugh deeply, my stitches stretching with a twinge of pain that I barely feel in the ease of this moment.

Tenya waves goodbye, off to tell Mythica about our conversation.

"What are you building?" I kick a rough-cut slab of wood.

Tyr and Maendril stand with twin smiles, and the same mischievous glint in their eyes.

"Booby traps," Maendril announces triumphantly with a chuckle that's cut short by Tyr elbowing him in the gut. "Oof."

"Platforms," Tyr replies more seriously. "Alana asked us to build a stable, wind-blocked platform for someone to sit on.

"How many?"

The predators of the mountains don't require such drastic measures. A chill runs down my spine, the ease of the moment lost. A secret understanding passes between Tyr and Maendril. There's something they don't want to tell me.

"Not many ... a few here and there. This is all precautionary."

I'm not convinced. Tyr flinches under my gaze and sighs.

"They're starting to stalk in pairs. One dark beast is not a problem. We can easily take on one in our hunting parties. But two? That complicates things ... we've had a few close calls."

Maendril pats the pile of chopped wood. "We're going to place these platforms in the trees to give the hunters a better vantage point." He swallows. "Or, a place to escape should they be overrun."

My anger over my own helplessness and my people's plight sets my blood boiling.

Kai

A ROUGH BANDAGE, POORLY wrapped around my head, leaks. My blood runs down my face, along my chin, and drips to the floor.

The cell is dark, the torch from across the dimly-lit hall burning low. It must be night. The dungeon is silent except for the ragged breathing on the other side of the wall I lean against.

Whoever shares my cell wall, they've chosen to suffer in quiet misery. With each passing minute spent rotting in this cell, I begin to lose hope of rescue.

Alana won't come back. I'm as good as dead.

Alana taught Cire and I everything we know about strategy and risk. Her voice echoes in my head as she explains the concept of sacrificing one battle, one position on the battlefield for the greater success of the mission.

Sacrificing one person for the good of the many.

They already risked one mission to rescue me. They played their hand, and if Vaiccar is as strategic as he is malicious and sadistic ... then he will be ready for them to try again.

I pray to the stars that they don't try again, and in the same breath I plead for them to. It's selfish, this desire to be saved, when I have no strategic value. Eliana is the priority, her safety from Vaiccar is the one thing that matters.

I served my role. I saved her. Cire would be proud. In the end, when it mattered most, I saved the auror ... and condemned myself.

Heavy footsteps echo through the dungeon, stopping in front of my cell.

Familiar green eyes with a new, evil glint stare at me from the other side of the door.

"Hello, Kai. Are you ready for your next treatment?" Vaiccar smiles, showing all of his teeth.

This is not Cire, it can't be.

Eliana

THE FLAMES OF THE torch dance off the crystals glittering overhead, casting the cavern and the still lake in a warm glow. Tenya sits beside me. Our boots dangle over the edge of an outcropped rock that juts out above the pool of clear water below. From here, it's easy to spot the stalagmites hidden deep beneath the water's surface.

Have you been to visit Pyria yet?

I shake my head, no.

She's withdrawn from everyone. Tenya's face is pinched with worry over her sister. Pyria lost her husband, Borielle, and her best friend, my mother, in the Morei guardian's attack on our home. She stayed with those that fled, her role as our healer too vital to risk in battle.

I think you should visit her. She misses you.

I will. It's not a lie, but I can't admit to Tenya I've been avoiding Pyria. Seeing her without my mother glued to her side, the two of them sitting with cups of steaming tea in their hands ... it's too much.

Alana mentioned you were reading your mother's journals. If you want to talk about what you read, Pyria will be able to discuss it with you. Your mother confided everything to her.

My time spent with Tenya tugs at my heart-strings. She reminds me of my mother. It aches at times to be with her. With Pyria I know it will be different. She was always around, always so supportive and nurturing. There is no one in this world my mother trusted more than Pyria. Their bond ran incredibly deep. Deep enough I fear a cavern would form under me, swallowing me whole in my grief.

I get up, patting Tenya's shoulder as I stand. She reaches up and grabs my wrist, forcing me to stop and turn back to her. Tenya smiles encouragingly, but the corners of her eyes are still pulled down with sorrow. My mother's loss weighs heavily on us both.

As I re-enter the main antechamber, a small light flickers in one of the tents along the far edge of the cavern. Pyria's personal tent is adjacent to a larger tent for patients. As I near the light pink tent, I take a deep, calming breath.

The shadow of a woman curled in a ball, lying on the ground, sends shivers down my back. I can't count on both hands how many nights I've spent curled up in the same manner, trying to block out the memories and the pain of losing my mother and my best friends, Brynne and Naomi.

I stop at the threshold of the tent's entrance, rapping my knuckles on the wooden stake helping to hold the structure in place. Pyria barely stirs, and I try again. On the third try she sits up, crawling to the entrance. Tears well in my eyes as her own blood-shot, blotchy eyes gaze into mine.

She opens her arms to me and I collapse into them, both of us sobbing and clutching one another for hours. Her tears mingle with mine, creating a pool of shared grief and comfort. I finally pull away, and the small amount of space leaves me cold and alone once more.

I'm so sorry, Pyria. I should have sought you out immediately.

Fresh tears stream down my face.

It's not an excuse, but I think I avoided finding you because it would have made losing my mother too real. I've been avoiding a lot of things these last few months.

Her small hands wrap around mine and she smiles softly, understanding. She lets go of my hands to sign a response.

Eliana, it's okay. If we're being honest, I wasn't ready either. Maendril brought you here when ... you were stabbed. I couldn't bring myself to find you after that. I couldn't support you, or offer any inspiring words. I have been in a very dark place since–

You don't have to be alone anymore, if you're ready.

I pull her into another deep hug.

You're my family now, if you'll have me.

We've always been family, Eliana. Your mother was everything to me.

She smiles more genuinely, leaving behind a small piece of the sadness.

Tell me all about your adventure. I know you've been quite busy.

We stay up all night as I share with her everything that's happened in the last six months, and what's to come. Being there with her feels as if I've gotten back a piece of my mom, and the sadness that sits with me always gets a little bit smaller.

I open my eyes to a rough stone pressed into my cheek. I fell asleep on the floor of Pyria's tent, a thick blanket lovingly tucked around me.

Pyria sits on her cot, a scrap of fabric and thread in her hands.

What are you making?

Nothing, clearly. Her eyes twinkle with the faintest hint of humor. *I was never talented with needle craft. Need stitches for an injury? Easy. Need a piece of clothing mended?* She snorts.

She sets it aside, patting the open spot on her cot and scooting over to give me space to sit beside her. A small clay tea cup is pressed into my hands, and my stomach drops. Pyria's smile is sad, sharing in the monumental weight of this moment. She handed me my mother's tea cup.

The tea pot rattles slightly in Pyria's hands as she pours fresh tea into my cup. The steam warms my face.

She would want you to have it. Pyria grabs my arm, giving it a soft, loving shake. The tea sloshes in the cup but doesn't spill.

I nod, my throat too thick with emotion to speak.

Pyria and I sit in comfortable silence sipping our morning tea. The moment is achingly familiar. Before ... we spent many mornings around my mother's table with tea and fresh bread. When I finish my cup, she offers me more, but I wave my hand. The cup is taken from my hands and set aside for use another day.

Tenya told me you read your mother's journal. I want to tell you about my uncle. She breathes deeply. *Oeseth.*

Your uncle?

Pyria nods. *Yes. Do you remember your mother explaining to you why Tenya and I are non-verbal when you asked as a child?*

I shake my head. *No, I'm sorry.*

It's okay. You were fairly young. Her face pulls down with a deep sadness. *And, it's not a happy story.*

Tenya and I were raised by Oeseth and our aunt, Anabelle.

Oeseth used to beat Anabelle in the privacy of our home. He would whip her over the smallest inconveniences, or whenever it fancied him.

She swallows. *When beating our aunt proved no longer entertaining enough for him ...* Pyria pauses. I reach and take her hand in mine, giving it an encouraging squeeze before letting go.

"He turned his attention to Tenya. Tenya was born deaf. It was the first time this had happened in our village. The elders didn't know how to help our family, and so she didn't have the means to communicate with anyone outside of the family. Our uncle refused to teach Tenya and I how to write.*

Oeseth would take her to his and Aunt Anabelle's room ... and I watched my older sister wither before my eyes.

One day when he took her hand to drag her away I spoke up and yelled at him. Until then, he had assumed I was oblivious to his abusive treatment of my aunt and Tenya.

He couldn't risk me telling anyone. If the elders found out, he would be stoned, exiled for his behavior.

Pyria pauses again, collecting a breath, and sips from the tea cup, clutched tightly in her clenched hands.

I take her hand back in mine. *Pyria, it's okay. You don't have to tell me.*

I'm okay. It's important you learn the whole truth. I had an 'accident' that evening. In the following days, Oeseth would tell everyone I foolishly cut my tongue on a knife and the cut turned infected. In truth, he forced Aunt Anabelle to hold me down while he cut out my tongue himself.

I suck in a shocked breath.

After that, Tenya and I developed a secret language so we could communicate. Oeseth never touched Tenya again. My 'accident' had drawn too much attention to our family. Rumors began to spread about her bruises.

Pyria, I'm so sorry. Tears well in my eyes and spill over.

I tell you this because his account of your mother's assault is false.

My blood runs cold. *False, how?*

The night the elders pressured your mother to pursue Ryder as a prospect ... the following events are all falsified by Oeseth.

The smudged ink in the journal. It was so out of place on the page.

My uncle was a bad man, obsessed with power and how much control he had over others. He desired your mother, coveted the place as her consort or Champion.

Your mother left to meet Ryder in the fields at the edge of the forest, to ask him to marry her and stay with her in the mountains.

They shared a beautiful, loving moment together. Ryder left her there to pray. He planned to return briefly to his home in Sandovell before relocating to Bellamere, to be with her.

Oeseth witnessed their embrace ,and in a fit of jealous rage he attacked your mother. Brutalized her. In the aftermath, your mother was in shock. Her memory was unreliable and jumbled.

Without her side of the events, Oeseth was free to bend the events to his favor. He claimed Ryder had attacked her, and that he found her afterward. It was Oeseth that initiated the manhunt against Ryder.

Your mother was so ashamed and frightened. By the time her memory cleared and she could recall the true order of events, Oeseth had buried the whole ordeal and Ryder was lost to the beasts of the wild.

The horror of Pyria's words slams into me. My father was murdered. My mother was assaulted. It's all too much. Pyria stops signing to me, and takes my hands in hers. She swipes a stray tear off my cheek, and tucks my unruly hair behind my ear.

I know this is hard. Knowledge is a burden. Your mother was trying to protect you.

It took several years for me to convince her to tell the elders the truth. When she came forward, so did I and Tenya. By that time, my good for nothing uncle was dying from a brutal, excruciating illness. The elders exiled him from the village, cursing him to live out his remaining days in blinding agony as the disease claimed him.

So my father–

Was Ryder. Pyria finishes for me with a certain finality. *Your mother truly loved him, and I see him in you. You possess none of my uncle's disgusting traits. Just your father's gentle spirit and your mother's fierce stubbornness.*

I laugh quietly, knowing how stubborn I can truly be.

Pyria begins to cry, and we clutch one another for a long time. She pats my back to help clear my throat from the phlegm of my sniffly nose and all of the crying.

She could never bring herself to tell you. It's why she was so protective of you.

Thank you for telling me. Relief washes over me. I was not born of hate, but of love. My mother loved my father, and loved me. She truly was the strongest woman I've ever met.

You're welcome, Eliana.

I have a question. If you and Tenya created this sign language, how do so many know it now?

Pyria smiles. *Your mother and Tyr learned sign language so they could befriend us as children. When your mother became Chieftess, she required everyone to learn it. She wanted to ensure our voices were heard in the village, so that no one could take advantage of us again.*

Pyria kisses my forehead. *Thank you for visiting me, Eliana. I missed you. Now go, Tenya will have my head if you miss your first day of training.*

Kai

THE CEILING STARES BACK at me, full of rusted chains and horrific instruments, all coated in dried, flaking blood. I don't know how long I've been lying here this time. I keep flashing in and out of consciousness from blood loss. Larsus woke me up moments ago to give me water, the freshness an unexpected surprise that was cool and delicious. I gulped the entire cup down, pleading with him for more, but he scurried off without so much as a 'no.'

I close my eyes again, trying to take myself away from the metallic-smelling room and the aches of my many injuries. Vaiccar's been bleeding me out, inflicting small cuts along my entire body. With every fresh bleed, I try to harness my magic, but it's gone. He's done something to take my magic from me, and the emptiness is more painful than the cuts.

When I open my eyes, I'm no longer in the dungeon of the Aceolevia, but instead, I'm standing in chest high grass and wildflowers as they sway in a soft breeze. Tall mountains rise up around me on all sides. I'm in a valley. I turn my face up to the *solari* and fall backward, letting the swaying field swallow me whole.

A soft laugh pulls my attention. In the distance, the black-haired girl with soft, copper skin and fierce eyes from Bellamere sits weaving the grass and wildflowers into a chain. She catches me staring, and her smile disappears. The flower chain is crushed underfoot as she marches toward me.

"It's you." Her voice is quiet and lethal. "What are you doing here?"

"Is this the Beyond?" I ask. The tickle of the breeze is warm against my chest and face. I sit up on my elbows.

She's glowing softly, ethereal. I reach out to touch her, and she smacks my hand away. I thought perhaps she was a figment of my imagination, but she's solid and real.

"Don't touch me," she snarls. "I thought this was the Beyond until you showed up."

"Oh," I exclaim, suddenly sad. "I was hoping I was finally free of the pain." I scan my body, expecting bloodied clothes, torn and frayed, my chest, arms, and legs covered in the hundreds of small cuts inflicted by Vaiccar, but instead, I wear a plain white shirt and tan trousers, my bare feet clean of grime and dried blood.

"You shouldn't be here." Her words are a hissed whisper as I'm forcibly dragged from the flowery valley and left sprawled on the damp floor of my dungeon cell.

Amber eyes glow from the darkened corner. I scramble to my knees and shuffle backward, away from their gaze. Princess Atrya steps closer, the red-hot flames Eliana told me about whipping wildly around her.

"How," I sputter out.

"Kai, I need you to focus." She snaps her fingers. "Vaiccar is trying to turn you. You must resist him. Don't let him into your mind."

"I don't understand," I respond, exasperated. "Stop being cryptic. I wouldn't be in this mess if you had been direct with me in the gauntlet. Eliana would have never stepped foot in the Aceolevia, and Vaiccar wouldn't be free if you were honest from the start."

She sighs, annoyed, fingers pressing into her temple. "That's not how it works. I can't tell you exactly what to do. That would be interfering too much. It would draw attention. Listen to me. Resist Vaiccar. Resist with every ounce of strength you have."

"Attention from who?" I ask, reaching out to grab her so I can shake her. I'm so pissed. But my hands grab thin air, and Princess Atrya is gone.

"Kai." Vaiccar's voice is sharp, annoyed. A hand slaps my face hard, and I open my eyes to Vaiccar staring stoney-eyed down at me, his mouth drawn in a thin line. "Focus, we have work to do."

"This is Naevys." The woman he points to has grayish purple skin, white hair that falls in dreads past her shoulders, and pale, blue eyes. She glances down, unwilling to meet my gaze. "Naevys is a time mage from Keladone. She's gifted in a particularly *delightful* magic." He smiles cruelly, the menacing grin spreading further with each word that passes through his stretched lips.

The table rattles as I buck against my restraints, trying to get away from Naevys as she walks toward me, standing above my head. Her face fills my line of sight as her cold, boney hands grab my temple. She holds my head tightly and my vision goes black. Her presence is a chilling hand in my head, digging around.

Every fiber in my body struggles against her invasion. Searing cold travels through my body, numbing me. Her face disappears from view. There's nothing but the void and my consciousness that struggles to free itself from her cold grasp.

Slowly, light returns and my body surges toward it, sucking me away from the darkness and into another memory.

Cire and I are five and seven, running and squealing in a game of chase in the temple garden. His laughter breaks through the calm summer air, and I find him hiding behind a statue.

We lie on the grass, daring one another to stare into the bright light of the solari the longest. When I stand back up I'm dizzy, spots forming in my vision from staring too long. We begin running again, but in the confusion Cire and I both come to a crashing stop in a tangled heap at the feet of two people. I gasp. They're Morei guardians. I recognize them from the last all-temple gathering.

The shorter person squats down, making eye contact with me. "Hello, Kai." They turn and greet Cire, too. "My name is Hama, and this is Alana." They point to the tall woman standing next to them.

"Hama, we need to go," Alana says, annoyed. "We don't have time to entertain two children."

"We're sorry, uh, for running into you. We were playing," Cire apologizes, nudging me in the gut to do the same.

"Sorry," I murmur, staring up at Alana.

"It's alright boys. Please, be more careful. There are few here who would be so forgiving, even of young children." Alana's voice softens, some of her aggravation from before dissipating.

Hama smiles, offering each of us a hand. Raised scars mark each palm, and I swallow down my nerves, glancing at Cire to check if he noticed. His face is pale and his shoulders are shaking. Hama gasps at our reaction to their hands and pulls them back. When I glance back at Alana, her eyes are narrowed, more annoyed than a moment ago.

"Shame, boys. Hama is my Morei. The work they do is an honor to the True Faith," Alana chides us, and I tuck my chin, waiting for the swat that usually accompanies this tone. "Apologize to them."

Cire and I slide closer together and bow our heads to Hama. "We're sorry, Hama."

Hama bends down and gives us each a hug in turn. "It's okay. You're new to your training, right?"

I nod my head. "Yes, Cire is going to be my Morei. We were selected two days ago."

Hama's hands are warm wrapped around mine and Cire's. They give them a small squeeze. "If you ever need anything, don't be afraid to seek out me or Alana." They smile warmly at us.

Naevys's presence is a cold hand as it enters the memory. Shadows slide over the warmth of the *solari*, choking out the light. Hama and Alana's faces begin to fade from my view, taking all the warmth with them. I reach out to grab them, but my fingers grab onto a bone chilling sensation as the shadow slips through my fingers and I am left alone in the dark.

The pressure from my temple releases and I open my eyes to the rusted chains hanging from the ceiling of the dungeon. Vaiccar clears his throat and I turn to face him.

"What did you do?" I ask, snarling at him. "How did she get into my head?"

"That's her gift, Kai. She's a memory charmer." Vaiccar smiles at me, sending a chill down my spine. "With Naevys's help, you will be reborn."

The manacles holding me to the table bite into my wrists as I throw myself against them. Vaiccar leans close as if we are two friends sharing a secret, his breath warming my cheek.

"I will take everything and everyone you've ever loved away from you."

Eliana

Twenty expectant, smiling faces stare at me and Mythica. Some shuffle from foot to foot, too nervous to stand still. We are gathered in the crystal cavern with the pristine lake that Tenya showed me two days ago. Initially, Mythica objected to showing the Burroughs this small haven. I eventually wore her down (or won her over) when I argued that it would be better put to use as a serene place for all of the recently awoken mages to practice harnessing their element.

With the revival of our Lady's gifts among several in our clan, I felt it was necessary that we aid those struggling to adjust to their newfound powers by holding training sessions and private lessons. Helping them has the added benefit of distracting me from worrying over my own inability to call forth my magic.

I have continued to pore over the ancient texts Mythica was able to bring with her when we fled Bellamere. After the last passage I read in my mother's journal, I decided to move on to the other journals in Mythica's chest. So far none of them have documented the auror's magic. I suppose being separate from the rest of Hevastia did not provide opportunities to witness the last auror, Princess Atrya, performing her magic.

My magic's been dormant since the initial rush of white-hot fire through my veins. It's been impossible to grasp, as elusive as smoke. Mythica promises me that my magic will come to me, and for all of our sakes I hope it's true.

"Princess," Raen calls to me, his face breaking into a wide smile, arms moving wildly. He stands next to Clyn, who is also calling for my attention and waving sheepishly.

I wave to them both, and to the rest who stand in front of me. Everyone gathered claimed to have felt a strange change come over them. There's a near-constant pull for something slightly beyond reach. It's just as Alana described her magic. The blood called to her. Her magic was the answering echo. Surprisingly, none of the refugees from Wildewell are among the crowd.

How strange.

"Welcome, everyone! Auror Eliana and I look forward to working with each of you to access your blessing from Lady Hevastia. Now, it's important that you understand this process may take time, and if you don't succeed at first, that is not a sign to give up. You have been given a sacred gift. It must be nurtured, and everyone's journey to fully realizing her Ladyship's purpose for you will be unique." Mythica's speech is met with cheers.

Nausea rolls in my stomach, the memory of the last time I addressed these same faces rushing back to me. It was hours prior to the slaughter of thirty of our friends and family. I open my mouth, but the words catch in my throat. With shaky fingers I reach up and clasp the pendant of Hevastia's Heart in my sweaty palm, taking three, deep, calming breaths.

A soft wrinkled hand slides into mine, pulling my attention back to the folks standing before me, faces alight with hope and the same nervous energy coursing through me.

"Everything Mythica said is true. I couldn't have said it better." I swallow, thrusting my nerves down. "Today marks a new chapter in our people's history. From the ashes of everything we've lost comes the promise of so much more to be gained. We honor the sacrifices of those who brought us to this moment, and I ask you to join me in thanking Lady Hevastia for gracing us with her blessing."

"There is promise in the Light." The voices of all gathered join me, and the prayer to Lady Hevastia echoes across the calm lake.

A hushed whisper falls over the crowd as Alana and Hama enter the cavern. Behind them are several of the other refugees from Wildewell. My people split the group, letting them through. They give the refugees a wide berth, distrusting Alana, Hama and the others from Wildewell. My heart pinches to think they are not being treated fairly in the Burroughs.

How much have I missed while on bed rest? Why hasn't anyone said anything to me?

I open my arms, beckoning Alana and Hama to join me and Mythica in front of everyone. Alana holds Hama back, hesitant, but Hama breaks her grip and walks quickly, nearly toppling me over in one of their signature hugs. I hug them back. Alana hovers at the edge of the large rock we're standing on, hesitant to join us. Hama stretches their hand out to their partner, and Alana steps up beside us.

"We thought that perhaps we could help instruct everyone on how to harness their gift. When we were still with the Council,

Hama and I worked with the young children to help them display their gifts. It won't be exactly the same, but we and a few other retired Morei have offered to help," Alana whispers to me. She glances nervously at the crowd, now agitated by the arrival of her and the other refugees in the cavern. "That is, if they're willing to work with us." She sighs.

I clear my throat, and everyone's attention snaps back to me. Alana and Hama are each holding one of my hands. "Everyone, our friends from Wildewell have offered to help us." A collective murmur moves through the crowd. "I was once nervous. But, I assure you, we have nothing to fear from Alana, Hama, or the other refugees. They have experience with developing magical gifts, and I believe that with their help, we will be able to harness our own gifts."

"Their magic is unnatural. They can't help us," shouts a man I cannot spot from the back of the group. More heads nod in agreement with him. "They'll bleed us and steal our gifts."

Hama flinches at the accusation, and Alana pulls them close. Fear begins to take hold of the group, all eyes nervously watching the refugees to see if they will retaliate for the accusation. The refugees are the most fearful, huddled closely together. I am losing control of the crowd, and I gaze fearfully to Mythica for guidance. She takes a deep breath.

"Shame on all of you," she yells, silencing the rest. "These folks came to us for sanctuary and in peace, and look at how you turn on them so easily.

"Yuriel," she calls to the man who spoke up, "was it not just three days ago that Daneth of Wildewell helped you harvest your vegetable garden?"

Yuriel bows his head, shrinking away from Mythica's harsh tone. "And Abigael, Hama made you a beautiful swaddle for your newborn. They showed you how to swaddle him to your chest." Abigael sheds a single tear. Mythica smiles, urging me to speak next.

"These folks are our friends and allies. We are no longer enemies. When I was injured and near death, Alana saved me and nursed me back to health. We would not be standing here today, blessed with magic, if not for the kindness of Alana and Hama who took me in as one of their own, despite the horrible way I treated them and their kin." I pause, looking each person in the eye. "We are better than this, and there are bigger problems than our prejudice and petty concerns to be focused on. Vaiccar is free. There is no way of knowing the unspeakable horrors he has planned for Hevastia, or all of Odora. We have to band together.

"If you are unwilling to work alongside the folks from Wildewell, then you can learn to access Lady Hevastia's blessing on your own, though you are undeserving of it. She calls us to walk in her Light, and here you stand deeply within the dark of your fears and prejudice."

Several people in the group shuffle their feet, and I hold my breath, wondering if anyone will leave or speak up against me. A low murmur spreads through the group, and soon everyone has their hand to their heart, thumb pressed to their chest, fingers spread wide, and they bow to me. I gasp in shock, *the blessing of the Chieftess.*

Raen grabs the hand of one of the Wildewell refugees, and soon everyone is standing before us with their hands clasped. I turn to Alana and Hama.

"Where do we begin?" I ask, a tear sliding down my cheek.

As I walk through the cavern, the sound of hushed whispers echoes through the large space. To my right, Yuriel is working with Daneth. The flame of the torch gripped by Daneth ripples as Yuriel concentrates on commanding the fire. Daneth smiles broadly and laughs, clasping Yuriel's hand. It's the first sign of his gift. Over the last several days, the refugees from Wildewell have been helping each of my people connect with their element through trial and error.

Raen squeals with excitement from across the cavern as the feather he's been staring at begins to float in the air between him, Clyn, and a refugee girl. They all fall into a fit of giggles when Raen makes the feather tickle Clyn's nose. Hama holds Abigael's hand as she works to coax a pebble on the ground to roll over.

It's been small steps these past few days, but there has been progress in nearly everyone here—except for me. Alana and I have been meditating with Mythica three times a day, trying to draw on my magic, but there's nothing. They both promise me that it will come eventually, but I'm starting to lose hope. It's been two months since magic has returned, and Vaiccar was set free. I have no power, and no plan.

Kai's been trapped by that monster for just as long, and I worry we may already be too late. Two months of torture is a lot for anyone to bear, even someone as strong as Kai. Every time I bring up returning to the Aceolevia to rescue him, my suggestion is met with a chorus of dissent from all my friends. Maendril is adamant that we stay far from the Temple of Clarity, and Tyr and Tenya follow his direction. I know they're all afraid of what will happen if I fall back into Vaiccar's grasp, but I promised Alana and Hama I would save Kai, and Cire, and I'm not ready to give up hope yet.

Kai

WARM AIR CARESSES MY face, and I open my eyes to the beautiful rolling fields haloed by golden light.

How is it possible that I'm leaving the dungeon? What is this place?

The girl from Bellamere stands several feet away, her eyes narrowed to slits as she stares at me with open contempt.

I deserve that.

"Why are you here?"

I'm glad you're okay. The memory of you dying in my arms haunts me, is what I want to say, but all I muster is, "I'm not sure."

My eyes flick to where her hand rests on her hip, half-expecting a knife strapped there, but there's nothing.

She huffs, annoyed, and turns her back to me.

"Please, I only want someone to talk to."

My words stop her hasty retreat, and she glares at me over her shoulder. "I don't owe you anything, least of all someone to unload your burdens on."

"I know," I sigh, running my hand through my hair. "You're right."

The wind plays with loose tendrils of her black curls that have come undone from their braids, pulling them across her face. Her expression is torn as she glances back at me with a sad smile.

"Eliana is alive," I blurt out. "At least, she was before I was brought down into this gods-forsaken dungeon."

At the mention of Eliana the briefest flash of hope flits across her face before she tamps it down and returns my pleading look with the same cold indifference as before.

"Dungeon?" She scoffs. "Aren't you the Morei's favored *pet*?" She places extra emphasis on the word 'pet,' a petty smirk on her face.

I swallow. "I was."

I take a tentative step toward her and she shuffles back immediately.

"What happened to your village, to you. I—" the words lodge in my throat temporarily, and I swallow again. "I wish, with every pained breath I now inhale, that I could take it all back. I would make different choices."

She snorts. "You expect me to believe that?"

"Eliana did."

She scoffs. "Eliana would never. I know my best friend."

"A lot has happened. Things change."

She shakes her head. "No, I don't believe that. Eliana is as stubborn and as intelligent as they come. She wouldn't allow herself to fall into our enemy's arms."

A blush rises in my cheeks. "You're right, she wouldn't. And, she didn't." I cough and mumble, "she held a dagger to my throat and turned me down."

At that, she laughs. "That's Eliana for you." She takes a small step forward. "Is she truly alive?"

"Yes, and she's fighting for you, for your people." I laugh quietly under my breath. "She's a fierce warrior, and an even better friend. She saved my life."

"But you're trapped in your people's dungeon? What's happened while I've been here?" She waves her arms in a dramatic arch over her head.

"A lot," I laugh, a smile breaking on my face.

"I saw the error of my ways, because of you. After–"

She snorts, cutting me off.

"I'm being serious, when I held you as your life faded ... it changed everything. You've haunted me, a manifestation of my guilt. I'm not asking for your forgiveness, or to forget all the pain I've caused you," I swallow. "I only ask that while I'm here–wherever this is–that I can sit in the grass, in peace."

She opens her mouth, but I cut her off with a raised hand.

"Please, I'm not requesting your company. I realize I'll never be fortunate enough to earn that right."

She turns her back to me, lost in her own thoughts as her hand reflexively draws up to her supple lips. She bites her nails, so lost in thought she's forgotten about me. Just as suddenly as she succumbed to her thoughts, she snaps back with a heavy sigh.

"I may regret this ... but, would you want to go for a walk? It's one of the ways I spend my time here."

"I'd appreciate that."

She holds up her hand as I take the first step toward her. "On one condition."

"Anything." The word slips out, and a blush creeps into my cheeks.

"You'll tell me everything that's happened since I died."

"Are you sure you want to know?"

She flashes me a stern, determined look. "Yes."

"I'll tell you everything I know," I reply with little reservation as I step up to walk next to her. From this close her eyes are a brilliant blue in the warm *solari's* light.

She leads me through the tall grass, and I begin at the beginning ... when High Priest Marius ordered us to march on her village.

There's a slight pinch as the needle glides under my skin. Its icy contents burn in my veins. Everything's a blur. The room comes in unfocused flashes, the shadows of Vaiccar and Naevys swimming in my view. I don't know how long I've been strapped to this table, but I worry I'll never leave it. I close my eyes and try to disappear into another memory, anything to escape the nightmare of my reality.

It's the same field as before, and I sigh with contentment. The *solari* are warm on my back as I wander the expansive space, running my hands through the tall, swaying fronds of grass. Out of the corner of my eye I spot long, dark curly hair and my heart skips a beat. I run to catch up to her, the village girl.

She was so brave to her bitter end, I need to know how she mustered that kind of strength. It's the kind of strength I must possess to endure this torture.

I've come to need her.

I find her standing with her back to me, head tilted to the sky. As I approach, she turns around slowly, smiling at me.

"You're back." Her voice is teasing, playful. "Couldn't stay away?"

"My mind keeps bringing me back to this place ..." I pause, shy, "to you." I take her hand in mine running my calloused thumb over her smooth, soft skin. "Where do you go when I'm not here?"

"Nowhere. I've been here ever since I died. I'm not sure why," she says wistfully, her eyes wide with wonder. "It's not the Beyond, at least I don't think it is. I'm alone here, and you're the only other person to appear."

She frowns with that admission, and takes her hand back.

"I'm sorry if my presence makes you uncomfortable." I run my hand through my shaggy dark curls. "I know I'm probably the last person you want invading your eternal peace."

She shakes her head. "That's not it. I thought if this is the Beyond ... that my father, mother, and brother would be here. I wish I could be with them again, even for a moment."

"I understand. I wish I could see my brother Cire's face, unmarred by the evil of Vaiccar, just one more time. I also wish I wasn't trapped in the dungeon of the Aceolevia, I long to be anywhere but there."

The field of grass and flowers sways softly in the breeze flowing down from the mountain. There's nothing but flowers stretching across the horizon. A trap of its own kind. We're both in a prison of sorts.

She nods her head, acknowledging my words, but not really hearing them. Her eyes have a far-off look in them. When she snaps out of it, she smiles sadly. "I suppose it's funny that the only other person here is the last face I saw in my life."

"Again, I apologize it had to be me." I laugh and she joins me, her laughter melodic and beautiful. I could listen to it every day and never tire of it.

"I'm Kai," I reply, holding my hand out to her.

She takes my hand in her own and shakes it softly. "I'm Naomi. It's a pleasure to meet you, Kai."

The sensation of a blade slicing my skin pulls me back to reality, and I groan with pain and sadness. I already miss the warmth of the *solari*, of her smile. Vaiccar is carving me up again. My blood runs slowly down my chest.

"Where do you go," he asks, not stopping his work of mutilating me, "when you lose consciousness?"

"None of your damn business," I shoot back, growling at him. He chuckles to himself.

A fresh pain erupts from my inner thigh as he carves a new line into my flesh, deeper than the last. Naevys sits to the side of the table, avoiding eye contact. She wears a metal collar around her neck, her own feet and legs dirty with grime.

She's a prisoner here, too.

She catches me staring and glares back, folding in on herself, trying to disappear. I turn back to Vaiccar, waiting for what he plans to do next. He puts down the blade to pick up a needle filled with strange, dark liquid.

Every time he bleeds me, he injects me with more of the same disgusting liquid. It's death and darkness itself being shot into my veins. I hate it. After I've been "treated," as he calls it, Naevys invades my mind. She's searching for something, but I'm not sure what. It's becoming increasingly difficult to remember much beyond this small, hellish room.

The one place my mind is free and clear is when I'm in the flowering field with Naomi. I repeat her name in my head, trying to will myself not to forget it, not to lose it as I have already lost so much.

My mind succumbs to Naevys's control.

Swords clang and ring as several potential Morei duel in the center of the room.

Cire's steady presence is on my left. He's a gangly fifteen-year-old, unsure in his own skin, with a face marred by a frown as he intently analyzes the fight, absorbing everything.

These duels are just practice before the Culling.

In two days' time, Cire and I will stand in the arena together against our entire class of potentials in a battle to the near-death to determine the most powerful among us.

The Haematitian Council will decide from the pool of victors who will receive their own regiment and become captains.

For now, we practice without magic and with dulled blades to conserve our tithe's blood–Cire's blood.

"Lighten up, Cire," I tease, "we have this in the bag."

He sighs, perpetually annoyed by my flippancy and bravado.

"We have the largest targets on us–if they're smart. And, some of them are. They'll team up and take us out first."

I chuckle quietly, "yes, but we both know it won't make a difference.

"Don't tell me you're getting cold feet about our strategy–it was your idea," I hiss.

Cire shakes his head, no. "It's a big risk. If we use all my blood right away ... when it exhausts, you'll either be standing alone in the arena or on the ground next to me."

"Then let's make sure it's the former." I clap my hand on his shoulder.

I'm pulled abruptly from the memory. It's disorienting. Metallic air and a cold, wet table greet me. My blood soaks my clothes. The room is dark. I'm alone, or so I think.

"You and Cire were once a force to be reckoned with, " Vaiccar whispers in my ear, as if we are sharing a secret.

"I'll kill you for what you've done to him." I snarl, blindly lashing out against my restraints.

"What I've done to him?" He laughs and it sends a chill down my spine. "You ought to be more concerned with what *you've* done to him, Kai."

Naevys's ice-cold hands grab back onto either side of my face.

It's the morning of the Culling.

We stand among our classmates, donned in matching leather armor, green armbands for Cire's favorite color. I sharpen my blades. Cire holds his sword, a whetstone striking the blade with faked concentration.

"Cire," I whisper, "are you ready?"

"Do I have a choice?" he asks bitterly.

"What's gotten into you?" I whisper harshly. "You're acting as if I'm forcing this on you."

"Aren't you?" Cire glares at me.

"Cire, we were hand-chosen by the High Priestess," I scoff.

"You mean you were," he snarls, "I think you're giving me a bit too much credit."

I shake my head, no.

"You begged her to pick me."

"In the selection?" I run my hand through my dark curls. "Cire, we were kids–I didn't want to leave my best friend behind. We swore to be brothers."

"What if I don't want to bleed for you anymore, brother?*"*

Smack! My hand cracks against his cheek.

"Are you mad?" I hiss, "don't let anyone ever hear you say that."

The memory fades, cold sweat running down my face, chest, arms, and back. I search wildly for Cire, the apology on the tip of my tongue. Vaiccar's sneers at me with victory.

"That's not what happened at the Culling. Cire and I worked flawlessly as a team, and I won the tournament in record-breaking time."

"Is that so?" Vaiccar smiles. "Perhaps that's all you remember of that day. But you see, I have his memories, and I saw a *completely* different side of that day."

He leans in very closely to me and whispers in my ear, "I thought I would share it with you, a nice trip down memory lane before I wipe the slate clean."

I spit in his face and he recoils with a snarl.

I smile triumphantly at him.

He's wrong. I would have never forced Cire to do something against his will ... right?

"Are you ready, Kai?" Vaiccar towers over me, smiling confidently. "We are so close to your rebirth."

I spit at him again.

He shakes his head in disappointment at my lackluster response to his declaration.

"You are about to serve a greater purpose than you could ever fathom, and that's how you thank me. I have big plans for you."

Eliana

NEXT WEEK A SMALL group of us leaves to begin traveling to other villages in Hevastia, hoping to find more who have been regifted with magic so that we can protect and train them. Those in the Burroughs with magic are making greater and greater progress, and soon they will have mastered their gifts. I want to make sure that their talents and the lessons they've learned are put to good use. We will need their strength against Vaiccar and whatever is to come.

Sweat trickles down my forehead, my breath coming in short pants. Tyr stands across from me, equally exhausted. We've been dueling for quite some time now, running different drills. I figured if my magic won't make itself known, I shouldn't let my physical strength and my combat skills dull.

He charges at me again, short sword low. As he brings it up to me in a fast arc, I bring my own blade down, trying to pin his sword. He dances backward, out of reach, and advances again, swinging the sword down and quickly back up. My heavier blade can't parry the quick attacks, and he gets past my blade, the tip of his sword tapping my chest.

"And, you're dead," he jokes, chuckling and sucking down gulps of air. We both collapse onto the cavern floor, breathing deeply. "I believe that makes the score Tyr two and Eliana with one."

I slightly raise my arm, pointing at him. "I'll get you next time, count on it."

We both laugh. Heavy footsteps ring through the small cavern and thick, large boots fill my vision. Maendril is towering over me, frowning.

"I thought you promised you would use the wooden staff I whittled for you?" he asks, exasperated.

I turn over and stand up, still several inches shorter than Maendril's shoulder. "And, I thought we agreed that you would pretend I heard you when you said I had to use it," I reply with a wink.

His booming laughter fills the small space. "How's training been?" His question is directed at Tyr, who is still lying on the ground collecting his breath. Tyr leans on his elbows and chuckles again. "It's going well. She's improving. I think Tenya could begin practicing with her now."

The jolt of shock at Tyr's words shuddered through me.

I'm strong enough to go against Tenya?

My chest swells with pride. Despite her small stature, Tenya is one of our fiercest warriors. She was sidelined from our battle against the Morei warriors at my mother's insistence. Tenya and Tyr have been trying for a baby, and my mother fought with Tenya to convince her to pursue that dream. My heart pinches with the memory of my own mother's traumatic journey to motherhood, and I'm silently grateful that she was still able to celebrate that choice with other women.

"Tyr, do you really think I should?" I ask, nervous. "I'm not sure I'm ready yet ... she's, uh, very intense." I rub the back of my head where I received a hearty whack from Tyr when we used the training staff. After seeing stars, I forced Tyr to use weapons, knowing we were more liable to pull our hits with real blades rather than large sticks.

"We could always tell Mythica you want to go back to meditating?" A knowing smirk lights on Tyr's face. I groan with frustration. I have continued to meditate with Alana and Mythica, secretly thankful I convinced them to let me use some of that time for dueling. It's been another week of trying to harness my magic, and nothing's changed. At least when I'm fighting I'm useful, capable. If I am to be the auror, then I need to be strong, for my people and for all of Hevastia.

I pick up my sword as Tenya walks in, holding her bow, no sword in sight. She smiles and waves to me before walking to Tyr, giving his cheek a quick peck. He smiles, pulling her in for a deeper kiss. I look away, giving them their moment.

"Did I forget to mention Tenya prefers shooting over dueling?" Tyr chuckles. "Good luck," he shouts as he and Maendril make a quick exit from the cavern, leaving me alone with Tenya.

Twenty second head start before I start shooting at you. Tenya signs to me. *I promise to go easy on you the first time.* She smiles.

Don't. I smile back, before turning and running. This particular cavern contains several smaller chambers and tunnel systems. We have plans to expand this area into a school someday. For now, it's Tenya's hunting ground.

I come to a crossroads and choose the left path, tossing a rock down the right path, the sound of it rolling echoing off the tight walls. Tucked behind a large outgrowth of rock, I wait patiently, listening for Tenya. The unmistakable sound of boots scraping on stone comes to a stop at the crossroads, accented by the soft twang of her bowstring going taunt.

Her arrow strikes the rock I'm hiding behind, and I clap a hand over my mouth to keep from crying out. I sit quietly, and after a few heart-pounding seconds, she takes the right path, her footfalls growing more faint.

I sheathe my sword, pulling my daggers from my belt. Silently, I slip each of my boots off, leaving them behind the rock I've been using to hide. I followed the direction Tenya disappeared to, my bare feet quieter on the stone path. I take three calming breaths, centering myself. I hurry silently down the tunnel, coming quickly to the next section of divergent tunnels.

Tossing another loose stone down the furthest right path I listen intently for sounds of Tenya's boots. The rock bounces down the tunnel, but nothing else. I pick up a second stone and toss it down the middle path, and still no sound returns.

Could Tenya be deeper into this tunnel system?

The third stone ricochets off the close walls of the left path, followed by the sound of boots scraping stone.

I've found her.

I duck into the closest tunnel, waiting. Tenya's bow and arrow come into view, drawn and ready. I pounce from the shadows, jumping in front of her and knocking her bow from her hands with a sweeping kick. She jumps with momentary shock before collecting herself and bringing up her fists.

My daggers slide back into my belt and I bring up my own fists. Tenya advances first, taking a large swing at my head. I duck and bring my right leg up, connecting with her side. She stumbles and regroups, dancing away from me. She takes a second before coming at me fast, her left fist clocking me in the jaw with a pop. I swat at her, my right fist punching her in the throat, forcing her to back off.

I shuffle forward, my bare feet cutting on the stone shards of the cave floor. She takes a few quick jabs at my face, and I block them easily. With my arms up to protect my face, my stomach is exposed and she pulls her knee up, hitting me in the gut.

I double over, and she sweeps her left leg under mine, bringing me to the ground. She leaps onto my chest, pinning me, bringing her dagger to my throat.

Panic floods my body at the familiar pose, and a chill spreads down my arms and back.

I scramble frantically out from under Tenya, sucking in deep breaths to calm my nerves.

Eliana, are you okay?

Tenya places a callused palm to my cheek and turns my face up to hers.

I nod my head, unable to meet her eyes. Cire's face, contorted into a cruel, sickening smile, fills my vision.

Eliana. Breathe. She breathes deeply with me.

One ... two ... three deep breaths.

I need to go.

I dart away from Tenya, winding my way back through the maze of tunnels, all of it becoming a blur through my teary eyes.

I collapse on the cot in my tent, sobs wracking my entire body as the memory of my dagger stabbing into my gut replays across my closed eyelids. Vaiccar haunts me night and day.

The day's come for us to leave. I lie on my cot, taking a few calming breaths before I join the others in preparing our supplies for the journey across Hevastia.

Lady Hevastia, please protect us and all of your gifted children.

Boot steps on stone pull me from my prayers. A tall shadow darkens the entrance to my tent.

"Are you awake, Eliana?" Alana asks, opening the flap to my tent and stepping inside. Hama follows closely behind her, a bundle of fabric in their arms. "We brought you a gift, a new outfit to wear on your travels."

Hama unfolds the package, and draped across their arms is a beautifully stitched pattern, the white stitches matching the same swirl and peaks of the charm hanging around my neck–Hevastia's Heart. "I figured since you're the auror, you should look the part as you introduce yourself to the rest of Hevastia."

I pick up the suit, its black fabric soft to the touch. I step behind my privacy curtain and slip on the skin tight black pants, running my hands along the stitching on each side–the runes of Hevastia's elemental gifts. I pull on the black jacket, lined with soft fur. It's even more luxurious than the last outfit Hama made me, perfectly sized to fit me. When I step out, Hama is smiling ear to ear with pride, holding one more piece of fabric.

"You know I love to add flare. You can hook this to your belt as a makeshift skirt, in case you want to really impress." They wink. Alana knocks her shoulder into theirs, rolling her eyes.

I take the skirt from Hama. Into the supple fabric they stitched tiny white and amethyst gemstones. It's the night sky.

"I love it, Hama," I whisper, in awe. I pull them in for a big hug. "You're coming though, right?" I ask, still smiling. Alana won't meet my eyes, and Hama pretends to make themself busy straightening their dress. "What is it?"

"We won't be joining you and the others on the trip across Hevastia," Alana announces, holding Hama's hand. "There's something else we need to do first."

"Is it because of Yuriel and the others' comments? I thought things have been improving for the refugees." My temper rises at the mere idea of mistreatment against sweet Hama or any of the other refugees who have selflessly been helping with magic training, daily chores, and the infrastructure and expansion of the Burroughs.

Hama places their hands on mine, calming me with a gentle squeeze. "Your people have been more welcoming since your speech. There have not been any problems that a simple discussion between friends hasn't been able to resolve."

"Then what is it?" I ask, pulling Hama to sit down next to me on my cot. "How can I help?"

Alana stands beside Hama, her hand on their shoulder. "Eliana, it's not your burden to bear. We can handle it ourselves." She smiles, but it's forced. She's trying to appear unworried.

"You're going after Kai, aren't you?" I stand up abruptly. "You were going to travel to the Aceolevia without me!" My temper is rising again, and Hama won't be able to cool it this time. "How could you!"

"We all thought it was best if you weren't involved–it's too risky." Alana's calm voice fuels my anger at them hiding this from me. "If you were captured, or worse, killed ..." she pauses. "We couldn't take the chance."

"That's not your choice to make." I glare at her. "I have unfinished business with the Haematitian Council. They still owe me a debt for massacring my family, and for Wildewell. Kai is my friend, too. You can't expect me to stand aside while you risk your lives for him without me."

"Eliana, listen," Alana shouts. "You are the *auror*. Your life is immeasurably valuable, We still don't know how to defeat Vaiccar, but I would stake my life on your magic being key to his demise." She sighs. "This is so much bigger than revenge, and I know you recognize that."

"Please, you can't potentially face Vaiccar without me. We have no idea what you will be walking into." A frustrated tear falls down my cheek. "What if it's a trap?"

"That is my point, Eliana! What if there is a trap and you walk right into it? You would be doing exactly what Vaiccar expects you to do. He knows you care for Kai. Of course Vaiccar wants you to come searching for him. We can't let Vaiccar capture you."

Of course Alana is right. It's the same argument we've been having for weeks now. The risk outweighs the benefits, and stubbornly I don't care. It pains me to think of my friends being captured by Vaiccar, and that I would be somewhere else, safe. It's an all too familiar guilt.

I should have died on the battlefield alongside my mother. Every breath I draw is because I survived against all odds. And, it's not fair. I always survive, and someone else pays the price of protecting me.

Then, a thought occurs to me.

"Alana, I'm the only one to have stood against Vaiccar. I drew his *blood*." I smile at the memory and it bolsters my spirit. "I can fight him. You said yourself, Kai almost bested him. I've bested Kai more times than I can count on one hand."

Alana groans with frustration. "Eliana, now is not the time for a pissing contest."

I snort. "I'm being serious. I can fight Vaiccar, if it comes to that."

"We don't know what new powers he may have."

Hama shifts uncomfortably next to Alana. Their hand rests on Alana's arm, holding her close. My heart pinches. I can't let anything happen to Alana, Hama would never recover.

"That's true, but I could still be of use. Please Alana, I want Kai safe as much as you do. I owe him my life."

She opens her mouth to argue, and an exasperated groan escapes. Hama smiles with gratitude from behind Alana's shoulder. Alana beckons me to follow her and Hama. Together, we find Maendril, Tyr, and Tenya.

Maendril's eyebrow shoots up when he spots me behind Hama. "What is she doing here?" He doesn't need to point. We all know he's referring to me.

"Eliana is joining us," Alana declares over a chorus of frustration and objection from everyone else. "Her knowledge of Vaiccar could prove valuable."

"If we encounter Vaiccar, I promise not to do anything too heroic." A few smiles break through the worried scowls of those I love most.

Maendril rolls his eyes over Alana's shoulder. "Do we have a choice?" he asks, chuckling.

"No." I shove his shoulder, laughing too. He nudges me back and I almost fall over. That sends all of us into riotous laughter, and the moment of anger is easily forgotten.

"Mythica and Daneth can lead the excursion across Hevastia in search of other mages. I will join you in rescuing Kai. Then, together, we will hunt down the solution to stopping Vaiccar and freeing Cire."

"I'll help Tyr and Tenya organize an extra supply pack," Maendril murmurs. The three of them leave to prepare for the trip.

"What do you think we will encounter when we get to the Aceolevia?"

Worried expressions cross over Alana and Hama's faces.

"I'm not sure. We have to be prepared for anything," Alana responds. "And, pray to Lady Hevastia that Kai is still alive, and we're not too late."

Kai

CIRE MARCHES NEXT TO me, his pack weighing nearly as much as him. My own pack is light, mostly consisting of a few days' worth of rations and weapons. Cire carries additional rations, our tent and bedrolls, his own weapons, and medicinal supplies.

As my Morei, he is responsible for ensuring my safety and success on the mission—our very first mission. Part of ensuring my success is maintaining his health and performance so that I may harness blood from him.

High Priest Marius ordered our regiment to march to Greenville, a small village in the grasslands. There has been a disruption among the villagers, and we're meant to settle it. Cire and I are fortunate our first mission is this simple peacekeeping effort.

Sefrina returned from her first mission a week ago, and she refuses to speak of it. Her haunted eyes said enough—the riot in Eternis was not a simple peacekeeping mission.

"Break for camp." The order from Captain Alana pulls me from my thoughts.

"Thank the stars," Cire mutters under his breath when he thinks I can't hear him.

I break away from Cire to join Captain Alana and the other warriors around the mess wagon. Alana's Morei, Hama, prepares us each a bowl of gruel. Cire and the other Morei are pitching tents and preparing the latrines.

We are less than a quarter day's march from Greenville. Tomorrow, I may finally have the chance to show my devotion to the True Faith.

Dinner passes quickly. We sit gathered around the fire, sharing stories. From over the rim of my first mug of ale, pilfered from the mess wagon when Hama was occupied with serving the Morei, a man stands in the shadows cast by the fire.

He's observing me with an unnerving attentiveness, never turning away. Another guardian walks past him carrying a torch, the fire illuminating his glowing red eyes.

I shake off the notion—it's insanity. When I gather the courage to investigate, he's gone, and there's no sign of him. The muddy ground surrounding the tent sits undisturbed, except for my fresh boot print.

After I turn in for the night, Cire sleeps quietly next to me on his own cot as I stare up at the ceiling of our tent. The red eyes stare back at me and I cannot sleep. It was a trick of the torchlight, I convince myself.

The solari had not yet fully risen when we set off for Greenville, carrying only essentials—weapons and medicinals.

Two Morei pull a large cart behind them containing various supplies for the citizens of Greenville. Hama excitedly told Cire and I before we left for our mission of the garments they included for the children, as well as cloth dolls and other toys.

Now, Hama marches alongside Captain Alana, a short sword strapped across their back. Two blades sit resting across my shoulders thanks to Captain Alana's insistence that, if I should ever rely on my weapons, I will be a dual wielder, like her.

I smile with pride.

The smoke from the chimneys of Greenville rises above the tall grass and brush of the horizon—we're close. Cire shifts uncomfortably next to me at the first sign of Greenville. He's been uncharacteristically quiet.

"Cire, what is it?" I ask quietly.

He doesn't immediately answer, and I grab his arm. His eyes widen in confusion. He's traversing.

I curse under my breath.

"What did you take?" I hiss, roughly shaking him. "How could you?"

"I was nervous, Kai."

I scoff. "Of what? We're delivering supplies."

"That's what Sefrina said, too." His voice trembles.

"You're wrong. She was trying to get under your skin." I grab his chin, his eyes still unfocused. "And by the looks of it, it worked," I utter with disgust.

"You're a disgrace to the True Faith."

What should I do? If I tell Captain Alana, she'll surely make us wait, and I'll miss out on this mission—my first mission. We'll be punished—that's unacceptable. Cire will not mess this up for me.

Greenville comes fully into view as we crest the last hill. Smoke rises lazily from several chimneys as the villagers bustle up and down the lanes of their small village.

A kindly man with bushy eyebrows walks through the main gate and greets Captain Alana. They exchange brief words before the signal to file into rank is given.

Cire and I stand side by side, waiting to march into Greenville under the captain's order. The horn blows, and we cross under the arched gate to Greenville, and toward the tehendra.

The tehendra is small. We gather in tight formation, Captain Alana, Hama, and the village elder standing above us on a raised platform. Villagers have gathered around the edge of the tehendra, packing the tight lanes that lead to the rest of the village.

"Welcome," announces the elder, "we are grateful to the Haematitian Council for their generosity."

"It is our honor," Captain Alana replies with a large smile. "It is good to see you again, Daneth."

"You as well, Captain."

A small commotion breaks out in the back of the tehendra. Several older Morei guardians draw blades, the metallic tang of fresh blood filling my nose.

"Sell out," cries a man hidden within the congested lane directly across from the platform. The cry is taken up by more villagers. A second cry of "death to the ruffira scum," is echoed, and the commotion swells into uncontrolled chaos.

Bursts of air and flashes of bright flames erupt at the back of the tehendra as the older Morei retaliate against the villagers. Screams rise above the shouts against our regiment. More warriors join the fray as villagers begin to attack us with crude weapons.

"Stand down," Captain Alana cries. She and Hama are already shielding Daneth from the violence. The skirmish is now a frenzy beyond order.

A villager armed with a pitchfork rushes at me and Cire. I scramble to unsheathe my swords from behind my back. They continue advancing, hate-filled eyes locked on us. I abandon my *weapons and snag a dagger from my belt. Without a warning, I snatch Cire's hand and draw the blade across his palm, calling on his blood to fuel my magic.*

I press my hand out to the villager as he draws close, and spikes rise from the ground, spearing him in place. His cries are cut short as he begins to choke on his own blood. I palm my dagger and stride to the captured villager. Hate-filled eyes glare into mine. I flash my dagger, and fear takes root in his eyes.

"Die, ruffira." His words are garbled by blood and spit.

"Traitor," I hiss. I don't hesitate, drawing my dagger across his throat in a smooth line, and his threats are cut short as he drowns in his blood.

A man stands on the edge of the skirmish, unphased by the violence that rages around him. He's only preoccupied with me. I pay him no attention.

Cire has fled, now hiding. I growl in frustration and embarrassment at Cire's behavior.

When the next armed villager rushes at me, I draw the blood of my first victim to further my magic and flash a wicked smile.

This is what I was born for.

Eliana

MAENDRIL FOLLOWS BEHIND ME as we step out of the portal into the ashen ruins of Wildewell. In the rising *solari's* light, the atmosphere of the broken huts and charred ground is more somber than the last time we were here over two short months ago. Soon, there are twelve of us gathered on the outskirts of the village. Mythica, Daneth, and a small group of mages will begin traveling to the nearest village, Greenfield. Maendril, Tyr, Tenya, Alana, Hama, and I will travel on foot to the Aceolevia to rescue Kai. The plan is to meet back at the Burroughs when we are successful. Mythica possesses the second traveler's stone. With it, they can easily spirit away any new mages to the Burroughs, out of harm's way.

I hug Mythica tightly. My heart aches to leave her. Her wrinkled hand cups my face, giving it a soft pat, and in her aged face is pride and love. A single tear slides down my cheek, threatening more, as I hug her fiercely again. Over Mythica's shoulder, Alana and Hama are saying goodbye to Daneth and to a few of the Wildewell refugees who volunteered to come on this mission. They're serving as guides for the Bellamere clan, who have never left the mountains. My people gaze with awe at the sky without mountains to block the view, and at how the forest rises up nearby, the largest thing for several miles.

"Take care of them," I whisper in Mythica's ear. "And, take care of yourself."

She pulls away from my crushing embrace, smiling. "I should be saying that to you." She laughs quietly. "Promise me, at the first sign of trouble you will leave–no matter what."

"I won't leave there without Kai. I can't." My words are strong and full of a lot more confidence than I truly feel. I'm terrified of what we may find when we arrive at the Temple of Clarity, of whether we will be too late.

She sighs heavily, shaking her head. "Your mother was equally headstrong and defiant." She gives my hand a squeeze. "And, loyal and brave. I'm so proud of how you've grown."

More tears begin to fall down my cheeks. I brush them off with my sleeve, sniffling. "I'll see you soon." She nods and begins walking away to join the others.

The large group walks through the ruins to the Thessimis Fields beyond. I press my thumb to my forehead and spread my fingers to the sky in prayer.

Lady Hevastia guide their quest, protect them.

Slowly, they disappear from view, and when they finally dip beyond the horizon, I take my first breath in minutes. Alana and Hama have been standing on either side of me, also watching their friends walk away.

"Are you ready?" Maendril asks, holding out my small supply pack.

"Would you believe me if I said yes?"

He chuckles quietly. "No, I wouldn't. It's a brave thing you're doing by going back. None of us asked, because … well it's hard to return to a place that's caused trauma."

I open my mouth to object, to tell Maendril it's okay, and that I'm fine. Rising anxiety clogs my throat, and the fear of Vaiccar washes over me. I shiver from the chill that's spread across my skin. My scar stings.

"I'm proud of you." His words are sincere.

Unable to speak, I swallow the lump in my throat with a nod to Maendril. I take my pack and follow Alana as she leads us back through the Hilwe Wildes and to the temple tucked within the forest.

We follow almost the same path as before, stopping once for a break before continuing. As we reach the temple, we split off into two groups. I follow Alana, Tenya, and Tyr, while Maendril and Hama wait in the shadows of the forest. We walk past the garden gate we used last time we broke into the temple, as Alana leads us around the garden wall and further into the temple's grounds. She stops abruptly, and we crouch down, hidden by the trees that run up to the edge of the temple's lawn. The grass here is dead, not the same lush green as the rest of the grounds.

"Are you sure this is the spot?" I ask. There's nothing but an underwhelming patch of grass and the stone wall of the garden. No guardians patrol this area.

I hand Alana the traveler's stone. She takes it with practiced ease after years of using it to escape the Aceolevia as a young captain. I blush, recalling how Hama once told me about their secret trysts in this very forest. They were given the stones by High Priest Marius as a reward for services rendered. Alana refuses to speak of the circumstances which led to her ownership of such powerful stones. In my gut, I know it's something terrible. Alana wears the shame of her service to the Haematitian Council on her sleeve. Asking would only cause her pain–no matter how curious I am.

"Yes," Alana replies, focusing on the traveler's stone. She begins to work a portal to appear hovering above the ground, a window into the dungeon below the lawn. I crawl toward it, careful not to make a sound as I peer down into the hole and the hidden world below between rusted chains hanging from the ceiling. Dried bloodstains lie splattered across everything, flaking off the chains and onto the metal slab below. The smell that assaults my senses almost causes me to audibly gag, but I swallow it down.

I shake my head, and Alana moves the portal several feet, allowing me to view more of the room we are sitting above. There's still no sign of Kai, and as we move through the dungeon I begin to lose hope. I am close to the garden wall now, having slunk across the wide open space of the lawn, completely without being spotted. I stare down into the last cell, and it's not Kai curled up, but an unfamiliar girl.

Shockingly white hair, tangled and knotted, falls past her waist. Her skin is a purplish gray color, adding to the allure. She hasn't spotted me spying on her, and I hesitate.

I've found someone–it's not Kai.

Before we left the Burroughs, Tenya and I taught Alana several words in sign language, but we brought Tyr with us in case we needed him to translate for Tenya. Alana was terrified of Hama being caught, so Maendril stayed back with them, out of harm's way.

Tyr tells Alana what I said and she hangs her head in her lap, shoulders bobbing as she begins to cry.

What should I do?

I know what I want to do. I want to jump down there and rescue this poor girl. But, is it worth the risk?

Tyr shakes his head no. *It's not why we're here.*

I can't leave her here. She's treated horribly, judging by the dirt caked on her scraps of clothing and her body. I mouth the words, *I won't leave her,* just as a guardian comes into view further down the wall. He hasn't spotted me yet, and it's too late for me to make a run for the protective cover of the forest. I lock eyes with Tenya's fearful gaze and sign *I'm sorry* before rolling out of view into the portal.

I land on the stone floor of the dungeon cell with a sickening pop, my shoulder dislocating. I choke back a sob and roll to face the cell's inhabitant. Wide, frightened eyes meet mine. I grab my right arm and set it back into place. The pain makes me want to black out, but I push through, keeping my focus on the girl two feet from me. From above, I didn't notice how cramped these cells are, and it's sheer luck that I landed on the floor and not the latrine bucket.

"Hi," I whisper, giving a small wave. "My name is," I pause, trying to think of a fake name, "uh, Olyvia."

"How did you do that?" She motions to me falling from the ceiling out of thin air. "Who sent you?" As she asked the question the faintest shimmer of hope crossed her face, her eyes brightening with excitement.

"I'm searching for someone, his name is Kai—have you seen him?" I ask, ignoring her questions.

She doesn't hide her disappointment well, the frown disfiguring her dirty face. My heart aches to think of how long she's been daydreaming about one of her loved ones coming to her rescue. I vow at this very moment that I'll do everything I can to help her.

"He's not here anymore," she says.

All the air leaves my body as I stagger against the wall to keep myself upright. "I was too late," I mumble to myself. A tear slides down my dirty cheek.

"He's upstairs now," she points to the ceiling. "Lord Vaiccar took him there last week."

"So, he's not dead?" That's such a relief. "Where is he? How do I find him?"

She reaches out to me, her bony hands clasping my arm tightly despite her frail appearance. "Don't," she whispers. "That's a bad idea. He's not, uh, right, anymore."

"What do you mean he's not right?" I pull my arm free. "How would you know that?" I'm taller than her, and standing so close I cast her into my shadow.

She flinches and tries to move further away, but the cell is small and I have her trapped against the other wall. I brace my arms on either side of her, pinning her in place with my fiercest stare. "Tell me."

"Please, you have to understand, I never wanted to do any of this. I didn't have a choice." Tears begin to fall down her face, desperately pleading with me. "Lord Vaiccar said I had to, if I didn't I would lose comforts, food."

"What did you do?" I enunciate each word, drawing the question out till it ends in a growl.

"I stole his memories," she whispers, her crying growing stronger and more inconsolable. "He is empty inside now, your friend is no more."

"How?" I grab her shoulders and shake her roughly. Her chipped nails dig into my arms as I hold her tightly.

"I'm a Keladonean, it's my gift."

"You're going to fix him," I plead with her. She shakes her head, large tears streaming down her face. Her body is so tiny in my arms that as I shake her, her neck snaps violently, and she hits her head on the wall, her body going limp in my arms. *Shit.* "No, no, no." I lightly tap her face, trying to wake her back up. Checking her pulse, it beats weakly under my thumb. I sigh in relief. She's alive, but unconscious.

I slide her gently to the ground. Guilt ripples through my gut at having hurt her.

From beyond the cell, the sound of a deadbolt scraping open screeches through the silence. The massive wood door of the dungeon is being opened. Panic floods my body, I can't be caught down here. I draw my daggers, ready to fight my way out, when several pebbles hit my head from above. Alana, Tyr, and Tenya stare down at me, relief spreading across each of their faces.

Climb. Tenya signs to me, pointing to the metal bars of the cell's door. *Hurry!*

I point to the unconscious girl at my feet, using my eyes to plead with my friends to take her with us. Another loud bang sounds from the front of the dungeon, iron manacles slamming against a metal table. I flinch at the sound and pull the girl up to my friend's outstretched arms.

Despite her frailty, she's a heavy deadweight, and I struggle with her. Bootsteps begin to echo down the stone hallway of the cell block. There's no time. I set her down gently on her makeshift bed, slipping the small dagger from my braid and tucking it under some loose rags, hoping she finds it when she wakes.

The guard is a cell or two away from discovering me. I place my boot on the metal door, and it creaks. I quickly hoist myself up, and launch myself off the cell door with a loud bang, my hands gripping tightly onto Tyr's as he hauls me up and out of the dungeon. I lie down on my back, the *solari* warming my skin once more, and gulp down deep breaths of fresh air.

I flip over and crawl back to the portal as Alana begins closing it.

"No, don't," I whisper. "Someone is down there, I want to know who it is."

Alana leaves a small portal open, enough for me to barely peer into the girl's cell. A familiar head of blonde hair opens her door and steps into her cell. He spits with utter disgust to find her lying on the dirty bed of cloths.

Fury builds in my stomach over Vaiccar's control of Cire's body, twisting him into something unrecognizable. The nightmare of his hands on my body, and the searing pain of my dagger stabbing my gut, rushes back to me.

Sickness rushes from my stomach, up my throat–choking me. I scramble back from the portal and gulp down deep breaths. I thought I was ready to face Vaiccar, that if I saw him again it would be fine. I was wrong, and the truth of that burns as much as the dull ache in my stitches from where he stabbed me.

I force myself to watch through the portal. I must know the fate of the poor girl I knocked unconscious.

He nudges her with the toe of his boot, and when she doesn't respond he kicks her. I flinch. "Naevys!" e snarls. "You're needed. Get up."

She lies still, not stirring. Only then does he bend down and flip her over. "The dumb girl knocked herself out," he mutters to someone standing out of view.

Fighting another bout of nausea at being so near Vaiccar, I try to tell Alana to move the portal so I can observe who Vaiccar is talking to, but the sound of a guard walking the wall and whistling pulls our attention out of the dungeon and to the temple grounds where we sit, completely exposed. Alana snaps the portal shut, stuffing the traveler's stone deep into her pocket. The whistling grows closer as we sprint across the open grass, diving for the shelter of the forest's shadows. The guardian continues by, unaware of us hiding in the treeline.

"Alana, we need to go back," I hiss. "That poor girl is being tortured. We can't leave her." I promised to get that girl out, and the reality that I abandoned her, like I've run away from everything and everyone is already beginning to tear away at me.

"It's too risky, I won't let you," she says with finality.

"Kai's alive," I blurt the words out, hoping to sway Alana to my cause. "He's in the temple somewhere, and that girl knows. She said she stole his memories, but he's *here*." I place emphasis on the word, pleading with Alana.

"What did she say?" Tyr asks, cutting in.

"She stole his memories," I repeat. "Does that mean something to you, Tyr?"

Tenya frantically signs to Tyr, worry written all over her features.

"What is she saying?" Worry begins to build within me, I can't keep up with how fast her fingers are moving.

Tyr sighs. "She said this magic is not from Hevastia. And that, if what the girl said is true, there's no way to bring Kai back. He's gone."

"What?" I stare dumbfounded at Tyr.

"No." I swallow. "No! He's *alive*." Three deep calming breaths. "She can undo it."

"Maybe, but probably not. Without his memories, the Kai you both knew," he motions to me and Alana, "he's no longer here. Our memories make us who we are. Without them ... Kai could be anything Vaiccar wants him to be. It's too dangerous."

I drop to my knees, fists pounding the dirt in frustration. Alana is staring off into the forest, eyes unfocused. The shock of Tenya's revelation may have finally broken her beaten spirit.

"You said Tenya's heard of this magic before. How?" I clench and unclench my fists, desiring to hit something really hard. My anger and anguish wash over me in equal waves, combined with guilt for Alana's hope these last two months.

"It's time magic, from Keladone," Tyr states. "Tenya's ancestor was one of the elders who received a Keladonean clan when they showed up in our village."

"They were the ones who gave my grandmother Sarlaine the prophecy," I whisper, my thoughts beginning to tumble and spiral as I try to connect unseen dots. "We need to find them."

"You mean to travel to Keladone?" Alana asks, her voice hoarse.

"Yes." My jumbled thoughts finally slow and sort themselves out. "If a Keladonean mage gave our people the prophecy then perhaps they know more about my magic, and how I can harness it. If the girl," I say pointing back to the patch of dirt above her cell, "used Keladonean magic to wipe Kai of his memories, then their auror will know how to cure it."

"We can't help her right now, and I understand why. It would draw Vaiccar out to hunt for us, and we're not ready." I swallow. "I'm not ready. We have to travel to Keladone, find their auror and beg for their help. It's our best option for saving Kai, and countless other victims of Vaiccar."

Alana, Tyr, and Tenya all regard me with various degrees of uncertainty. None of us have ever left Hevastia, and we know so little of what to expect beyond our own shores. One thing is for certain, I'm not ready to face Vaiccar, yet. I will travel to Keladone and find the answers to what I need to unlock my magic. And, when I do, I will be ready, and Vaiccar will burn.

Kai

LORD VAICCAR RETURNS FROM the dungeon aggravated. He paces back and forth, grumbling under his breath. He will call me from the corner of the room to his side if he needs me. I am perfectly content to stand and await orders. His anger washes over me, my body responding to his emotions as if they are my own. The torrent of anger rises and ebbs away as he calms himself once more.

"She's too weak," he spits out. A simple flick of his wrist beckons me forward and I stride across the grand hall, kneeling before my Lord. He resumes pacing in front of me, and I keep my gaze downcast. I try to think of something to occupy my mind, but it's blank ... *has it always been?* I concentrate deeply, and still nothing arises.

My first memory is of Lord Vaiccar standing over me, a black uniform in his arms. He smiled, explaining to me my purpose. I am his right hand, executor of his will. High Priest Marius, the advisor, is afraid of me. He arrived moments ago to discuss strategies with Lord Vaiccar. As he entered the grand hall, he glanced at me with fearful eyes, not daring to stand too close, as if he was seeing a ghost.

I am a shadow, an extension of Lord Vaiccar's grand influence. His will is my own, his command my creed. I desire nothing, unless granted to me by him.

"Kai." My name pulls my attention, and I gaze back to my Lord as he stands before me. His blonde hair is neatly combed, a jacket of dark velvet fitted perfectly across his chest. I wear his insignia, a black jacket with deep blue trim, a red drop of blood on my right sleeve by the cuff. It's a simple uniform, but standing amongst my fellow guardians, we are a dark tide.

"I need you to retrieve something for me." His smile shows no hint of kindness.

I bow my head in reverence. "What is it I shall retrieve for you, my Lord?"

"Not an 'it,' a person," he states. "You will travel to the country of Keladone and retrieve their auror for me."

"But what of the Hevastian Auror?" High Priest Marius interjects. "She's been walking free for nearly two months now. She needs to be captured."

Lord Vaiccar turns sharply toward High Priest Marius, all but having forgotten he was still in the room. "You dare question my judgment?" His voice is a hiss that sends Marius shrinking back. Lord Vaiccar crosses the hall quickly to High Priest Marius, getting in his face. "Well," he barks, making High Priest Marius jump.

"No, not at all." He swallows, nervous eyes scanning the room for any sort of escape. When they land on me he quickly looks away. "She's a direct threat to your plans. Shouldn't we focus on capturing her first?"

"She will come crawling to us, like the worm she is." Lord Vaiccar's face twitches as he stares down High Priest Marius. "The Hevastian Auror is weak. She poses no threat to our plans." He raises his hand to backhand High Priest Marius, who draws his own arms up in defense. "Never question me again, Marius. You won't live to regret it."

High Priest Marius flinches at the threat, his throat bobbing as he swallows. He bows deeply and begins to walk backward, away from Lord Vaiccar. He doesn't take his eyes off of him until he nears the large doors of the great hall, bowing once more before opening them and slipping through, shutting the doors with a loud bang.

"When shall I leave?" I ask, turning my focus back to Lord Vaiccar.

"Immediately," he orders. "Gather your supplies and travel to Sandovell to commandeer a ship."

I rise from my knees and bow deeply at the waist. "As you command."

The pack on my back is light. The sole supplies I need are my own bare hands, my swords, and some loose coins from Lord Vaiccar. Sandovell lies on the coast of Hevastia, the only remaining trade port of the land. I walk through the Dartnuae Hills, the mid-day *solari* high in the sky but concealed behind storm-laden clouds.

The grass sways in the breeze, the rain-scented air flowing down from the Hilwe Wildes. I stop to gaze at the Ventemere Mountain Range far off in the distance. The mountains stand tall and proud, eternal. Soon, Lord Vaiccar's influence will overshadow their strength as he controls all of Hevastia.

As I continue walking, a flash of bright light blinds me, and I stumble to the ground. I stare at my hands, now illuminated by a bright, cloud-free day. My name echoes in the wind, the voice of an unseen woman. I find myself standing in the Thessimis Fields. Contentment washes over me. As I try to stand, I stumble again, and once more the world is cast in the storm's shadow, the warmth of the *solari* gone.

What was that?

My temple throbs, and I press a dirty palm to my head, trying to make it stop. I don't understand what I saw, if it was even real. But I felt the heat of the *solari*, the breeze smelled of fresh flowers, and the woman's voice was so close. I shake my head, dust my hands on my pants and continue walking, hurrying to put as much distance as possible between myself and the strange effects of the Hilwe Wildes.

I walk all day and night, arriving at the outskirts of Sandovell as the *solari* break the horizon once more. The clay buildings sit packed tightly along a crumbling coast, the colorful huts bordering either side of the road into the port city. A nagging thought in the back of my mind whispers that I've traveled this exact road before, but for what purpose I can't recall.

I follow the dusty path, slowly becoming engulfed in the cacophony of the city as grubby children run wild in the streets, chasing one another and shouting. Women with ratty clothes and rotting baskets wander the market with day-old bread to sell, and smelly fishermen with old catches try to pass off the fish as fresh.

I walk purposefully through the throng of people, ignoring the cat calls of the younger women, focused on making it to the sailyard. I arrive some time later, annoyed at the gall of the folks in this city and their shameless behavior in begging for coins and food. A young boy stands by a small ship, untying it from the dock. I stop a short distance away and watch, waiting.

He loads the last crate and net into the boat, ready to set sail. I casually approach him, drawing no attention to myself. Several other Morei guardians wander the dock in similar uniforms. When my shadow is upon him, a greeting forms on the boy's lips–until he spots my cold, hungry gaze. Fear flickers across his face, and he begins to back away from me, but not fast enough. I grab a hold of his collar, bringing the pommel of my sword down on his head, knocking him unconscious. I toss his body into the boat and jump in, pushing off from the dock.

The channel network leading out of Sandovell and into the open water is a maze. Several times I find myself stuck in too shallow of water, and I have to backtrack and try a different path. Half a day is lost in my efforts to reach open water.

When we're far enough into the bay, I pull the scruffy, malnourished boy up from the bottom of the boat and tie him to the small mast. I draw my dagger cleanly across his palm, letting his blood drip into my hand. I call on my power, commanding control of the water to pull the current in my favor, directing the water to carry the boat away from Hevastia and to Keladone.

Hours pass on the open ocean, and I relax into the calm sway of the boat as my magic carries us effortlessly over the waves. I grab the boy's hand once more, drawing a fifth line to keep track of how many times I bleed him, careful not to overdo it. His blood is not as strong as the guardians of the temple, but it's a better option than having to fish for every tithe, which would have proven difficult.

I drop his hand. Beyond the front of the boat, the horizon stretches endlessly in front of me. The boy stirs, waking from the hit on his head. His wide eyes take in the blue water on all sides of us. Seeing his blood drying on his pants, hand, and the bottom of the boat, he screams. It's the screech of a wild animal as he thrashes against his bindings, yelling foul curses at me.

"*Ruffira! Ruffira,*" he yells, his body quaking with the force of him struggling against the ropes around his chest.

I sit patiently, waiting several long, annoying minutes for him to tire himself out and calm down. When he finally relaxes, his breath comes in short pants. He's given himself rope burn where it touched his bare skin. I grit my teeth in annoyance, those injuries could cost me precious opportunities to harness his blood to propel the boat.

"What do you want with me?" he asks, frosty eyes glaring at me in defiance.

"I wanted your boat," I say, "and your blood."

At the mention of his blood the boy's face pales and his bottom lip quivers.

"I have a Ma and Pa back home. They'll notice when I go missing. There will be trouble to pay for when we return." He holds his chin high, deepening his voice to threaten me. I laugh, and his bravado falters.

"*We* won't be returning to Hevastia." I smile at him, showing all of my teeth and he flinches away, tears building in his eyes. I find myself already bored of tormenting him, and close my eyes, ignoring the boy.

A weak whimper is the only sound aside from the boat effortlessly cutting through the water.

"T-this boat is not made for o-open water. It's a channel skiff modified with a small sail, it can't handle big swells."

I snicker. "That's fine. The boat doesn't have to. That's what I have you for."

He whimpers again.

A bright light flashes behind my eyelids, and I find myself in the Thessimis Fields once more, experiencing the same sensations of warm air and springtime flowers in the breeze.

There is a dark-haired girl with long braids and dark skin standing a few feet away, relief washing over her at the sight of me. She's not any of the guardians in the temple I have crossed paths with.

So, why do I feel as if I know her from somewhere?

"Kai!" She runs toward me. She wraps her arms tightly around me as we collide, sending us both tumbling to the ground. She laughs, smiling down at me. I stare back at her, confused, and her smile fades.

"They finally got all of you, didn't they?" Her fingers gently run over my shaved head, the hair a finger tips' length. "What did they do to you?"

"Who are you?" I ask.

"Kai–I don't understand. You know me." She takes my hand in hers, drawing small circles in my palm. "It's Naomi. We met in Bellamere in my lifetime, but you've been visiting me here for several weeks now. I'm your friend. You can trust me."

"I've never seen you in my life," I retorted. "Where are we? Why are you lying to me?"

I push her off of my chest and stand, eyes scanning the grassy field surrounding me on all sides. "Where is the ocean, and the boat?"

Turning my gaze sharply to her, she shrinks away from me, terror in her eyes.

"What have you done to me," I growl out, towering over her.

"Nothing, Kai, I swear." She pleads with me, "you need to listen to me. You're being manipulated. You've been telling me for weeks now that they've been stealing your memories. You were afraid."

"You're lying," I spit out, turning away from her.

"Vaiccar is evil, Kai. You can't trust him!" She reaches for my hand, and I push her back to the ground. Her cheeks are stained with fresh tears that fall freely down her face as she whispers, "Kai, come back to me."

I sit up abruptly, nearly capsizing the boat. I must have fallen asleep. It was simply a vivid dream, I tell myself, as the memory of her fingers in mine lingers on my skin. The boat is rocking in the high waves and taking on water, at the mercy of the ocean once more. My magic must have worn off while I slept.

I grab my dagger and the boy's hand, making my sixth cut. He whimpers in his sleep, but doesn't open his eyes. When the boat resumes its journey across the waves, I force myself to stay awake, too afraid to fall back asleep and see the dream girl again.

Eliana

TENYA HELPS ME FLIP through every journal in Mythica's tent, searching for any information on Keladone, or a world map to help guide us on our journey to the unknown country. Alana and Hama are sitting in the gemstone lake cavern, taking some time alone to come to terms with Kai's horrific fate. I stop unrolling another scroll detailing a past lifetime's crop yield, my fist crushing it. Tenya looks up, concern written all over her face.

I'm fine. Sighing, I admit, *I need a moment. Keep searching?*

She nods her head in response to my question, turning back to the scroll in her hands.

I step out of Mythica's tent, avoiding Maendril and Tyr who sit around a low-burning fire, roasting meats to take with us as supplies for the boat. I follow the path into the deeper caverns, the very same one I walked with my friends three months ago when all the pieces of the prophecy suddenly began to take shape and make sense. I grab the last torch fastened to the wall of the main antechamber, disappearing into the dark depths of the cave's extensive tunnel system.

Soon, there's no sound except for my own breathing and the ping of pebbles bouncing on the stone floor as my boots shuffle along. I reach the deep pit with the etchings in minutes, finding it easier now that I don't have everyone else to keep pace with. I climb down into the hole, sitting in the center of the pit, holding the torch above my head.

The script my grandmother recorded here shortly before her death glows faintly in the fire's light. I take a deep cleansing breath, holding it for three seconds as it settles into my gut, creating a heavy rock before I expel it quickly. I do this several more times, trying to center myself and stave off the anxiety that threatens to overtake me.

I balance my torch against several rocks and place my hands on my heart center and forehead, fingers extended out.

Lady Hevastia, I don't understand. If I am truly Fate's Guardian, your reincarnation, why am I powerless? How am I supposed to be expected to save everyone without magic? I can't even protect my friends. A tear slides down my cheek. *What if you chose the wrong daughter of Bellamere?*

The sound of rocks rolling down the side of the pit snaps my attention back to the darkness I'm sitting in. The hairs on the back of my arms raise. Eyes stalk me from beyond the torchlight. I stand abruptly and snatch the torch, holding it out to peer further into the pit, for whatever is lurking in the shadows.

It's probably a small cave rodent.

When nothing jumps out at me, I sigh with relief. I find the path leading out of the pit and begin following it back to the main tunnel that leads to the Burroughs. The sensation of predatory eyes suddenly returns, and I stop, turning slowly. This time, yellowed, cloudy eyes stare at me from further down the tunnel.

The creature yowls furiously and pounces at me, knocking me to the floor. Naomi's disfigured face fills my vision. The memory of her attack in Bellamere's ruins rushes back to me, how she nearly killed me last time. I use the torch to burn her rotting skin.

She screeches in pain, stepping away from me. I reach reflexively for my daggers and realize with sickening dread that I don't have any of my usual weapons. Naomi's dark, monstrous form hisses at me. Black blood oozes from open sores, and yellow puss flies out of the nasty cavity that is her mouth. She rushes at me again and knocks the torch out of my hands, pinning me to the ground once more.

There is Promise in the Light.

I yell out, and she screams back at me, more of the black blood landing in wet, sticky globs on my face. I place my hands on her chest to shove her off, and something else rises within me in response. A bright light forms in my hand, shooting out of my palm and at Naomi. She falls off of me, and I scramble to climb on top of her, putting my hands on her disgusting flesh once more. I take a deep breath, hoping I'm not being stupid. Immense relief washes over me as the power burning under my skin rushes forward and out of my palms into Naomi.

She thrashes on the ground, the light moving under her skin and spreading. Soon, it covers her entire body and she glows as bright as a small *solari*, illuminating the entire tunnel.

Pounding boots echo in the tunnel as Maendril and Tyr run up behind me, stopping abruptly when they spot Naomi's body absorbed by the ball of light.

"Eliana!" Maendril pulls me into a crushing embrace, simultaneously putting himself between me and Naomi. His eyes roam over my body, touching the black blood on my face, relief in his gaze as he realizes it's not mine.

"Are you okay? What is happening?"

Naomi stopped moving, the glow slowly fading from under her skin.

Tyr's sword is drawn, the blade extended toward Naomi's chest. As the burning light finally disappears, I hold the torch out to her unconscious body, sucking in a shocked breath. Similar gasps of shock come from Maendril and Tyr, and I know at that moment that I am not dreaming.

Naomi lies at my feet, completely healed. Gone is the rotting, disgusting flesh that was falling off her bones, the black blood and vile ooze no longer mar her skin. She's been renewed.

"Maendril, pick her up. We need to take her back to the Burroughs." He doesn't move, still staring at Naomi's marvelous, inexplicable transformation. "Hurry!"

I push him, snapping him from his daze. He bends down and gingerly picks up Naomi, careful to support her head and neck as if she is a newborn babe. I follow Tyr as we quickly make our way out of the tunnel and back to Mythica's tent. Up ahead, Alana, Hama, and Tenya are standing guard, weapons drawn. They all must have heard my screams.

I shout, waving my arms to draw their attention to us. "Quick, grab blankets and some fresh clothes!"

Alana's eyes grow wide with shock before she rushes off to my tent to grab spare clothes and blankets. Tenya and Hama stand still, watching us approach. Hama's face is blotchy and red. They must have been crying. My heart pulls as I remember the original reason I went down to the pit of carvings. I wanted to beg Lady Hevastia to spare Kai.

Alana rushes forward, holding an old dress from my trunk, gifted to me by another survivor. Maendril lies Naomi on the blankets Tenya laid in front of the fire, stepping back to give her privacy as we rip off the dirty, bloodstain-crusted rags hanging from Naomi's limp body. I try not to think about which stains are Naomi's blood, and which aren't. I hold her head gently in my lap as Tenya pulls the dress on her before wrapping her in another spare blanket.

She makes eye contact with me, and I know the question behind her gaze–it's the same one playing on repeat in my own mind.

How is this possible?

"Eliana, I know this must be a rather large shock to you, but you need to tell us what happened." Tyr is squatting down beside me, offering me a hand to help me sit beside the fire. I take his hand and let him lead me to the log a few feet away. My mind is still spinning.

"I-I don't know. She attacked me. I wasn't thinking. I thrust my hands out in front of me and the power surged out of me." All the anxiety from before rushes up, bringing tears of relief to my eyes. "I didn't know what I was doing, whether or not it would hurt her. I," I pause, realization dawning in my mind, "I whispered 'there is Promise in the Light,' the same as when I was in the Heart Chamber of the Aceolevia when the magic initially rushed into me."

"How is she healed?" Hama asks, their hand gently grazing Naomi's smooth, healthy skin. "It's a miracle," they whisper in awe.

"The light, it must have purged the darkness from her. The prophecy said my touch would burn true, I never understood what that meant ... until now. What if I am able to purge the black plague from all of the monsters across Hevastia?"

"And, what if you died trying?" Maendril shoots back. "You nearly died up against her. You can't expect every time to be so easy. What if you got lucky?"

I flinch at this tone. "You're right. It won't be easy. I would be a fool to believe the enormous task placed on my shoulders is simple. We all know it's not." I breathe deeply. "I have to believe this was not just a stroke of luck, but a breakthrough. I have *magic*. I'm not powerless." A tear of relief slides down my cheek, and soon, more follow. "I've been so terrified of letting you all down. This gives me hope."

"Eliana," Maendril's voice cracks. "I didn't mean to–"

"It's okay. I forgive you. I know all of your concern comes from a place of love."

Maendril hugs me tightly.

"I'll be cautious. I still don't know enough about my magic. That's why we have to travel to Keladone. Not only to find answers about my magic, but to also find a cure for Kai."

Hama grasps Alana's hands, tears in the corner of both their eyes. I made a promise to them, and I intend to keep it. There are already too many broken promises haunting my conscience.

"You all get some rest. I'll take the first watch over Naomi." I say, placing my dagger in my lap. "I'll yell if anything changes."

Maendril and Tyr hesitate, but Tenya places a firm hand on their shoulders, leading them away to their respective tents. Hama and Alana both hug me before leaving for their own tent across the Burroughs, where the other refugees from Wildewell stay.

In the morning, I'll have to explain to everyone what all of the raucousness tonight was about. I hope that I won't have to show them Naomi fully healed, and yet still dead. That won't win me much favor, and I fear panic will set in. They've all been made aware of the dangers Vaiccar poses and the necessity of our mission to save other elemental mages across Hevastia, and now our newest mission of traveling to Keladone.

But, what if this failure makes the lose all the trust they've placed in me?

I've worked so hard to live up to the expectations.

I stare at Naomi, searching for any sign of life, but her body does not stir. It feels as if years pass as the night wears on, and still no change. As the *solari* rise in the sky, peeking through a crack in the outer antechamber wall that allows for the briefest sliver of natural light, something miraculous happens.

Her chest begins rising and falling, breathing. I try to recall if she had been breathing all night, and I know that every time I checked for a pulse or a breath, her skin was warm, but without a pulse, and her chest never moved. I take her hand in mine, laying a finger along the veins in her wrist, a strong pulse thrumming against my finger.

I gasp in shock, dropping her hand. Her fingers twitch as I reach to take her hand back in mine. Her eyes open slowly, blinking against the fire's light. When her eyes meet mine they widen in surprise and she yelps.

"Eliana?" She reaches a shaky hand out to me, her soft fingers cupping my face, fingers pulling my auburn hair through them. "This is a dream. I'm finally dreaming."

"You're alive," I say in awe, pulling her tightly against me, tears spilling over my cheeks as I sob in relief. Her shoulders shake as she hugs me back, crying too.

She pulls back first, swiping her eyes with the back of her hand. "How is this possible? I died."

"You were a dark beast. Even scarier than the ones Jasath warned us about before the attack on Bellamere," I say, clasping her hands tightly within my own. "I think I purged the darkness from you."

I laugh as confusion crosses her features. "It's hard to explain. I have so much to catch you up on. I can't believe you're here. I've missed you so much."

I pull her into another hug, laughing and crying with relief. "You tried to kill me—twice. Can you believe it?" I chuckle, wiping away my own tears.

Naomi shakes her head in disbelief. "I don't believe any of this. It doesn't feel real yet." She runs her fingers along her arms, amazed. "How long has it been? Since the village battle."

Her mouth forms a small 'o' of surprise as she takes in the scale of the large cave, realizing for the first time that we are not in a house in Bellamere. "Where are we? Where is everyone else?"

The unspoken question of whether we are the lone survivors hangs in the air between us.

"The others are still asleep. Everyone who evacuated before the guardians attacked is alive, and safe, here. They rebuilt in the mountains surrounding Bellamere. We call this place the Burroughs." I pull her to her feet, leading her toward the pools for a bath. "It's been almost six months since the battle. We all thought you had perished in the blood bath … until I found you in the ruins, turned into a dark monster."

I swallow before carrying on, glancing back to check that Naomi is okay. She's taking in everything with mixed awe and wonder as we enter the tunnel that leads to the baths. I keep talking, "you were the only one I saw. Everyone else was burned in a pyre."

"Kai," Naomi says the name so quietly I almost don't catch it. I lose focus and trip on a rock jutting out from the tunnel wall.

"Naomi, what did you just say?" I ask in disbelief.

She doesn't hear my question, but extends a hand to help me stand again before continuing to follow me into the tunnel. When we arrive at the bath, I help her remove the dress, setting her gently into the hot spring. She sighs in relief before dipping under the water, staying under for several seconds. I panic that she's drowning when she finally reemerges. I hand her some scented oils for her skin, beckoning her to the edge of the pool so I can help her wash her hair.

Naomi swims over, laying her head against the edge of the pool. "Thank you, Eliana." She sighs in relief, or sadness. "I don't understand how I'm here ... I missed you too. I didn't go to the Beyond. It was a space removed. I was all alone ... except for one visitor." Her eyes soften under a small, sad smile on her face.

"His name was Kai," she stops and turns to me, giving me a very serious look. "Before you get mad at me, he was one of the guardians that attacked our village. I don't know how he found me, but he did. I met him, in the aftermath of the battle, and once before that when he spared my life. He had such a deep sadness wrapped around him. But, in the golden place I've been in for the last six months," she chokes on the word months, recognizing how long she's been gone. "In the golden place, he was kinder, gentler. We became friends."

"You saw Kai in the in-between place?" Hope spreads over every inch of me. "How?"

Her eyebrow raises, questioning. "So it's true. You knew him, too. He told me he met you ... but I thought perhaps it was my mind trying to make sense of everything around me." She laughs. "He's real. I didn't make him up."

I tell her everything from the last six months–discovering the prophecy of Hevastia and my role in it, accepting my enemy's help, uncovering the truth of the prophecy, and finally releasing magic.

"Kai was lost to us in the skirmish. Alana said he didn't make it before her hold on the portal broke. And when she went back, he was gone, and we couldn't risk running into Vaiccar." At the thought of Kai being a shell of himself, his memories stolen I begin sobbing.

"We will get him back, El," Naomi consoles me, wiping away my tears. "He's not all gone."

"What do you mean?" I ask, gazing at her with tear-blurred eyes.

"When I was in the In-Between, as you called it, he would visit me. He told me all about how Vaiccar was using a mage to steal his memories, how he was tortured and bled. But, I saw him recently, I think. He didn't remember me, but he still visited me in the golden fields."

"That's horrific," I whisper. "Oh my stars, I let that happen to him?" My mind begins to spiral, and Naomi grabs my hands. She looks me directly in the eyes. "Eliana, you didn't let anything happen to him. None of this is your fault. It's Vaiccar's. Don't blame yourself, please."

"I'm going to make it right."

She squeezes my fingers. "I know you will."

Naomi dips under the water, rinsing out the oils, leaving me alone momentarily with my thoughts. Relief and fear collide in my gut, but above all such deep gratitude to have Naomi back, one of my best friends. When she resurfaces, she's smiling.

"So, what's the plan, Eliana?" She smirks. "What? Don't act surprised! You always have a scheme. Tell me everything." We fall into a fit of giggles while she dries herself and redresses.

We walk arm in arm back to the main antechamber.

"Are you sure you want to face everyone? We can keep it a secret for now if you want. It could be a lot. We all thought you were dead, and you thought you were gone too–those are heavy emotions."

"I'll be fine, El." She squeezes my fingers. "I can handle it. I've missed everyone so much. Are you sure you're ready to explain how you brought me back?"

I stopped walking. The thought hadn't occurred to me.

Naomi smirks. "Are you coming?"

"No, I'll catch up. I just need a second."

"Don't be long, otherwise I might embellish the whole thing, and suddenly people will think you can fly or something."

Naomi's laugh echoes in the tunnel, reaching me after she's already turned the corner out of view.

I close my eyes, searching deep within myself, trying to call forth my magic.

"There is Promise in the Light," I whisper to myself, opening my senses up to feel *anything*.

Nothing happens. Three deep breaths, in and out, before trying again. I clear my mind of everything and try to call forth the same ball of light from before. Still, nothing changes.

What if it was a one-time opportunity, and I used it to free Naomi instead of banishing Vaiccar? How will I tell everyone. What could I possibly say?

My thoughts spiral, and I collapse on the tunnel floor.

"Eliana, wake up. I don't have much time," a familiar voice whispers as ice cold hands wrap around my face. My eyes burst open, staring directly into the dark, black pools of Atrya's eyes.

"Princess Atrya?" I push her away, giving myself the needed space from her frigid touch. "What are you doing here?"

"You accessed your powers. I can sense it." She offers me her hand, pulling me on my feet. "How did it feel?" The excitement in her voice is obvious, and a sickening suspicion spreads in my chest.

"Wait, wait—why are you asking me?" I start pacing. "Didn't you use your magic when you were alive?"

She frowns, ashamed. "Well, no, not exactly. I never learned how to call forth my magic. I'm not even sure if I had any gifts other than the blood in my veins."

"Your blood—what does that have to do with anything?" I stop pacing to stare at her. "And if you didn't have any magic, then why were you considered the god-touched of your time?"

She reaches out with both hands to hold mine, but I brush them off and resume my nervous steps. None of this is making any sense.

"Eliana, please stop pacing. I have but a moment before they realize I'm interfering again. And this is important." Atrya grabs my wrist and pulls, forcing me to look at her. Her ice cold hands burn against my skin, but I can't shake her grip.

"*Lady Hevastia was half mortal. She and Soran, the first deity of this land, started a mortal bloodline, a very powerful one. Those mortals became the royal family of Hevastia, and one of their descendants, the auror for Lady Hevastia's magic. My family–*"

"*Stop, that doesn't make sense,*" I interrupt her. "*There was a clan from another nation that visited here and told my ancestors of the prophecy, that the 'chosen one' would come from their bloodline.*"

"*And that part is true. Fate's Guardian, you, were born to the Bellamere clan, just as the Keladoneans 'predicted'. But, they also told that same prophecy to villages and cities all across Hevastia. They didn't know where the auror would truly be born next, so they told everyone.*"

I laugh in disbelief. "*So, you're telling me that the 'prophecy' was a hoax? That this is all random, and I happened to fit the criteria of the prophecy's text–born of blood, forged by fire, risen from the ashes? My village burned and suddenly I became the auror?*"

"*No, not exactly. My bloodline carries the potential of the auror, the gift of Lady Hevastia. So, if you're to be the auror, and you are, then your blood and my blood are one in the same.*"

"*We're related?*" *A laugh bursts out of me. Her whole story sounds ridiculous, less so than a clan from another deity's land professing the return of our goddess born to a no-name family in the mountains, but still, it's far-fetched. I can't believe I let myself believe I was something more. This whole time it was random.*

"*Stop it,*" *Atrya says firmly.* "*Your mind is probably racing, and you don't believe me. But, it's the truth.*" *She sighs, pulling me to sit on a large rock jutting out from the tunnel's wall.* "*When the siege of the royal palace started, my mother hid me away. I was supposed to escape the palace at all costs. I couldn't allow myself to be* captured. I fled, leaving Eternis behind. I escaped into the Ventemere Mountains. Word traveled quickly that the entire Helesatra royal line was murdered, and I thought I was safe."

"I found your ancestor's clan deep within the mountains, and they took me in. I was already several months pregnant when I abandoned my mother and father, and near time to give birth when I was rescued by your people. They never knew my true identity. I couldn't risk word spreading that I was still alive. I was afraid the rebels would hunt me down and use me, again."

"I gave birth in your valley, to a beautiful, healthy baby girl. The chieftess at the time was a kind, generous leader." A single tear rolls down Atrya's cheek as she pauses. "It was my opportunity to disappear. The bloodline would be protected, safe, far from the rebels and the insurrection's rising influence. So, I took my leave in the middle of the night, leaving a note that begged the chieftess to take my daughter in as her own."

Tears flow freely down both of our cheeks as Atrya continues. "Your great grandmother was royal. Her bloodline is the very same one you were born to. I'm your ancestor, Eliana, your family."

"I don't understand. Why didn't you stay? You were safe." I squeeze her hands. "And why are you just now telling me all of this?"

"My grief and my fear of being recognized were too great. I loved my baby so deeply. I loved all of Hevastia as if it were her. I couldn't risk exposing myself or her, and losing everything." She sniffles. "I couldn't tell you because you weren't ready to hear it. You didn't yet fully believe you were the auror. I needed to wait for you to accept that part of yourself, otherwise you wouldn't have trusted what I'm telling you. I may not have had access to any of Lady Hevastia's *magic because the time to use it wasn't in my lifetime, but it is in yours. You are a far greater force than you realize, Eliana.*

"Promise me you will learn everything you can about your magic. I wish I could tell you more, but I myself don't know anything about it. All I know is that the Keladonean's prophecy is real, and you will need the aurors of the other deities in order to defeat Vaiccar."

"I can't harness my magic. I was trying before you found me," I reply, exasperated.

She lightly touches my face, a deep longing in her black, endless eyes. How did I never notice that before? She lightly plants a kiss on my forehead, standing up. Her flames burn brightly further down the tunnel, ready to take her away.

"Remember Eliana, there is Promise, Power in the Light. You are the Light."

She is swallowed by the flames, leaving me alone in the tunnel once more.

Music and excited chatter carry down the tunnel. My people are throwing a celebration. The main cavern is illuminated in a warm glow by *eternia* lanterns. They sit scattered all over, a sign of gratitude and reverence to Lady Hevastia, painted *solari* glowing in the light. Everyone is gathered in the new *tehendra,* and I follow the colorful lanterns to my people, standing on the sidelines as they holler and chant, stomping their feet and dancing with joy. All of this must be for Naomi, the beloved daughter of our clan, returned to us. She's in the middle of the crowd, wearing a crown of mountain lace, laughing. She twirls in a circle, the dress she was wearing before now exchanged for a more lavish style with colorful patches sewn randomly on the skirt. I recognize it instantly as a Hama original.

Naomi spots me and smiles as I wave to her. She beckons me to join the group. I reluctantly step into the dance, awkwardly moving at first, but soon I close my eyes, relax my mind, and let the music take me. I dance with my people, my friends, and my chosen family, letting the larger worries and fears of the last several months take a seat on the sidelines, if only for the briefest of moments.

When I'm done dancing, my legs ready to give out from under me, I collapse on the ground next to the fire Maendril, Tyr, and Tenya are seated at, chest heaving from the fast pace of the last dance. They all smile as I join them.

Tyr and Tenya are holding hands. One of Tenya's hands rests lightly on her stomach. She's tired and wasn't out dancing earlier. Tenya catches my eye as I've been staring at her for the last several minutes. I blush, ashamed to be caught. She squeezes Tyr's hand, pulling his attention back to me, and she signs something into the palm of his hand.

Hama and Alana approach the campfire, holding hands. Maendril offers them the log he's sitting on, and goes to stand beside Tyr. "We're not interrupting anything, are we?" Hama asks.

"I'm grateful you're here. It saves me the task of telling you later." Tyr winks at Alana and Hama. "You've become dear friends to us. We want you to share in our news.

"Tenya is pregnant!" Tyr sits proudly, smiling ear to ear. "It's something we've both wanted for a long time," he exclaims, holding Tenya close.

Her smile widens, eyes bright with joy as she hugs her stomach.

I throw my hands up in celebration, smiling broadly, and cheering. "That's such fantastic news. I'm so happy for you both!" Suddenly, I remember my skirmish with Tenya in the tunnels the other day.

"Oh stars! Tenya, I didn't hurt you or the baby when we fought, did I? I would never forgive myself–" I sign and talk at the same time.

Tenya shakes her head no, cutting me short from my ramble.

I'm fine, baby is okay. You don't need to worry about us, sweet girl.

Oh good, that's good.

How far along? Hama's signing is clumsy, but improving.

Seven months. Tenya signs and Tyr translates.

"Seven months ..."

"You're mother is the first person we told. It's why she wouldn't allow us to join the battle against the Morei. She insisted we stay with everyone else ... We owe her our lives, and the life of this little one." Tyr explains and signs to translate for Tenya.

Tenya's hand gently rubs her stomach.

My throat grows thick with emotion. With gratitude, I stare at my loved ones, safe and huddled close around the fire.

My mother would have loved this. This is all too much.

I need to be alone.

"Good night everyone." The words are strained, emotions already clawing up my throat, threatening to spill out. My mother would have loved to sit by this very fire.

A chorus of good nights and well wishes settle in my heart as I leave the warmth of the fire. My friends' excited chatter follows me as Hama and Alana discuss potential baby names with Tyr and Maendril, their suggestions becoming more wild with every new name. Maendril's booming laughter is a low rolling thunder that follows me all the way to my tent.

"Can I join you?" Naomi breaks away from a group of villagers she was chatting with to walk alongside me.

"I'll probably be some lousy company."

Naomi shrugs. "I don't mind. I'm out of practice being 'good company.'" She laughs, but it's hollow.

"Was it hard?"

She shrugs. "Before Kai started visiting me, I had my hope to cling to. The hope that I would be reunited with my family and Brynne in the Beyond, that the empty, golden place I found myself trapped in was wholly temporary.

"After Kai began popping up randomly, spending sometimes hours, sometimes mere minutes, disrupting my solitude and keeping me company, I began to feel lonely when he was gone." Naomi sniffles. "Thank you for saving me from that existence, Eliana."

"You're welcome." I throw my arms around her and hug her close while we walk to my tent.

Curled on my cot next to Naomi I sleep peacefully for the first time since returning from the Aceolevia. Vaiccar does not haunt my dreams tonight.

Kai

THE START OF THE fifth day on the open ocean proves not nearly as uneventful as the first four. The day began with the boy refusing to eat the apple I offered him, and spitting the water I forced into his mouth in my face.

Now, he sits with eyes closed, pretending to be asleep as I concentrate on controlling my magic against the large swells that threaten to tip the boat.

Another swell rocks the boat, nearly capsizing us. I lose the grip on my magic, and the boat is once again at the mercy of the violent water. I grab the boy's arm and he fights me, trying to keep his arm away from my blade.

A giant wave crests next to our small boat, sending me into the deep water and capsizing our boat.

I swim back to the boat. The boy's supply crates are carried off by the crushing waves that now hammer the bottom of the boat. I dive, struggling against the churning ocean, to reach the boy tied to the mast now submerged in the dark water.

I pull my dagger from my belt and cut through all of his bindings, dragging him to the surface. He's unconscious, having swallowed too much sea water. I cut his arm for the ninth time, letting his blood fuel my own strength.

I struggle to keep us both afloat as I battle the tossing waves. A large wave slams against the skiff, sending it further away. I curse and take a deep breath before diving, dragging the boy down with me. Submerged, I swim under the side of the boat and wedge my shoulder on the rail, kicking furiously against the waves. Calling forth my magic, I propel myself upward faster than normally possible. The boat pops above the waves, righted once more.

I drag us both aboard. The boy's limp body falls onto the deck with a wet smack, and I smile satisfactorily. Let this be a lesson to him if he ever tries to fight me again. The supplies are lost, and I groan with frustration at my current position. This stupid brat is hardly worth his contributions to my journey. I retie him to the mast, and cut him for a tenth time. Instead of calling forth the waves, I summon the wind and fill the sails, slowly propelling us across the wild, tossing waves.

Hours pass, and still the boy does not wake. I check his pulse again. It beats faintly under my thumb, he's alive.

Perhaps I've drained too much blood from him.

I press my fingers to my temple, everything about this first mission for Lord Vaiccar is proving far more troublesome than I had hoped. I will prove to him that I have earned my position as his favored warrior, that I can be trusted to carry out his will no matter the circumstances.

The wind continues to fill the sails, and the precarious battle with the waves quickly gives way to a smooth trip gliding through the water. I close my eyes once more, hoping for a moment's peace. There is nothing but a black, blank expanse. No memories bubble to the surface to replay in my dreams, no thoughts beyond Lord Vaiccar and my mission. I frown, disappointed that the beautiful girl with black hair hasn't revisited me.

She spoke against Lord Vaiccar, acting as though she knew me. Why would I care about a stranger?

I try to shake the thoughts, but questions nag me. *What did she mean to me? And why can't I remember?*

I wake with a start as something jolts the boat, nearly capsizing us once more. The waves are eerily calm. The boat rocks violently again, and I stare out into the water. From the corner of my right eye, a dark shadow crests the water and dives back down.

I laugh to myself, thinking it's probably a young, curious *jorol*, a whale, when the dark shape rams the boat, sending me sprawling on the deck. I scramble to my feet, grabbing my swords, anger and annoyance brewing in my gut.

With the blood of an animal this large I will be at Keladone in a matter of mere minutes. It will be a power beyond my wildest dreams.

I scream at the open water, taunting the animal to return. The boy stirs, frightened eyes staring at my drawn swords. He begins whimpering, begging for his life.

"Hush, fool," I growl. "I'm hunting a prize far more valuable than your measly blood. Be quiet, or you'll be bait."

This only furthers his whimpering, now combined with quiet sobs that rack his whole body as he shakes in his bindings. I ignore him, tightening my grip on my blades, waiting for the beast to show itself once more.

A dark shadow surges toward us, barely under the water's surface. I climb the mast, ignoring the insipid boy as I gain higher ground. When the beast draws closer, I launch myself from the mast, shouting and hollering with the sheer rush of free falling through the air. I land on the creature's back, stabbing both of my swords deep within its scaled flesh.

The beast rears itself up out of the water. It's not a whale but a water demon, a serpent monster. It roars, thrashing its massive head and back, trying to shake me loose. I hold fast to my swords, still embedded deeply within its flesh. In the chaos, it bashes its head into the mast, shattering it into oblivion. Large chunks of wood bob in the water all around us, the wreckage adding to the mayhem of the beast's struggle. I grip my swords, bracing my body as the beast bucks, unsuccessful in knocking me off its back. I pull one of my swords free and stab the serpent again, its metallic blue blood gushing from its wounds, coating the water in the oily substance.

It roars and dives into the water, sucking me along with it under the waves. It continues to dive deeper, the light from the *solari* barely reaching the depths where it stops, The water is ice cold, my body spasming from the frigid, abrupt temperature change. I manage to pull both of my swords free, breaking for the surface and the warmth of the *solari* now high in the sky.

Powerful jaws clamp around my body, dragging me to the surface before tossing me in the air. As I fall back toward its awaiting teeth and my death, a vision of the black-haired girl smiling flashes behind my closed eyelids, the heat of the *solari* where she is warming me, too.

I can't die, not without knowing who she is.

I open my eyes, and thrust my swords in front of me, diving right for the serpent monster and its open jaws. The first rows of the monster's sharp teeth close around me as my sword pierces the back of its throat. Several teeth pierce my back and gut. I yell out from the searing pain.

The monster lets out one final, guttural shriek before collapsing, dead, and crushing the remains of my boat with a gigantic splash. I drag myself out from its maw, tearing my flesh and clothes on the sharp teeth.

The water surrounding the wreck shimmers metallic with the beast's blood. When I try to harness it, nothing happens. I pound a fist on the boat deck, now quickly filling with the murky, blood-filled water. All the trouble of killing the stupid beast and its blood is useless to me. Now, I'm without a boat and without a plan.

I get up, sheathing my swords as I pick my way across the ruined remains of the vessel. I roll up my sleeves, beginning to clear the rubble from the broken mast. I pull several large beams away, and sticking out from under one is the hand of the boy. I had all but forgotten about him in my skirmish with the beast. I continue to clear the debris, finding his broken body pinned to the deck by a large piece of the rigging beam.

Checking his pulse, I snarl, disappointed. His red blood mixes with the oily metallic blue of the monster's. Useless.

I should have picked someone stronger. This child was a waste of breath and resources. Hardly worth the headache and not even capable of saving himself.

Weak. Pathetic.

He's dead, and I am alone once more. Stuck on open water with a boat quickly taking on water.

Eliana

THE *SOLARI* BARELY CREST over the mountain peaks as their soft heat warms my skin when I slip from the Burroughs's entrance and out into the rocky landscape of the mountainside. Breathing deeply, I tip my face to the sky, and the gentle kiss of the mountain breeze caresses my skin. The sound of shifting rocks pulls my attention to the cave behind me. Naomi stands arms outstretched, blooming under the *solari*, just as I had. I extend my hand to her as she picks her way across the loose stone.

"In the In-Between, where I was trapped, it was bright and warm all the time. It could be easily mistaken for a paradise. Flowers danced in the breeze, their smell thick in the air. It was peaceful and intoxicating," she says, wistfully, smiling up to the sky with her eyes closed.

"It almost sounds as if you miss it?" Concerned, I gently shake her hand, grabbing her attention.

She laughs softly, and shakes her head. "I'm so grateful to be back as myself, and to no longer be a dangerous monster. But, I miss the peace and the ease of that place." Her smile is sad. "I miss Kai." She laughs in disbelief. "I can't believe I said that."

I shrug my shoulders, smiling knowingly at her with a wiggle of my eyebrows. "I've never heard you say that of anyone, and I've known you too long to think this doesn't mean something."

"How can someone be the reason for the worst moment of my life, and also the person who brought me the most joy I've ever experienced?" Naomi shakes her head in disbelief.

"I think life is weird like that. The world is cruel and violent, but the moments where you experience true joy, that's what makes all of the darkness and pain worth it. Sometimes, those are inexplicably intertwined." I kick a rock, and it tumbles down the slope.

"Do you think you can save him?" My best friend's eyes brim with hope when she meets mine. "I mean, you helped me, so–"

"I promise, Naomi, I will do everything I can to bring Kai back to us. I promised Alana and Hama, and now I'm promising the same to you." I squeeze her fingers, still locked in mine.

"You don't have to do it alone." She squeezes my fingers back. "I know–"

Naomi pierces me with a familiar, knowing stare and I fall silent. It's *the gaze* reserved for when I'm being *particularly* stubborn. I know it well, always given to me by Naomi after another escapade that landed us in trouble with my mother. Memories from a shared childhood of skinned knees flit across my mind. Adventures born from boredom and the desire for an existence beyond the confines of our village. Adventures that resulted in "told you so's" from Naomi, and conspiratorial snickers between me and Brynne.

"El." My childhood nickname has never been said in such a serious tone. "You're not alone, okay? I know the prophecy didn't mention the 'chosen one's best friend,' but she's standing right here. I'm right here."

Emotions swell within me—gratitude, love.

I'm not alone. I want so badly to believe that.

"No more of this 'I' business, okay?" Naomi opens her arms to me. "Hug on it."

Laughter bubbles up, and soon Naomi joins me. As children, we sealed all of our promises with hugs. There was nothing a hug between best friends couldn't resolve. Promises cast in each other's arms were sacred.

I eagerly step in her arms as they fold around me, holding me tightly. I return her embrace with a squeeze. As we separate, Naomi quickly swipes a tear from her cheek.

"Thank you, Naomi. I needed that reminder."

She shrugs. "You are who you are, El. I know you think you have to bear it all on your own, but you don't. The people," she pauses and tips her thumb over her shoulder, pointing behind us, "in there love you, and they'll follow you to the ends of Odora if you ask. Now, I'm going back inside to take one final, hot bath before we leave for Sandovell. Are you coming, too?"

I shake my head. "In a minute. I'm going to take a short walk."

"Do you want company?" Naomi's face is tilted toward the sky, absorbing a bit more of the warmth before ducking into the cold caves we now call home.

"No, that's alright. Go enjoy your bath." I pretend to hold my nose. "You smell."

She playfully shoves me, laughing. "Rude!"

I gently push her back, laughing too. Soon we are in a fit of giggles, and hugging.

Stars. I've missed Naomi so much.

"Don't be too long. I heard Maendril say last night that he wanted to leave before the *solari* fully breach the mountains," she calls out to me.

I wave back to her over my head, already picking my steps down the rocky slope and toward the lush forest at the base of the mountain. I pat my hip, Fate's Guardian secured there, just in case I come across any beasts. Soon I leave behind the warmth of the *solari* for the cool shade of the forest's canopy. The dried leaves crunch softly under my boots as I walk among the trees, enjoying the peace of the forest in the morning.

It was always my favorite time of day, the best opportunity to slip away from the village and have a moment for myself. An escape from the life I felt trapped by, the expectations I wanted no part in. Now, I would do anything to go back to that time and place. I wouldn't take it for granted.

A twig snaps to my left, and I unsheathe my sword, holding it out in front of me as I turn to address the sound. A dark shadow stands concealed by a thick copse of trees, ten paces from me. It lumbers slowly forward and I hold my ground, tightening my grip.

A large, burgundy head pokes into the light breaking through the canopy and I relax. I sheathe Fate's Guardian and run up to Vendeekta. I bury my face in her soft scruff. She grumbles and nuzzles me, searching for berries or other hidden treats.

"Vendeekta, settle girl. I don't have any treats for you." I scratch her fuzzy ears and another rumble of pleasure echoes in her throat.

"We're leaving today for Sandovell, and from there to Keladone." She tilts her head, as if she's truly listening to me. "My world's become so much bigger these past six months, and so much has changed. I'm both thrilled and terrified of leaving Hevastia. What if it's a major waste of time? Or something horrible happens while I'm away? I don't know if I can bear the idea of that."

I start pacing, my anxious thoughts trailing behind me. If I keep moving then they won't catch up and swallow me whole. I glance at Vendeekta, and she's visibly nervous by my anxious pacing in front of her.

"I'm alright, girl. Maybe a little overwhelmed." She huffs, not believing me.

"I mean, I brought someone back to life! I expelled the darkness from my best friend's body, and now she's alive again. What if word spreads and people think I can do it again? Oh stars, what if I can't?"

A sob chokes out of me. "Atrya doesn't know how my magic works. She was my last remaining hope of understanding any of this, and she's a dead end." I throw my hands up. "She's my great-great-grandmother. How insane must I be to experience visions of my ancestor who is my same age and talks to me? And, how pathetic that I have this miraculous gift and no idea of how to harness it? What if everyone dies while I'm still trying to figure it out?"

I turn and run into a wall of thick, soft fur. Vendeekta moved to sit in the path of my pacing steps. I hug her tightly, and scream into her chest. She sits patiently, letting me scream out all of my frustrations.

I sigh, knowing it's time. "It's time for me to go." I give Vendeekta more scratches behind her ears. "Watch out for everyone here while I'm gone, okay?"

She shakes her head and lays her head against my chest for another hug.

"Okay, one final hug." She nuzzles close and I squeeze her head tightly.

Vendeekta lumbers into the dense forest, her nose already twitching as she hunts for berries.

When I enter the Burroughs, everyone's awake and the daily hustle and noise is in full swing. I join the fray, following the current of bodies that move about their daily activities. It doesn't take me long to reach my tent, where I find Hama packing my satchel.

"Hama, what are you doing?" I ask, smiling.

They jump, my sketch journal and quill flying from their hands. "Eliana! You startled me." They laugh and pick up the items they dropped. "I was helping to pack your belongings. Naomi mentioned you went for a walk, and I wasn't sure how long you would be gone for. I didn't want you to leave anything behind on your trip."

"Wait, you're not coming with me?" This is the first I'm hearing of this.

"Alana and I have decided to stay back. Tyr and Tenya are going to need help preparing for their baby." They take my hands and pull me down to sit beside them. "We'll watch over everyone in your absence. Mythica and Daneth should arrive soon with new refugees, they'll all need our help, too."

"But, what if I need you?" My heart's heavy with sadness. I hadn't thought of what Tenya's pregnancy news would mean for our journey. And, I'm ashamed I wasn't thinking of the new refugees.

"I selfishly hope you'll always need us, but I also know you can do this on your own." They open their arms for a hug and I collapse into them, immediately comforted by their warm, strong embrace.

"Thank you, for everything you've done for me and for everything you're doing now for our people." I give Hama's forehead a kiss, a sign of deep respect in our clan. "You've made me stronger."

"The strength was in you all along, Hevastia's chosen or not. You have such a pure heart, Eliana, and that love, it's not a weakness. It's your greatest strength. You envision something more out there for all of us. That vision, combined with your passionate, loyal heart is what gives us all the strength to stand beside you."

"Thank you, Hama. I'm still not sure I deserve your belief in me, but I will work to earn it."

"And, that's precisely why you have it. You take nothing for granted. I've watched you bloom and come into your own these last six months. There's a hunger inside of you willing to burn the world for those you love."

We wave goodbye to the crowd gathered at the entrance of the Burroughs before stepping into a portal leading to Sandovell. Salty sea air attacks my senses as I emerge from the portal on the outskirts of the port city. Everyone follows closely behind, and Alana steps through the portal last.

"Are you sure you don't want me to wait until you've boarded a ship?" Alana's eyes squint against the bright *solari* high in the sky. When I follow her gaze, I gasp at the beautiful ships of all different sizes bobbing in the harbor. The water beyond the harbor stretches for as far as the horizon. It's limitless.

"We're not leaving this port unless it's on a boat, but I appreciate the offer." I open my arms to Alana and she steps into them, folding me into a long hug.

"Be careful, Eliana," she whispers in my ear as she steps back, already forming a portal back to the Burroughs.

Maendril, Naomi, and I wave one final time as she disappears from view. When we turn back to take in the city of Sandovell from the hill we're on, a wave of anxiety washes over me. I've never seen so many people in one place before, and I don't know the first thing about manning a boat. All three of us are horribly out of our element. We need to find someone who's not loyal to the Haematites, a minion of the Haematitian Council. That shouldn't be too hard.

I lead the way down the sandy path to the main gate. I can't help my jaw from dropping as we walk under its massive shadow. A sentry in shiny chainmail and a red and black uniform holds out a spear, blocking my path.

"Papers?" They ask in a bored tone as they barely glance at me and my friends.

"Papers?" I repeat, dumbfounded. "I don't have any papers. We're hoping to go down to the port. We're in need of a ship."

They laugh. "Well, miss 'in need of a ship,' that's too bad. I can't let you through without documents, Haematitian Council's orders."

"No, I don't think you are listening. I don't care about the Haematitian Council or the dumb papers. I need a ship, so, you need to let us go."

Two more sentries take interest in our conversation. We've been standing here arguing for too long. It's becoming suspicious. The sentry I'm in front of jerks their head, motioning for the other two to join them. The two additional sentries walk up, fists clenched around the shafts of their dull, ill-maintained spears.

"Buna, what's the problem?" The taller one's voice is gruff, and his beard unwashed and scraggly. The shorter one is not much cleaner with stains from an earlier meal smeared all over his clothes.

"Claims they need to enter the city without the proper paperwork, acting all defiant of the Council's will," Buna explains, turning their nose up at me.

"Please." I swallow down my disgust when the tall one's beady eyes land on me, full of desire. "We just need to get to the port and hire a boat. We're not looking for any trouble."

He studies me up and down, and I find myself suddenly regretting how tightly my new dress fits my lithe frame. My fingers reflexively reach for the dagger on my belt, ready to carve his repulsive eyes out of his nasty skull.

"I don't know how folks handle their business in the shit-hole villages, but Sandovell is the crown jewel of Hevastia. We don't take kindly to troublemakers and rule naysayers." He snorts and spits a disgusting ball of snot onto the ground by my boot. "It's our duty," he pokes either thumb at Buna and the shorter man, "to maintain the peace. We're guardians of the Haematitian Council."

I clench my fist, ready to bring it violently up to meet his nose, hoping to knock the predatory smile right off his ugly face. Maendril's hand lands on my shoulder, pulling me back from the guardians and out of swinging reach. Naomi steps up, smiling and flaunting her curves.

He turns his attention to her immediately, assessing her with the same predatory gaze he used on me. Naomi places a hand on his chest, running her fingers up it, and I want to retch. Buna rolls their eyes, but the other guardian is pissed to not be the one Naomi is flirting with. She was always better at talking her way out of situations. I usually swing first and talk last.

"Captain Kai sent us from the Aceolevia. He wouldn't appreciate it if he knew we were held up at the gate. I'll let him know you were amenable to the situation, just this once." Naomi winks and twirls her hair with her left hand, the right one still placed on his chest.

"I'm sorry miss, but we're not to let anyone into Sandovell without papers. *Captain* Kai's *friends* are no exception."

All at once Maendril's hand lifts off my shoulder and Naomi steps back away from the guardian. It's the opening I need to bring my fist up, connecting a right hook with the guardian's face, dazing him.

He staggers, falling back into the other two guardians, who are stunned at what's happened. All three are knocked down, helmets and spears clattering to the ground.

Buna recollects themself first, shoving the tall one off and running at, me bare fists raised, having lost their spear in the confusion. I set my stance and let Buna advance. As they draw closer, I swing out my right leg, catching the left side of their body and sending them sprawling to the ground.

Buna drops to the ground, and I leave them for Naomi to handle. She pounces on Buna immediately, tying their wrists together, and apologizing when Buna hisses from the rope being drawn too tight.

This is the fight my body's been craving ever since we lost Kai in the temple. I was born to kick the Haematite's asses.

The shorter guardian and Maendril are locked in a sword fight. Maendril is barely breaking a sweat as the smaller guy comes at him repeatedly with everything he has. They really don't have the best fighters outside the elite Morei. The tall one I first punched finally collects himself. He spots me and comes barrelling at me, screaming. His fist comes at me from the left, and I dodge it easily, crouching low and bringing my own fist up, connecting with his gut. He doubles over and I grab his head as I stand back up, driving my knee into his face, knocking him out.

Buna and the short one sit to the side tied up, and soon I have the tall one restrained as well.

A slow clap sounds off from behind us, and I turn, my hand already resting on the hilt of Fate's Guardian. I didn't work nearly enough frustrations out, and could use another fight. Standing in the shade of a tree along the path is a man in a funny outfit. His pants are loose and flowing, with knee high boots and a sash for a belt. His shirt is more or less a fitted vest, bare chest proudly displayed. He wears his hair long and tied back, deep black shadow smudged under both eyes.

"Can I help you?"

"No, but I think I may be of service to you." He smirks. His smile is cocky and confident, but not predatory. He bows dramatically. "Captain Zayne Kipp, m'lady."

"And I should know who you are?" I laugh, shaking my head. Maendril and Naomi are equally unamused by the stranger's interruption, or that he witnessed our entire fight with the guardians. "Are all Sandovellians so pretentious?"

"I couldn't help but overhear you needing a ship. Or, was I mistaken?" He chuckles. "Because, I would be willing to sail with someone who beats the snot out of the Council's lap dogs anywhere they want to go."

Kai

B Y SHEER LUCK, I manage to stay on a piece of driftwood from the ship's wreck, now floating aimlessly with the waves. I lie with my back on the board, my face to the *solari* beating down mercilessly, eyes closed. Their heat warms my skin and dries my dripping wet clothes, soaked from the chilled waters I plunged into while battling the serpent monster.

Its metallic blood still coats my hands, but the monster's corpse and that of the boy from Sandovell were claimed by the water long ago. I am utterly alone, without a plan. I search my mind for any sign of the black-haired girl and the peaceful place with flowers, but I find nothing. I lay my arm over my eyes, blocking out the world.

Hours later I sit scanning the horizon, lips chapped and dehydrated. In the distance, something rises above the water. Squinting, I can barely make out the shape of trees, a forest of them.

Impossible, my mind is tricking me.

I continue to stare at the trees as they grow larger, the waves working in my favor, carrying me closer to the shoreline and my salvation. My boots splash into the shallows, and I stagger toward the beach, collapsing onto the sand, relief flooding my body. All hope is not yet lost. I've made it to Keladone. I dust the sand off my pants and walk with purpose toward the treeline, in need of shelter from the unforgiving solari that continue to beat down on me.

Instant relief washes over my skin as I leave the bright light in favor of the shaded forest. It would be easy to mistake the dense trees around me as the Hilwe Wildes surrounding the Aceolevia, and brief panic spikes in my chest at the thought of having washed up on the shores of my homeland, empty-handed.

Lord Vaiccar would not take lightly to me failing his request, I shudder at the thought of disappointing him. So far from the temple, his influence still has its claim over me. His will runs through my veins. It is my entire purpose for being alive. Without it, I am nothing. I will not fail him.

There's movement in my left periphery, and I draw my sword, stalking forward. The undergrowth is minimal, and it's easy to pick my way through the forest following the shadow that weaves itself between the trees and bushes dotting the forest floor. I reach a low spot, the ground rising on all sides, roots and rocks sticking out from the loose, red dirt. I sheathe my sword and grab the largest root in front of me, yanking on it to check that it's secure before climbing over the side of the outcropping and back to level ground.

Frustration builds in my gut at the thought of losing my mark, but the shadow is ahead, continuing to wind its way through the forest. I stare down at my blood-red hands from the soft clay this forest grows on.

Suddenly, the forest is gone, and I find myself in a shadowy place, darkness surrounding me. I stand and redraw my sword, a deep unease creeping into my bones. This vision is nothing like the kind girl and the field of flowers. It's sinister. Something scuttles across the ground, the sound of feet shuffling on stone, scattering loose rocks.

"Hello?" I call out, voice raspy, my throat raw from sucking down so much salt water. "Come out and face me," I yell, my demand ending in a cough.

The scuttling sound stops, and I pivot to face the direction I last heard the noise come from. I squint my eyes, peering into the darkness. The faint outline of a person stands within the darkness, barely distinguishable from the shadows that pool all around me, slowly creeping up my own body.

"What are you?" I ask. I hold my sword out. The shadows now lick up and down my body, chilling me to my bones. I try to shake them off, but they come right back, exploring every inch of me. Suffocating me.

The large shape steps forward from the darkness, and a nervous, confused laugh escapes my own mouth.

What in the hateful stars is this?

Stepping from the darkness is a reflection of myself, eyes the color of freshly spilled blood, face ashen as if it was never touched by the *solari's* warm rays. It stops several paces in front of me, staring silently. I continue to struggle against the shadows that coil themselves around me.

"What do you want with me?" I snarl and twist against the shadows, trying to reach for my sinister reflection. It remains silent.

"Answer me," I bellow. A painful shock shudders through my body, and I drop to my knees at my reflection's feet.

Red eyes–*the shadow man.*

It's him. I can't recall why, but I know with every fiber of my being this tall, red-eyed man is not my friend.

My hands land in the soft red clay of the forest, and I find myself free of the shadowy realm. As unexpectedly as they arrived, the shadows disappeared. My sword drops from my hands, and I sink with disbelief down to the ground, fingers digging into the red clay.

I drank too much salt water. This is all a dehydration fueled illusion.

***

I sit concealed by thick brush, while below me a small group of people collect flowers from a clearing filled with the strange blood-red blooms. They move about carefree, children weaving between the neatly planted rows, squealing and chasing one another. The women in the group wear long flowing dresses of black, their hooded cloaks various shades of red and orange, the men simple white shifts and flowing white pants. Their skin is alabaster white, hair a shockingly dark black, and their eyes a piercing amber.

These are not the Keladoneans.

A twig snaps behind me, and I make eye contact with a boy of twelve years. He possesses the same features as the people below, but painted under his eyes are three red, vertical lines. I place a finger to my lips as I stand, towering over him and casting him in my shadow.

He holds his right hand out to me, staring at me with intense concentration. I take a step toward him, and a weird sensation passes over my body, suddenly immobile. Stepping back from me now, he continues to hold his arm out, eyes never leaving mine. My mind commands my body to move, but nothing responds. I am completely aware of my body and yet have no power over it.

When he's nearly ten feet from me, he drops his arm and takes off running. My body collapses as I gain control of it again, and I pant, hands shaking as I run them over my body with relief.

I turn back to continue observing the group gathered in the clearing, hoping to learn more about them, assessing my next move. I count the red cloaks among the group and realize three of them are missing. In my commotion with the boy, I lost track of them.

Cold steel presses into my back. Three women in red, each holding their own red blade, all pointed at me, stand behind me. I hold my hands up and away from my own blades. The blade poking my back digs deeper, and I hiss as the tip brushes over my spine.

"Hands and forehead to the red," the tallest woman says in the common tongue, flicking her blade from my head to the red clay I am kneeling in. "Now," she commands.

I kneel, pressing my palms and forehead into the ground. "I don't want any trouble," I reply. "This is a misunderstanding."

"I shall be the judge of that, *ruffira*." She spits out the insult. The heat of her stare burns into the back of my neck, juxtaposed by the cold, steady pressure of her blade.

The blade tip breaks the skin below my shoulder. I hiss at the pain. I try to turn my neck, but a boot comes down on the back of my head, pushing my face back to the red clay.

"Forehead to the red," the first woman snarls.

"You will regret this." I swallow against the pain building in my shoulder from the blade that continues to press into it.

"This grove is sacred to our people. Your presence here is not permitted," the third woman says, her voice strong and confident. "*Venaripa*, what shall you have us do with him?"

"Return him to the red," she states, digging her blade into my shoulder as I cry out in pain.

Eliana

AFTER SOME CONVINCING, MAENDRIL agreed to hire Captain Zayne for our trip to Keladone. We boarded his boat alongside a ragtag crew of ten, all experienced sailors according to the Captain.

Now, Naomi and I stand leaning against the railing overlooking the complicated network of channels leading out of the port, waiting to launch and begin the journey. Maendril and Zayne are arguing over something. Maendril's thunderous voice carries from all the way across the boat. When I glance back, Maendril is waving his arms over his head and Zayne's arms are crossed, but an amused smirk lights up his face.

Naomi nudges me, pointing to a group gathered on the dock, all wearing the same uniforms of the Haematitian guardians we beat up outside the gate. These guardians are talking with a distraught woman, her wails carrying over the breeze. A stone-faced man stands next to her, watching her antics with obvious annoyance.

Three guardians disperse from the group listening to the crying woman, coming right for our boat. I lock eyes with one of them, and they shout something at us. When I don't respond, the guardians begin running toward our boat.

"Captain, we have company," I shout, getting both his and Maendril's attention. "Haematitian guardians on the dock."

"What?" Captain Zayne marches to where Naomi and I stand, following her pointed finger. "That's unfortunate," he mutters.

The sound of jingling chainmail stops in front of our ship. Standing on the boardwalk are three guardians, swords drawn and pointed at us. I push Naomi behind me, even as she draws a dagger from a fold of her cloak.

Captain Zayne shouts unfamiliar commands to his crew and they disperse. I stand at the rail, locked in a staring contest with the guardians. The boat jolts under us and begins to head out into the harbor as the sails are dropped and it backs away from the dock. The Haematitian guards run along the boardwalk as it wobbles, threatening to collapse into the water.

I peel my eyes away from the guardians and find Captain Zayne is watching them from the helm. It's with relief I notice how comfortable he is standing up there. Although, I can't help but have a small, nagging thought.

"This is your ship, right?" The wind is in my favor, carrying my words to him.

He smirks, and winks. "It is now."

Maendril booms, "I knew it!" He huffs, trying to take a calming breath. "Eliana, this man is a conman and a thief. He commandeered this ship. It's not his."

Sandovell is already growing smaller behind us. I silently apologize to the merchant whose ship we stole. On second thought, I don't pity them knowing that Sandovell is loyal to the Haematitian Council, and by extension, Vaiccar.

"Maendril, it's fine." I make eye contact with Captain Zayne. "You can sail this ship, right?"

"Absolutely, m'lady. My crew are some of the finest sailors in all of Sandovell." He pulls his collar again, a mischievous smile on his lips. "We happen to also be some of the unluckiest gamblers." He puts an arm around me, and I reflexively lean closer, distracted by the smell of the sea that wraps his body in an aura. "I lost my ship in a bad game of cards."

Coming to my senses, I shove his arm off of me and step away. "I don't really care about how you lost your own ship so long as you can successfully sail this one. We need to get to Keladone, and quickly."

He bows deeply, a smirk on his lips. "As the lady wishes."

Grunts accompanied by the sound of clanging metal alert us to the Haematitian guardians that managed to board the boat before we left port. The three of them stand with their swords drawn.

I step next to Captain Zayne, my own sword drawn, and we rush the guardians, meeting our blades with theirs. Two against three shouldn't be a fair fight, but without a *sanguinar* to support them, these guardians are poorly skilled swordsmen.

I dispatch the first one easily, locking blades with him, and using my own leg to pull his legs out from under him. He falls to the deck, sword clattering from his hand, and I hold my blade to his neck. With murderous eyes, he screams and tries to swipe at me, but I dance out of the way, knicking his neck with my blade. He flashes me a triumphant smile and closes his eyes with concentration. There's the smallest tremor of air in front of him, but before he can so much as push a breeze to ruffle my hair, Maendril steps up and picks the guardian up by his scruff, throwing him overboard.

Captain Zayne is fighting off the remaining two guardians, and doing a fine job of it. His long sword is impressive compared to the short swords of the guardians, who are no match for his skills. He grunts and pushes them back, giving me an opening to engage with the shortest one.

I hold out my hand, waggling my finger at the guard, beckoning him to ignore Captain Zayne for me. He smiles, thinking he'll have an easier fight.

As if.

Our swords meet, and I dance back, forcing the guardian to step closer. As he arcs his sword, slashing toward my right shoulder I slide to the left, and he misses, giving me the perfect opportunity to rush into his open right side. Bringing up my sword, I smack him on the butt with the flat side of my blade, and he yells a string of curses at me.

Laughing, I dance away, and he turns to face me head-on once more. He rushes at me, his sword in front of him, but his footwork is clumsy and unbalanced. When he raises his sword to swipe at me, I knock it away easily with my own, throwing him off balance. He lands with a wet smack on the deck, and I bring my sword down on his neck.

"Surrender," I command, chin held high. He glares back at me, a challenge in his eyes. I smirk, and call for Maendril with a flick of my wrist over my shoulder.

Maendril's large form casts the man in shadow, and the guardian's cocky grin fades to terror as he realizes Maendril means to throw him overboard into the rough water of the outer bay.

I smile and wink. "Bye," I casually remark as Maendril picks up the guardian and pitches him over the side of the boat. He lands in the water with a gigantic splash.

Captain Zayne also incapacitated his opponent, his own men heaving the remaining guardian into the black water. With the threat gone, the sailors return to their tasks, as if the skirmish with the guardians never happened.

The Daughter of the Seas cuts easily through the large waves that rock the boat as we journey toward Keladone, leaving Sandovell a small speck behind us. Naomi and I share a bunk below deck, playing a card game Alana and Hama taught me in Wildewell. It's a good distraction, and I welcome it. Sitting with Naomi makes it easier to forget everything that's happened these last six months, everything I've lost.

After our fifth game, Naomi's eyes blink slowly with sleep and I leave her to rest while I go on deck. As I open the door, I'm overcome with the wild wind of the open ocean whipping my braid and loose hair. I open my arms to the cool breeze and breathe deeply of the salty air. It's a sensation I've never experienced before, this sense of ultimate freedom. The world appears infinite from the middle of the crystal blue waters we sail on, and I feel so small, almost insignificant.

What I wouldn't give to stay here on the open ocean, the spray of salt water washing away all my worries, the solari heating me to my core. Stars, this is incredible. I think to myself, face upturned to the sky, arms open wide as if I could embrace the entire ocean.

Captain Zayne stands at the bow of the ship, leaning casually against the railings. As I approach, he glances back, and smiles when he realizes it's me.

"M'lady," he half bows, his eyes running up my entire body as he stands. I roll my own, and shove him.

"None of that, please, Captain" I beg, laughing.

"Only on the condition you stop using my title. It's just Zayne. Titles are unnecessary." He smiles.

I couldn't agree more. Here, I can be Eliana. Not the daughter of the chieftess, not the auror. Just Eliana. But I can't say any of this to him, or to anyone. I will bear this new title with all the strength and confidence I can muster. I will not let them down.

"What are you doing out here alone, anyways?" I ask, following his gaze to the vast, blue horizon ahead of us and the *solari* setting.

"When it's just me and the water, I think more clearly. The waves know how to wash off all my worries." A gentle smile rests on his face. His hair is ruffled from the sea spray that shimmers on his vest and strong cheekbones. I stare back at him and smile, content to stand next to him in silence.

Maybe the waves will wash all of my worries away, too.

"You think it's odd," he mumbles, not meeting my eye.

"No." My hands are intertwined and I fidget folding and unfolding my index fingers, debating what to say. "It's not that. It actually sounds really nice ... do you think the water could carry my concerns away alongside yours?"

Curiously, a veil falls from Zayne's demeanor and he relaxes. Gone is the showboating, over-the-top pirate. Standing before me is just a man. I smile to myself.

"Perhaps. Look," he pauses, running his hand through his tangled dark curls. The motion reminds me of Kai, and I think of Naomi asleep below deck, and Alana and Hama left behind in the Burroughs, all worried for him.

"Are you running from something?" He stands, and his gaze catches my eyes, trying to hold contact. I break first, looking away. He stands next to me while I stay leaning against the railing, taking three deep breaths, trying to decide how to respond.

"Not exactly, more or less running to something." I sigh. "Answers, hope, some way out of the impossible position I've found myself in."

"It's not my business, and that's why I never asked, but usually people don't accept the help of the first stranger who offers a boat leaving Hevastia."

"Well, I'm not most people," I admit.

Even if I sometimes still wish I was.

Shame heats my cheeks in a deep blush.

His smile softens, and he leans next to me, our shoulders almost brushing. Staring out at the water, he talks to the ocean. "Well, you're someone I would enjoy getting to know." He chuckles, and it's a pleasant sound. "I've never heard of someone handing the Haematitian scum what they had coming to them quite the way you did. It was ... impressive." He blushes.

I place a hand on my chest, pitching my voice higher as I retort in a mocking tone, "why Captain Zayne, are you saying I'm a good fighter?"

"It's Zayne." He rolls his eyes, laughing under his breath. "Don't get ahead of yourself. Let's just agree I would rather stay on the 'good side' of your blade."

"A wise decision," I state, smiling.

"What had you going toe to toe against the guardians anyways? They're not exactly well received in Sandovell, but their word is law, and they maintain order and protection from the dark beasts, so most people at least respect them enough not to get in their way."

"Are you familiar with what's been happening in villages across Hevastia?" I ask, my voice falling quiet.

"Unfortunately." He runs his hand through his hair again. "Lot of refugees walk through the same gate you shit-kicked those guardians under. They're treated worse than garbage by the city's native citizens. Relations are strained. There's already so few resources to go around as it is with the droughts, rotten harvests, and the prey in the plains scared off by the dark beasts."

"It's not much better in the villages, but they find ways to make do." I think back to the time I spent in Wildewell, how although their harvests struggled, and they could barely hunt due to the dark beasts, they celebrated, and they danced. Wildewell was rebuilt once on its own ruins, a monument to tenacity and resilience, and now it lies in ashes, abandoned.

"The Haematitian Council does nothing while its people are starved and hunted by dark beasts. Stars, the Council itself hunts its own people all in the name of its 'True Faith,' the promise of cleansing the darkness from the land."

I shudder. "It's barbaric, and it's only going to get worse. There is a greater evil at work in the Haematitian's ranks."

At the mention of greater evil, Zayne stands up once more, his eyes clouded with concern. "How do you know any of this?"

A condition of hiring Zayne was that I promised Maendril not to tell him who I was, just to be safe. But, standing here with Zayne, I feel myself wanting to tell him all about it. We're in the middle of an ocean, traveling across the world.

If I trust Zayne to get us safely to Keladone, maybe I can trust him with this, too?

"Are you familiar with the prophecy of the return of Lady Hevastia's reincarnation?" I stand and square my feet to his, staring him dead in the face, my tone serious.

He laughs, thinking I'm joking but as his eyes roam my face, the seriousness of my question sinks in. "I mean, everyone's grandparents told them the tale of the return of Princess Atrya. But, it's merely a story."

My eyebrow shoots up in disbelief.

"I'm not loyal to the True Faith, but those of us who live by the sea have tales of our own, and those are far more real to me than some lost princess."

"If I thought you were loyal to the Haematitian guardians, we would be having a very different conversation right now," I jest. The tension between us eases and we both relax a little.

"Whatever version you've heard of the prophecy, it's probably only partly correct anyways. And, that's not really the point I'm trying to make."

I sigh, nervous. I realize this is the first time I'm telling a stranger about what I've gone through and learned in the last six months, and somehow that makes it all the more real.

"I'm the descendant of Lady Hevastia, the one destined to save us all." The words tumble out of me quickly, and I look away from Zayne, afraid of his reaction, worried he'll be disappointed somehow to know it's me.

Zayne laughs, letting out a long exhale at the end. "Well, that's a relief." His arm drapes across my shoulders pulling me closer to him. With his other hand he tips my chin up toward his face and smiles. "You're the most courageous woman I've ever met. If I had to bet on anyone, I'm glad to know I'm betting on you." He lets go of my chin and catches a stray hair caught in the ocean's breeze, tucking it back behind my ear.

A heat rises from my toes to my chest and finally finds a home on my cheeks that now burn bright red. Embarrassed, I step out of his arms, and hug my own. "Thank you, Zayne." I laugh. "I, uh, haven't told anyone that before. I mean, a stranger."

"I don't think we're strangers, Eliana," he replies softly, a gentle smile on his face.

"No, I suppose we're not anymore." I smile. "You don't think it's insane?"

He laughs softly and shakes his head no. "I told you, I grew up listening to sea tales. Those are far crazier than a prophecy where a strong, powerful woman saves our land." His voice is soft and kind, and I smile despite myself.

"Maybe you can tell me about those sea tales, someday," I offer. The subtle warmth of another blush rises in my cheeks.

"I'd enjoy that." Zayne gazes across the water before continuing to talk. "About two months ago, I was working on the dock, reeling in a haul of fish for my neighbor, and as I was fighting the bobbing boat and the thrashing catch I felt something shudder through me, and suddenly the water around the dingy, and only my dingy, was calm." He chuckles. "Strange, right? I suppose you might know something about this?"

"Ah, you've got me there." I laugh. "Hardly the strangest thing I've heard of these last six months." I find myself wanting to tell him everything, the beginning of the story forming on the tip of my tongue.

Heavy boot steps stop right behind Zayne and I, breaking our focus on one another, and I turn to Maendril standing with his arms crossed. "Eliana, I was hoping to have a word with the Captain." Maendril's voice is gruff, but his face shows mild concern to find me shoulder to shoulder with Zayne.

"Anything I can help with?" I ask, slightly challenging Maendril to show his hand. He shakes his head no, and I know from experience when Maendril falls into this silent mood it's best not to try your luck. He can be more stubborn than Vendeekta when he wants something.

Does Maendril have some sixth sense for when I'm about to break a promise?

I jokingly think to myself, stepping back from the railing and giving a small wave to Zayne and Maendril before returning below deck to the bunk I share with Naomi.

It's the fifth morning traveling aboard the Daughter of the Seas, and as I climb the steps to the deck the smell of the salty air hits my nostrils and I breathe deeply. The *solari* are barely rising over the horizon, and the choppy water is a bright orange, the sky a soft pink–it's beautiful and mesmerizing. The boat sways greatly as another large wave crashes over the deck, soaking the wood.

Zayne's crew moves quickly around the boat as they execute various tasks. On the breeze their voices harmonize as they all sing together.

It began on a warm spring's evening:
I was the unluckiest pirate around,

She was the destined princess.
She was a beauty,
My beautiful danger,
My princess.
We could fight so well together,
Run away.
We wanted to sail together, around the world,
We wanted it all.
But one evening, one lovely evening,
We conspired to forget it all.
Together we gave our worries to the water.
It was beautiful, so beautiful.

When they finished their shanty I stopped one of the older gentlemen and asked him where to find Zayne. I follow his gaze as he points to the cabin at the other end of the ship. He winks at me before walking away, picking back up the tune as his shipmates restart their shanty.

I stop in front of the door, my knuckles barely brushing the wood as I hesitate to knock.

What am I doing here? I think to myself, running my hand down my face, embarrassment heating my cheeks. I take three deep breaths and knock on the door, holding my breath.

Boot steps echo from inside the cabin, and when they stop on the other side of the door, I let out the breath I'd been holding, nerves jumping through my body.

Zayne opens the door. His hair is ruffled, clothes wrinkled as though he slept in them, and his eyes have shadows forming under them. When his eyes meet mine, he frowns and begins to close the door, but I stop him, putting my own boot in the door's path.

"Zayne, what's wrong?"

"Nothing, m'lady." He tries once more to close the door, annoyed when I don't remove my boot. He sighs. "Eliana, go away."

"I won't." I stare at him, my hand now resting on the door frame. I'm halfway into the doorway, if he wants me to leave he'll have to remove me himself. Slowly, he comes to the same conclusion, and finally gives in and opens the door to let me walk in. "What's happened?"

"The water is unsettled." He offers me a comfy chair next to a small table, a book closed with a feather to mark its page on the table. "I've been up all night battling the waves."

"By yourself?" I shake my head in disbelief. "That's impossible."

"The crew needed their sleep, they're handling it well enough now on their own while I rest."

He sits on the bed across from the reading chair I'm seated in. The cabin is a rather small space, made even smaller by all of the bookshelves covering every available wall and books stacked at various heights on the floor of the cabin.

I blush as I realize he's staring at me. "Do you read?"

I shake my head, no. There weren't many books in Bellamere. "I was the scribe of my clan, the recorder of history. It was my mother's attempt at grounding me to our clan and my future as chieftess. I rebelled every chance I got, slipping away from our valley to the mountains or the forest. I enjoy sketching and painting." I wave my hand at the stacks of books. "This ship's real captain surely loves reading, or at least hoarding books."

Zayne laughs, and for the first time this morning he's more himself. "He does."

"This is your ship, isn't it?" I laugh. "You stole your own boat. That's why the crew is so comfortable–they know this ship."

He winks at me, smirking. "Guilty as charged. I really did lose her in a bad game of cards, but the idiot who won her doesn't know the first thing about sailing." Zayne rolls his eyes. "The dumb bloke wanted to show off to his mistress."

"Why did you bet your boat?"

"Leverage. We needed the money. The Haematitian Council continues to raise taxes in the refugee camps, exploiting the weakest of us. The money was supposed to help ease conditions for the refugees, give them a chance to make a life for themselves so they could get out from under the guardians' boots."

"That's very noble of you," I whisper, shocked at how generous he is.

Zayne shrugs and responds, "it's the right thing to do. I grew up poor. My mother struggled to support us. When the dockmaster offered me an apprenticeship at ten years old, that hand up was the very thing my mother and I needed to pull ourselves from poverty. My mother would want these refugees to be cared for."

He's talking about his mother in the past-tense. My heart clenches.

"I'm sorry to hear she's gone," I whisper, grief over the loss of my own mother and the truth of her horrific history washing over me. "I lost my mother, too."

"How?" We both ask at the same time.

Zayne opens his mouth to speak first and I nod my head, encouraging him. "When I was fourteen the Haematitian Council called for a 'tithe.' My mother and I were devoted followers back then. She had been courting a guardian who was permanently stationed in Sandovell. He didn't tell us what the 'tithe' meant.

"They had all the citizens of Sandovell gather in the largest square in the city, and they separated us into different groups—men on one side of the square and women on the other. They tried to dismiss all of the men, but most stayed, our wives, sisters, and mothers were there.

"All of the women were split into different age groups." He pauses, a dark shadow passing over his face as his memory takes him away from me and back to that day. When he blinks again, he's back, but a single tear streaks down his cheek. "The guardians randomly pulled women from every adult age group. And then, they executed them."

I gasp, tears falling down my cheeks. I think of the guardian that slit Brynne's throat, how I sunk my dagger between his eyes. How so many more of my people fell by a Haematitian guardian's blades.

"It happened so quickly. One minute my mother was standing at the front of the group, holding hands with the other younger women, smiling. We all thought they were going to be rewarded, and then a blade was thrust through her chest and she dropped, still holding the other girls' hands.

"We rioted. All the men around me screamed in anger and agony, charging the Haematitian guardians with their bare hands. We had never seen the *sanguinars* before. We didn't know what they could do. They used the blood of our own families to slaughter more of us, calling forth their magic to destroy that city square and anyone who put a hand up in defiance of them.

"When it was all over, they commanded us to gather all of our dead and burn their bodies. Anyone caught trying to give them a burial at sea would be executed. They denied us our burial rights, and we desecrated our loved ones' spirits in that foul smelling pyre."

I take his hand, squeezing it. He glances up from his hands and at my face. Our cheeks are both wet with tears, sharing in the grief of having witnessed the massacre of our people.

"The Haematitian guardians came to my clan as well. We had heard rumors of their work across Hevastia, but my mother believed the Ventemere Mountains would keep us safe. When they found us, some of my people stayed to fight, giving our women, children, and injured a chance to escape. They fought valiantly, destroying the squad of guardians that attacked us, and losing their lives in the process.

"Naomi is the lone survivor of the battle. I lost one of my best friends and my mother to the guardians' blades and blood magic. That loss is what triggered everything I've gone through these last six months."

"You lost your mother six months ago?" Zayne's face falls. He holds my hands in one of his own, using the other to brush the tears from my eyes and to tuck the hair stuck to my tear-stained cheeks behind my ears.

"And learned I'm the destined guardian of Lady Hevastia, fought beasts, faced a monster who used my blood to gain full access to our world, unlocked elemental magic for all of Hevastia, learned I have powers of my own, and stole a boat."

At the last item on my list, Zayne laughs quietly and I join him. It feels good to laugh, despite all the darkness and pain we've both felt. I cherish knowing we both can still find small moments of joy.

A squawk rings from the far corner of the room and I spin around, my dagger in hand. I scan the room, spotting a golden cage in the corner covered by a red cape.

"Zayne, what is that?" I point to the cage.

He laughs under his breath and strides across the room, beckoning me to follow. Zayne grabs the soft red cape in his hands and pulls it away revealing a beautiful bird of iridescent wings and sharp, intelligent eyes.

"It's beautiful," I whisper in awe.

"Her name is Akiko. She's a *cantowauksi*, a cousin of the *crost bird*. They're extremely intelligent birds. Able to track their mark for hundreds of miles."

I reach into the cage, my finger gently brushing against her feathers. They're softer than anything I've ever touched before.

A sharp prick sends pain shooting through my finger. Akiko bit me. "Ouch," I hissed, pulling my hand from the cage.

"Ah, yeah, I should have warned you. She's also temperamental." Zayne runs his hands through his hair and it falls into his eyes. "She has your scent now. She could track you hundreds of miles."

I laugh, lightly shoving Zayne's shoulder. "Are you implying you're going to keep tabs on my whereabouts from now on, Captain?"

He grabs my hand, holding it to his chest.

"Mmmm ... Perhaps I shall, my lady." His eyebrow quirks up, a mischievous grin on his face. "I would be a fool not to."

His hand reaches toward my face, his eyes meeting mine. My heart rate quickens and my breath hitches. Zayne leans closer, so close I smell the saltiness of the sea wafting off of him. Nervous energy courses through me.

His fingers curl around something behind me, and the nervous energy becomes charged with crackling fire. My fingers wrap around the cool hilt of my dagger. The scent of salt and sweat grows stronger as he leans closer.

I draw my dagger and place it against his neck. My heart beats wildly in my chest. We stand so close I can practically hear Zayne's heart stop as he sucks in a surprised breath.

He chuckles. "I told you I wanted to stay on the 'good side' of your blade. So before you cut me and make a mess of my quarters, and my books, let me explain."

I retract the dagger enough that the blade barely kisses his throat as he breathes. Zayne pulls his hand back, and pinched between two fingers is a beautiful iridescent feather.

"This feather was in your hair," he says with a devilishly amused smirk.

Kai

THE TALLEST WOMAN, THE one called the *Venaripa*, left some time ago after binding my arms behind my back. The two other women now sit staring at me as I glare back at them. Their milken skin and black hair give them the appearance of shrouded shades, and my mind wanders back to the shadowy man.

"Who are you?" the shorter woman with the soft-spoken voice asks.

"No one of concern. I was shipwrecked here on my way to Keladone from Hevastia."

She shifts closer, her amber eyes boring into me as if they are peering at my very soul. The weight of her stare makes me uncomfortable, but I sit still, unwilling to show discomfort in front of them. She leans over to the other woman and whispers something in her ear.

"The *Venaripa* called you a *ruffira*, a blasphemer. Do you have a connection to the red?" the other woman asks, her voice deep with commanding authority.

"What does that matter to you?" I ask.

The second woman stands and strides to me, placing her blade on my shoulder against my neck. "It's not so much what matters to us–the true question is, how much does your own life matter to you?"

I debate internally what to do. *I could die here, in service to Lord Vaiccar and without consorting with a potential enemy. I will have failed him, just to die a coward's death. Or, I could play their game, learn what they know before escaping. If I gather useful intelligence, perhaps Lord Vaiccar will not be disappointed in me for failing my mission.*

The decision is simple–I'm not a coward.

"My life is purely to serve my lord, Vaiccar." I tip my head forward, exposing the back of my neck. "My body is his weapon. I am his Will in flesh. If blood must be spilled, I will gladly do so in service to my lord and his Grand Design."

The cold steel leaves my neck, the pressure of the blade resting on my shoulder now gone. Both women stand before me, smiling cruelly.

"A warrior." The second woman smiles, showing her teeth. "You will serve a new lord now, *ruffira*. The Red Queen, the *Venaripa*, is the holiest servant of Raephe, and you belong to her now." She snaps her fingers and two men wearing all white emerge from the shadows. Pulling me roughly to my feet, the brutes drag me between them, deeper into the forest.

They lead me away from the grove of red blooms, and soon the undergrowth disappears, leaving nothing but the exposed red clay of the forest floor. The smoke of fires and the smell of burning meat greets us. They drag me through the camp, one hundred pairs of eyes following my shameful trip to the center of camp. The men in white dump me onto the ground, and I lie face down in the red clay, unable to sit up.

A throat clears from somewhere above me, and the strong hands are back under my arms, pulling me up to my knees. I've been forced to kneel in front of the Red Queen, the *Venaripa*. Her red robe from before was replaced by a deep red gown, a crown of bone and red gems atop her head. With her black hair falling freely, and the fire glinting off the red gems and her amber eyes, she is a terrifying sight to behold.

"Badriyah, Callidora—what is the meaning of this?" The *Venaripa's* voice comes out almost a hiss. "I explicitly told you to return this *ruffira* to the red. Why is he alive?"

"Our Queen, I propose a different, more intriguing opportunity. He is connected to the red. Perhaps he knows something of use?" The taller woman replies. "He said he is a weapon, so let us wield him against our enemies."

"Interesting, Badriyah," the *Venaripa* says as she curls her long fingers, tipped in black nails sharp as spikes, around the arms of her throne. "Bring him to me. He must swear fealty on the *blud*."

The two men in white pull me to my feet and walk me forward. As I enter the long shadow cast by the *Venaripa's* throne, I stare unflinching into her cold, amber eyes. I stop a few feet from her dais, and the men kick the back of my knees, sending me to the ground abruptly.

"What is your name, *ruffira*?" she asks.

"Kai, your majesty." I bow my head.

"Who do you serve, Kai of Hevastia?" As she asks the question, the weight of cold steel presses against my neck on both sides. Badriyah and Callidora stand behind me, their blades on my neck.

"I serve you, *Venaripa*." Even as I say the words, I know them not to be true in my heart. My fealty is to Vaiccar. He is my lord. His desires are my own and his Will is my command. I shall never forsake him. I am nothing without him.

She laughs, and it is a horrible sound–the cackle of a wild beast in the thrill of the hunt.

"The *blud* will determine that," she states, smiling down at me.

The pressure of the blades lifts from my shoulders, and I relax. A searing pain tears through my neck as each blade leaves a deep cut, my blood pouring down my shoulders and chest.

"If Raephe shall see him as a loyal servant, she will save Kai of Hevastia from death and share with him the sacred *blud*. If not, may Kai be returned to the red to nourish our lands and serve our people."

Rough hands grab my arms, wrenching them behind my back as I'm dragged away from the *Venaripa* and to a dirty tent at the edge of the camp. The men drop me on a bloodstained blanket and leave, closing the flap of the tent behind them.

The blood seeps from my neck wounds, down my back and onto my bound hands.

They call me a leech and yet still drew my blood. The fools.

Closing my eyes I concentrate on calling a small shard of earth from the ground, sharp and lethal. The cool stone spike grows between my hands, and I lower my bindings to the rock, using it to cut through the ties. They snap, and I bring my arms forward, rubbing my sore wrists. Quietly I rummage through the items in the tent, searching for anything remotely clean to wrap my neck with.

I find a strip of cloth, dirty in one spot, and decide to risk the infection. With my neck wounds dressed, I open the tent flap, gazing out into the camp. Most of the Raepheans are sitting around various fires, drunken chatter and songs echoing across the camp. The two men in white from earlier are now gone. Badriyah and Callidora are scarce as well.

I slip out of the tent, keeping to the shadows as I creep away from the camp and into the dark forest. Without a fire to light my path, I struggle to keep my footsteps quiet. The snap of twigs accompanies nearly every step I take.

Stopping to crouch behind a bush, I listen for anyone who may have followed me. Through the brush burns a single torchlight illuminating the man carrying it. He wanders directly toward me, stumbling every few steps–drunk. He stops directly in front of the bush I'm hidden behind, and as his torchlight moves to expose me, we lock eyes. He's surprised to see me, taking a drunken moment to recognize I'm the man he recently witnessed his queen order to death.

He opens his mouth, and I pounce on him, driving my dagger into his throat. Instead of shouting, he lets out a wet gurgled gasp, hands dropping his torch and groping his neck. I feel no pity for him as I place my own hands upon his bleeding neck and draw the blood from the wound and into myself. The surge of magic is immense, more than I've ever felt from a fellow Morei guardian.

His pulse weakens under my pull and stops. His body is limp in my arms, drained dry of all its blood. I dump it to the ground with a soft thud and pick up his torch. Using my earth magic, I clear the ground in front of me, creating a clean path for me to follow, covering my tracks behind me. I wander deeper into the forest, leaving the Raephean camp behind me.

I walk until my own blood loss catches up to me, and the blood of the Raephean wears off, leaving my body sluggish and tired. A large tree rises from the forest floor ahead, its roots growing out of a hill and forming a sort of shelter against the red clay of the hill.

I crawl into the tight space, my back against the hill, eyes scanning the dark forest around me. No noise comes from the trees. The birds and beasts of this forest must be asleep. I snuff out the torch, not wanting to draw attention to myself. With the quiet darkness surrounding me, I pass out.

⸙

A cold chill kisses my skin, my eyes bursting open. I'm surrounded by darkness, but it's not the same as in the forest. This is endless. The same sickly shadows from before slither out of the vast blackness and begin to coil around my legs and arms.

I shiver at their icy touch wrapping itself around me. As I stand, the shadows fall off of me, re-pooling at my boots, an ink splotch on the ground. I rub my arms, trying to bring warmth back to my body. Gazing into the darkness, there is nothing.

Where is the red-eyed version of me? He must lurk in the darkness.

"Come out and face me, coward," I snarl, frustrated. My swords are drawn, ready.

As I peer into the inky blackness, red eyes peer back. I jump, startled. My monstrous reflection glides up to me, smiling down at me with a sickening expression. My stomach clenches.

The red-eyed man glances at my drawn blades with mild amusement.

"Pr–" he rasps.

I don't let it finish speaking–I have no interest in exchanging words. My swords slice through the air with lethal precision at the shadowy man, and as they cross, ready to intersect and dislocate his head from his neck, they pass through him. I snarl and lunge again, my swords once more passing between the shadows.

"Sir–"

"Leave me alone," I bellow. The swords drop from my hands, clattering to the invisible stone floor.

The dark expanse shrinks down, confining me. I lunge at the man, and he slides out of the way. Catching nothing but air, I land hard on the stone floor and skid.

"Until next time, sir."

I scramble to my feet, prepared to–I don't know what exactly, but I'm never given the opportunity before the shadows and darkness recede, leaving me once more alone in the forest. My discarded swords sit resting against the exposed roots of the tree.

Crawling from my makeshift shelter, I suck in a pained breath. The wounds inflicted by the crazed Raepheans weep fresh blood.

What are my options?

All I know for certain is I do not want to risk recapture by the *Venaripa* and her people. I still have my mission from Lord Vaiccar to complete.

I resheathe my swords, and their familiar weight on my back is a comfort.

The Raephean forest is reminiscent of the Hilwe Wildes. Lush green brush and small flowers create a pleasant ground cover, the trees above full of bird song and vibrant greens catching the *solari's* light. A gurgling stream cuts through the underbrush, and I follow it, hoping to find something useful at the end–be it a Leomarisian settlement or the open waters. So long as I leave the Raepheans' territory.

A shadow passes between two trees ahead of me. My swords slide silently out of their scabbard. The red-eyed shadow will not get the best of me this time.

Crouching low, I wait for him to expose himself. Minutes pass, but the shadow never reshows itself. I sheathe one sword, still waiting–albeit impatiently.

Another five minutes and no sign of the shadow man.

A twig snaps behind me–*finally*.

Before I can turn to confront the shadow man, I am slammed into, my body pitching forward and smashing into the brush I've crouched behind. My sword slips from my hand, getting lost in the brush.

A low growl sounds behind me, the weight on my back not letting up. Foul-smelling, hot breath brushes my neck.

Piercing pain lances my back and travels as the beast claws me. The claws hook on my scabbard, throwing me. I roll and crash into a tree, the air knocked from my lungs.

A glint of steel in the *solari's* light catches my eye. My sword–barely out of reach.

I scramble to my knees, lunging for my sword. The beast's claws catch my leg, piercing into the flesh of my calf.

As it begins dragging me back toward it, my fingers wrap around my sword's hilt. Dirt and sticks dig into my chest as the beast paws at me.

I roll onto my back, kicking the beast in the face. It yowls in anger and pain, following with a menacing growl.

My sword now hangs in the air between me and the open maw of the forest beast, its yellow fangs bared, snarling at me.

I clamber to my feet as it swipes at me. I easily dance out of the way–finally gaining the upper hand.

The beast lowers to its haunches, preparing to strike. When it leaps, I bring my sword up, my blade slicing open its gut. Intestines and blood spill to the forest floor.

The beast sags to the ground, its breathing labored and slowing. I watch with smug satisfaction as life fades from its eyes.

The forest blurs around me, exhaustion and blood loss setting in from my newly sustained injuries. My knees slam into the ground. It's all I can do to catch myself before I faceplant into the blood-stained flowers of the forest floor.

The red eyes of the shadow man stalk me from behind a tree as I lose consciousness.

Eliana

Z AYNE AND I HAVEN'T spoken since I drew my dagger on him two days ago. My cheeks burn with embarrassment at the mere memory of it, how reckless I was to have pulled a dagger on the Captain. I told Naomi everything immediately, knowing it was useless to try to keep it from her.

"Eliana. Are you listening to me?" Naomi asks, poking me in the ribs with her finger.

She's wearing the same goofy, knowing smile she's had on her face ever since I told her about the incident. I roll my eyes at her, and she winks.

We've been helping one of the sailors, Pilo, tie knots to form a net. He hasn't told us what the net is for yet. In fact he doesn't speak to us at all. I've seen him laugh and joke with the rest of the crew. It doesn't bother Naomi. She chatters away nonstop without so much as glancing at Pilo, content to talk with me as if he's not there.

A loud boom echoes through the boat, and Pilo turns to the mast where Zayne, Maendril and the rest of the crew are gathered. Zayne holds a large staff in his hand, and he slams it into the deck, another loud bang pulling everyone's attention to him.

"There is a storm brewing. I've felt it building in the water. The currents are shifting, and we risk being sucked off course. Man your stations!"

Pilo jumps up, abandoning the net, me, and Naomi. Naomi stays seated across the tangled pile of rope and shrugs her shoulders, bowing her head as she returns to forming knots. Naomi and I work in silence for several minutes, both listening to the commotion of the crew as they rush to prepare the ship for a storm. Pilo works fast to fasten a cannon to the deck before scurrying off below deck to tie down the others.

The boat begins to rock more violently, and large, white-capped waves crash against the ship, spraying water on me and Naomi. She squeals as the ice cold water splashes over both of us, drenching us to the bones. Maendril battles the large waves, clumsily walking in our direction from across the ship.

"Girls, go below deck where it's safer! Can't risk you washing over the side of the ship," he bellows, pointing to the door twenty feet from us.

Naomi wastes no time. She drops the net and scrambles for the door. The boat rocks on another large swell, and she crashes to the floor, laughing. I crawl behind her, not trusting myself to stand against the violent waves.

I kneel by her, helping her to her hands and knees. Our wet hair and clothes stick to our bodies, and a chilling cold spreads across my body. I grab her hand and pull her forward. Naomi follows me to the door and down the stairs.

"Why did it suddenly get so-so cold?" Her teeth chatter, her face a frosty shade of blue. She stands hugging one of the beams, using it to keep upright.

I pull a large blanket from one of the crates near our bunk, wrapping it around Naomi. She sighs with relief, as the blanket begins to warm her frozen body. Taking her hand I guide her to our bunk, helping her lay down on the bed that's bolted to the floor of the boat.

"Stay here and try to warm up, okay?" I brush her wet hair from her face, and she sighs.

Her arms open, offering me some of the thick blanket, but I shake my head no. Zayne and Maendril may need help on deck. The thought of leaving them and the crew to face the storm alone doesn't sit well with me.

"I'm going to go back up," I announce, pointing to the stairs. "I want to check that they don't need help."

Naomi rolls her eyes, and snuggles deeper into the blanket. I laugh, shaking my head. She is a fiend for blankets, always has been. I climb the steps, almost tumbling back to the bottom as a large wave rocks the boat and it dips sharply to the right.

Above deck, Zayne is shouting orders to the crew. Maendril helps to tie down crates and other various pieces of cargo that slide around on the wet deck. Violent waves continue to spray icy water over everyone. I blink water from my eyes and stagger toward Zayne.

"Eliana, you're supposed to be below deck," he shouts, anger flashing across his face. "It's not safe up here."

"I can handle myself," I shoot back at him, glaring. My breath sends puffs of mist into the cold air. "Why is it suddenly so cold?"

Zayne shakes his head, eyes roaming the white-capped waves. "It's out there," he replies, voice growing quieter.

I grab his arm, pulling his attention back to me. "What's out there?"

He cups my face with his calloused hand, rubbing some warmth back into my ice cold cheek. "Please, Eliana, go back below deck. I'm begging you."

"No–" My argument is cut short by a shrill shriek that echoes through the water and air, piercing my ears. I lock frightened eyes with Zayne, all the color now drained from his face.

"Zayne, what was that?"

"A *sciros,* a water serpent." Zayne shoves me toward the door. "Go, Eliana, now," he orders, his eyes frantically searching the water.

"I'm not leaving you to fight a water demon by yourself," I growl.

The boat lurches as something unseen rams into it, the ship pitching to the right, nearly capsizing. Another shriek echoes right through my bones, and a fearful chill spreads down my spine. As the waves crash over the deck, the standing water starts to freeze. The cold air drops in temperature, and my breath creates a thick cloud as I breathe, the air burning my lungs. It's so cold.

"How is this possible?" I ask, teeth chattering.

"*Sciros* control water and weather. This one must be gifted in ice and cold–it's creating a winter storm in the calm spring sea." Zayne's voice is resigned.

"Battle positions," he shouts, drawing a small horn from under his vest. He blows the horn and the sound mimics the shrill screech of the monster.

A white-capped wave washes over the deck, soaking me. In the violent water a dark shape swims below the surface directly at the boat. I grab onto Zayne with one arm and the rope wrapped around the mast with the other as the serpent rams the ship and it pitches to the left. My boots slide on the wet deck, the rope burning my palm as I hold onto it for dear life.

The monster bursts from the water, its golden eyes and white teeth flashing in the lightning that cracks across the sky. The storm builds, and blinding rain pelts us. The serpent shrieks again.

Zayne lets go of me to cover his ears, and I do the same. My head might explode with the pressure of the noise.

The water demon is covered in iridescent blue scales, two golden horns protrude from its head, and white spines form a large crown. It's the most beautiful and terrifying monster I've ever seen.

Is this one of the sea tales Zayne was telling me about?

The serpent dives once more, and I lose track of it in the dark water and rolling waves. The boat shudders from the impact of the monster ramming it under water. Across the boat, the crew and Zayne are arming themselves with large crossbows and bolts with barbed tips. Pilo hands one to Maendril, showing him how to trigger the crossbow.

Water and chunks of ice rain from the sky, and I dodge a large piece of ice that falls directly toward my head, rolling across the deck and bouncing back to my feet. I'm soaked to the bone, and my fingers are going numb, but I unsheathe my sword and stand, ready to fight.

The monster rears its ugly head out of the water once more, rising twenty feet above the boat. Zayne shouts and points at the serpent. Pilo, Maendril and the others all launch their arrows at the beast. Three pierce its scales, the rest glance off its body and fall to the waves.

They struggle to reload the mechanism, their own fingers numb and clumsy. The beast thrashes from being hit. Its massive head swoops down, white teeth clamping down on the nearest person, pulling them from the boat and biting them in half. Red blood sprays across the boat, both halves of our crewmate falling to the ocean's waves.

Zayne's scream is furious and feral as he calls for another attack on the beast. The next volley of arrows is more successful, with five arrows finding purchase in the serpent's softer under scales. It roars in pain and dives toward the ship once more. The crew are ready this time, and as it surges toward the deck, Zayne and Maendril draw their swords and slash at the monster's face.

I sprint forward, stabbing my own sword into its eye, blinding it. Metallic blue blood sprays from the wound as I withdraw my sword. It shrieks in pain and rams its head into my chest, knocking me down. I fall into the net Naomi and I had been working on earlier. I sheathe my sword and grab the net.

"Maendril, the net," I call.

Anger glows in Maendril's eyes over me disobeying his orders. Maendril grabs the other end of the net and I run around the serpent's head, sliding on its blood that coats the deck. Maendril and I toss the net over the monster's head, and the loops hook on its spines. With a massive pull, Maendril manages to wrestle it down, the rest of the crew helping to keep it pinned as it thrashes and tries to escape.

Zayne slashes at the serpent, more metallic blood spilling onto the deck and drenching all of us as we struggle to hold the beast's head down. I stand on the side of its good eye, and it stares back at me, full of hate and rage.

I grunt with the effort of holding onto the net, wrapping a loose strand around my arm, giving me a better grip. Water splashes the deck, and my fingers tense up under the cold shock. Several of the crew let go of the net as their hands cramp from the icy water, and the serpent rears its head, throwing everyone else to the deck.

As It thrashes around, trying to shake off the net, I fight to unwrap the rope from my arm, becoming more entangled. The water demon roars, and I have to cover my ears, my brain squeezing under the pressure. Maendril lets the net go to cover his ears, and it's the opening the serpent needs to rise from the boat, bringing the net, and me, with it. I cling to the net, the boat growing smaller as the monster stands tall once more. It dives for the ship, the net sucked back in the force of its drop, pulling me with it. I smack into the side of the monster's head, seeing stars. I pull a dagger from my belt and stab at the serpent's head, holding desperately to the net with the other hand.

"Eliana." Maendril's worried cry carries from the ship. I stab my dagger into the monster once more, my dagger finding purchase in its good eye.

It screams, and blindly grabs another crewmate from the boat, biting them in half. Red splashes the deck. Maendril calls for me again, his voice joined by Zayne's.

I pull my dagger from the monster's eye, and try to cut my tangled arm free. The beast thrashes, causing me to lose my grip on the dagger, and it falls into the metallic, blood-coated water below with a small splash.

I try to reach for my favorite dagger in my boot, but I can't pull myself up as the monster throws its head, trying to knock me free. Maendril and Zayne stand on the deck holding the mechanism armed with barbed arrows. They fire them at the serpent's soft underside, and it screeches, shaking its head as both arrows pierce its scales. The net snags on more of its spines, and I hold onto them as I try to unwrap my arm. The monster sways and begins to fall forward.

Horrified, I realize it's going to crash into the ship, crushing me against the deck. I scramble to unhook my arm, and with a painful pull I finally free my arm. The water demon falls with a final, weak roar into the ship, wood splintering under the impact. I narrowly avoid hitting the boat and fall into the deep, dark water. I kick furiously for the surface, breaking the water and sputtering for air.

A large wave comes crashing down, smashing me against the boat, and the air in my lungs is forced out, bubbles rising to the surface. Garbled by the water and the roaring waves, I faintly hear the sound of Maendril calling for me as the violent waves carry me away from the ship and any hope of rescue.

Rough sand scratches my cheek, and warm water laps at my boots. I blink open my eyes to an expansive beach and crystal blue waves. The *solari* are high in the sky, and the frigid cold I felt in my bones is now replaced with their gentle warmth. I bolt upright, panic surging in my body as I realize I went overboard during the *sciros* attack, washing up on this shore—alone.

On the edge of the beach lies a dense forest, and I worry I've returned to Hevastia. A large piece of driftwood lies in the sand a few feet from me. Walking up to it, I relax. It's not from the Daughter of the Seas. That ship is painted a deep teal, and this board is well worn, from an ill-maintained boat, and not Zayne's prized ship.

I wander toward the forest, conscious of the fact that I'm sitting too exposed on the wide open beach. Under the canopy of the trees, the heat of the *solari* cools to a more comfortable temperature, and I'm reminded of wandering the forest that surrounds Bellamere and the Burroughs.

The underbrush is sparse, the forest floor coated in a spongy green moss that dampens the sound of my steps as I travel farther away from the beach. The sound of birdsong echoes from the canopy, and the familiarity helps to calm my racing nerves.

I'm all alone, and I have no idea where I've washed up. I need to find fresh water and shelter. Lady Hevastia, save me. And help my friends to find me.

The snap of a twig makes me pause, and I crouch low, drawing my sword. A shadow passes several yards in front of me, and I relax. It reminds me of a *nazelle,* a hoofed, grazing beast. I keep still, anxious to frighten it and scare off my chance at a juicy meal.

I pick my steps carefully, trying to keep each step on the soft moss to conceal my movement. I'm two feet from it now, and as I stand, the *nazelle* senses me and bolts, darting through the trees quick as lightning.

I groan in frustration and sheathe my sword. The hair on the back of my neck raises, and I turn around slowly, expecting a *laseron* or *severn.* Instead, it's a young boy with three red vertical lines painted under each eye.

He smiles at me, and motions me to come closer. I hesitate, the raised hair on my neck telling me something about him is ... off.

Was the nazelle running from him and not me?

He eyes me with a predator's hungry stare, and my stomach turns. I try to take a step back, but my body stiffens. I've lost control of my own body. His hand is held out in front of him, eyes concentrated on me.

Is he doing this to me?

Two men step out from behind trees on either side of me, grabbing me roughly by the arms. The boy continues to hold me in place as a large sack is thrown over my head, and my vision goes dark. Sensation returns to my body, and I know I'm back in control, except for the men who have a firm grip on both of my arms and pull me between them as I trip on every unseen obstacle in the forest.

We walk for hours before stopping. The sack is pulled off my head, and I find myself surrounded by thirty or so men, all of them with red lines tattooed under their eyes. The boy who stopped me is standing in the middle of the group, next to another man who could be his older brother. When they smile, it's with all their teeth.

Who are these people?

Kai

THERE'S NOTHING BUT AN endless void of darkness. Gone is the lush forest. I have been swallowed by the pitch blackness of the dark place with the red-eyed man. I sit up, wincing in anticipation of painful wounds, and am surprised to find myself miraculously healed. Not a sign of pain or scars.

"How ..."

Movement to my left alerts me to the presence of someone else in the darkness. The red-eyed man hovers off to the side.

"Did you heal me?"

"Not exactly. Your worldly injuries are unfelt here in the Shadow Realm."

"Excellent." I smile to myself.

The red-eyed man steps closer, misinterpreting my statement as acceptance of the circumstances–his mistake. I roll onto the balls of my feet and spring forward, my arms reaching for the red-eyed man.

As my arms wrap around him, a cold current shocks through me, and I land on the black floor, spasming. Several minutes pass as the icy shocks reverberate through my body.

"Sir, please don't try that again."

I groan. I don't understand what happened. How was this trick of my mind able to do that?

"What are you?"

"I'm the Keeper of the realm, and you, sir, are the Shadow Prince," the reflection rasps. He bows slightly at his hips. "You may call me Noras. What brings you to the Shadow Realm, my lord?"

"You brought me here." I groan as the last of the shocks leave my body. Noras holds out his hand, offering to help me stand, but I wave him away. "Don't come close to me," I snarl.

He flinches away at my tone, but his ghoulish face softens. "I understand sir. This will all take some getting used to."

"Getting used to it?" I scoff, "there is no 'getting used to it.' There is only 'the exit' and where it's located."

Noras makes a terrible choking sound, and I'm startled to realize it's a laugh. "Prince, I am not holding you here. You have come here of your own volition."

"That's not possible. Why would I come here?" I ask. "How?"

"This is your realm. You are able to travel between here and the Light Realm at will," he explains, his tone taking a scholarly note–like Cire's used to when he was annoyed at having to explain something "obvious" to me.

The thought of him comes so easily to my mind at this moment, but I can't recall him on my own. Cire? Who is that? And, why does my heart ache at the memory of him? Who was he to me?

"My lord, are you listening?" Noras asks. "I was explaining the shades to you." He points to the pool of shadows at my feet, and they ripple as if they know they're being talked about. "The shades, and myself, are at your bidding."

"This is too much. None of this is real." I shut my eyes, trying to block out the cold of the darkness, the shadows coiled at my feet, and Noras's red eyes staring at me. Opening them, I'm disappointed to find myself still standing in front of Noras.

He snaps his fingers and the shadows at my feet are joined by more rushing from the darkness. They pool together and form a dark, shadowy throne.

"Sit, my Lord," Noras commands with a bow.

"How–" I sputter.

Noras's face contorts, and similar to when he laughed, it takes me a moment to realize it's a smile.

"With the *dominanturi*, the sway. As the Keeper of the realm, I hold dominion over the lesser shades, such as these." Noras points to the swirling mass of darkness at my feet. "These shades, the *corpuscu*, are able to conjure into a solid object." He smiles. "Please, sit."

The shades that make up the throne still move and shift past one another, yet the shape of the throne holds.

"They will not shock you as I had. That was in self defense. These *corpuscu* have no need for such defense tactics." His words should not mean much, and yet, I trust he's being honest.

I ease myself into the throne, and the chill of the shadows now wraps around every inch of me as I settle into the seat. I grimace as their tendrils reach out to gently touch me, sending icy chills throughout my body.

"Shadow Prince–" Noras says as I cut him off.

"Kai, please." I clench my jaw, fighting the urge to jump from the throne as the shadows continue to lick against me.

Noras is alarmed by the informality, clearing his throat with a disgusting sucking noise. "Lord Kai, you hold dominion over the Shadow Realm, the space between the Light Realm and the Beyond."

"But what does that mean? And how?"

"It's your birthright. You are of the shadows. The Shadow Realm is as much your home as the Light." He steps toward me, his hand extended. "May I touch you, sir?"

I swallow.

Should I let him touch me? Do I honestly believe any of this?

"I won't shock you, sir. I promise that was a one-time occurrence."

I wince, but sit very still as Noras presses his frigid thumb to my forehead. A searing pain travels through my entire body, and I collapse out of the throne, writhing on the ground. As fast as the pain appears, it dissipates, leaving me on the ground panting. As the shock recedes, I reach for the dagger on my belt.

"You said you wouldn't do that," I snarl.

"Sir–"

The dagger clatters to the ground with a sharp ringing sound. Where there used to be an endless abyss of darkness, now stands a beautiful hall of black marble. Pillars rise from either side of the open floor, accented by a deep red rug that runs the entire length of the hall. A dark marble throne replaces my shadow-made one.

"What–" I ask, and Noras interrupts.

"I unlocked your shadow vision." He smiles. "Welcome home, my Lord. Beyond your palace lie the different shadow folds, each of them containing the spirits of those who are not yet crossed over to the Beyond."

Something pinches at the back of my mind. My head bursts and I clench my eyes shut, attempting to block out the pain.

When I open my eyes, I'm no longer in the Shadow Realm. The warmth of the *solari* breaks through the forest canopy, and I sigh with relief. It was all a weird dream. It's not real. The forest is slowly becoming alive with birdsong and critters in the trees.

A dark shadow stands in between two trees, and I jump. The more closely I gaze at the forest around me, the more I notice shades intermingled with the living. A bird swoops down, shadows falling off of it as it dives. Its feathers are ink-black, and when it stops on a branch across from me, its red, beady eyes peer at me.

The corpse of the striped forest beast lies rotting where I felled it. The pattern and size resembles that of a *severn*.

I half expected its ghost waiting for me to return. I breathe out a sigh of relief.

My thoughts are interrupted by a twig snap, and the sound of footsteps crunching through the dried leaves of the forest floor. I draw my swords.

Breaking through the underbrush are Callidora and several other women, all wearing the same red cloak. When she spots me, Callidora smiles.

"Kai, you survived." Her voice is gentle, and soft. She holds her arms up, the red sleeves of her cloak falling back to expose dozens of raised scars along both of her arms. "Praise Raephe," she announces, her voice strong and steady.

The other women in the group all raise their arms and join her in praising their goddess. "Through sacrifice may you find strength," they say in unison, bringing their arms down.

I slowly raise my drawn swords, and my body seizes. All sensation leaves me, and I stand frozen in place, as I did once before with the young mage.

Callidora's good-natured smile is replaced with an annoyed frown.

"Stand down, Kai."

I glare at her, my muscles still straining against her hold in a futile effort to reach my sword.

Callidora rushes toward me, grabbing my arm gently as she steers me toward the other women. "Come Kai, we must tell the *Venaripa* of your success."

I try to fight her off of me, but her grip tightens, and as soon as I'm surrounded by all the women, their red cloaks become a blur, and I can't distinguish them from one another. It's mesmerizing and confusing.

Once we are in the camp, the other women disperse, and I'm left with Callidora. The Raepheans are bustling around the camp, rarely stopping to talk with one another as they carry out a variety of tasks.

My mind pulls, unable to resurface the memory of a similar scene.

It's as if part of myself is locked away out of reach, Mere slivers of it slip through to my consciousness.

Callidora stops me in front of a large, ornate tent at the center of camp. Two men wearing all white stand on either side of the tent's entrance. As we approach, the one on the left raises his eyebrow, surprised to see me. The one on the right reaches out quickly to the other, and a red gem passes between the two of them.

Those bastards, they made a bet on whether I would survive.

"Kai of Hevastia is here to sit with the *Venaripa,*" Callidora announces.

From within the tent a sharp whistle erupts, and the two guards step aside, holding the tent flaps open for me and Callidora. As we enter the tent, my breath hitches. The tent is full of plants in various shades of red. Nestled among them is the *Venaripa,* her body draped over a throne of polished, white bone.

Callidora steps forward, dragging me along with her. My feet snag on an ornate rug, and I trip, my knees driving into the ground. The *Venaripa's* eyes pierce mine, and she smiles, showing all her teeth.

"Hello, pet," she purrs, undraping herself from her throne and sitting on it properly. "I must say, I am surprised Raephe favored you. You must be something *extraordinary.*"

The way she said the last word sends chills down my spine. I hold her gaze, unwilling to show my fear. She smiles again, and I grimace, gritting my teeth.

As she stands, her long red sleeves fall back, and like Callidora, her arms are covered in raised scars, standing out against her porcelain skin. She stalks toward me, her movements predatory.

"Stand, warrior," she commands.

Callidora pulls me to my feet and shoves me forward. I stumble, stopping a few feet from the *Venaripa.*

Her long nails cup my chin as she draws my gaze directly into hers. They bite into my skin, and I flinch, sucking a breath through my clenched jaw. She turns my head side to side and tugs off the strip of cloth I used to cover my wounds dealt at her command.

"You're very strong. I wonder what you're truly capable of," she whispers to me, smiling. "We'll find out soon enough what bloody work you can do."

Zayne

THE WATERS ON THE shores of Raephe are a crystal clear blue on this cloudless day. I lean against the deck railing overlooking the wide open expanse, my thoughts on Eliana and the time she and I stood at this very spot overlooking the waves.

Maendril and Naomi left us two hours ago to search for Eliana. *I should have gone with them.*

My duty lies here, with my crew, and with the responsibility of repairing our ship. We took significant damage in the *sciros* attack, and it will take several days before Daughter of the Seas is truly capable of weathering a return trip to Hevastia.

I only hope that is enough time for Maendril and Naomi to locate Eliana. My crew is restless to leave this land. They whisper that it's cursed.

I roll my eyes, another nightmare tale parents whispered to their children, carried down from the days before the Great War, when the nations openly traded with one another and Hevastians were masters of the Great Oshia.

The memory of the stolen moment with Eliana flits across my mind, warming my cheeks and the back of my neck. Alongside the tales of monsters from the deep and lands that bleed, the legend of the lost princess was a folktale told to the children of Sandovell.

I still can't believe she's truly alive. More than that, she's incredible.

I shake the memory from my mind, trying to reconcentrate on the repair of the railing.

It's best to be friends … there's nothing worthwhile I could offer her as the disgraced captain of a stolen ship.

The plank I was nailing to the railing to stabilize the broken wood splits, the splinter falling into the blue water with a small splash.

"Curses," I mutter under my breath.

Eliana is powerful, the most powerful mage of our land. She has no use for a washed up pirate with a few water magic tricks up his sleeve.

I take another piece of scrap wood and slam the hammer into the nail, finishing the work of patching the railing. We don't want anyone going overboard if we hit rough waves on our return voyage.

The thought of that brings my mind back to Eliana, and I press the hammer to my temple, willing myself to stop thinking about her.

"Captain! We have company," Pilo shouts, pointing off the port side of the ship toward shore.

The Daughter of the Seas sits anchored several hundred yards from the beach, in the deep waters where we wouldn't run aground.

Gathered on the beach is a small band of men with shaved heads and tattered clothes. Standing huddled behind them is a group of women and children bound in chains.

Lady save me.

I've heard my fair share of rumors surrounding the brutality of the Raephean clans.

But to enslave and chain your own women and young? Sickening.

"What should we do, Captain?"

"Daughter of the Seas can't get any closer to the shore. They would have to be mighty reckless to make an attempt at us. We can wait them out. They'll lose interest eventually."

The largest man on the beach grabs a short woman from the group, dragging her by her hair as she kicks and screams.

He drags her to the edge of the beach, raising a crude sword above his head before sliding it across her throat. Blood spurts from the wound onto the wet sand.

There's a series of splashes as two of my crew jump overboard and begin swimming to shore.

"Get back on this boat, right now!"

Pilo stops swimming and shouts back, "we can't leave those prisoners, Captain–it's not right."

"Pilo, Nita–come back," I command.

Nita reaches the shore first, she runs at the Raephean man, sword drawn.

There's a sickening crack, and then Nita drops to the sand, sword falling from her hand. I watch closely, waiting for her to rise again, but she doesn't move. Pilo screams a war cry, rushing the blood mage. The Raephean man holds out his hand, and Pilo drops to the ground, his war cry cut short.

It's all I need to be convinced we are not safe on the boat.

"Anchor up–now."

The crew rush to pull up the anchor, drop the sails and prep the ship to set sail. Chaos ensues on deck as several other crew members try to jump ship to aid our lost friends. They find themselves quickly disarmed and tied to the mast—for their own safety. There's no time to mourn the loss of Nita and Pilo right now.

"We're ready, Captain," Loith, my new first mate announces.

Together, my crew and I stand on either side of the ship and begin coaxing the tide to pull us out. Loith adds wind to the sails, pushing us toward deeper water.

Soon, Raephe is a small part of the fading horizon.

I'm sorry, Eliana. Forgive us.

Kai

BEFORE LEAVING THE *VENARIPA*, I was stripped of all my blades. Now, I sit in a small tent in the middle of her camp, guards posted outside at all hours. My eyes trace the pattern I've drawn in the floor of my tent, four loops interlocked–something nags at the back of my mind, that I should know what it means, but no clarity comes forward.

I should be plotting how to escape, but the *Venaripa's* last words to me haunt my thoughts, and I'm morbidly curious to know what she has in store for me.

"We will find out soon enough what bloody work you can do."

The Red Queen, what a formidable title. I wonder what she did to deserve something so wicked? I think to myself, falling back on the cot and soft furs the guards laid in my tent. She's terrifying, and yet so ... alluring.

There's the kiss of cold air, and I open my eyes, knowing I've left my tent behind and unwittingly traveled to the Shadow Realm.

Noras stands at attention several feet away, shadows pooling at his feet.

"Lord Kai, you've returned," he states, smiling. It distorts his face, sending a chill down my spine. He steps forward, offering me a hand, and I realize I've arrived lying on the ground.

"So I have." I shake my head in disbelief. I am no closer to understanding how I travel to and from the Shadow Realm than I am to explaining the large gaps in my memory.

His hand is cold and boney, but his grip is firm as he yanks me to my feet and dusts me off. I brush his hands away, not comfortable with him touching me. He's hurt by my briskness, but hides it quickly.

"Shall I give you a tour of the palace?" he asks, ushering me from the dark room. "Follow me. I will show you the library and the kitchens."

The image of the girl with black hair illuminated by the *solari's* bright light flashes before my eyes.

I still don't know who she is to me, but perhaps Noras will know...

"Noras, you mentioned I could visit the shades stuck in the In-Between—take me there. Please."

His face lights with joy over me taking a genuine interest in the Shadow Realm, and he pulls me along, gliding quickly down a grand hallway of black marble, a thick black runner stretching the length of the entire hallway. We arrive at a grand staircase, a large candelabra illuminating the stairwell and the foyer below.

"The *umbrasinum*, the shadow folds, or as you referred to them, the 'In-Between,' lie beyond your palace, my Lord." Noras opens the ten-foot tall door at the end of the foyer, and I expect to be blinded by the *solari's* light, only to be surprised as the soft light of the *lunei* illuminates a massive garden outside the door. "The shades held within the folds are called *hadefari*.

"Your Highness is able to walk the folds, if you wish. Though, I must warn you sir, some of the *hadefari* held in the folds are not ... stable. They have been trapped here for nearly a century. Their minds are fractured."

"Trapped? Why would you trap souls in the shadow folds?"

He flinches under my accusation, sputtering for words. "I did no such thing, my Lord. Their souls are stuck here because they haven't met the true death in the Light Realm. They are kept safe until they are able to ascend to the Beyond. As the Keeper, it is my sacred responsibility to care for them.

"I would never hurt a *hadefari*. These trapped souls are under our protection for their stay in the Shadow Realm. The *umbrasinum* are merely special places of their own conjuring, meant to keep the tormented souls at ease.

"Like seeing something comforting in the final moments before death?" Lord Vaiccar's most recent lecture on the proper technique for keeping a tithe at the unique space between consciousness and death—what he called the *sanguinis tenere*—whispers across my memory.

To achieve sanguinis tenere is to hold your tithe's life in your palm.

"Yes." Noras brightens, impressed that I have been paying attention. "It is usually a very brief flash. Some experience the *umbrasinum* for longer. For those that lie in the fields surrounding the palace, it's been much longer—a century. But, even a century in paradise is still a prison, and their minds are unwell."

He leads me through a hedge garden, the bushes in bloom with flowers of deep blood-red. As we leave the hedge maze, ahead of us lies a wide open field dotted with the shimmer of a soft, pulsing light similar to *sparkflies*, hundreds of them.

"More shadow folds appear every day, Lord Kai. And they do not leave. There have never been so many before. I worry something is not right in the Light Realm. Do you know of anything, sir?"

"The dark plague."

"A plague? I assure you, sir, there have been several plagues and no plague could hold so many on the brink of death for longer than their natural lifespan. As the Keeper, I have no knowledge of something so powerful." Worry washes over Noras. He takes his responsibility very seriously, that much is obvious.

"There's no need to worry." I stand tall, proud. "Lord Vaiccar is working to clear the dark plague and remake Hevastia in his image. He works to maintain order among the ungifted, ungrateful citizens of the land. They dare to stand against him, and soon they will all know the true glory of his might."

A pain sears through my brain and I clench my eyes shut. Opening them, I find myself back in the Light Realm, still under guard.

The umbrasinum is a place for the dead, or nearly dead. So the dark-haired girl of my vision is one of the dying souls.

Somehow this revelation does not bring me any comfort. She is now most likely dead and unable to torment me any longer ... or answer my questions.

The tent flap folds back, and one of the guards steps in holding a tray of strange fruit and roasted meat. "Eat," he commands in a gruff voice.

I take the tray from him, and wait for him to leave, but he stands firm with his arms crossed.

"You're not going to leave until I eat, are you?"

He shakes his head no. "The *Venaripa* ordered me to stand watch, to ensure you eat. You must fuel your body for the *Rubruliem,* the Red Battle."

"You want me to fight for you?" I scoff, "why?"

"You will face the Champion of the Blud Revel clan. We must settle the debate on who is to lead the warriors in our war against the Leomarisian scum's invasion of our land. Chosen warriors will determine our leader through shows of strength."

I bite into the roast meat, the tangy juices bursting in my mouth and dripping down my chin. It's delicious. I bite into the meaty fruit with a fleshy texture next, expecting a savory flavor, but finding it to be sweet and fragrant.

"What happens if I refuse to fight?" I ask through a mouthful of juicy fruit.

The guard glances down at me with disdain. "Then may the *Venaripa* have mercy on you. Raephe does not suffer cowards."

He swats the fruit from my hand and it bounces in the dirt.

I snarl at him and he draws a short, razor sharp blade.

"Go ahead, cut me and make my day," I taunt.

He swallows but keeps his weapon outstretched between us.

"You will fight for us and win the Red Clan glory, or be returned to the red."

He resheathes his sword with a smug expression. I roll my eyes, bored.

"What happens after I win?" I ask through mouthfuls of food.

The guard laughs. "After we prove where our true strength lies, we shall wage war against the Leomarisians and stop their abuse of our land once and for all."

I finish the tray of food in silence, and hold out the empty plate to the guard. He nods, satisfied, and takes the tray back, exiting the tent immediately. And once more, I'm all alone. With a full stomach for the first time in days, I fall asleep easily.

Strong hands rattle me awake, and I open my eyes to the same guard from last night shaking me. I shove him off of me and sit up. He hands me a hard biscuit and another piece of roasted meat.

"It is time to leave for the *Rubruliem*. The *Venaripa* wants you to travel with her." His voice is gruff, and he sits impatiently as I finish eating and pull on my boots and jacket.

The other guard steps aside to let me through, and the warm light of the early morning *solari* shines down on the camp. Where there used to be a sprawling camp full of tents and campfires, there is red clay and cooling embers. Red cloaks and white tunics stand in a large group across the barren field, and the two guards walk alongside me to the gathered campers.

In all black, I stand out amongst the crowd, but so does the *Venaripa*. She wears a black gown of thin lace, a deep neckline, and a long, flowing train. Her black hair is pulled back, spilling down her back in soft waves. Her red jeweled crown glows in the light, making her a terrifying and beautiful vision.

"My champion arrives at last," she cheers, smiling. For all her beauty, she is still dangerous and untrustworthy.

"Walk with me, Kai."

She snaps her fingers and the guards shove me forward before falling in line behind their queen. She drapes her arm through mine and smiles once more. I grimace.

"Good morning, your majesty." My voice is strong. I won't show my unease at being so close to her.

The large group marches ahead. The men in white tunics pulling the carts of supplies make up the rear of the company, led by the women in red robes, their hoods up, and their queen and myself. We travel through the forest, away from the red blossoms in their small grove.

The red clay and soft moss of the forest floor give way to dry dirt and shriveled plants the farther we travel from their camp. My boots crunch on dried leaves, the canopy above us dying out.

What happened here?

The *Venaripa* maintains a strong, commanding grip on my arm, but when I glance over she wears a saddened expression. I open my mouth to ask, but close it as a massive city rises from the edge of the forest.

"Where are we?" My voice drips with awe-struck wonder.

"Puhlmia, the heart of Raephe." She sighs. "This used to be our home, before the Leomarisians destroyed it."

The entire city is built of smooth white stone with red ore veining throughout. Beyond the impressive homes and neatly lined streets we now wander, a tall castle rises from the center of the city. The homes and storefronts are abandoned, but there is no damage to any of the buildings from what I can tell.

"Destroyed? It's pristine."

The *Venaripa* shakes her head. "The damage is not to the buildings, but to the land on which the city rests. The Leomarisians are leeches. They are mining the land of its resources, sapping our lifeforce.

"You will stand alongside us in our battle to wrench control of our land from their greedy hands. But first, you must beat the Blud Revel's champion."

The ladies in red hoods lead us deeper into the city, toward the castle. A tunnel descends under the street, and we follow it, swallowed by the darkness. They walk without fire to light the way, familiar with this tunnel. I stumble on unforeseen rocks, and steps. The *Venaripa* laughs at my plight, but never lets go of my arm or slows down.

The tunnel opens to a large pit lined with torches. Along the edge of the pit are ropes, and in half of the cavern stand a group of men in red, their heads shaved, red vertical lines tattooed under their eyes.

The boy from the forest had those same tattoos.

Behind the men stand several women, manacles clamped around their wrists. All of them except one have the same dark hair and amber eyes, Raepheans, but the tallest woman on the end has fiery auburn hair and bright blue eyes. And she's staring slack-jawed right at me.

Why is she acting as if she knows me?

"Kai." My name echoes from her lips across the wide cavern, and she smiles.

Her face falls as I ignore her and turn to the *Venaripa*. The Red Queen leads me and the rest of our group to the other viewing platform across from the group of men and the strange woman.

The booming echo of a staff striking stone reverberates throughout the cavern, and all eyes turn to an old woman in deep red, hair streaked with white and gray, holding a spear at the far end of the pit.

"The Red and the Blud Revel Clans gather today in the sacred *Rubruliem* at the heart of *Puhlmia*, under Raephe's watchful eye, to determine Her champion."

Cheers erupt from both clans. The women scream battle cries, and the men beat their chests and boast with guttural screams. The elder woman holds up her hand, and the noise quiets, attention turning back to her.

"For too long, our neighbors, the Leomarisians–"

"*Ruffira,*" a man yells, interrupting the woman. His cheers turn to a cry of agony as her intense gaze seeks him out, and he drops to the stone floor, holding his head in pain.

The elder clears her throat. "The Leomarisians have desecrated our way of life, disrespected our traditions, and stole our lifeblood from us. That all ends today. We honor Raephe, Goddess of Life, in the *Rubruliem*. The Champion of the battle shall lead the Raephean people against the Leomarisian scourge as ruler of Her people.

"Are the warriors of each clan ready?" Her booming question rattles me to my very bones.

The *Venaripa* steps forward, her arm still tucked in mine, and I step with her to the front of the Red Clan. She holds up my hand and smiles.

"I present our Champion, Elder." She raises my hand higher, nearly tipping us into the deep, dark pit we teeter on the edge of. "We fight for the honorable path, following Raephe's most sacred laws."

The same young boy from the forest steps forward, an identical, older copy of him at his side. "I present our Champion, Elder. We fight for the assured path, evolving is the only course to success."

"So be it," the Elder replies, striking her spear on the stone three times. "Through sacrifice may you find strength."

Hama

MY TORCHLIGHT FLICKERS AGAINST the walls of the tunnel, casting eerie shadows on Tenya's back as I follow her to the training space.

She and Tyr have been leading combat training with the refugees. Daneth and Mythica escort new groups of two or three to the Burroughs almost every other day. Alana's been teaching them how to harness their magic, and a few of the more capable students from the Burroughs have been assisting.

My work as the primary seamstress for the entire village has kept me plenty busy. The most recent refugees to arrive fled their homes and left all their worldly possessions behind. It's been several days since I've left my tent to walk the Burroughs and visit the training spaces.

The clang of metal striking against metal and the soft thud of wooden staves hitting travels down the tunnel.

Tenya's belly is starting to show, but she's not let it slow her down. Her fingers twitch at her side, itching to grab her blade and join the skirmish.

I tap her on her shoulder. Her bright eyes smile as she turns, always so joyous to see me. How quickly she's become a sister to me.

Go on ahead. I'll catch up.

Are you sure? What about your foot?

I had been assisting Alana in training the new mages until my accident. Abigael was practicing her control of moving large stones around the perimeter of the arena.

She lost focus and sent the boulder forward too quickly, not giving me enough time to move out of the way before it rolled onto my foot and crushed it.

I'm fine. I can make it. I swat playfully at her with my walking staff, a gift from Tyr.

Pyria, Tenya's sister, patched me up as well as she could, but resetting bones is tricky business, and a foot worst of all.

Tenya disappears down the tunnel. The other refugees shout with surprise and gladness at her entrance. They adore her.

Within the mere minutes it takes me to catch up, she's already pinned one of the biggest men in the Burroughs, Pityr. She offers him her hand, and he takes it with a booming laugh that reminds me of Maendril.

I hope he is taking good care of Eliana and Naomi, keeping them out of trouble. Eliana is very headstrong, so I know she's giving him a run for his worth, I think to myself.

Hama, Tenya signs as she walks up, barely breaking a sweat. *Do you think they're starting to go easy on me?*

Her hand rests on her distended stomach, rubbing it slowly.

And face your wrath? No, I don't think anyone is foolish enough to treat you differently. Despite Tyr's threats.

She laughs and throws an arm over my shoulder, guiding me into the training space and to a rock situated as a bench on the far wall.

Don't tell Tyr.

Your secret is safe with me.

She smiles before turning back toward the group of refugees holding various weapons at the center of the room.

To my surprise, several of them sign a greeting to her. They must have been teaching themselves. Tyr is usually her interpreter.

They huddle close to her as she draws out a battle strategy in the loose dirt of the cavern floor. Several break away from the group and go to assigned positions, the rest facing off against one another in close combat.

Those at the corners of the space hold training bows and arrows tipped with a soft bulb of fabric dipped in dye—my doing. As their comrades engage in close combat with the "enemy," their goal is to hit the target without also hitting their allies. When the exercise is done, we will check each team for dye spots.

Soon the cavern echoes with the cacophony of noise as they fight, shouting instructions and direction to one another.

Tenya sits down next to me, studying her students' movements with a proud smile.

I told them whoever wins this battle can have first turn at the baths and use the good soap.

I chuckle. *That is a good motivator.*

The battle is over soon after it begins, with the team on the left successfully subduing their enemy. Together, Tenya and I inspected all fighters for dye—no one hit their ally.

Excellent work, everyone. The red team won and may head to the baths. Blue team, run through your drills once more.

Firm handshakes and hugs are shared by all before the teams go their separate ways.

How does Alana's mage training fare?

Well. She thinks they will be ready for a public demonstration soon.

Excellent. We will need to train everyone together soon. Our greatest chance of success will be if they can fight alongside one another.

Do you truly think they're ready to face trained warriors and whatever monstrosities Vaiccar has created? I ask.

They have to. Tenya signs, her mouth pulling down into a slight frown. *We don't have a choice.*

Eliana

I WALK WITH SICKENING dread down the treacherous steps carved into the side of the massive pit. The boy and his brother lead me and the other women prisoners down to the arena. With every step, my worry and confusion grow–a mess of thoughts swirl in my brain.

How is Kai here, and why? What is the Rubruliem, *and what role do I play? What role does Kai play? Why are they fighting the Leomarisians?*

Nearing the bottom, the man holding our chain yanks it, causing the women in front of me to stumble down the remaining steps. I try to keep my balance, but the short chain causes me to tumble as well. I help the woman closest to me to her feet. She's now covered in several shallow cuts. The sting of my own injuries sends fresh worry through my body.

Kai follows a woman with long black hair wearing a beautiful black gown. They're striking in their matching attire. I try to catch Kai's attention once more, but he glances right past me, unaffected.

The older brother steps to the center of the arena, the stone stained a dirty brown color–*the color of dried blood.* The woman on the other end of our chain is released, and the guard drags her kicking and screaming to the man at the center of the arena. Once there, a large metal cylinder lined with stained spikes is clamped around her torso, and she screams in agony. Blood begins to drip from every place the spikes pierced her body, and the older brother breathes deeply, calling her blood to his hands.

A sanguinar.

The woman collapses to the ground, screaming in pain as the metal clamp is jarred by her fall. The sanguinar ignores her, his focus on harvesting her blood. He doesn't see Kai step to the center of the ring as he also draws the woman's blood, robbing the Blud Revel man of his unfortunate power source.

The air grows very still as Kai focuses his energy on channeling one of his elements. Unaware, the Blud Revel screams a battle cry and rushes Kai, the blood he absorbed granting him heightened strength—judging by his bulging muscles. He's about to land a powerful punch against Kai when Kai releases the air he's gathered in a concentrated blast that sends the Blud Revel Champion tumbling across the arena.

Kai smiles, smug. He calls forth more of the dying woman's blood, and she moans in pain. The air balls in his hands once more, and before the Blud Revel Champion can stand, he hits him with another torrent of air, tossing the man several feet.

I glance across the arena to the leader of the Red Clan, and she is smiling widely, pride radiating off of her as she watches hungrily.

How did she find Kai? Why is he fighting for her?

Kai continues to advance on the Blud Revel Champion, not letting the man land a single blow. He stands above him, funneling air directly onto him, simultaneously suffocating and crushing him.

Kai fights with a ferocity unmatched by anything he's done before. He's always been brutal in battle, but he never tortured his opponents as he is now. He yawns, bored with the fight and the man he is slowly murdering.

What happened to you, Kai?

I call his name, trying to catch his attention, but his focus is singular.

I need to get over there.

The guard holding our chain is paying attention to the fight. The brother of the champion is also distracted as he faces his brother's murder. I slowly raise my arms, the chains softly jingling, catching the attention of the other women I'm chained to. I press my fingers to my lips and mouth—*I am getting us out of here.* They watch me, hope blooming in their eyes. They also raise their chains, stepping closer and allowing me enough slack to reach behind my head and grab the thin dagger I always keep secure in my braid.

I hold the dagger between my teeth, using the thin blade to trigger the lock mechanism in the manacles. I listen intently for the soft click of the release, holding my breath. The woman next to me stands watch, ready to warn me should the brother or guard decide to check on us.

Click.

The manacles loosen around my wrists, and I slip my hands free, silently rushing to the next woman and her bonds. I'm able to get all the other women free quickly, and they disappear into the shadowy corner of the arena that's not lit by the torches above us. Perhaps they know another way out of the pit.

Kai continues to pummel the Blud Revel Champion. The air around them is thick with dark, pulsating shadows. The other man lies bruised and bloody, his broken bones sticking out at unnatural angles from his skin.

Gripping the thin dagger, I rush the boy who captured me and slice the back of his calves, my dagger tearing through muscle. He drops, screaming in pain—unable to pursue me. His cries alert the burly guard, who turns his thick neck too slow and misses me pouncing on him. He tries to pull me off, but I plunge the dagger into his neck, all the way to the hilt. He drops dead, and I step away covered in his blood.

Bile rises in my throat, but I choke it back down.

The commotion I've caused has drawn the attention of the other faction standing across from us in the pit and the rest of the Blud Revel Clan watching from above. Several men shout at me, rushing for the stairs. A loud boom draws everyone's attention.

The elder strikes her spear once more and commands, "None shall enter the *Rubruliem*. What has passed is ordained by Raephe in her most sacred battle ground. The girl has proven herself mighty and fierce. Let her stand for the Blud Revel Clan."

The raucousness from above dies down. Kai stands, panting, above the Blud Revel Champion's dead body. Dust and shadows hover in the air around his boots. He turns and spots me, covered in blood. I freeze as he strides across the arena, stopping a few feet from me. His brown eyes burn into mine as he stares me down.

"Why do you know my name?" he asks, eyeing me with suspicion.

I open my mouth to answer, but no sound comes out.

He doesn't recognize me? Is this what the Keladonean mage did to him?

"Kai, you know me. It's Eliana. I've been searching for you. How did you end up here?"

"I don't know you." He steps closer. "Do you serve Lord Vaiccar?"

I gasp, sick dread spreading through my body. I peer into his cold, dead eyes and whisper, "what happened to you, Kai?"

My hand reaches for his cheek, and he grabs my wrist, squeezing tightly. Panic races through my body.

Kai wouldn't hurt me, would he?

The woman dressed in all black shouts from across the arena, grabbing Kai's attention. I wrench my hand from his and step back, stumbling on the dead guard's body. The stone floor jars my bones as I hit the ground with a loud thud. My eyes never leave Kai as I scramble to my feet. While he's distracted, I run toward the dark shadowy corner the other prisoners disappeared to.

His heavy footsteps echo ominously as he pursues me, and I run faster, hoping to find the tunnel before Kai catches me. The sound of several sets of boots running toward me causes me to slow down.

Who could be running into the arena?

Three people emerge from the shadows, and I scream with surprise. Maendril and Naomi follow another woman with the same pale skin and black hair as the Raepheans.

"Naomi, Maendril—be careful. She's dangerous." I point to the woman. "We need to leave, now."

Naomi runs up and hugs me. She holds me out at arms length, and worry washes over her at the blood coating my clothes.

"It's not mine. I'm fine." I push Naomi back toward the shadows. "Please, we need to leave."

The footsteps pursuing me slow to a walk, and Kai steps into the shadows. Naomi's eyes grow wide, a smile spreading across her face. She moves to run toward Kai, and I put my arm out, stopping her.

"Kai–" she says.

"Naomi, don't. It's not Kai, not really." I step into her path, blocking her from him.

"*Ruffira*," the strange woman with Naomi and Maendril growls. She turns to Naomi and Maendril. "Your friend is right. We need to leave. The Red and Blud Revel Clans are dangerous."

"You're not going anywhere," growls Kai. "The *Venaripa* said no one is to live."

"Look–" Maendril he clenches his fists. "I don't want to fight you, but I will. Eliana is my priority. You don't mean anything to me."

I move to stand in front of Maendril. "Stop–don't fight him. Please."

The Raephean woman cuts her palm, and mutters something under her breath. Kai cries out, dropping to the ground and clutching his head. She twists her hand and his body contorts, writhing in agony.

"Move, now," She orders, her eyes never leaving Kai's body.

I grab Naomi's hand and drag her behind me, following Maendril into the shadows of the arena. The Raephean woman follows closely behind, her boots shuffling on the stone floor. Shouts of frustration at missing Kai's attack against me carry from above down to where we run, and I worry we will be discovered before we escape.

"Eliana, we can't leave him," Naomi pleads with me as she pulls against me, trying to run to Kai. "He needs us. We can't leave him with these monsters–look what they would have him do. He doesn't want to be a killer anymore, please."

I sigh. This might be our chance with Kai, and if I walk away without trying, then I'll never forgive myself for going back on my promise.

"Maendril, grab Kai," I order him, and then add "please," to soften the blow.

He grunts with frustration but stops running to turn around and scoop Kai's unconscious body from the floor of the arena.

Stars. That Raephean woman did a number on him.

She glares at me as she runs past us, now taking the lead on our escape. We all follow, entering a partially collapsed tunnel in the far corner of the pit. Glancing back, I am relieved to find that no one pursues us.

The *Rubruliem* is over, I survived it.

The Raephean woman leads us out of the deserted city and into a grassy field, reminiscent of the Thessimis Fields of home. Up ahead is another forest full of barren trees, the red clay dry and cracking. It's the opposite in every sense from the lush, healthy forest I wandered through on my way from the beach.

"How did you find me?" I ask my friends, still not believing they're here.

"Captain Zayne tracked the currents to figure out which one sucked you away from us. He and the crew harnessed the waves and propelled the ship to the shores of Raephe without stopping to rest their magic," Maendril states, sheepish.

He was never a fan of Zayne, but I can tell he's come around to the pirate.

"Where–"

"They're in the shallows, repairing the ship from the *sciros* attack. We left them to come searching for you, because of course you wouldn't just sit on the beach waiting for us." Naomi teases, nudging me. "Zayne's bird was leading us through the island when it suddenly veered out of view and disappeared.

"Isadora found us wandering the forest." Naomi points to the woman we've been following. So that's her name.

Stepping into the shadow of the dead trees, the Raephean woman makes an animal call. We all stop, the return call coming from the left. She turns in the direction of the screech.

I stop walking. Naomi slows, and turns back to me. "El?"

Isadora glances back, annoyed to see me lagging behind. "What's wrong? We can't stop yet, it's not safe."

"Thank you, Isadora, for your help. But, this is where we go separate ways."

Naomi grabs my hand, pulling my attention away from Isadora and back to her. "What are you doing?" she asks in a harsh whisper.

"We need to find Zayne and set sail for Keladone," I whisper. I haven't forgotten our mission. Louder, I say, "we have a boat waiting for us. Can you point us toward the beach?"

She hesitates. The same call and response echoes through the trees. Isadora responds with a different call than last time.

"I'll escort you. We're still in the Blud Revel Clan's territory."

I don't exactly know what she means by that, but the memory of watching the men in the arena gut a woman without hesitation is fresh in my mind, and that's the only warning I need.

"Thank you, Isadora." Naomi says on my behalf.

Maendril jostles Kai's unconscious body from one shoulder to the other.

Isadora grimaces. "We don't have long before your *friend* wakes up. Follow me."

As we climb a small hill, the forest clears, and a sprawling, sandy beach meets the trees and stretches to the sparkling, blue water. White-capped waves crash against the sand.

"That's odd," Naomi murmurs. Her eyes scan the shallows.

"I knew that the damned pirate couldn't be trusted," Maendril grumbles, mostly to himself, but still within earshot of me.

My heart plummets to my feet. This doesn't make sense. "Zayne wouldn't just abandon us."

Something rolls in the waves and is left behind on the beach.

Is that?

A body in a familiar loose shirt, ripped pants, and calf-high boots lies face down in the surf. The waves pummel Pilo's body.

"Your friends were attacked." Isadora points to several splotches of stained sand, the color a dull brown. "Blud Revel Clan from the looks of it. We need to go, this beach is deep within their territory. You can stay with us."

Naomi and Maendril follow Isadora off the beach and back into the shadows of the forest. I glance back one last time, secretly hoping to see the sails of the Daughter of the Seas on the horizon. We're stranded, without a boat or a way to communicate with anyone on Hevastia.

How will I contact the Keladonean Auror now? What about everyone back in the Burroughs?

Isadora leads us through the forest and into a clearing. Tucked within the grove is a small village of crudely-built huts made of mismatched wood and stone. There are approximately twenty in total.

She beckons us to follow her through the entire village to the largest hut in the far corner. We haven't spoken a word since she led us from the beach.

"The *ruffira* stays out here. Secure him with these." She spits out the insult, handing Naomi several strips of leather. "Join us by the fire when you're ready."

I help Maendril strip Kai of all his weapons, a small armory quickly piling at our boots, while Naomi stands to the side. As the last dagger is slipped from a secret pocket on his leg, Naomi steps up and offers Maendril the leather strips. We bind his arms and legs tightly, confident that he's secured.

Once Kai's secured, Maendril climbs the stairs, and I follow him. When I glance back at Naomi, she's hovering next to Kai's unconscious body. "Naomi?"

"I think I'll stay out here, in case he wakes up. You go on without me." She smiles, encouraging me. "I'll be fine." She points to Kai, bound hand and foot. "He's not going to hurt me."

"Be careful."

"I will."

I saw darkness rolling off of him. Naomi didn't. I'm not sure how to begin explaining that to her, so I don't. I hope she knows what she's doing. I'll never forgive myself if I lose her a second time.

I nod my head and enter the building with Maendril, finding a group gathered around a large fire in the center of the building, smoke billowing and climbing through a hole in the roof.

The hut is more of a lodge with a high ceiling and deep carved-out floors, making the space feel twice as large. There are several doors on the perimeter of the main room that lead to adjacent rooms, and a staircase leading to a landing with several closed doors. It's an impressive structure.

Isadora stands, motioning for us to follow her away from the fire and to another room beyond the large hall. I rest my hand casually on the hilt of my sword, still unsure of Isadora or her intentions.

"The Auror of Hevastia, we've been expecting you."

Kai

I WAKE TO MY hands and feet bound, a blanket draped over my shoulders, and a dying fire several feet away. Someone else is seated by the fire, asleep. I squint in the dark, trying to make out their features.

And it all comes back to me.

I was stalking the auburn-haired prisoner through the arena, planning to corner her in the shadows and finish her off. It would be a declared victory for the Venaripa, *and perhaps my chance to beg for release from her service.*

I was ambushed by a different Raephean woman who shot pain through my entire body. As I lay writhing on the ground, I saw the black-haired girl, the one from my visions, standing in front of me, her eyes full of concern. She was begging the auburn-haired girl to take me with them. Where have they brought me?

The person sitting across the flames from me shifts and wakes. Her blue eyes meet mine and she smiles, nervous. She stands and leaves, her shape disappearing into the night for several minutes.

She returns with an armful of fresh wood for the fire, careful to keep the fire between us as she lays the logs in the embers. Bending down, she blows life into the embers. They glow and pop, burning brighter with each breath until a spark forms turning into a fire that licks the logs.

Through the fire, I'm able to make out her features more clearly. *It's truly her, the girl from my visions.*

An unexpected relief washes over me that my earlier assumption she had died was incorrect. She opens her mouth to speak, thinks better of it, and instead, bites her chapped lip. We sit in silence for several long minutes as I wrack my brain for what to say.

Why do I care? She's a distraction. She may very well be an enemy of Lord Vaiccar. I must focus on that.

But I can't help the way my mind yearns for her, some hidden part of me truly knows her. And selfishly, I need to know why.

"True or false, have we met before?" I ask, finally breaking the heavy silence between us.

She frowns, disappointed in my question. "True, we've met in two lives."

"Two lives?"

"You don't remember?" Her voice grows quiet. She shifts closer, the fire no longer between us.

Her gaze is filled with hope as her eyes search mine. When I stare back at her, unable to give her the recognition she's looking for, a single tear slides down her smooth cheek.

"We met on the battlefield that was my village, Bellamere. You had the opportunity to kill me then ... but you didn't. I watched you chase after your Morei, Cire, leaving me and the battle behind."

There is the mention of Cire, again. My heart tugs at the sound of his name.

"The second time we met was in the ruins of the village, both burdened with the survivor's responsibility of tending to the dead. You threatened to kill me then, too, but I could tell your heart wasn't in it. You showed me mercy, and as I lay dying in your arms by my own hand you were gentle, remorseful even."

She stops, searching my face again for something I can't give her—recognition. I shake my head, and she sighs.

"I don't recall being with you there," I offer.

Another tear slides down her cheek. She breathes deeply.

"I didn't die from my injuries, although we both thought I did. I was corrupted by the dark plague that's consuming Hevastia and turning it dark and bleak. We met a third time in my 'second life,' when I was trapped in the In-Between."

"I know of the darkness. Lord Vaiccar is developing the cure to the blight."

"Lord Vaiccar—" She shakes her head with disbelief. "Vaiccar isn't curing the plague that's ravaging Hevastia—he's engineered it. Kai, he's lying to you."

I scowl at her. "Liar."

She flinches at the word, her cheeks wet with tears.

"You were different then, too. Kinder, gentler." She reaches out to me, her hand almost touching mine before she pulls back, letting it fall empty into her lap. "You don't remember any of this?"

"When we met in the In-Between, were you in a bright field of flowers?"

Hope springs in her eyes. "Yes, the Thessimis Fields. It was always warm, peaceful. You found me there when you were trapped in the dungeon of the Aceolevia."

"I would never be a prisoner of the Aceolevia, I'm the trusted hand of Lord Vaiccar." I sit tall, my words low and commanding.

"You weren't always," she whispers. "You used to think for yourself. You never would have followed Vaiccar. I don't know what's happened to you, but we'll fix it."

"No. You will let me go, immediately." As I say the words, the part of me I try to ignore flares in argument, and I find myself drawn to her.

"I can't free you, Kai. I won't." She sighs. "I'm not sorry–this is for your own good."

"Hardly. You have no right," I growl. "I don't even know your name."

"I'm Naomi. It's a pleasure to meet you, Kai." She's smiling, the corners not quite turning up to meet her eyes.

Where have I heard that before?

I turn away from her, no longer interested in talking.

The fire disappears, and Naomi with it. I find myself back in the Shadow Realm, in the grand hall of the palace.

"Lord Kai, you've returned." Noras appears from thin air, shadows zipping across the floor from him to me.

The *corpuscu's* cold touch doesn't bite as much as it once did, and I wonder if I'm growing accustomed to this place.

"Yes ... somehow." I shake my head. I still don't understand how I end up in the Shadow Realm or how I leave.

"How can I assist you?"

I wave my hand, ushering him away. "I think I'll sit here, alone, for a while."

"As you wish, Lord Kai."

Noras leaves the grand hall through a side door, and I find myself in the company of a few *corpuscu* who flit around my boots. My steps echo as I march through the hall, then the foyer, and finally out onto the balcony overlooking the gardens.

If what Naomi said is true, then is the golden field of her fold now gone? And if so, how did she overcome her condition?

I reopen my eyes to Naomi's bright blue eyes hovering right above my own. At the sight of my open eyes she squeaks and falls back, dropping me from her arms in the process. I fall to the ground with a loud thud, jarring my head.

"Kai, you're back," she laughs, nervous. "You really frightened me there. Here, let me help you sit back up."

She hesitates to touch me now that I'm awake, and her hands shake as she grabs my shirt and yanks me up out of the dirt. When I'm no longer at risk of tipping over once more, she sits back, putting space between us.

"Where did you go?" she asks. "Do you ... see other people? Like how I was, I mean."

"No," I reply, uninterested in telling her more, though I suspect the version of me she is familiar with used to tell her all sorts of things. Her disappointment is evident in the slump of her shoulders and the frown on her face.

"Kai ... you can trust me." She smiles encouragingly. "Eliana and Maendril are your friends, too. I won't pretend to know what's happened to you since ... I lost contact with you.

"However, I promise to help you figure it out. You think nothing's happened, but I swear to you, this isn't you." She waves her hand up and down my body. "You would never follow Vaiccar."

"You've said that already," I snarl.

"Well, at least you're listening." She laughs, shaking her head. "I'll answer any questions you have and try to fill in the blanks."

"How–"

How did she know there are holes in my memory? Could everything she's claiming be true? And, how did she escape the shadow fold without dying?

"The last time we met in the In-Between ... you told me you were afraid Naevys and Vaiccar were stealing your memories. Judging by your reaction to seeing Eliana, I think that's exactly what happened."

"Who is she to me, this auburn-haired girl?"

"She's the Hevastian Auror, the living conduit to our goddess, Lady Hevastia." She explains, "I won't pretend to know what you may have meant to each other. You'd have to ask Eliana. But I know you were at least friends. She risked her life trying to rescue you from the Aceolevia."

"Why would I care about a follower of the *Old Ways*," I spit out the words, my lip curling in disgust. "Lord Vaiccar plans to eliminate the faithless from the land, making way for those of the True Faith and his Ascension."

"What?" Naomi squeaks. She clears her throat. "What did you say?"

I glare at her, my stare making her uncomfortable. She shrinks away from me.

She's of the Old Ways. She cannot be trusted.

"Kai—"

"Go away," I growl. "I'm no longer interested in talking."

She stands, stepping over the dying fire. She scoffs and turns, kicking over the logs, killing the remaining flames. With a satisfied smirk, she walks away, leaving me alone in the dark.

I entered the Shadow Realm on purpose this time. Striding across the great hall, I shout for Noras. He appears at my side, shadows jumping from him to come to me, gliding down my back and forming a cape.

"Lord Kai, welcome back." Noras smiles, and it's less offensive than before.

Perhaps the Shadow Realm is growing on me, because it's the only place I feel whole. The shock of that realization stops me in my tracks.

Could it be true?

"How did I come to find the Shadow Realm?"

"I sought you out, sir. We've been waiting for you." Noras snaps his fingers and a peculiar shadow of a faint gray rather than the deep black of the other shades darts from a far corner and into his palm. "We sent messenger shades, but you never took notice of them.

"In recent months you began making journeys to the Shadow Realm at random, visiting one of the shadow folds. It wasn't until I began to directly interact with you that you stepped over to the palace, and not the shadow folds. I've been watching over you your whole life."

"The shadows that followed me all my life, that was your doing ..." My voice fades.

"Why yes, that's how the messengers work. We sent you messengers frequently in your dreams, but you never interacted with them."

"You haunted me ..." Something in the back of my mind recognizes this sensation, the terrors that trapped me in my sleep, frozen and unable to wake. "All that time ... you were trying to make contact with me."

In my distracted pacing I stumble, and the shadows fall from my shoulders to form a chair. I collapse into their cold embrace, their icy touch no longer biting as it once had.

"Noras, how does a soul leave their shadow fold?"

"To leave their *umbrasinum*, a soul must die in the Light Realm. Then, their soul is released. Why do you ask, sir?"

"I think ... no it's not possible." I return to pacing, my steps echoing on the stone floor. "Is it possible to meet someone who returned from the shadow fold, alive?"

"I've never heard of that before, sir. But perhaps?" Noras hovers, gliding closer. "Why the sudden interest?"

"There's a girl in the Light Realm ... she claims I met her in a 'second life' while she walked the Light Realm as a dark monster and resided in an *umbrasinum* at the same time. Could everything you've been trying to tell me ... be real?"

He scoffs, offended. "Of course it is real. Everything in this realm is your inheritance. May I remind you, the shadows are at your disposal, sir. Including in the Light Realm."

I pivot on the heel of my boot to face him. "Is that so?"

My brain hurts every time I try to recall something beyond my time as Lord Vaiccar's trusted hand. It's as if nothing's there.

Could Naomi be telling the truth—my memories were stolen? But, why?

Naomi's gone and I'm alone. The fire's nearly burned out, and I shiver at the cold that's settled into my bones.

I bring my wrists to the embers of the fire, letting the small flames lick at the leather strip binding my hands together. Several minutes later the ties are weakened and I break them, rubbing my sore wrists. I undo the bindings at my ankles easily and stand up.

My weapons are gone, taken from me while I was unconscious. I growl with frustration, anger rising in my chest at their treatment of me, until I realize it's my own doing.

If I want answers on what's really happening, I will need to set aside my aversion to the *Old Ways* and listen to Naomi, Eliana, and Maendril. My instincts whisper to turn and disappear into the shadows of the forest surrounding the village. It's my opportunity to escape and return to my quest of finding the Keladonean Auror.

But the Hevastian Auror is within my grasp ... Lord Vaiccar said she wasn't a threat, merely a weak girl with no hope of stopping his Grand Design.

Yet, if that's true, why is she here? And, why is she nothing like what I've been told?

I walk up the steps of the large hut and find a roaring fire burning in the center of the great hall beyond the door. As I step into the room, several seated around the fire spot me with surprised expressions. A shout goes up, and those gathered scramble for their weapons, all aimed at me.

I hold my hands out low, surrendering.

"I am here to speak with Naomi," I state, my voice clear and calm.

Across the room, a large door opens, and Naomi and Eliana run into the room, weapons drawn. When Naomi sees me she sheathes her sword and calls for the others to stand down. When they don't, she turns to Eliana and whispers something.

Eliana sheathes her own sword, her eyes never leaving mine. "Stand down. Let Kai through."

I step slowly, walking past the warriors gathered around the fire, stopping several feet from Eliana and Naomi.

"Naomi promised to answer my questions." I glance at her from the corner of my eye, and she's smiling.

Eliana frowns, but nods her head. "Very well then." She turns to Naomi and places a hand on her shoulder. More quietly, she tells Naomi, "keep an eye on him. Call out if you need anything."

Naomi places her hand on top of Eliana's and squeezes her fingers. "I'll be okay, El."

Eliana shakes her head and disappears through the door and into the room beyond the grand hall.

Naomi steps up beside me, hesitating before grabbing my wrist and pulling me from the bright fire and the staring faces. She leads me up a stairwell and through a door that opens to a small room lined with bookshelves and a fireplace.

"Sit," she commands. "So, what do you want to know?

"Everything."

Eliana

ISADORA AND SEVERAL OTHER Raepheans stand on the other side of a large table. The absence of Naomi is immediately noticeable. Since having her back, we've been inseparable.

"Are you sure we should leave Naomi alone with him?" Maendril leans close and whispers.

"She can handle herself," I state, trying to sound confident. "Besides, she has the best chance of getting through to him ... he seems to trust her."

"I wouldn't trust him as far as I can throw him," he murmurs to himself.

I laugh quietly, covering the sound with my hand.

Isadora clears her throat, pulling my attention back to her and the other Raepheans standing alongside her on the other side of the room.

"You were telling us about the situation in Hevastia," she prompts, motioning for me to continue.

"Yes. As I was saying, Vaiccar is destroying the land. He's corrupted Lady Hevastia's magic, somehow, and he's raising a dark, monstrous army."

"And why is that of any concern to Raephe?" she challenges me, her eyebrow quirked up.

"Because I don't think he plans to stop with Hevastia. He wants to become a god. He's leeching all the magic he can from our land, but if it's not enough, he will come for more. You're our closest neighbor. What's to stop him from destroying Raephe? And if he succeeds in becoming a god, why stop with one land—why not conquer them all?"

"We have our own concerns with land and magic feuds, ones that are much closer to home."

Isadora unrolls a worn map onto the table, dark red ink etched into the fraying parchment in various locations. I step closer. On the map X's are drawn through several spots with dates.

"What is this?" I ask, my eyes roaming the map.

"It's the Leomarisians' warpath of destruction they've carved into our land. You claim Vaiccar is leeching your goddess's power? Well, the Leomarisians are draining our land of its resources, and Raephe's lifeblood—our magic source."

"What—how?" I whisper.

"Murder, what else?" Isadora growls. "They're slaying our people and mining our land for gemstones. It's sucking the ground dry of lifeblood. With every inch of land they gain they further weaken us.

"They'll kill our entire continent in pursuit of these." Isadora tosses a small rock onto the table, and my breath hitches.

In front of me lies an unremarkable purple gemstone, except it's indistinguishable from the ones lining the walls of Hevastia's Heart Chamber ... siphoning her magic and powering Vaiccar's disgusting scheme.

It can't be.

"Isadora, I think our problems are more interconnected than either of us bargained for," I say, shock rocking my body. "I know that stone … it's what Vaiccar used to siphon Hevastia's magic from the land and from our people."

"Impossible," she declares, slamming her fist to the table. "Why would the Leomarisians share something so powerful with a Hevastian?" She spits out the names.

"Why would a Hevastian know Raephean magic?" I throw her insult back at her.

"How dare you?" She leans over the table, and one of her companions pulls her back. I stand taller, meeting her sharp amber eyes.

"You called Kai a *ruffira*, a leech. In Hevastia, that's the insult we use for a sanguinar, a blood mage." I point to her. "Like you. I saw what the other Raepheans can do. It's the same magic the Haematitian Council's 'guardians' used against my people when they burnt my village to the ground."

"That's it. Do not come into my home and spout lies. That *ruffira* has as much in common with true Raephean magic as you do, *Auror of Hevastia*." Her words ring with anger and derision. "You see our spilled blood and assume it's all the same, but you're wrong. The One Mother does not condone the kind of senseless violence your friend inflicts."

Shame heats my cheeks. She's right. I jumped to conclusions about their magic based on fear and my experience on Hevastia. But, even so, I can't shake this suspicion that their magic and the Morei guardian's are somehow all related.

"I'm sorry, Isadora. It was wrong of me to accuse you in that way."

Maendril places his hand on my shoulder, pulling me back. I shake off his strong grip.

I have this under control ... I hope.

"This," I point to her map. "It's bigger than a land feud, It's all related." I hold my hand out to her. "Join me, Isadora. We can help one another."

She growls in frustration, running her fingers through her long, black hair. Stepping around the large table between us, her rests her hands on her head as she paces. Her amber eyes lock onto mine–full of barely suppressed rage ... and fear. I step toward her, and her arm darts out to grab my wrist, twisting it.

"Why should I trust you?"

"You shouldn't, but what other choice do you have?"

I pull my arm from hers, using the other to hold Maendril back as he steps toward us.

"We can return to this in the morning. I think it's time to rest." I catch Isadora's eyes. "There's a lot to be considered."

"Wren can show you to your sleeping quarters." She pauses and frowns. "The *ruffira* is under your guard. If he lays a finger against anyone in this camp–your heads will be mine."

Maendril bristles next to me, but I shake on her terms.

A tall woman with cropped hair steps forward and opens the large door back to the main hall, gesturing for us to follow her.

We walk up a stairwell, stopping at an unmarked door. The others on either side of the hall have carvings etched into the wood by the handle. Wren spots me eyeing the weird markings.

"It means warrior." She points to the etching. "Isadora has one spare room in this barrack. You'll have to share."

The door opens to a small room lined with bookshelves and a fireplace. Kai and Naomi sit across from one another on the two pieces of furniture in the room–a frayed chair and a settee.

"Oh, and there's no bed," Wren adds as she yanks the door closed with a loud thud that shakes the rafters and scatters dust onto our shoulders and hair.

"Charming," Maendril murmurs to himself, his eyes never leaving Kai.

"How did it go with Isadora?" Naomi asks, turning on the settee to face me.

I shake my head, *not now.*

"She's something else. I've never met someone so rude," Maendril grumbles.

I place my hand on his dirty forearm. "She is being more than generous letting us stay here. She doesn't owe us anything. We have no idea what she's been through."

I turn to Kai, who matches my stare with obvious indifference. "You are allowed freedom so long as you swear not to lay a hand on anyone under Isadora's protection."

Naomi opens her mouth to accept on his behalf, but I glare at her and she slowly closes her mouth. When I return my gaze to Kai, he nods, accepting the terms.

"I'll take the first watch–everyone get some rest."

Maendril makes a face suggesting he wants to object, but thinks better of it. He waves his arm, brushing it off and settling against the far wall. With a strong yank, the red curtain releases itself from the window for him to use as a blanket. Naomi settles on the settee, warm by the fire.

Kai stays seated by the fire, staring at me. I sit against the door, the wood rough against my back. Naomi may trust Kai, but I have no idea what he's capable of now, and I won't take any chances.

I pull my journal from my satchel. Maendril brought it with him from the ship, and I'm so happy to have it back. My fingers have been itching to draw the strange plants and trees of Raephe.

"Eliana," my name spoken in Kai's voice pulls my attention back to him. "Could we talk?"

I'm surprised, but nod my head yes. He stands and walks over, sitting down on the floor across from me.

"What do you want to know?" My journal falls closed in my lap.

"Who are you?"

I can't help myself, I laugh. Of every question, I honestly did not expect something so simple.

He clears his throat and clarifies, "to me, who are you to me?"

I pause, deciding how to respond. "I would like to think I'm a friend, but in truth, we barely know one another. Your family, Hama and Alana, asked me to protect you. We met because your Morei partner, Cire, was helping me. You were helping me, too ... before you were captured.

"What happened to you during those two months, Kai?" My last question is a whisper, the painful memory of Hama and Alana crying, their anguish when we failed to rescue him all bubbling back to the surface. A single tear falls down my cheek.

"Cire ... I don't recognize that name." Kai eyes me suspiciously. "I don't have a Morei partner."

"No, I suppose you wouldn't now." I sigh. "Kai, I don't know how else to say this–Cire is gone. Vaiccar destroyed him."

Recognition does not light his eyes ... it's as if Cire never existed to him. But then, he twitches.

Kai doubles over, clutching his skull and muttering to himself. I hesitate to touch him as he spasms in front of me. Horrified, I see shadows zip from the corners of the room and fold around his body, soaking into his skin. Kai twitches one final time and lies still. His breathing returns to normal, and his eyes remain closed.

"What just happened?" I whisper to myself, my hands shaking.

I sit staring at Kai's unconscious body, not sure what to do.

Do I dare touch him? Is this one of the side effects from Vaiccar's brainwashing?

There's a soft knock on the door that draws my attention. I move back from the door and stand, cracking it open enough to spy on who's standing on the other side. It's Isadora.

"Eliana, I was hoping you had a moment to talk?"

I open the door farther and step out from the room, softly closing the door behind me. "What is it?" I whisper.

"Not here," she whispers, motioning to my sleeping friends, and Kai, unconscious, behind the door. "Follow me."

I hesitate, glancing back at the door. I hope I'm not making a mistake in leaving. Isadora stands farther down the hallway, waiting impatiently. I slip back into the room, grabbing my satchel. I nudge Naomi awake.

She opens bleary eyes, red around the edges from tears.

She's been crying.

"What is it?" she murmurs, her voice groggy.

"I'm sorry I woke you. Isadora is waiting outside the room. She wants to talk."

"Alone?"

The implication that Isadora shouldn't be trusted is thick with that one word. Naomi gives me her best mothering, scolding look. I smirk in response, and she rolls her eyes. She was always the mother of the group.

"I'll be fine."

"You better," she replies, a smile of her own creeping into her voice.

"Can you watch over Kai?"

She nods her head, and her eyes widen with surprise as she takes in his slumped over form. I forgot I didn't bother to prop him back up after he fell unconscious.

"Is he alright?" The whispered question is laced with worry.

She was crying over Kai.

I shrug, trying to play off the eerie incident with Kai I witnessed moments ago. I'm almost certain he wouldn't hurt Naomi. He had an opportunity earlier and didn't take it. Maybe selfishly–stupidly–I hope they can work through whatever happened to him.

"I think so. He collapsed without any warning." I leave out the part about the shadows, convincing myself I was seeing things, again.

Naomi nods her head, easily accepting my explanation. Her nonchalant reaction has me wanting to ask more questions, but Isadora is waiting for me. If Naomi is not concerned about Kai's weird incident, then I won't be either–for now.

"I'll keep an eye on him and Maendril."

I get up, and Naomi catches my wrist. "Please, El. Be careful."

I bend down and plant a soft kiss on her forehead. "Aren't I always?"

Naomi snorts, and I laugh under my breath as I slip from the room and quietly close the door behind me.

Isadora stands waiting impatiently, hands on her hips, an annoyed scowl on her face.

"Sorry," I mutter.

"Let's go," she commands, already walking away from me.

I follow Isadora down a different staircase at the end of the hall, poorly lit by a single torch at the top step. Isadora grabs the torch and leads me deeper into the building. We wind down the stairs for several minutes before stopping at a rotting door.

The hair on the back of my neck bristles as the stench of stale air attacks my senses with the force of the door opening into a dank, dingy basement.

Isadora steps into the filthy room and looks back at me expectantly. "I'm not going to kill you, if that's what you're thinking." She chuckles and smiles.

I step into the dark basement, and Isadora shuts the door behind us. We wander farther into the dank space, the smell growing stronger.

My boot squishes as I step on a thick, black mucus that sticks to the floor in disgusting globs. I scowl, shaking it off my boot. The stench nearly causes me to vomit.

"What is this place?"

"Just a basement, but also a great way to leave the village without being seen." Isadora points at the rotting, black goo. "That would be the world rot, a rather 'delightful' side effect of the Leomarisians rampage through Raephe."

"You weren't kidding about them killing off your land—that was literal."

"You saw the devastation yourself in the forest. Our land's been sucked dry of its lifeblood–Raephe's lifeblood."

"Where are you taking me?" I step to avoid another pile of rot.

"To meet someone." She pauses. "They're very reclusive ... not many of my people know of their existence within our borders."

She stops at a stone wall at the far end of the basement. "It's through here. Give me a hand?"

I stand next to her, and together we push away the wall, revealing a moss-covered tunnel. The smell of rot is stronger in the tunnel, blasting me in the face with the rush of air as we break the seal.

I gag, and Isadora chuckles. She leads the way through the tunnel that exits into the dead forest. We walk deeper into the trees, now kindling and hollow logs, and across a slow-moving stream with clear blue water.

"This way," Isadora announces, pointing to a thick copse of dried bushes. "It's just beyond here."

I push through the bramble behind Isadora, careful not to let her torch touch the dried wood. This whole forest would easily go up in flames.

On the other side of the thicket lies a small, abandoned, wooden cottage. Isadora approaches slowly, making a bird call in the back of her throat. A soft bell jingles from within the cottage.

She holds out her hand for me to wait as she opens the door, shining light into the dark interior. A pair of white eyes gleam in the light. A chair scrapes, and heavy footsteps echo across the wooden floor.

A large shadow passes in front of her torch, and I stumble back. The person standing in front of us is rocky in complexion, as though they're made of stone. A scream is trapped in my throat, and I try to swallow it down as Isadora embraces the rock-skinned person.

"Birvat," she says quietly, hugging them fiercely.

A twig snaps under my boot and their head pivots to me, white eyes blank and unreadable. A cold sweat spreads down my back.

Who is this person? Why has Isadora brought me here?

They step forward, twigs and dried logs breaking under their large feet. In four strides Birvat stands in front of me, casting me in their long shadow. White eyes stare down at me, their mouth pulled back in a snarl.

"Who are you?" Their voice the sound of gravel crushing against itself.

Isadora rushes to Birvat. She places a reassuring hand on their arm, drawing their attention. Brivat's gaze instantly softens.

"Issa, who is this?" The question is surprisingly gentle.

"Birvat, meet the Auror of Hevastia." Isadora grabs my arm and pulls me forward, placing my hand in Birvat's massive palm. "Eliana, meet the Auror of Leomaris."

"Excuse me?" I blurt out, shocked.

"So it's finally coming to pass ..." Birvat mumbles to themself, their milky white eyes staring down at me.

"Isadora, why are you hiding the Leomarisian Auror?"

"Birvat is my partner," Isadora explains, glancing lovingly at Birvat. "They're not a threat ... let us explain."

I nod my head, my eyes never leaving Birvat's endless stare.

Isadora takes my hand back and pulls me toward the cottage. Inside there's sparse furniture—a rickety chair, a large cot made of wood, and a large pillow on the ground. She points to the large pillow, "You can sit there."

Birvat settles onto the floor across from me with a loud thud that rattles the rafters. Isadora pulls two blankets from a chest under the cot, handing one to me and draping the other around herself.

"Birvat doesn't get cold, or eat," she laughs, "so there's very little comforts here. I stash that pillow and these blankets for myself."

"Okay ..." I reply, apprehensive. My brain is tumbling over itself trying to figure this out.

"Your arrival was foretold," Birvat explains in the same rock-crushing tone. "One century, nearly to the day."

Isadora rolls her eyes, patting their hand. "They believe in the mystical 'prophecy.' I believe in action and results. But, you were right—we can help one another save our lands. Birvat is a part of that too."

I gesture at Birvat's tremendous form taking up most of the small cabin. "How did you two find one another? And, why aren't you enemies?"

Birvat shares a look with Isadora, an entire conversation happening in their brief eye contact. Isadora nods her head.

"You can tell her. It's okay."

Birvat's eerie gaze falls on me, sending a chill down my spine. When they clear their throat, it sounds like rocks scraping against one another.

"My people disowned me when I stood in opposition to the continued desolation of Raephe. I found Issa injured from battling another Leomarisian raid that destroyed a bordertown.

"I nursed her back to health–"

"They were terrible at it," Isadora cuts in, laughing softly. "Leomarisians don't bleed, and they don't eat. I nearly bled out and starved to death from their 'help.'" She smiles up at Birvat, whose face is turned into an awkward jumble, what must be the equivalent of a smile.

"Horrible nursemaid aside, I wouldn't be here if it weren't for Birvat. They overlooked our differences and showed me genuine care. It's more than I can say for some of my own people."

"The Blud Revel Clan?"

Isadora flinches at the mention of the cutthroat men who murder their people for power.

"Raephean culture is founded on a matriarchy. Women are celebrated as being made in Raephe's own image–the Life Bringer, One Mother. Men serve in the clan as caregivers, supporters, hunters and gatherers. The women are the warriors, the leaders, and the lifeblood wielders.

"The Blud Revel Clan deny Raephe as the One Mother, favoring their own strength through the bloodsport of robbing our women of their lifeblood. It's a disgusting perversion of our gifts, a defiance of our most sacred laws."

And that's what Kai and the other Morei guardians do to harness the elements.

"Then who is the *Venaripa*?"

"My younger sister," Isadora replies quietly. "Iamara calls herself the Red Queen. She believes she is the direct descendant of Raephe, blessed with the power to restore our land.

"In truth, she's a power-hungry religious zealot." She shrugs. "But, she has her uses."

"So, she's the Raephean Auror?" I ask.

Birvat sits taller at the mention of the Raephean Auror and I flinch under their looming shadow. "Issa is the Raephean Auror, not her crazy sister."

Isadora leans closer to Birvat, and they settle back down. "It's true. I'm the auror. When I returned from my time with Birvat, I tried to convince my people that not all Leomarisians are a threat, that there was another way." She slams her fist down on Birvat, who doesn't flinch at being hit.

"I was deposed for my 'heresy,' and Iamara took the throne, recrowning herself the Red Queen. Of course, everyone knows she's not the true auror, but I'm dead to them, so she's second best." Isadora scoffs.

"Those that didn't want to kneel to her followed me, and we've been working in secret to end the land feud ever since."

"For how long?"

"That was five years ago, and nothing's changed for the better."

"So you're both rejects of your own people?" I laugh, shaking my head. "We have more in common than you think."

Birvat "smiles" again, and Isadora and I both laugh at their expression. Birvat's laughter is an avalanche of noise, putting Maendril's booming laughter to shame. I clap my hands over my ears to dampen the noise.

"Tell us what brought you here," Isadora says gently.

"I need your help."

Birvat smiles and I flinch, anticipating that they will laugh again. Instead, they nod their head, encouraging me to share my story.

"Most of Hevastia doesn't worship Lady Hevastia anymore ... they were made to worship the Haematitian Council's 'True Faith,' which is a perversion of Raephean lifeblood magic.

"The Morei guardians use Raephean magic to harness elemental magic, our birth right. My people have been without Hevastian magic for one hundred years."

At the mention of Raephean magic, Isadora's face turns down into a dark scowl. I recall in the war room how rage radiated from her at the insinuation of her power being connected to the despicable crimes committed in Hevastia.

"This is all very new to me–I found out I was the auror six months ago, and gained access to my magic almost three months ago. I'm not sure what my magic is, let alone how to wield it against Vaiccar and the True Faith." I sigh, placing my head in my hands.

"Vaiccar's been systematically weakening Hevastia for nearly a century, using the purple gemstone you showed me, Isadora. He used it, somehow, to siphon Hevastia's magic and store it. They're broken and gone now. Our magic is free once more. But, so is Vaiccar."

Isadora leans over to Birvat and explains the moment in the war room where she showed me the purple gemstone–the moment where another piece of Vaiccar's grand scheme clicked into place.

"Birvat, what is this magic? How can a gemstone siphon an entire nation's magic?"

Birvat's face twists into a grimace. Another secret conversation happens between him and Isadora in the span of a glance.

"That's best left to be explained another time. It's ... complicated."

I bite my tongue from a sharp remark. My own fear spurs the anxiety that rises in my gut, the inner voice that rages against Birvat's evasion to my question.

I settle for a simple nod of my head in response.

An involuntary yawn escapes my lips.

"Let's rest. We can continue this discussion in the morning." Isadora says, her own voice thick with sleep.

"Shouldn't we return to the village?"

Isadora kneels beside me, looking me directly in the eye.

"Eliana, I took a great risk bringing you along on this trip to meet Birvat. We don't have many opportunities to spend time with one another."

Her eyes plead silently with me as her words grow quiet, yearning.

"I know you have little reason to trust us, but please try to." She bites her lip. "I'm not ready to return home yet."

I nod my head and yawn again.

"Thank you, Eliana."

I lay down on the pillow next to the roaring fire, Isadora settled on Birvat's chest like a small laseron curled up on their favorite rock. She's so at home with them.

I wish I knew how that felt.

Zayne

THE SANDOVELL WE RETURNED to is not the same city we left one week ago. The presence of the Haematitian guardians has increased. We are a city under occupation.

Rumors have spread like wildfire that the guardians are hunting for those whose gifts have resurfaced since the auror restored our connection to Lady Hevastia. An undercurrent of anger at the auror for restoring magic and causing this *magavenari*, a mage hunt, ripples through the city. Many resent the return of magic, blaming their lost loved ones on the auror. More don't believe the auror is real. If I had not met Eliana myself … it's hard to know what I would believe.

There is an underground network, the *Absconditi*, that is working to gather all the known mages of the city and aid them and their loved ones in avoiding notice of the guardians.

I have taken refuge in their camp within the underbelly of the city—the sewers. The *Abskonditi's* ranks have swelled to nearly one hundred, with some hearing of us in the outer hamlets.

"Captain." Loith's voice pulls my attention back to the packed room full of masked figures crowding a large oak table.

I adjust my mask, hoping it conceals the roll of my eyes.

The masks are for our *protection*. Anonymity ensures that if our secret society is compromised by the Haematitian scum that infests Sandovell, we can reconvene in a new location without losing everything this ragtag council of disgruntled merchants, shop owners, and common citizens is working toward. The one thing we have in common—a desire for freedom from the Haematitian Council and whatever twisted fate awaits us if they discover we are all mages of Hevastian origin, not the perversion they call the "True Faith."

"We must evacuate the camp below the central *tehendra*," a woman wearing a *laseron* mask demands, her fist slamming the table to emphasize her point.

"Where do you propose we relocate nearly thirty individuals?" a broad-chested man retorts. Several nod their heads in agreement.

"There must be some pocket of Sandovell the accursed Haematitian guardians have not infested," the woman replies, her open hand slapping the table with less emphasis than her former statement.

Grumbling ripples through the crowded room. This meeting is losing direction. Soon it will dissolve into a bitching fest as the richer among us complain of how the Haematitian guardians' occupation has disrupted their—illegal—business dealings.

Loith jabs me in the ribs, conveying a warning with her eyes behind her *crost* bird mask. My own mask is made from Akiko's shed feathers.

I clear my throat. "There may be a place beyond Sandovell where we can seek refuge."

Twenty pairs of eyes flick to me with guarded expressions. It's the first time I've ever spoken in these meetings.

"The Hevastian Auror has been gathering refugees in a secluded location. I could request her assistance."

I have not heard of Eliana's fate since we abandoned her on Raephe. I hope she's truly alive and well.

"The Hevastian Auror?" The laseron mask snorts. "Where is the supposed prophesied savior of Hevastia? She's more myth than flesh and blood."

My hackles rise, my cheeks flushed with annoyance as a low-simmering rage builds within me. This is not the first comment of this sort. Many among this group are displeased with Eliana's lack of presence or proof of her existence.

"The auror is occupied with another mission," I bite out each word slowly, barely biting back the rage.

"What could be more important than the protection of her people?" an unknown voice chimes in.

I open my mouth to argue, but Loith places a warning hand on my arm, shaking her head, no.

I hope Eliana knows what she's doing by leaving Hevastia. We need her.

"I will contact her."

A few in the room nod their heads in appreciation of my offer, but most of them eye me with varying degrees of mistrust behind their masks. The conversation continues on with more complaints of business interruptions, but Loith and I turn to leave.

I have a letter to draft.

The quill scratches across the page as I cross out the words, "my beautiful, dangerous princess."

"Zayne, you hopeless flirt," I mutter to myself.

Akiko chirps from her perch, most likely laughing at me.

"I know, girl. Eliana made her stance clear. I will respect that."

I quickly pen the letter I've agonized over writing for the past two days, the words consuming nearly every waking minute.

My whistle summons Akiko to my shoulder. She bumps her beak against my cheek, and I stroke her colorful throat.

"Chirrup," she squawks with joy for the pets.

I tap the top of her foot, and she holds out her left leg. I secure the note with a ribbon, and it rests snuggly around her ankle.

"Fly true, girl."

Akiko chirps, taking flight through the large window behind my desk. Her brilliant colors reflect the *solari's* light high in the sky.

A knock at the door.

"Sir?"

"Enter."

"I saw Akiko depart. Did you finally finish professing your love for her Highness?" Loith's cheeks heat to a soft pink.

"No." I suddenly find myself in a sour mood.

"Right." Loith straightens up, clearing her throat. "There's news of another meeting tonight. What shall I respond with?"

"Not tonight," I sigh. "I would like to take a walk."

Loith turns, probably to run off and fetch her coat.

"Alone, Loith. Please."

"Of course, Captain."

I grit my teeth at the use of my old title. I'm hardly a captain without a crew. They abandoned the Daughter of the Seas when we made port in Sandovell. Many disagreed with my decision to abandon Nita and Pilo's corpses on the accursed beach. The remaining few requested leave to secure their family's safety.

All except Loith. Loyal to her very marrow—even after witnessing the love of her life die on that beach.

"Take the night for yourself, Loith. That's an order."

"As you wish, Captain."

"Wishing has nothing to do with it, and stop calling me that. It's Zayne."

Loith nods and makes a quick exit from my cabin.

Kai

BESIDE ME SITS A young boy with short-cropped blonde hair, a flower pinched in his thin fingers. We are sitting in a garden, our backs resting against a stone fountain, taking turns tossing pebbles at a statue of a woman holding a yellow orb. The game was to get the pebble to land in her upturned palm—a tight space to toss a rock with the yellow glass blocking a clear shot.

The boy laughs, plucking petals from the flower. "Remember me, remember me not," he chants in an upbeat, silly tune.

"What are you doing?" I ask.

"Seeing if you'll regain your memories."

"What?" I sputter out. "Who are you?"

He turns away from the flower, now missing half of its petals, to stare at me. I'm caught off guard by how bright his green eyes are as he matches my gaze. He wears his hair short, slicked back. He's wearing the same black uniform as me. Judging by the sharp angles of his face, and that the sleeves of his uniform are too short, I would say he's thirteen and growing.

How can I piece together all of that and not recall his name?

There's a joyous shout from behind us, and I scramble to my feet. Two Morei guardians have found us in the garden. I don't recognize them, but the blonde boy runs to greet them. They each hug him in turn, opening their arms for me to receive a hug as well. I brush them off, not interested in something so ... soft-hearted.

The summoning horn blows three short bursts—the order for all potentials to assemble. The blonde boy follows me as we leave the garden, taking an arched hallway to a large training room not far from the garden. Large racks of every conceivable weapon line the walls of the large room, a makeshift arena of dirt and rope in the center of the wide open space.

In the center of the room stands an imposing woman in a red robe shouting orders to the others gathered around the perimeter of the arena.

"You two," she commands, pointing to me and the blonde boy, "swords." She snaps her fingers dismissing us to scramble for our assigned weapons.

I am instructed to grab twin blades by another priestess in black with a red stole and to stand next to the blonde boy. His face has paled since our time in the garden. A trickle of sweat builds on the back of his neck. He doesn't have a weapon.

We stand facing another pair—a fiery red-haired girl with a long sword, and a small, sickly, black-haired girl.

"On my mark you will face your opponents and show no mercy," the woman in red commands.

"She wants us to fight them?" The blonde-haired boy whimpers next to me. "With real weapons?"

I scowl at him. "Of course we duel with real weapons. What were you expecting?"

The command is shouted for us to begin fighting. Reflexively, I snatch the boy's hand, and he yelps, trying to yank it back. I hold firm and draw a thin blade across his scarred palm, blood blooming on his pale skin.

He hisses from the pain, but stops trying to pull his hand away as I lock our palms together and chant under my breath.

The movements are all as natural as breathing, something I've been doing my whole life, was always meant to do.

His blood pours from the wound, making both our hands slick, but still he holds on, and a surge of strength shudders through my body. The air around us has grown very still, and I reach out to touch it, bending it to my will. With my hand thrust out, I shoot a current of air at the girls, throwing them both to the ground.

I smile to myself, the addictive power coursing through me. There's a weighted pause in the arena, as if the air itself is holding its breath for what I'll do next. I grab onto it once more with zeal, pummeling them again and again.

Inky darkness oozes from the walls, bubbling and spurting. The first drips land on my hands, and I gaze up, blinking as several more drops of the black, mysterious liquid drip all over me.

The blonde boy's hand slips from mine, cutting my magic off. The air I had turned into a current crashes down, kicking up the dust of the arena floor. The dirt sticks to the black liquid, leaving me speckled.

I turn to chide the boy for letting go of my hand and suck in a surprised breath. He lies on the ground, dead.

Cire.

The throbbing in my head spikes as the name comes forth, breaking through an invisible barrier that locks my mind away from me. The young blonde boy, his name was Cire. Eliana called him my Morei partner.

My brother.

My eyes shoot open, leaving behind the bleeding walls of the arena and Cire's dead body. I wake to find Eliana gone and Naomi and Maendril still sleeping soundly. The fire's burned down, and I add fresh logs, staring at the low flames.

The throbbing headache in the back of my head confirms I had another episode, but I didn't travel to the Shadow Realm. Instead it felt like a dream.

What is happening to me? My mind is fracturing.

A soft hand briefly touches my shoulder, and I glance up to Naomi's concerned expression staring down at me.

"Is everything okay, Kai?"

Is everything I know a lie? How am I supposed to know what's real anymore?

"Cire is dead," I whisper.

Naomi folds herself neatly to the floor beside me, pulling me to her. I fall into her embrace with a small sob, the softness unfamiliar to me.

Was it always?

Naomi's touch is gentle, comfortable. She moves around me as if we've always shared the same air. For the time being, this is strategically a good position. I'm deep within enemy ranks.

Naomi is not your enemy.

I stiffen as the betraying thought whispers across my mind. The hand caressing my face pauses for a breath before continuing.

Pull yourself together, Kai.

I can't let a girl, a worshiper of the Old Ways, cloud my judgment. She's the Hevsastian Auror's best friend. She stands opposed to everything Lord Vaiccar stands for–everything I stand in service to. I would be a fool to abandon my mission. Lord Vaiccar does not tolerate insubordination. Worse yet, my betrayal would risk Lord Vaiccar's Grand Design, his plan to save Hevastia from the monstrous plague and ruin.

"Kai, what's happening?" She strokes my hair, her fingers gently raking through my short curls. "You can tell me."

I shake my head, unable to voice the horrors I witnessed in my dream. Unwilling to tell her how her touch gets under my skin. How it comforts me.

"Shhh," she hushes me, continuing to pet my head. "I don't know how, Kai, but I swear we will fix it. Eliana, Maendril, and I are on a mission to find the Keladonean Auror. We believe they'll know how to reverse whatever Vaiccar's done to you."

They're going to the Keladonean Auror ... could it be so simple?

Hama

MY NEEDLE SLIDES EASILY through the soft yarn I am working with, stitching the two pieces together to form a sleeve.

The tent flap opens abruptly, startling me. Alana smiles, her face flushed from another hard day's work. She's been assisting a few of the other Wildewell refugees in building a new forge in one of the caverns off the main antechamber with a small skylight, perfect for a furnace.

"It's nearly complete. We only need to finish carving a large boulder into a table and move the anvil."

"What anvil?"

Alana breaks eye contact, her hand rubbing the back of her neck as she bites her lip, shuffling back and forth.

"Alana, what anvil?"

She sighs. "A few of us are going to venture into Bellamere to find their anvil and bring it back. We've already built a cart to carry it with–"

"Absolutely not." I stand, my project falling from my lap. "It's too dangerous. We don't know that Naomi was the last dark beast roaming the valley."

She takes my hands in hers, bringing them to her lips, and slowly she kisses each finger.

"My *Amorei*, we are armed. We'll be fine. We need a forge, and we won't be able to craft anything without that anvil."

"When do you go?"

"Tomorrow."

Alana kisses my forehead once more and holds me tightly to her chest. Her hands wrap around my head and pull me back, tilting my chin up to meet her eyes.

"Without fail. I have made that promise to you since the very first day we met. I won't break it now."

She bends down and hands me the sweater I dropped. The thread and fabric is a soft pink I dyed in secret as a surprise for Tenya. She is due any day now, but you wouldn't know it.

"There's a demonstration tonight. Are you coming?"

"I wouldn't miss it."

Alana kisses my forehead once more before ducking out of our shared tent and into the bustle of the Burroughs right outside our little haven.

I plop back down on the soft bench Tenya helped me make and finish the stitching of the first sleeve before moving to the next. I have an hour or so before I need to join Alana and the others in the *tehendra* for the demonstration.

My fingers gingerly graze the buttons I fashioned from the sturdy reeds that grow along the stream. The yarn is made from the soft, sturdy fibers within the thick stalks.

I built my own carding tool, brush, and spindle to process the harvested fibers.

The children of the Burroughs will soon outgrow their clothes, and replacements are in short supply. I have my work cut out for me.

I add the finished sweater to the pile of baby clothes I've made for Tenya. Tomorrow I will start on new knitted trousers for Raen and Clyn. Those boys follow Alana, Tenya, and Tyr around like lost pups, working so hard they've worn sizable holes in all of their pants.

No boys of mine wear scraps.

My heart constricts at the memory of Kai and Cire, how they had the same reckless, wild energy when they were that age.

A hot tear slides down my cheek, splashing onto my hand. I sniffle.

Pull yourself together old girl, there's no time for sentimentality right now.

Bootsteps alert me to the presence of someone behind me, and I'm greeted by Tenya's round stomach and her smiling face.

She immediately notices my wet cheeks and rushes over.

What's wrong, Hama?

She dabs my cheeks with her sleeve, a soft, gentle smile on her face.

You will be an excellent mother, I sign, laughing. *I was thinking of Kai and Cire.*

Tenya opens her arms, and I scootch over on the bench, letting her strong arms envelope me in a hug.

Walk with me to the demonstration? Tenya asks, taking my hand in hers.

I nod my head, and she smiles wider. Her other hand rests comfortably on her stomach, tracing small circles.

I'm due any day now. Do you think my baby will be the first born with a gift?

I smile, patting Tenya's hand that holds mine. *Absolutely. With you and Tyr as the parents, that child is surely blessed to be born into your home.*

She rolls her eyes. *That's not what I meant, and you know it.*

I chuckle quietly. My heart pinches with envy at Tenya's fortune, but I will never allow that to stand in the way of celebrating her joy.

When we arrived at the *tehendra*, a large crowd had already formed, leaving the very center open as they gathered around the makeshift stage.

Do you know what's being shown today? Tenya asks me.

I shake my head no. Even though Alana is in charge of these spectacles, she keeps them secret, unwilling to ruin the surprise for me. I know she's incredibly proud of the progress being made in the training sessions.

Raen, Clyn, Abigael, and Yuriel step into the center of the group. Each is holding an object they'll use in their demonstration.

The boys spot us in the crowd and blush, giving us each a tiny wave.

Yuriel steps forward first, an unlit torch in his hand. Several burning torches line the *tehendra* and its various tables.

He closes his eyes, sucking in a deep breath. The torches around us begin to flicker, the flames responding to Yuriel's magic. One by one they snuff out, their fire flying into Yuriel's mouth and down into his gut.

Yuriel opens his eyes and the fire he's absorbed burns in his eyes, twin infernos. He holds the torch out in front of him and bellows, sending all the fire he swallowed out of his gut and at the torch, lighting it.

He's breathing fire.

Many in the crowd gasp in shock, the children squealing with delight. It's an impressive show of his gift. As he rejoins the crowd, several men clap him on his back, and he smiles with pride.

Yuriel started his journey very apprehensive about receiving Daneth's and then Alana's guidance, but he's flourished under their instruction, and his gift is incredible. None of the Morei guardians were ever able to absorb their element and project it.

Abigael steps forward next holding a plant, its roots dangling from her fist. Her left hand reaches in front of her and the ground begins to quake under our boots. Her lip trembles.

If she loses control of her gift, she could send us all falling into a pit.

Clyn places a comforting hand on her shoulder, and she breathes. The ground stops trembling as she regains control and focuses her magic on the spot of ground directly in front of her.

A small hole forms under the space where her hand hovers. She bends down and places the plant in the hole, guiding the dirt to refill the gaps around the plant.

Standing back up she dusts herself off, and we all begin to clap.

Abigael shakes her head. "That's not my demonstration—this is."

Her gaze now focused on the plant, what was once a small sprout doubles, triples, quadruples in size within seconds, vines shooting out from the plant in all directions. She flicks her wrist and the vines respond, darting out at the crowd, wrapping around several folks in the front row.

They scream as the vines lift them from the ground. Abigael bows, smiling ear to ear before she sets her audience down, wrapping the vines back up and releasing the plant from her influence. Once again it sits in the hole, a plain, little sprout.

We roar with applause. Abigael bows again, her cheeks wet with tears. Her partner rushes from the crowd carrying their daughter. She hugs them both, and they escort her to the crowd.

She controlled the plant. Never has there been a Morei warrior able to manipulate a living thing. Is this true elemental power?

Clyn steps forward next, the handle for a bucket of water clutched in his fist. He waves again at me and Tenya before setting down the bucket.

He calls the water from the bucket, sending a geyser shooting toward the ceiling of the antechamber. As it falls, Clyn catches the droplets, collecting them in his hand, the ball of water growing as more of it is sucked in.

He smiles mischievously and tosses the ball of water, catching it in his other hand. The water is juggled back and forth several times before Clyn drops it to the ground and it splashes over his boots.

In a humorous fashion, Clyn shrugs his shoulders and scratches his head as he taps his boot. He flashes a surprised face, holding a hand up in victory. His right hand hovers over the ground where the water landed and he wiggles his fingers.

The water slowly beads to the surface and rushes to Clyn's hand, reforming in a ball. He sends the ball into the bucket with a satisfied plop and bows.

The crowd erupts with cheers and laughter, several whooping and whistling. Clyn smiles ear to ear before stepping back to usher Raen to the front.

Raen steps forward holding a large feather. He tosses the feather in the air, and it begins to slowly float to the ground. As Raen's magic coaxes the air to catch the feather, it begins to spin slowly in a circle, hovering in place.

He sends the feather around the front of the crowd, tickling several children who giggle and squeal with delight.

In the distraction of Raen's trick, Clyn disappeared, and I know in my gut something is up. These boys are tricksters. They have something up their sleeves.

Tenya nudges my side and points up. She had the same idea as me, and had been searching for Clyn. She spotted him tucked into a crevice in the wall behind the vendor tables.

He's holding his bucket of water, a devious look on his face as he laughs to himself.

Raen continues to distract everyone with the feather as Clyn slowly guides the ball of water from his bucket out over the crowd.

Clyn drops the ball of water, soaking unsuspecting audience members, who glance up searching for the source of the cave leak. Raen drops his feather, gathering more wind in his arms before sending it out to the corner of the crowd that met Clyn's water bomb.

Raen's wind wraps around them, circling their bodies, pulling at their clothes and hair as it whips around them, drying them off.

When the water's been dried from their clothes, Raen stands before everyone circling a silo of air and water, the force of the air keeping the water circling in a funnel.

Clyn hops down from his hiding spot, holding the bucket. Raen guides his funnel of air over the bucket and then releases it, sending the trapped water down into the bucket.

Raen and Clyn hold hands and bow to roaring applause, everyone in the crowd flabbergasted at the display.

Did you know? Tenya asks, her eyes wide with shock.

I shake my head. *No, Alana does not tell me anything about the demonstrations. I'm surprised she managed to keep this one a secret.*

Strong arms wrap around my shoulders as a soft kiss pecks my cheek.

"What did you think?" Alana asks, turning me to face her.

"It was incredible, Alana–did you know the boys were planning that prank?"

"I didn't know they had figured out how to combine their gifts. That was incredible. They have a much stronger connection to their gifts than any Morei ever did. It's phenomenal."

Eliana

THE *SOLARI'S* LIGHT PEEKS through the window, warming my face. The smell of roasted fruit wafts across the room, and I open my eyes to Isadora holding a large yellow fruit over the fire.

"Morning, mother's blessing," she offers. "I hope you're hungry." She chuckles. "Birvat's collected enough food to last a week."

The only other piece of furniture in the small cabin is an old table, now piled high with an assortment of fruits, root vegetables, and fungi.

"They don't know how much we eat, do they?" I ask, hiding another giggle behind my hand.

She shakes her head, no. An easy, joyful smile alights on her face. "Thankfully, they've stopped trying to feed me twigs and leaves."

I cackle, and Isadora joins in.

Birvat enters the cabin, their hulking frame barely fitting through the small doorway. They watch us eat, holding their own skewer of fruit-courtesy of Isadora.

Between bites of fruit I ask, "what do you know of the Hevastian prophecy?"

"Birvat is a self-proclaimed expert on the 'prophecy,'" Isadora explains in a light, teasing tone. "The Auror of Keladone is very prophetic. Birvat enjoys her storytelling."

I perk up at the mention of the Keladonean Auror. "You know the Auror of Keladone?"

Isadora shrugs. "Not directly. She visited my predecessor nearly one hundred years ago. The visit and the 'prophecies' she shared are sacred to our people. I've shared her tales with Birvat."

"I'm teaching myself to read." Birvat sits taller and sets aside their uneaten fruit.

"What do the Keladonean tales mention?" I choke down the nervous energy coursing through me.

"The last Auror of Hevastia was proclaimed to unite the aurors of all lands in a world-saving battle. We were told by our deities to prepare ourselves for your arrival."

At the mention of 'world-saving battle' my stomach drops. "Do you know why I'm the last auror?"

Birvat and Isadora both glance away, and the pit in my stomach grows.

"No, we don't," she sighs. "It's ominous-sounding though. If I were you I would be shitting myself."

My stomach clenches. "I'll do whatever it takes to free my people and avenge the lost and brutalized."

Silence falls over the breakfast table for several agonizingly long heartbeats.

"So you've been waiting for someone to wash up on your shores claiming to be the Hevastian Auror?"

Isadora laughs, Birvat joining in. This time, I don't cover my ears at the thunderous sound.

"Not exactly," Isadora responds between giggles.

"Then–"

"Your amulet, where did you get it?"

"I suppose it's a family heirloom?" I run my thumb over it. "Honestly, I'm not sure how my mother came to possess it. All I know is that it depicts Hevastia's Heart, the gate that once held Vaiccar back."

"It's your *mendott.*"

Isadora pulls the chain around her neck to reveal an amulet similar to my own. "This is my *mendott.* They're each unique to their deity."

"You call yours Hevastia's Heart. We know that pattern as Soran's Soul–the first deity of your land. Mine is known as Mother's Womb, and Birvat's is Leomaris's Fist.

"The *mendott* helps you focus your power."

I stare more closely at my amulet. It doesn't appear special to me in any obvious way. The memory of holding it for the first time flashes through my mind–the instant recognition of its twisting pattern, the same design I had drawn countlessly from my haunting dreams. Dreams that ceased after I unlocked the gate and freed Vaiccar.

"It is rumored that the *mendotts* can be combined to unlock an ancient, mythic shield."

Birvat speaks so quickly I almost miss what they said, still lost in my own thoughts.

"A shield?" I scoff, "what is so great about a shield?"

Isadora smirks. "Spoken like a truly inexperienced warrior."

She leans forward, elbows resting on the table. "A shield is a powerful tool on the battlefield, when wielded properly. Only someone who was trained to rely on brute strength and their magic would scoff as you did."

The hair on the back of my neck bristles, and immediately I think of several truly nasty remarks. Birvat interrupts me before I say something regrettable.

"This shield is said to have the power to withstand the might of the gods. It's called the *Imortei Novemendott,* or the Nine Souls Shield." Birvat's milky white eyes gleam with pride as they share this with me. Isadora was not kidding about Birvat's fascination with the prophecy.

"How does one find this all powerful shield?"

"That's a bit ... tricky," Isadora replies, no longer meeting my eyes. "When I asked you yesterday what benefit my people would have in helping you, it was because helping you leaves my own people vulnerable."

"I don't understand."

"The *Imortei Novemendott* can be wielded only once. And, only if all the *mendotts* from each deity are connected to it."

"So that's what the prophecy meant about uniting the aurors," I murmur under my breath.

"You'll have a hard time convincing some of the aurors. Not everyone believes your side of this feud is the 'righteous side.'"

"Are you telling me the other auror's will take Vaiccar's side?"

"Potentially," Birvat answers.

"Do you really not know?" Isadora stares at me, dumbfounded.

"Know what?"

"Your goddess, Hevastia, is not favored among the gods. There are those that blame her for Soran's death."

"What?" I scoff, "*Vaiccar* murdered Soran, not Hevastia."

"Vaiccar would have never challenged Soran if he had not weakened himself by giving Hevastia part of his immortality. They blame her for their eldest brother's death."

"That's ridiculous."

"Maybe to you, but not to them. They are gods, Eliana. Time is irrelevant to them. They can hold a grudge for eternity, and some do. If you want the help of their chosen, then you'll need to convince their aurors to turn their back on their deities."

"I convinced *you*." I don't say it with much conviction.

"I've always known on what side of injustice Raephe would want me to stand on, the side in favor of life, and freedom."

"I would never betray Isadora," Birvat states. They add with a smirk, "I have no loyalty to Leomaris."

"How will I convince the others?" I ask quietly.

"Not sure, but I think it is worth contacting the other aurors about the situation."

We sit around the grand fire in the main hall of Isadora's officer barracks. Most of her warriors are out scouting, tracking where the Leomarisians plan to attack next and evacuating the area.

Isadora is regaling a tale of a skirmish between the Blud Revel Clan and her warriors. The women and men cheer in equal measure at the memory of their victory over the blasphemers. Naomi listens with rapt attention. Maendril is also sucked into the story, his whetstone and sword forgotten on his lap.

We had recently finished our first practice duel since coming to Raephe. Several of the Raephean warriors observed from the sidelines, eyes wide with excitement and the thrill—so similar to their expressions now as their leader honors them with this tale.

"What is the word for the magic the Blud Revel Clan uses against you?"

If Naomi's question catches Isadora off-guard, she's good at hiding it. Several people groan at the story being cut off. Naomi blushes, embarrassed to have shouted out the question. I pat her knee in reassurance.

At the question, Kai perks up. He's also experienced the effects of the uncomfortable magic. My skin crawls with the memory.

"It's called *bludinflexi*, blood bending. It's blasphemous to use it in combat as the Blud Revel Clan does. The ability to still a person's body, it was meant as a merciful practice during times of crisis, or to ease the pain of death. For mercy killings, not blood sport.

"It sickens me. I'm so sorry you endured that," she says to me, and to my surprise, even acknowledges Kai, who sits apart from everyone. "It's those very heinous acts that make stopping the Blud Revel Clan so difficult. They use that against their own people in order to subdue them and then murder them in the name of 'protecting' the very people they slaughter—it's insane."

"So *bludinflexi* doesn't work on the Leomarisians?" Maendril asks.

"How could it? They don't have circulatory systems. Leomarisians don't bleed."

"So how do you take them down?" Maendril asks. He uses the skewer his dinner roasted on to pick his teeth, comfortably reclined against a large log seated around the fire.

Isadora flinches at his question. "The most we've been able to do is separate them from the crystal they channel. Without it, they fall into a trance-like sleep."

"So they channel the same kind of crystals that siphoned all of Hevastia's magic as a lifeforce?" I ask, intrigued.

Isadora's glance pleads with me, *please don't press this,* before answering aloud. "That's what we think, but we're not sure. Leomarisians are incredibly strong. Taking one down is near impossible."

The door bursts open with a bang as it crashes into the wall. All eyes turn to the messenger in the doorway, his hands on his knees as he takes deep breaths.

"Isadora, there's been an attack," he wheezes in another deep breath.

That's when the smell of blood hits my nostrils. He's covered in it.

"Grantt, what is it?" Isadora asks, already rushing to his side.

"The *Venaripa*, her camp." Grantt collapses.

Isadora shakes his shoulders, but he's already gone, his blood beginning to pool on the ground around us.

"I need to go," Isadora announces.

"Let us go with you," I offer.

She nods her head. It's the only command Maendril, Naomi, Kai and I need to begin gathering our weapons.

"Maendril, keep an eye on Kai," I request under my breath as he joins me in gathering supplies. He grunts in response, but I can't help but notice the satisfied smirk. I know I can trust Maendril to incapacitate Kai if it comes to that.

In minutes, we're all following Isadora through the forest, our boots crushing dried twigs and brush without a care for the noise.

The dead forest gives way to the lush moss and vibrant red clay. I smell the smoke first. The *Venaripa's* camp is ablaze, the fire reaching beyond the camp to the forest surrounding it.

Survivors in soot-covered clothes run frantically with buckets of water trying to put out the flames, but they can't keep up with its ravenous path as it carves its way into the surrounding area.

"Iamara," Isaodra yells, frightened eyes scanning the camp for the Red Queen's crown of bone. She runs into the chaos and I call after her, running to catch up.

A strong hand grips my wrist and pulls me back.

"I can't let you do that, Eliana," Maendril states. His resolve is absolute. He truly means to prevent me from joining Isadora in helping the others.

I yank my arm free and whirl on him, anger flaring in my eyes. "What was the point of coming if we're not going to help them? They're our allies, Maendril. I'm sorry, but I won't let them suffer."

He stares down at me, stunned. Naomi and Kai shove past him as well, joining me. We leave Maendril behind, running into the burning camp.

My steps falter. Flashes of Bellamere burning streak across my mind's eye. I understand now Maendril's hesitation. He did not witness the brutality of the Morei warriors. He only worries for me. Naomi charges past me, and her bravery gives me strength. I can't let the past hold me back from making a difference here, now. I may not have been able to save my people, but I can save Isadora's.

The thick smoke chokes our lungs. Isadora is helping women in red cloaks lift a fallen tree off of a brightly colored tent. I grab the trunk, straining to lift alongside the other women. Glancing at the woman to my left, her hands are stained red with the blood that flows down her arms, the sleeves of her cloak soaked in it.

It's with sickening dread I realize why the women wear red cloaks … *to hide the blood stains from self-tithing.* The men must wear white to ensure they're not practicing sacrilege as the Blud Revel Clan does.

Naomi runs up next to me, her arms gripping the trunk and lifting. Kai taps her on the shoulder and takes her place. With his help the tree lifts far enough off the ground to peer into the wreckage.

"Iamara," Isadora calls for her sister.

"Naomi, crawl in there and find the *Venaripa*," Kai grunts out, straining with the weight of the tree.

"Are you crazy?" I snap, my head whirling to meet his gaze with fire in my eyes. "Absolutely not."

"Cut me," Kai commands, matching my gaze.

"What–"

"Cut me. Now," he growls.

I let go of the tree and pulled my dagger from my belt, rolling up Kai's sleeve to expose his forearm. I gasp–it's covered in raised scars, the lines criss-crossing over themselves.

Stars. What happened to you, Kai?

He glances away, and I snap back to the present. I gently slide the tip of my dagger down his arm, drawing a line of red blood that beads along the wound. I glance up and Kai nods his head in thanks.

I step in to help lift the tree as he steps away. Kai's blood is pulled from the wound and into his hands. His face is scrunched in concentration as he focuses on the pull of his magic.

The ground quakes under my boots as Kai draws it up, building a makeshift shelf of clay and stone to rest the massive tree on. We all step away, my eyes never leaving Kai.

He draws more blood, and the air begins to ruffle my hair as a breeze flows into the camp. The breeze crescendos, growing into a powerful gust.

Panic courses through me. *What is Kai thinking? This much air will stoke the fire until there's nothing left. We'll all be consumed by it.*

The fire is sucked into the frenzy of the whipping air, becoming an inferno of rolling flames. Kai strains against it as he folds his hands together, constraining the storm, forcing it to shrink in on itself. The fire begins to suffocate with the lack of air, and the ball of wind grows smaller, choking out the flames until they're all gone.

The camp is left smoking, but the fire is gone.

Bodies scrape against the crisp ground and ash, and I turn to the sight of a soot-stained Naomi pulling the *Venaripa* from the wreckage of the collapsed tent. The *Venaripa* is unconscious, and her skin is burnt in several places, but she will recover.

The thud of something heavy hitting the ground pulls my attention away from Isadora as she weeps over her sister's body–Kai lies collapsed on the ground.

Naomi runs to his side, dropping to her knees and pulling him into her lap. His head lolls in her lap. He's unconscious.

Shadows pull off the trees surrounding the camp, flooding the ground as they rush to Kai. Naomi squeals, setting Kai down as the first shadow touches her, recoiling as if she was burnt.

"They're freezing cold. It was like being kissed by death." Her voice fades to a whisper.

I kneel down beside her, pulling her into my arms. "He'll be okay, Naomi, Kai's incredibly strong. What he did ... he saved everyone here."

Frightened eyes watch Kai's body be absorbed into a living darkness that writhes on the ground, swallowing him whole. Footsteps approach us, and a heavy hand falls onto my shoulder. Maendil stands still behind me, his eyes on Kai's shadowy form.

"What happened to him?" he whispers under his breath, genuine fear in his eyes.

"Maendril, we need to get Kai out of here." He looks at me, but it's as if he's not really listening. I place my hand on his. "Maendril please."

I get up and walk to a singed tent, now smoldering. I tear the fabric, gathering a large section of it. With Naomi's help we wrap Kai in it, the icy shadows burning our fingers every time we accidentally touch them directly.

Maendril stands in shock, and I give up on hoping for his help.

Naomi lifts Kai's head and shoulders, I gather his legs and feet in my arms and we lift, stumbling away from the camp and to the shelter of the forest–away from prying eyes.

Behind a thick copse of trees, we set Kai down before sitting next to him. Naomi sniffles, tears falling silently down her cheeks.

"It will be okay. He will be okay."

Why did Kai help us?

I shake the thought away. Now is not the time to worry over his reasons. He lays still, chest barely rising with shallow breaths.

Lady Hevastia, save him.

Kai

A ROUGH POKE AND then a shove wake me, and Noras's face fills my vision. I cry out in shock and flinch away. He smiles with relief.

"Sir, you're okay." He offers me his hand. "I was worried. I sent the shadows to protect you."

"What happened, Noras?" I ask, my mind groggy. "One minute the fireball is bending to my command, the air funnel choking the flames, and the next the world fades to black."

"I don't know, sir. I sensed your distress and called the shadows on your behalf to your aid. They're protecting you now as we speak."

"Protecting me—they won't hurt someone if they touch me, will they?" I ask, thinking immediately of Naomi.

"No-no, nothing like that. Your body needs rest. You're in stasis." Noras meets my frustrated glare and stammers, "temporarily. Only temporary, sir. I promise. Matters have gotten worse while you were away. Perhaps we can use this time to discuss the Shadow Realm?"

I sigh, rubbing the back of my neck. "Sure, Noras. What is it?"

"It's the shadow folds, sir. They grow in number every day. I've had to begin opening the garden surrounding the palace to them, otherwise they risk overlap. If the trapped souls overlap, both could be lost or fractured."

He leads me from the great hall where we stand to a small library wing adjacent to the hall. "I've read of a magic that corrupts the soul by stealing parts of it. It makes the victim a shell of oneself, open to the influence of another entity. If these trapped souls are under this sort of influence, they would be alive, but not under their own volition."

"What happens to someone under this sort of dark influence?"

"I don't know, sir, but I imagine they would be capable of great harm without so much as a hesitation or conscious thought against it. They may not even be aware of such influence."

"Noras, study this. I think you may be onto something."

"Where are you going sir?"

"To visit the shadow folds. I want to visit them for myself."

"Sir, I don't think that is wise. These folds, unlike the one your friend was trapped in, contain souls that are not in a happy place of their own creation. They're suspended in a vicious darkness." He reaches out to stop me, and I shrug off his hand.

"Please, I can't guarantee your safety should you enter one. I merely study them from the outside to record every soul to step foot in the Shadow Realm."

"I understand your concern, and I'm grateful for it. You're a loyal friend." Noras glances at my hand resting on his shoulder, and smiles. It is the first time in my memory that I've called someone my friend.

I leave the palace, my boots sloshing in puddles along the garden from where Noras must have recently cared for the hedges and various dark blooms that line the walkways. Where the hedge garden used to extend far beyond the palace's shadow, Noras's trimmed them all away and created a wide open space dotted with the thin sliver of light that is the entrance to a shadow fold.

However, these folds are not split by the bright, airy light of Naomi's fold, or those that fill the shadow field. The light glows an ominous red. My gut clenches as I step close to one, the sinister presence within the fold emanating outward.

I clench my fist at my side, taking a deep breath. Extending my arm I reach into the fold and something on the other side grabs me, claws ripping into my arm.

I struggle against the unseen foe, trying to pull my arm free. Losing my balance, I fall forward, and the palace garden disappears, to be replaced by dark stone, glinting red under the light of a blood-red *lunei* suspended in the sky. It's a world of darkest obsidian.

I hold my injured arm to my chest. In my fall, the monster that grabbed me let go, and now it stalks me from the shadows.

"I don't want to hurt you," I call out, standing tall. "I'm here to help."

"Trespasser," hisses a garbled voice. "Leave."

"Why are you here?"

"Where is here," it responds.

I step forward, and claws scrape against stone as it moves farther away from me.

"Stay away," it snarls.

I hold my hands out in front of me, apologetically. "I'm sorry. I won't come any closer."

It snarls, and I catch a glimpse of white teeth before the soul moves, shuffling away further into the darkness.

"Who are you?" I ask. I spin in a slow circle, trying to determine where it's hidden.

"Remember nothing," it whines, a lonely, sad sound. "Makes my head hurt, no more."

When I try to recall my own memories, my head splits with pain. Could Noras be right and I've encountered this same sinister magic, too?

"Leave … before it … is too–" the voice's strangled vocals cut off with a sickening shriek.

"Run," it bellows with animal-like ferocity.

I stumble backward, catching the edge of the shadow fold and stepping back through it, the obsidian giving way to the gray sky of the Shadow Realm and the palace garden.

I find Noras in the library, several books open in front of him. From the doorway, I watch as he opens another tome, his eyes roaming the worn text before slamming it shut with a disgusted snarl.

I laugh, and his head shoots up, shame giving way to shock and worry at the sight of my mangled arm.

"Lord Kai, what happened?" Noras asks as he rushes around the desk piled with books and floats to my side.

"I went inside one of the folds. When I reached my arm in, something grabbed me and was tearing me to shreds. But, the soul trapped in there, they were too afraid to come close to me. I don't think they attacked me. I think the fold itself did."

"A shadow fold attacked you?" He mumbles under his breath, "most strange."

"Noras, what does that mean?" I ask.

"I'm not sure, sir. I will continue to pore over the texts. You need to return to the Light Realm. There is nothing I or the shadows can do here to heal that wound."

He points to my arm, the shredded skin turning a diseased black color.

Eliana

"EL, DO SOMETHING," NAOMI whispers, her frantic eyes never leaving Kai's shadow-entombed body. "Maybe you can help him."

"Naomi, I don't know. I'm not sure how I reached you when you were a dark beast."

I stare down at Ka. He hasn't moved since we laid him down. The shadows move slowly over his body, slithering along him to create a living cocoon.

"What if I make it worse?" I ask, turning to face my best friend.

"You won't," she replies, trying to convince herself and me, too. "You wouldn't do that."

"We don't know what my magic is capable of. What if it's fundamentally not compatible with his? He's not like us, Naomi. There is a darkness in him."

"Put there by Vaiccar," she retorts, her face serious. "It could be the very same darkness I had in me. You have to try. Please, El."

I sigh. Naomi won't stop until she's worn me down, and the more I stall, the more I fear she'll resent me when it doesn't work. Like there's a timeline on this sort of thing.

The shadows are ice cold to the touch as I graze them with my fingers. My breath hitches as I force my hands through their barrier, feeling them slide over my hands and arms. I take a shaky breath, closing my eyes. I try to channel the same sense of urgency and fear I felt when Naomi's monstrous form attacked me in the Burroughs.

The power within me remains dormant, and I squeeze my eyes shut searching for a push or pull, something buried deep within me. *Nothing.*

Lady Hevastia, I beg you, please help me.

Three deep breaths to center myself and I try once more, calming my mind to open myself up to Her influence. The shadows have grown still around me, and Kai's heart beats steadily under my palms.

"C'mon," I mutter under my breath.

There is Promise in the Light. I recite the prayer, remembering how I whispered it to the soul gem sitting on Hevastia's Heart, how I pleaded with it when I fought Naomi.

A warm glow builds in my chest, and I want to scream with joy. Slowly, cautiously, I gather the warmth into my hands, pulling it down along my arms, similar to the trickle of water in a bubbling stream.

Opening my eyes, I sigh with relief. My palms glow through the shadows that lie still against Kai. I whisper the prayer and push the light from my palms into Kai.

The glow fades under his skin, and the shadows shift away, some darting off his body and into the night. I pull more of the light to my hands and press them into his chest once more, the glow spreading further along his body before fading.

More shadows leave, and Kai stirs ever so slightly under my touch. Naomi's hand rests on my shoulder, and when I glance at her, she's smiling, tears shining in her eyes.

I send one final push of golden light into Kai before removing my hands. The glow spreads across his entire body, staying right under his skin for several breaths before finally fading.

I sit back, the golden power in my heart center fading, and my energy waivers. I press a palm to my head, the rush of the power leaving a vacuum of nothingness in its place. Naomi's arms fold around me, holding me close, and I relax into her support.

We sit and stare at Kai's still form. Maendril remains silent, standing guard behind us. His face wears an expression of deep shame at having refused to help us, and I remind myself to talk to him later when Kai wakes.

Naomi shakes my shoulder, and I flutter my eyes open. I must have fallen asleep. I scan Kai's body, searching for any sign of a change, but he appears to be the same as before—although no longer covered by shadows.

"Naomi, I'm sorry. I really wanted it to work," I whisper, choking back tears.

Naomi sits hugging her knees, tears glistening on her cheeks. She stares with dead eyes at Kai, sorrow plain on her face.

"It's not your fault, El." She sniffles. "I was foolish to think it would work."

I slide closer and take her hands in mine.

"Shh, no you weren't." I tilt her chin up so her eyes gaze into mine. "We'll figure this out, okay?"

Maendril clears his throat and we both look at him, but he's staring wide-eyed at Kai.

I turn my body, and to my surprise, Kai's stirring. Naomi scrambles to her knees, kneeling at his side as she pulls his head into her lap. Her fingers gently stroke his head, untangling his thick, dark curls.

"Come back to me," she whispers to him.

I stand and step back to stand next to Maendril, giving her some room. Her loyalty and love for Kai are obvious.

Kai's eyes blink open, and a slow, surprised smile spreads across his face at the sight of Naomi.

"My light," he whispers to her, his voice hoarse. He reaches his hand up and takes hers in his, interlocking their fingers.

She cries with joy, and nods her head. "I'm here. You're okay."

She smiles up at me, and I smile back. Perhaps there is hope for me yet. I won't give up on understanding my magic.

Naomi helps Kai sit up, and he nods his head in acknowledgement of me and Maendril.

"Something isn't right in Hevastia." Kai's face is full of worry. "I think Vaiccar is creating an army."

"What?" I ask. "How would you know that?"

"You went to the In-Between again, didn't you?" Naomi asks.

Kai nods, wincing with some lingering pain.

"I did. Noras pulled me there when I went unconscious. He called the shadows to protect me."

"Why do you think Vaiccar is building an army?" I dread the answer immediately after asking. Nothing good comes from that sort of question.

"The shadow folds, they're multiplying at an alarming rate. They're not the same as Naomi's. I don't think Vaiccar's manipulating the souls of those on the brink of death any longer. I think he's harvesting live people."

Naomi sucks in a shocked gasp.

"So not only is Vaiccar able to steal souls on their way to eternal rest in the Beyond, he's murdering people to create monsters to do his bidding?"

I scoff, the urge to shriek and pull out my hair in frustration punching me in the gut. I'm completely powerless against this knowledge.

"How is that possible?" Naomi asks. She hugs her knees, trying to stave off the cold chill that's spread down both our spines.

"Vaiccar's influence–it's gone." Kai's eyes widened with wonder and shock. "It used to be a heavy presence in my mind. When I was with him at the Aceolevia I felt his emotions." He laughs. "It's gone, how?"

"I used my magic on you. It purged the darkness from you, like with Naomi." I try not to sound too hopeful as I ask, "do you remember your life from before?"

"No," Kai shakes his head. "I'm sorry."

Naomi leaned in, hopeful. Her shoulders slump in defeat with that one word.

I shrug, playing off my own disappointment. "It was a long shot."

"There's still hope," Naomi interjects.

"Of course, my light," Kai responds softly. Naomi blushes.

He leans close to her and plants a quick peck on her forehead. Naomi's blush deepens to a dark red, the shock of his sudden affectionate turn catching her by surprise.

"So, what now?" Kai doesn't look away from Naomi. It takes me a moment to realize the question was directed at me.

"We tried once to rescue you from the Aceolevia. Vaiccar had a Keladonean mage locked away in a dirty cell. I tried to take her with us, but I wasn't able to." My voice falls quiet. The guilt of leaving her behind continues to gnaw at me.

"Is that why you were going to Keladone?" Kai asks.

"Yes, I thought perhaps their auror could tell us what had been done to you, or how to reverse it."

"Thank you," he replies quietly.

"You're welcome. I made a promise to Alana and Hama to get you back. It just so happened that we also need the Keladonean Auror's help in fighting Vaiccar."

A chilling thought occurs to me. I bite my lip, chewing over whether or not to voice it, and finally settle on clearing all the air between us, even if I worry the answer may hurt Naomi.

"You've never told us what Vaiccar ordered you to do. How did you end up here?"

Kai flinches.

"Would you believe me if I told you I was attacked by a water serpent and washed up here?"

At that, Maendril laughs, and some of the tension holding our small group hostage dissipates. "Yes, actually." Maendril says through chuckles.

Kai sighs, a small laugh slipping out at the end. He rubs the back of his neck, his eyes no longer meeting even Naomi's focused gaze.

"I was shipwrecked here ... but this wasn't my final destination. Vaiccar sent me on a mission to capture the Keladonean Auror."

My anger surges. "And you were simply going to keep this to yourself?"

Shame heats Kai's cheeks. "What good would it do telling you? You already don't trust me, Eliana. Admitting I was after another auror–that wasn't going to win me any support. And, until just now ... I didn't trust you either."

I glare at him. Maendril shifts next to me, ready on my command to subdue Kai–if it comes to that.

"What does Vaiccar intend to do with the Keladonean Auror?"

"I'm not sure."

His answer sounds sincere. If what Tenya told me of the Keladonean's time magic is true, it's possible Kai doesn't even recall meeting the prisoner in the Aceolevia's dungeon.

"Why did you help us just now?"

"Eliana–" Naomi begins to plead, but I cut off her cries with a strong stare.

Maendril probably feels vindicated after warning me about Kai on several occasions. Naomi frowns, clearly annoyed with me, and I know we'll be talking more about this later.

"Naomi." Kai's voice is clear and strong. "There's just something about her that I couldn't ignore."

Naomi blushes. Maendril rolls his eyes. I hesitate to react. I want to trust him, I do, but there's one more thing nagging me.

"I have one final question. Is Vaiccar hunting me, too?"

Silence. Maendril's hand moves an inch closer to the blade on his belt, and Naomi holds her breath as we all wait for Kai's response.

"No."

I breathe out in relief.

"At least he wasn't when he sent me on this mission. He's not ... worried you're a threat."

I scoff and smirk. "Well, that's just rude. However, it's good news. Hopefully he continues to underestimate me, underestimate the Hevastian people. I'm not ready to go toe to toe with him again, yet, but I will be soon."

"Thank you for healing me. Yy arm is much better." He waves his hand in front of him in wonder. I want to ask what he means, his arm was perfectly fine—but decide not to question it.

I take Kai's outstretched hand and pull him to his feet.

"That couldn't have been easy for you," he offers, peering down at my face. "I know I've wronged you."

"It's good to have you back," I say with a smile. Naomi beams and slips past Kai to envelope me in a tight hug. I hug her fiercely back, my heart full despite the growing dread that is spreading in my gut.

What does it mean for us if Vaiccar is truly building an army?

The *solari* break through the canopy of the forest as we walk back to the *Venaripa's* camp. It's the morning after the attack. Women in red cloaks and men in white rush around the smoldering remains, gathering the remnants of anything that survived the fire.

A small pile of salvageable items lies stacked in the center of the camp.

Isadora spots us, getting up from her sister's side to march across the grounds toward us. She roughly grabs my arm and drags me to the side, hissing, "what is he still doing alive?"

She's glaring at Kai, who stands with Naomi and Maendril as they take in the damage done to the camp.

"He saved all of their lives," I retort, challenging her. "Without his quick thinking, there wouldn't be anything to salvage or anyone to collect it."

"I saw the shadows. He is a monster."

"They're not dangerous. If you let Kai explain, he'll tell you anything you wish to know."

She eyes him suspiciously, letting go of my arm. "Fine."

"What happened, Isadora? Why was their camp burning?"

"Iamara said the Blud Revel Clan attacked, claiming 'retribution' for her *Champion*, Kai, beating one of their 'princes' in the *Rubruliem*. Still think this isn't Kai's fault?"

"He's no longer under Vaiccar's influence. His actions are his own now. What he did to the Blud Revel in the arena, he was acting on pure, murderous instinct and the influence of a very corrupt, twisted man."

"Agree to disagree. I think he was fully aware of his choices. You're just blind to it."

I sigh. "I don't want to argue over this. There are far more pressing matters to be concerned over."

"That," she says, "we can agree on."

"How can we help?" I ask.

"Iamara agreed to reinstate my position as the auror and the true leader of our people. My warriors could use assistance moving the refugees from her camp to our base in the village."

"Consider it done."

A screech pierces the air as a colorful bird swoops down from the sky and perches on a branch near my head. The iridescent wings are familiar, and I realize it's a *cantowauksi*. There's only one of these I know, and I smile to myself.

Zayne.

Akiko screeches again and ruffles her feathers, shaking them out after her flight. I approach her slowly, remembering all too well how she bit me last time.

She extends her leg to expose a small note tied around her ankle. I pluck it free and she chirps with pride, preening at having successfully delivered her charge.

"Is this your bird?" Isadora asks, slowly extending her hand to Akiko. The bird's sharp eyes turn to Isadora as she talks, and she chirps.

"No, she's a friend's bird." I stroke her feathers, my mind wandering back to Zayne.

I hope he's okay.

"Ah, I thought that perhaps she was your *animtah*."

"My what?"

"Your aurorian spirit guardian, something to protect and aid you as the auror. My *animtah* is a keen-eyed *peatsa*—a serpent of the forest. Sespa found me when I was a child. It was her appearance that confirmed the rumors in Puhlmia of my gifts and my potential as Raephe's chosen daughter. You can imagine the shock a giant serpent caused traveling through the city and wrapping herself protectively around a small child."

Isadora scans the canopy, "I imagine she is nearby. Sespa does not stray far from my side. Although harmless, most don't appreciate her company." She laughs. "Peatsas have the same power to control lifeblood that we do. They use it as a hunting technique—we use it in medicine.

"Such fascinating creatures." She smiles at me. "So, do you have an *animtah*?"

"I'm not sure," I answered honestly. "How do you know any of this Isadora? Was there a handbook I missed?"

She laughs. "Of course not. I learned from the previous aurors. When the rumors grew too large to quell, the elders of the city temple took me under their wing. I underwent years of trials and challenges to prove my inheritance. I honed a connection to my ancestors through that study. It was two years before Puhlmia fell to Leomaris that I was officially crowned our auror."

"And when you refused to fight Leomaris, your people just set aside those beliefs and traditions?"

"People do strange things when they're afraid. I was still young then. I didn't know what to do. I never used to have the backbone for such gruesome things. My sister, on the other hand, was more than willing to be whatever the elders wanted of her—that is until they were all killed. She took the power for herself rather easily after that.

"But now ... she realizes the danger we're all in, and she's not equipped to handle it as I am." Isadora stares at her hands, frowning. "It's a terrible burden we've been given by the gods, the ability to draw such tremendous power, decide the fate of so many so easily."

Isadora gazes at me expectantly, but I don't know how to respond. My powers have yet to truly reveal themselves, and I don't have the benefit of a decade of study and practice to draw from. Perhaps I am fighting a losing battle against Vaiccar–he's had centuries to plan his revenge.

She points to the note in my hand. "I'll give you some privacy to read that. Find me when you're ready."

"Thanks."

I unroll the note, and Zayne's handwriting is cleaner than I expected from a poor, uneducated boy.

Eliana,

~~**My beautiful, dangerous princess.**~~ **After you went overboard, my crew and I worked tirelessly to track the current that stole you away, only to find this gods-forsaken land.**

Lady Hevastia wills it, Maendril and Naomi have found you unscathed. Should you be injured, goddess help the souls of those who harm you.

Please send a sign of your condition. I shall wait anxiously for Akiko's return and your response.

I beg you to be careful. There are dangerous mages that roam these lands. Rumors say that the ground of their land bleeds.

The Daughter of the Seas is docked in Sandovell once again. We faced ruffiras on the beach where we deposited Maendril and Naomi. Pilo and Nita were lost to us.

Please send news of when you'll be returning to Hevastia. The tides have grown dark in Sandovell as more Haematitian guardians flood the city's streets.

There are many here who could use your guidance and reassurance. Fear flows rampant through every corner of the land.

Where is it safe to go? Your people are trapped in a slowly tightening net cast over the city. We need to make our escape while we can.

I await news of your fate, and your aid in determining the fate of nearly one hundred mages.

At the earliest opportunity, should you bid it, I will come back for you. Though I think you shall fare well on your own.

Yours faithfully,

Zayne

A smile breaks across my face, and my cheeks heat in a blush. The great hall is empty. All of Isadora's warriors are busy helping the refugees from Iamara's camp. There's no one in the hall to witness me run up the steps two at a time, grab my satchel and rush out through the kitchen. I run through the forest and to the beach.

I tug my boots off, tossing them aside. The sand is rough under my bare feet as I dig them in, anchoring myself in place.

The worn leather of my journal is supple under my fingers and I trace the fraying cover. Images of wildflowers, the constellations above our village, and the beginning of a portrait of Vendeekta all fly by as I flip to a fresh page.

Akiko sits perched on a fallen log, watching me. Her keen eyes are partially closed. I imagine she must be exhausted from batting the winds over the wide open water of the Oshia.

"Rest girl," I whisper soothingly to her.

She chirps quietly in response. Her feathers rustle as she settles in. The waves softly lap the shore behind her.

Inspiration strikes. A thin piece of charcoal pinched between my fingers is all I need. I glance up regularly to my subject, capturing the reflective light of the bright *solari* burning down from above. My fingers are tinted black, leaving smudges along my hand and forehead from wiping sweat. I turn to the next page and begin writing.

Zayne

TWELVE BLACK CLOAKS SURROUND the perimeter of the southern *tehendra*. Three more stand above the crowd on a crudely built platform. Behind them are seven hooded figures shackled together.

Loith sucks in her breath next to me, her eyes never leaving the stage. The leader of the Haematitian scum steps forward and tosses several homemade masks to the floor of the platform. Loith stiffens next to me, and a cold sweat builds on the back of my neck.

"Enemies of the Haematitian Council and the citizens of Sandovell have been identified conspiring with the 'unblessed.'"

These assholes are trying to claim the newly, naturally gifted among us are unnatural monsters creeping through the city and murdering innocents—oh wait.

"Use of unsanctioned magic is illegal under Order 27 from the New Orders by-laws. The Haematitian Council decrees only those under direction of the Morei order are to exercise use of magic. All others identified breaking this law are punishable by the appropriate measure due for their crime, under the Morei captain's discretion."

The captain's face twists into an almost gleeful smirk as she turns to address the prisoners. "I hereby sentence these dangerous traitors to death for their actions in conspiring against the law-abiding citizens of Sandovell. Their traitorous acts directly risk the safety of the citizens of Sandovell."

"More like the power of these scumbags," I mutter under my breath.

Several in the crowd clench their fists and I pray they're smarter than they appear. This entire public display is a trap meant to expose mages.

The black cloaks surrounding the *tehendra* are waiting for any sign of resistance or dissent. Those with defiant anger in their eyes, those who can't bear to watch–all will be suspected. And especially any stupid enough to unleash magic on the Haematitian guardians.

Loith's hand slowly shifts to her blade on her hip, and I stop her hand, gently gripping her fist within my own.

No. I mouth to her.

The captain commands the two guardians on either side of the platform to force the hooded prisoners to their knees. They shove them down, bowing them at the hips to expose their necks.

My jaw clenches.

The captain slits the palm of the closest guardian.

"We are the Morei of the New Order, the Council's right arm. No one shall escape our righteous deliverance. Kneel and be saved, for the Council sees all and saves all who need to be cleansed."

Her blade lights ablaze in her unnatural fire. She raises the glowing blade, arching it down in a smooth, unremorseful swing on the first prisoner's neck.

On the seventh thud, the stench of burnt flesh finally reaches our nostrils and Loith wretches.

The tension in the crowd continues to build and is about to burst. Black cloaks have their weapons drawn.

"Loith, move," I whisper fiercely. "Now."

"But–"

"Move, or lose your head. There's nothing we can do for them, but I won't be caught next."

She swallows and follows me out of the growing mob.

As we turn down a deserted lane a shout rises in the *tehendra*, followed by the staccato of screams of the innocent and angry as they are cut down by the Haematitian guardians in equal measure.

Eliana

S EVERAL DAYS PASS AS we wait for the messengers Isadora dispatched to return with replies from the other aurors. Apparently, she is in semi-regular contact with the other aurors, a precaution instilled by our ancestors after after the suspicious death of Atrya, the last Hevastian Auror. Of course, none of them knew about me or my whereabouts.

Isadora and I have not gone to visit Birvat since the first night. She's been busy directing small squads of her people to track the Leomarisians advance into healthy parts of Raephe and help the new arrivals settle into their homes. It's been quiet lately. The Leomarisians have not advanced, and there have been no sightings of the Blud Revel Clan members. Isadora assured Maendril it would be safe to leave the village. It was the only way he would let us leave.

An hour later, Naomi and I wander through the dead forest arm in arm. It's eerily quiet, no birdsong or animals breaking through the dried brush.

"Naomi ... shadows wrapped around Kai when he was unconscious. It was terrifying."

"El, something horrible happened to him–"

"Yeah, Vaiccar happened." I breathe out heavily. "He twisted Kai up, reformed him to his will. It's disgusting."

"What if it's something more than that?" Naomi asks, pulling on my arm to stop me from walking.

"What do you mean?"

"I can't shake the suspicion that there's more to it than just Vaiccar messing with his memories. How could Kai visit me in the In-Between?" She waves her hands in the air. "Can you travel to the In-Between?"

I laugh, shoving her arm playfully. "You know I have no idea whether or not I can."

"That's my point. You're Hevastia's *auror*. You have a connection to soul magic. You brought me back from the darkness and corruption of Vaiccar's influence. What if ... somehow ... Kai can see into that darkness? Because he's been affected by it so greatly."

"Well the darkness is gone now, so perhaps he will lose his connection." As I say the words, I know them to be false. There's something achingly familiar about Kai and this shadowy otherworld. Like me and my magic, they're inexplicably linked. I can only hope with time we'll both finally learn the truth behind our inheritances.

We continue walking, the dried clay giving way to soft, green moss. A bubbling stream cuts across our path, and Naomi winks at me before dramatically jumping over it. I laugh under my breath before leaping over it myself. My boots squelch into the soft mud of the stream's bank.

"Where is this coming from?" I ask.

"Every time I bring up our shared time in the In-Between, it's as if he vaguely remembers it, but doesn't want to admit it. I think he's hiding things from us," she states, very matter-of-fact.

A twig snaps to the right of us, and we both freeze, our heads pivoting toward the sound. I search the surrounding trees for movement, but everything is quiet and still.

Naomi grips my arm tightly, her nails digging into my skin. "El," she whispers, "something is watching us."

The hairs on the back of my neck raise.

There.

A shadow passes between the trees.

I pull Naomi to stand behind me, slowly reaching for the dagger on my belt, cursing myself for leaving Fate's Guardian behind when we left for our walk.

The shadow steps out from behind a tree, and the blood rushes to my toes as dread builds in my gut. It's a man, his head shaved, white clothes stained brown, with red lines tattooed under his eyes.

Blud Revel Clan.

A strange, numbing sensation begins to wash over my body. I stumble backward, pushing Naomi, and she trips, falling to the ground, pulling me down with her. The numbing sensation increases, stinging my skin with needle pricks everywhere, all at once.

Bootsteps muffled by soft moss and clay stop a few paces from where we fell, and the buzzing intensifies. The pressure builds to an unbearable level. Naomi writhes on the ground next to me, screaming in agony.

Our attacker meets my panicked gaze with malicious glee. He smiles down at me. I open my mouth to plead with him, but I can't speak, the pressure squeezing my lungs, and my words are no more than a wheeze.

The Blud Revel man drops to the ground, and the pressure in my head subsides. I search frantically for the cause of his downfall. Dark shapes fly across the ground, drowning out the light surrounding us.

Past the tree where the man appeared stands Kai, his face strained in concentration as he stares at the Blud Revel man. The shadows rush from Kai's hands, as if he is controlling them.

My pain completely disappears as the Blud Revel mage is swallowed by the shadows, writhing and screaming in fear and confusion. Kai continues to call shadows to attack him, the forest growing dark and ominous around us.

I peer into Kai's eyes, but they're all black.

"Kai," I whisper, my eyelids fluttering shut.

Kai

THIS MORNING, NAOMI VOUCHED for me to be allowed an unsupervised walk outside of the village perimeter. As I walk, the forest floor changes from the dry, cracked clay to a vibrant, healthy red with moss and small brush sprouting from it.

What am I supposed to believe? I think to myself as I wander aimlessly through the trees.

Could Naomi be telling the truth, that I can gain back my lost memories–but what then? I shake my head. *Do I want them back? It's hard to say.*

My boot splashes down into a thin stream, the water a muted red. I walk along its bank, not sure what I'm searching for. Ahead, face down in the stream, is a young woman. She doesn't move as I approach, and my gut clenches.

She's dead.

The water ahead of her body flows a clean, clear blue that becomes murky with her blood as it flows around her lifeless form. I kneel down and roll her body over with a soft splash.

Red blood seeps from a deliberate slash across her throat. The skin is cut deep enough to expose the bone of her spine. No animal of Hevastia could inflict such a precise wound, and I doubt such a creature exists in Raephe either.

My memory flashes back to the man in the *Rubruliem* as he bled a prisoner and used her blood to further his magic. She had died from her injuries, a waste. I shudder to recall how L–Vaiccar taught me the purpose of balance. What it felt like to bring the *tithe* to the brink of death without crossing it. How small wounds repeatedly inflicted is a more resourceful use of a bleeder.

Whoever cut this woman is ruthless ... and wasteful. My gut clenches. I step over her body, there's nothing I can do for her now. The forest beyond the stream is healthy and bright.

A shadow passes in the trees ahead of me, and I crouch down. They step out from behind the tree's shade. It's a man. On his face is the familiar red tattoo of the Blud Revel Clan.

He must be the one who killed the woman in the stream.

Moans of pain reach my ears. I creep forward, careful to keep my distance, and not alert the mage to my presence. If he recently gorged on that woman's blood, he will be more powerful than me.

My gut twists with dread as I spot his new quarry–Eliana ... and Naomi. They lie on the ground writhing in pain, frightened eyes locked on the mage as he slowly advances toward them. An agonized scream rings through the trees as Naomi's body is contorted.

The shadows are at your service.

The memory of Noras's words flits across my mind, and the cold sensation that accompanies the shadows caresses my hands and arms.

I close my eyes and concentrate, reaching for the cold, smooth shadows. My mind grazes against cool stone–the shadows beyond the barrier. I punch it repeatedly. The stone wall crumbling to dust in my mind.

On the other side, there is nothing but endless darkness and a frigid breeze that whispers over me, gently tickling my ear and ruffling my hair. The memory of Naomi's terrified scream echoes through me. A chill spreads over me, as the fear for her safety spurs me on. I step into the vast expanse of nothing.

Dark forms whip past me as I free fall, their cold touch grazing my skin and slowing my fall. I land on solid ground. The cold of the shades' touch settles into my skin. Their power becomes my own.

The Blud Revel mage is standing directly over Eliana.

Dark tendrils of shadow weave themselves through my fingers and along my arms. These shades are not the same as the small, shapeless *corpuscu* I've interacted with before. They're ... hungry. I don't stop to think what that means. I react. My hands rise, pointed directly at the mage, and, without uttering a command, the ravenous shadows respond to my direction.

They fly off my body, zooming across the ground before easily overtaking their prey. The Blud Revel man drops to the ground as the shadows consume him in their cold, dark embrace. He screams in fear, and I smile to myself.

Eliana's frantic eyes search my face for an explanation, but I ignore her. My focus is solely on destroying the mage who dared to attack Naomi.

The mage writhes on the ground–flailing his arms against the shadows that tighten around him, locking him in. His screams mimic the sound of a frightened animal's final death mew. He twitches one final time and stops moving.

The shadows fall off of him, satiated. The dark swarm darts across the ground, absorbing back into my skin, and sending a shiver down my spine.

I rush to Naomi and fall to my knees in the soft red clay. My eyes search her body for injuries, but she's unmarked. Her breath falls in even pants, her eyes closed. I pick her up, cradling her gently to my chest, and walk away from the mutilated Blud Revel mage.

Eliana lies unconscious next to him. Her dagger rests on the ground close to her hand. I know in the back of my mind that Naomi will be furious at me for leaving her best friend, but my thoughts are all consumed with the need to get her as far from the mage as possible.

I don't dare enter the village with Naomi in my arms. Maendril and Isadora will surely try to take my head before I can explain. I wander deeper into the forest, away from the village.

Naomi stirs in my arms, her eyes barely flitting open before closing once more, as she nestles into my chest with a contented sigh.

A brief flash blinds me. In the vision, Naomi and I are lying in the grass of the Thessimis Fields. We stare up at the solari. The sky bright with a cloudless, perfectly clear day. Her hand is small and fragile in mine as she traces my callouses with her finger.

I roll my head to the side, and she's smiling with her chin tipped to the warm sky.

"Do you think this will last?" she asks quietly. "When Naevys finishes her work on you, will you still visit me?"

"Are you worried I will forget about you?"

A solitary tear falls down her cheek as she turns her head to gaze at me. "You're not?"

I bring my hand to catch her tear, wiping it off her cheek. "I could never forget you, Naomi. You're the lone bright spot in my life. Nothing could ever snuff you out."

She laughs in relief, and I pull her close, kissing the top of her head.

I stumble on a rock, nearly dropping the real Naomi, as the memory releases me, and I'm back in reality. Up ahead lies a small grove. The *solari* breaking through the canopy and illuminating a small patch of soft moss dotted with tiny purple flowers.

I carefully lay Naomi down. Her features are soft in her sleep, no longer creased with the worry that seems to be her most constant companion. Gently, I lift her head into my lap and stare down at her beautiful face. I cannot fathom ever forgetting her face.

The 'old Kai,' as I've come to refer to myself when recalling the time before Vaiccar, was weak. He gave up his connection to Naomi. A notion I cannot possibly accept. She is my tether, and with this new life I will do anything within my power to spend it with her.

An hour passes before she slowly opens her eyes, blinking at the *solari* blinding her from above. The memory of the Blud Revel mage must rush back to her, because she scrambles to her knees, frantic.

"Kai, what–"

"The Blud Revel man can't hurt you any longer. I took care of him."

"You ... took care of him?" she whispers, nervous. "What does that mean?"

She turns in a circle, searching for something.

"Kai, where's Eliana?" She chokes back a sob. "No, no, no. She can't be–"

I take Naomi's hand, and her head whips back to face me. Shock lies plain on her face at my boldness in touching her.

The memory of the Thessimis Fields is fresh in my mind–I can't bear for her to be pained any longer. I won't deny my connection to her ever again.

"She's fine. I promise. I could only carry one of you away, and I chose you Naomi."

I reach out and swipe the tear from her cheek. She sucks in a surprised breath.

"It will always be you, Naomi."

"What?" She squeaks.

"You were right. It took me a while, and I can't imagine how much that must have hurt you, but I never forgot you, not truly. You're my bright light."

A joyful smile spreads widely over her face. I take her hands and pull her to me. We crash into one another, and she laughs. Her calloused fingers grab my face gently, pulling it down to hers. Our lips brush, and she leans in, kissing me deeply, desperately.

We hold one another, tears falling freely down both of our cheeks. I break the kiss and breathe out. I catch her eye, brushing a stray piece of hair behind her ear, and she blushes deeply.

"Is this real?" she whispers, her eyes frantically searching my own for answers.

I place a gentle kiss on her forehead. "Yes. It's real. I don't know what spell you've placed on me, but not even all-consuming darkness was able to overcome it."

She giggles. "I never gave up," she whispers. "I knew you would find your way back to me."

"Always." I tip her chin up, bringing my lips gently down to hers.

She smiles as she kisses me back. All too soon, she breaks the kiss short.

"Does this mean you're renouncing your loyalty to Vaiccar? That you believe me?"

"It means I want to." I kiss her again.

"It's a start," she murmurs against my lips.

"I don't know what's come over me, Naomi, but some part of me clings to you."

"Hold onto that, Kai. Hold onto me. I'm not going anywhere. We'll face this together.

"I want to stay hidden here forever, but I know we can't." She runs her fingers through my hair once more.

I stand and offer my hand to pull her to her feet.

"As my lady wishes."

She rolls her eyes, hitting me lightly in the arm.

"If you remember me … are your memories back now?"

I glance away, my hand coming up to rub the back of my neck. "Not exactly."

"Kai?"

"I don't have my memories back … not even the ones of us in the In-Between. Everything is coming back in short bursts, but never the whole picture. All I know for certain is how I feel about you, and that's enough for me."

"Are you sure?"

"For now."

Naomi nods her head, her mind already lost to other thoughts. "Eliana said there was a chance you may never get them back, but I don't believe it.

"Oh my stars, Eliana," she cries with an outburst, her eyes widening in mild panic. "I completely forgot about her. We need to go find her. The Blud Revel–"

Eliana

THE BLUD REVEL MAN lies dead at my feet. I kick over his body, and bile rises in my throat. The skin of his face is shredded, his fingernails caked with his own blood–he tore himself apart.

Did Kai's shadows do this to him?

A cold sweat trickles down my back. When I woke, Naomi was gone, and Kai along with her. Now, she's out there alone with him after he brutally murdered a man. I don't pity the Blud Revel man. He was probably going to kill me and Naomi. But I worry for Naomi's safety. Kai killed a man with powerful magic he's never disclosed to us.

Could Naomi be telling the truth? How is any of that possible ... Vaiccar's magic is the perversion of Raephean magic. It's not tortuous shadows and darkness.

I purged him ... he shouldn't be under Vaiccar's dark influence any longer. Right?

I shake my head. Kai said he could no longer feel Vaiccar's influence. I need to trust he was being honest ... because if he is still truly evil ...

I can't think like that. Naomi is fine. She has to be.

My eyes roam the ground, searching for any hint as to where they've gone. Boot marks lead away from the area, their imprint deeper than those of the Blud Revel man or myself. There's only one set–Kai must have carried Naomi out of here.

Oh stars. What if this was all a ploy to get her alone so he could steal her away? I know Naomi trusts him, but she wouldn't be so stupid to put her guard down enough to disappear into unknown territory with him. Right?

I draw my dagger and begin trailing Kai's footsteps. I run through the trees, completely ignoring discretion. I just got Naomi back. I won't lose her again to a murderer whose allegiance is to the very person we're trying to destroy. My promises to Alana and Hama give me pause, but I shake them off. I can't risk everything we're working for, everything I'm asking Isadora and Birvat to do, because of one person.

I've already chosen him over everyone else once. I won't make the same mistake again.

The repercussions of my choices are vast, and painful. When I chose to save Kai I ignored duty, not to mention my own safety. Now, every day my people pay the price for Vaiccar's freedom, the price for my actions. I put Kai before everyone once before, and now we're all on the hook for the price of Vaiccar's freedom. I put myself and my desires before the safety of my people, and nearly half of them perished, my mother included.

Up ahead, a large form weaves through the trees, and I slow my running. Panting, I stalk through the shadows, flanking the person. A flash of long dark hair catches in the waning light, and I nearly choke out a sob.

"Naomi," I call for her, my voice breaking.

She turns and spots me, her eyes growing wide with surprise and joy. I run to her and crush her against me.

"You're okay," I sigh with relief. I hold her away from me and scan her for any injuries. "Oh thank Lady Hevastia, you're alright."

"El, I'm fine. Kai carried me away from the Blud Revel man. We've been searching for you."

"He's here?" I ask, surveying the surrounding area. "Where?"

"Eliana, why are you acting weird?" Naomi glances behind me, expecting something to jump out at her.

"Listen to me, Naomi. You were right. Kai's been hiding things from us. He doesn't only see into the In-Between–"

"I also command the shadows." Kai's voice cuts me off and I freeze.

Reflexively, I grab Naomi to pull her behind me, but she brushes me off. Flabbergasted, I stare at my best friend. She's standing between me and Kai, unphased by his admission.

"Eliana, I'm glad you're alright," Kai greets me.

He opens his arms, and Naomi enters them. As if that's always been her place. Made just for her.

"Naomi, he brutally slaughtered the Blud Revel man." I stare at him, daring him with my eyes to deny it.

"I know," she says, disappointed.

"I'll tell you everything I know. Give me the chance to explain myself," Kai pleads, "please."

"If I get any sense that you're withholding something from us, I will not hesitate."

Kai meets my eyes and nods, a sad smile on his face. "I wouldn't expect anything different from you."

"How would you know? You claim to not remember me at all. So, what's the truth–are you pretending not to remember or have you truly lost your memories and you're lying about this?"

"Eliana," Naomi barks out, shaming me into silence. "Give him a chance to explain. He saved both of our lives–you owe him that."

I sigh, breathing out slowly. I motion for them to lead the way. Kai leads us to a small grove in a dense part of the forest. He and Naomi enter first, sitting next to one another, with me across from them.

"What do you want to know?" Kai asks.

"Start at the beginning."

"I'm starting to remember more beyond these past several weeks under Vaiccar's service. I remember Naomi mostly, and my time with her when she was in the In-Between."

Naomi places a gentle, loving hand on Kai's, squeezing his fingers.

"I didn't realize I was in a different place. I thought she was a figment of my imagination to help me cope during Vaiccar's torture.

"The In-Between and the Shadow Realm are essentially the same place. Trapped souls reside in pockets of the Shadow Realm. In places conjured by their own subconscious. While Naomi was possessed as a dark beast, her true soul was safely in the Shadow Realm. I visited her because I am ... part of that world."

"How is that possible? If you've always been a part of that world, why is this all happening now?" I ask.

"I'm not entirely sure–and that's the truth." Kai sighs. "Noras, he's the only shade in the realm I can talk to, claims they've been trying to reach me my whole life. Haunting me. I've merely been tuning it out.

"I don't know why I'm connected to it, or what it all means. Attacking the Blud Revel mage, that was the first time I've been able to summon the shadows. I didn't know what they would do. I reacted on instinct–"

"That was not the first time you harnessed your shadow magic," I interrupt him, my voice quiet and even. I'm barely able to conceal my simmering anger.

"What?" Kai asks. His eyes widen with genuine surprise.

"In the *Rubruliem*. I didn't understand at the time, but the air around you was dark, shadowy–you killed the Blud Revel Champion with shadow magic.

"Afterward, I convinced myself I was imagining the dark tendrils wrapping his body as he bled out on the arena floor, but I wasn't."

Kai stutters. "I–I didn't know."

"Maybe you didn't use the shadows consciously, but you have wielded them."

Naomi is staring at me, fear and anger burning in her gaze. Fear of losing Kai, and anger over my treatment of him.

Am I willing to risk Naomi's safety?

I swallow. That's not the right question and I know it. I glance away from her.

Am I willing to trust her judgment over my own?

"It worries me, that's all," I murmur, turning my gaze back to Kai.

"I would never hurt Naomi, or you, Eliana."

I frown, not convinced.

"Naomi was in danger. I couldn't let her get hurt. I don't remember everything about my time in the shadow fold with her, but it's my lifeline."

"The shadows caused that man to shred his own skin. It may not have been on purpose, but that power is incredibly dangerous."

"I understand what you're implying. That I'll use it in service of L-Vaiccar. I won't."

"Kai, you don't know that."

Kai stands and kneels in front of me, his head bowed. "From henceforth, I pledge fealty to you, Eliana of Bellamere, Chosen Daughter of Hevastia. May my blade and my might be in faithful service to you, without fail."

I stammer, unsure of how to respond.

He gazes up at me, "I know you have no reason to trust me, but I would never put Naomi at risk. If serving you ensures her safety, I forsake all ties to Vaiccar. His will is no longer my own. I choose to forge my own path."

"El, please," Naomi begs. "Give Kai time to figure this all out. I swear to you he won't be a danger to anyone here. I'm your oldest friend, Eliana. I owe you my life, and I would never do something to endanger anyone if I didn't think there was another way. Kai is safer with us than on his own."

I stand and pace. Nervous, I run my hands through my hair and try to untangle the twigs snagged in my hair from the attack by the Blud Revel man. My thoughts are a swirled jumble. He seems genuine.

Kai and I are in the same shoes. We've both been thrown into inheritances we don't understand. It's entirely possible my powers from Lady Hevastia are just as dangerous. I have no idea what I'm truly capable of. But, can I trust him? Do I trust my magic enough to be sure he's free of Vaiccar's influence? How would I even prove it?

Naomi and Kai sit in the soft moss, talking quietly. Where only a few days ago Kai was all hard edges and cold eyes, he's now gentle. His eyes seem clear of the fog that's clouded them. Perhaps he is truly out from under Vaiccar's sinister influence.

We need to learn more about the Shadow Realm, and what Kai called the shadow folds. If there are more of those places, then perhaps there are more souls in Hevastia that I can save from their imprisonment under Vaiccar's dark influence.

"Kai," I say, and he turns expectantly to meet my gaze.

"I accept your allegiance."

Naomi smiles widely, hugging Kai to her, and he wraps his arms around her, nuzzling into her hair. He lets her go, her arms slowly falling away from him, as he stands and faces me.

"I won't let you down, Eliana. I know I need to atone for my actions, and I intend to."

"Don't make me regret this, Kai."

Kai

It's been a week since the Blud Revel Clan's attack. The refugees from the *Venaripa's* camp are slowly integrating into Isadora's settlement, and several new huts are under construction to provide permanent shelter. Maendril and I have been assisting. Using our strength to cut timber and haul stone.

Eliana waits impatiently for word from the other aurors. All of the messengers have yet to return from their journeys to the other lands. She paces the settlement. Sometimes slipping away when she thinks no one is watching, to walk in the forest or sit on the beach. Naomi has followed her on several occasions to ensure she would be safe, but she doesn't do anything—just sits and stares out at the waves.

I spot Naomi and Eliana entering the main gate of the village and I jog over.

Eliana meets my gaze with a cool indifference. We haven't exactly become friends since she used her magic to save me, but there's less hostility.

"Naomi, I was wondering if we could talk?"

Eliana pauses, waiting for Naomi to decide whether she will walk with me or continue on with her.

"It's alright Eliana," Naomi says, touching her best friend on the shoulder before turning to me.

Eliana gives me one more wary glance before continuing into the village, waving down Maendril.

I sweep my arm out, pointing in the direction Naomi came from. There's a trail outside the village that leads to a bench nestled among several flowering bushes.

Naomi walks on my left side. She hugs her arm while we walk, keeping her right hand from reaching for me, and making it impossible for me to take her hand in mine.

"What is it Kai?" she asks quietly.

I turn back to the trail. My boot scuffs the ground and upsets a stone, sending it rolling into a nearby bush, startling a small animal that scampers away, unseen.

"We haven't spoken much since that day in the grove." I swallow.

She stops walking alongside me, gazing up at me with saddened eyes.

"I appreciated you coming to me defense with Eliana." I sigh, running my hand through my hair. "I can't help but feel like you were more upset than you let on when you found out what happened to the Blud Revel mage."

Naomi begins walking again, her head hung low.

"I know why you did it, and it was probably the right move." She sucks in a deep breath. "When we were in the In-Between, you had sworn to me you had left that part of you behind."

"What part?" I ask quietly.

Her lip trembles. "The killing part."

The side of me that was capable of killing her family.

I still don't remember the siege on her village, or the conversations Naomi told me of when we were in her shadow fold, but I know I was once a very bad person.

"Ah, that part." I take a ragged breath.

"I want that part to be dead and gone, too." My hand reaches for hers, stopping short and dropping back down beside me. "I've caused so much hurt in my life. I'm a different man now. I would never hurt you.

"That version of me, he did bad things too, but he wasn't *me*." I run my hand through my hair. "At least, that's what I keep telling myself."

We reach the bench and sit down, a foot of space between us. It could have been an entire canyon for how much it hurt me.

"It's not just a bad dream. What I did while I was under Vaiccar's dark influence ... I can't write it off as something out of my control, and that terrifies me. That darkness, what if it wasn't all Vaiccar? What if some of it is me?"

Naomi turns on the bench to face me, tucking her right knee under her chin. Tears glisten in her eyes.

"You're not evil, Kai."

Her hand is soft as it rests on top of mine, and all at once the smallest touch closes the chasm between us.

I lunge across the bench and pull her into me, kissing her desperately. She's crying. The hot tears run over my hands as they cup her cheeks pulling her into a soft, long kiss. Her hands are knotted in my hair, clinging to me.

She pulls away, breathless. "I mean it, Kai. You're not evil."

I breathe in deeply, trying to slow my racing heart and my hungry thoughts.

"I'm sorry I scared you. I'm sorry for all the hurt I've caused you."

It feels wrong to apologize for actions I don't remember taking. There's no true remorse if it's an apology made on behalf of another person. But, I know those are the words Naomi needs to hear.

I stroke my thumb over her cheek, catching stray tears. "You'll be my undoing. I'm sure of it."

"I forgive you," she whispers.

Why must I atone for the actions taken by another man?

I shake the thought from my head. Naomi wishes for a kind, sweet man—and I will be him. I grip her head and kiss her fiercely on the forehead before pulling her to my chest, hugging her body tightly to my own.

"I'll never forgive myself. I don't deserve you."

She wiggles against my crushing embrace. She breaks free of my grip to bring her hand up to my face, pulling my gaze down to meet hers.

"I know." She guides my face down to hers and kisses me deeply, lovingly. "It's not about what we deserve, but about what we're willing to fight for. And I will fight for you, Kai. Always."

Hama

SOOT-COVERED HANDS COME ACROSS my vision and rest over my eyes. Warm breath tickles my ear.

"Surprise, my *Amorei*," Alana whispers in my ear.

I melt into a fit of giggles.

"Hello, love."

"I have a surprise for you. Follow me—but don't open your eyes."

"Alana, what is it?"

"A surprise. Did you not hear me?" She chuckles. "Trust me."

"Without fail," I respond, taking her hand and squeezing my eyes shut.

Alana leads me out of our tent and down the main path in the antechamber, the sounds of our friends and neighbors echo loudly in the wide open space.

"How much farther, Alana?"

"Only a bit farther."

The warmth of the *solari* touches my hands and travels up my arms as Alana leads me from the Burroughs and out onto the mountainside.

"Are you sure this is safe?"

"Perfectly. Tyr is here."

"Hi Hama," Tyr says, a smile in his voice.

"Okay. You may open your eyes now." Alana's voice is practically giddy with excitement, something I have not heard in a very long time.

As I open my eyes, a soft, warm, wiggly bundle is pressed into my chest. A small *lupiquin* squirms in my arms. Its sweet face, framed by oversized ears, a soft, wet black nose, and big black eyes, peers up at me. A soft tail thumps against my hip, wagging continuously.

I hold it out from me, and it wiggles furiously, trying to come close once more–it's small pink tongue lolling out the side of its mouth.

"I don't understand. Where did you find it, and why am I holding it?"

"It's an orphan. Tyr and I found its mother and littermates slaughtered. We tracked down the dark beast and killed it before it could destroy more of the animals seeking refuge on the mountain."

Alana steps closer, suddenly nervous. She places her hands over mine, gently pushing the small pup back into my arms. She lowers her voice so Tyr won't hear.

"I thought that perhaps, since we have no children of our own, you might appreciate a companion. This little one needs a home, and I know of no one more compassionate and loving than you, my *Amorei*."

"Alana, don't you see? We have raised many children–Kai, Cire, Eliana for a time, and now Raen and Clyn. They have all turned to us for guidance and support. My life's been filled with the joy of their growth and discovery."

"So, you don't want this little one?"

I hug the pup closer, its tiny tongue giving me soft kisses on the underside of my chin.

"I never said that."

Alana laughs. "What shall we call it?"

I hold the pup out, confirming its sex. "We shall call him Orfuhno."

Orfuhno licks my face and yips in agreement. "I think it's settled. He likes his name."

Orfuhno's yip echoes through the tunnel as he bounces along beside me, trying to reach the makeshift toy tucked under my arm.

I shuffle along slowly, my injured foot sore from more time spent on it chasing after this pup. I can't tell Alana that I'm in pain. I know it will distress her. And besides, I adore Orfuhno. The slight pain is worth it.

Squeals of joy reach my ears as Orfuhno finds the boys, Raen and Clyn, walking toward us. They've been a secret blessing in helping wear out Orfuhno's tireless well of energy. As an added bonus, playing with the pup is helping the boys master their gifts.

"Hama," Raen calls, smiling. "Look what Orfuhno can do."

Raen and Clyn share a knowing, wicked smile, and my gut clenches.

"Boys–" my warning is cut short by Orfuhno flying toward me, sailing on a gust of wind courtesy of Raen's gifts.

The pup's tongue lolled out, enjoying every moment of being in the air.

Orfuhno sails toward me at an alarming pace, and I drop his toy, catching the excited pup in my arms as the force drives me backward, and we fall.

A soft, wet tongue licks my face. I open my eyes to Orfuhno investigating every inch of my body for injury.

"Hama?" Clyn's voice waivers. "Are you okay?"

I try to sit up, a piercing pain radiating down my neck. My head throbs with a head-splitting ache.

"No, don't. You hit your head." Clyn touches my shoulder, trying to guide me back down.

My fingers come back sticky with blood as I touch the back of my head.

"Raen is going to get Pyria."

A soft whine emits from Orfuhno as he curls in a ball beside me, his head resting on my chest.

"We're so sorry Hama–" Clyn's apology is cut short by the arrival of Pyria.

She ushers the boys out of her way as she kneels down beside me. Orfuhno's lips peel back with a soft growl. Pyria is patient, letting him inspect her hand for approval. His fluffy tail thumps against my leg, and Pyria is able to lean closer.

Soft hands cup the sides of my face as she lifts my head and slides a soft band over my wound. She snaps her fingers, and the boys grab under each of my arms, helping me to stand.

They escort me back to my tent where Alana is waiting for us. Raen and Clyn share a terrified look between them, and Clyn trips, almost sending me back to the ground before Pyria catches me.

Alana inhales, ready to explode at the boys, and I place a hand on her arm. Her worried eyes find mine.

"*Amorei*, it's okay. It was an accident. I think they've already punished themselves enough."

Alana sighs, resigned. "As you wish, my *Amorei*."

"We're so sorry," Raen blurts out before Clyn can cover his mouth. Clyn grabs ahold of Raen's arm and drags him away under Alana's piercing gaze.

Alana's strong arms wrap around my waist and help me limp to our bed. As I settle into the covers, she tucks me in, her motions gentle and loving.

I place my hand on hers, and she stops, meeting my gaze. The worry hasn't left her eyes.

"I'm fine, Alana."

She frowns and redirects her gaze over her shoulder to Pyria.

"Will they be okay, Pyria?" Alana asks and signs at the same time.

Pyria beckons Alana to her, and Alana stands, effectively blocking my view of their conversation as they sign to one another.

"Of course," Alana says with a nod.

Pyria hands Alana a small pouch of herbs before leaving.

"I was sitting right here. You could have clued me into the conversation," I grumble, arms crossed. My eye twitches with the acute pain it causes me to move my shoulders, and my neck is sore and stiff.

Alana kneels beside our bed, brushing a stray hair from my face.

"She ordered you on strict bed rest." She presses her calloused finger to my lips, keeping me from objecting. "You took a nasty fall."

I open my mouth to argue, but Alana's finger still rests against my lips, and her eyes warn me not to argue. She's in one of *those* moods.

"Please, *Amorei*. Rest."

I swallow my frustration at being bedridden and nod my head in acceptance.

Alana places a firm kiss on my forehead. "Thank you."

The tent flap swings shut behind Alana. At least there is always knitting to keep my mind busy.

Kai

"**K**AI," ELIANA'S VOICE PULLS me from my thoughts. She calls up to me from the bottom of the stairs that lead to our shared quarters. "Could we talk?"

"Of course." I trot down the stairs, stopping by her side. "Lead the way."

The forest surrounding the village is eerily quiet as we step away. Her eyes scan the darkness beyond our torches, wary.

"The Blud Revel Clan would have to be truly mad to attempt an attack here. Isadora maintains strong defenses, and now our numbers have grown with the arrival of the *Venaripa* Clan."

"It's not that," she shakes her head. "I can't shake the suspicion that something horrible is happening at home. I sense it, a burning sensation churns under my skin. I don't have much time to find the answers I seek. What is the Shadow Realm like?"

The question catches me off guard. Ever since Eliana purged me of Vaiccar's dark influence, she's kept her distance. This is the first time we've spoken in days.

"It's similar to home in a lot of ways. A gray haze hangs over everything. It's much darker. Why do you ask?"

"I still don't understand what it means ... that you're able to travel to a different realm. It's all a little strange. When I touched your shadows, they didn't hurt me. It was almost as if they sensed what I was trying to do. That I wanted to help. The more I healed you, the more they left."

I shrug my shoulders. "Noras said they were there to guard me while I was unconscious. So I suppose as you healed me, I was waking up, and that's why they left.

"I'm not sure what answer you're searching for, Eliana. I barely understand what my connection to the Shadow Realm means. I don't have answers for you."

"I understand that," she swallows. "That's why I want you to take me there."

My jaw drops. "Take you to the Shadow Realm? Are you insane?"

She scowls at me, crossing her arms. Somehow I know I've received this very look before.

"Why not? We're both connected to it. The prophecy mentioned a shadow-touched being ... at least that's how I interpreted the symbol."

She paces with her head facing down. Her thoughts tumble out of her as she creates a small divot in the ground from pivoting back and forth.

"I always thought it was referring to you or Cire, someone who was walking in the darkness of the Haematitian Council's influence–but what if it was literal? You said so yourself, Noras refers to you as the lord of the realm.

"I bring people back from the shadow folds. You protect them while they're there. You can protect me there. I'm sure of it."

"What if it kills you, or you lose your connection to your magic?" I throw up my hands, anger coursing through me.

"What if the missing piece to understanding my magic *is* there? I'm tired of waiting–for the aurors to decide to show up, for my magic to make itself known, for everyone to stop treating me like a child."

She glares daggered eyes at me. I know she's waiting for me to respond, her next argument already churning in her head.

"I am the Hevastian Auror. I'm done making excuses for my inaction. There is nothing I won't do to ensure Vaiccar rots for eternity in some far off corner of the Beyond.

"Even if it costs me my life."

"Eliana–"

She holds up her hand, cutting me short. "Kai, you will take me to the Shadow Realm. You offered your loyalty and service to me and our cause. If you meant that, then please do this for me."

I sigh. There's no point in arguing with her at this point. She's beyond listening.

"When do you want to go?"

"Immediately."

I open my mouth to barter for time and think better of it. Eliana stands beside me with her arms crossed, as if she also knows I want to argue further with her.

"Close your eyes. Relax your body," I instruct. "I usually travel there, on purpose, when I'm in a relaxed state."

I reach out and take her hand in mine before closing my eyes. Breathing in deeply, I picture the inky darkness of the Shadow Realm. I imagine Eliana and I standing in the Grand Hall of the palace. I silently pray she'll be safe and protected there.

The air cools, and, before I open my eyes, I know we've crossed over.

Eliana's hand is warm in mine. She lets go first. Her boots click against the stone, echoing through the Grand Hall. My black throne sits on the dais. Nothing's changed.

A faint aura of light shines around Eliana as she moves through the hall, getting a sense for her surroundings. At the first sign of trouble I will take her away from here.

The heavy door from the library adjacent to the hall creeks open, and Eliana's eyes widen in shock as she takes in Noras for the first time. I recall the first time I saw him, and how he repulsed me.

She strides confidently up to him, and extends her hand. "Noras, I'm Eliana."

At the sound of her voice, Noras spots her for the first time and lets out an ear-splitting wail. I clap my hands over my ears.

"Noras," I call out, trying to draw his attention to me. "Noras, it's alright. Eliana is a friend."

Eliana draws her dagger, holding it out between her and Noras, as she stares at him, unphased by the cacophony of noise erupting from his throat.

"You shouldn't be here. You must go," he wails, pointing to Eliana.

"Not until you tell me everything you know about the prophecy, my magic, and its connection to this place. I've been studying the prophecy. I think my magic is somehow connected to this place, and to the shadows."

Noras stops, peering with curiosity at Eliana. "You're not Lord Kai's mortal friend … are you?"

"Mortal friend?" Eliana asks quietly. The color drains from her face. More loudly she responds, "you mean Naomi? What would happen to Naomi if she came here?"

Noras observes Eliana with growing curiosity. "It would be very bad for her. But you … your light is brighter. You are the god-touched auror." He nods his head. "Yes, that is why you are not dissipating."

I step toward Noras. "Dissipating, how? What do you mean, Noras?"

"This place isn't the Light Realm. The living cannot exist outside the *umbrasinum*. Not unless they are god-touched, like Miss Eliana." Noras sighs, a wet, phlegmy noise in the back of his throat. He whispers, so quietly that I almost don't hear him, "Lady Hevastia, it can't be."

He ducks back into the small library, beckoning us to follow him. Eliana takes in the overflowing library, with its stacks of books and brick fireplace, with amazement. Her eyes widen at the sheer size of Noras's collection, and her hand twitches to pick up the book sitting on top of the stack closest to her.

I sit in an oversized reading chair situated by the fireplace. Fresh logs crackle as the flames lick against them. Eliana stands beside my chair. Noras hovers in the center of the room. He wrings his hands, clearly nervous.

"What brings you here, Miss Eliana?"

"I want to learn more about this place, and about whatever connection it may have to the Aurorian Prophecy," and more quietly she whispers, "and to my fate."

"I don't know much about your destiny, Miss Eliana. It's clear to me that you're already on your way to discovering those answers."

Eliana opens her mouth to object, but Noras continues speaking. "However, I do have some information that you might find of interest."

"First, you must promise to listen." Noras looks at me as he says this. He swallows. "I had no choice, sir. I tried to help steer you in the right direction."

"I swear to listen." I glance up at Eliana, and she nods in agreement. "We will listen."

Noras quakes, his form wavering between translucent and fully present. "A change has come over you ... Lord Vaiccar will be so displeased."

Eliana takes a step toward Noras. "Vaiccar?" She snarls, "what does he have to do with this?"

Noras knots his fingers together, fidgeting. "Lord Vaiccar's been to the Shadow Realm. This was his home since the Unjust Banishment."

"Unjust Banishment," Eliana snorts. "He deserved everything he got for killing a god. In my opinion, Lady Hevastia should have killed him."

The fire sizzles and pops, the only sound in the room. Eliana is in a showdown with Noras, piercing him with daggered eyes. He hovers in the center of the room, uncertain of how to escape her gaze.

This is not going as I expected. In truth, I planned to give Eliana a tour, and bring her right back to the Light Realm. I had no idea Noras had been withholding information.

"Noras, please." My voice is soft and encouraging. It's the soft 'please' that breaks the spell Eliana's fierce reaction has cast over Noras. He nods his head.

"Lady Hevastia banished Lord Vaiccar from the Light Realm and made a gate to hold him here, in my realm. He's been trapped in the Shadow Realm for centuries, waiting for the opportunity to return to the Light Realm. When the curse was broken, and the gate destroyed, Lord Vaiccar left this realm. But he still possesses *dominanturi* over the shades.

"Before he left, Lord Vaiccar released me with explicit instructions to train Lord Kai." Noras turns to address me. "You were meant to be part of Lord Vaiccar's plan to use the shades of the Shadow Realm to overtake the Light Realm."

"What?" Eliana takes another step closer.

Noras shakes, terrified of Eliana. "When Lady Hevastia trapped Vaiccar here, he locked me away. This realm is my home. The shades are my responsibility. Vaiccar saw the power I wielded, and he tricked me. I taught him how to use the *dominanturi*." Noras's voice falls in deep remorse. "When I let my guard down, he captured me and crowned himself the King. I spent centuries not knowing what had become of my home or the shades." Noras wails in despair.

"Lord Vaiccar threatened to end my existence if I didn't aid him in training you. Deceiving him, and you, was the only way to keep this realm safe. I couldn't abandon the shades. They need protection. I was hoping to appeal to you, Lord Kai, so that you might take my side and defend this place."

"It all makes sense." Eliana paces in front of the fireplace.

"What does?" My own head is spinning.

Would the 'old Kai' believe Noras and want to help the Shadow Realm?

"Why Vaiccar kept you alive. It's always bothered me why he didn't kill you once you were captured. There are so many Morei warriors loyal to him, without the need for brainwashing. So, why would he go through all the effort for you?"

A sick dread builds in my gut. "He knew I was the heir–but how?"

"I'm not sure, probably nothing good. It still doesn't explain what you're meant to do. The dark beasts have been roaming for nearly one hundred years. If he could control them this whole time–"

"I didn't know," Noras whispers, eyes sorrowful.

"Didn't know what, Noras?" I ask, getting up from my chair. Eliana tenses next to me.

"I didn't know Lord Vaiccar planned to use the shades in such a despicable way. He's emptying living vessels and replacing their essence with a dark shade. The shadow folds I told you about, sir, are Lord Vaiccar's doing. I tried to explain to you. Warn you."

"You said he commanded you to instruct me? Noras, am I able to control the dark beasts?"

Noras shakes his head. "No. The dark beasts are merely trapped souls. Their bodies rot because they're trapped here, and unable to pass on to the Beyond. You have no sway over them. Only the ability to visit the true soul trapped in the shadow fold.

"These new creatures are made of malicious shadows from the Shadow Realm, called *maligni*. As the heir, they fall under your command."

"Are you saying that these shadow-souls can't be purged? That they're lost forever?"

"I'm not sure," he flinches when Eliana flips her dagger in her hand, taunting him. "They are from this realm ... I don't know enough about the Hevastian Auror's gifts."

"It's true. I saw one of them with my own eyes. Whatever Vaiccar is doing to them, it's warping them," I explain, placing my hand on Eliana's shoulder.

Her eyes are wide with fear and remorse. "How many?" She whispers quietly, "how many dark folds are there already?"

Noras chokes out a wet, disgusting-sounding sob, and turns a dark greenish gray. "Roughly two thousand."

"No," she whispers, tears brimming in her eyes. "That's not possible."

"Miss Eliana," Noras says, "you can free those trapped from finding eternal rest in the Beyond ... perhaps you can also reach the shadow-touched."

"Take me to the shadow folds," she commands, turning on her heel to march from the library.

"Absolutely not." I step into her path. "I can't let you risk it, Eliana. Those folds are dangerous. One attacked me last time. What if it hurts you?"

"I have to try. I can't go back home, and ask our friends to march to their deaths." She peers into my face, pleading with me, "this has to work."

"Eliana, you don't know what you're doing." I grip her shoulders.

"I know that!" Tears brim in her eyes. "I know that better than anyone. I'm supposed to save us all, but I don't know how–" her voice breaks. "This could be how. Please."

I sigh, running my hand down my face in exasperation. "Then I'm coming with you."

I lead her from the library to the garden. Noras has cut back more of the hedges. The dark shadow folds now encroach on the very edge of the flower garden. The wall of hedges is all but completely gone.

We step up to the first fold. The red light pulses ominously. Eliana, with weary eyes and trembling shoulders, flashes me a nervous smile. We both draw our weapons.

I reach into the fold, tensing as I brace for an attack from the other side, but nothing happens. I glance back at Eliana one last time before stepping fully into the fold. On the other side, it's pitch black and empty.

Seconds later, Eliana's hand lands on my shoulder as she steps in behind me.

"What next?" Her voice is a quiet whisper.

"I'm not sure. I never made it past this point before."

The faint aura of light from Eliana illuminates the area around us. We are standing in a small unfurnished hut.

"It's almost like back home." Eliana's voice sounds far away even as she stands right next to me in the inky darkness. This place does not feel at all like home.

The door is in the far corner. I shuffle toward it, taking Eliana's hand in mine and leading her along. Our boots send bones and stones clattering into the dark corners of the room, and a shiver runs down my spine.

"What do you think lurks in this fold?"

"I'm not sure I want to find out."

She laughs quietly.

We step through the door of the hut and into a village. An eerie fog rolls silently across our boots, blanketing the ground. With every step it swirls up, the wispy edges of it curling toward our hands.

I swallow down my apprehension.

Eliana holds her sword out in front of her, eyes roaming the shadows cast by the dilapidated buildings we walk past. As we walk, the buildings fall into further disrepair with walls toppled in and wood beams sticking out like broken bones from the wreckage.

A wet crunching sound echoing through the wreckage draws us to a stop. We crouch low, hugging a collapsed wall, as we sneak closer to the sound—equal parts curious and fearful of what we might find.

We reach the end of the wall, and I peer over the side, spotting a dark form in the middle of the town square.

A winged creature is hunched over something. Its back turned toward us. Its wings are the color of darkest night tinged with a shimmering purple. The creature shuffles around its prey, its beak gripping another chunk of flesh as it rips and tears at the body, furiously shaking its head back and forth to break its bite free.

Eliana gags softly beside me, clapping her hand over her mouth.

The slight noise is enough to draw the creature's attention to us. As it spins the fog gathered around its body swirls up in an angry cloud, adding to the ominous and frightening sight of the creature. Its beak is the length of my forearm and lined with small, razor-sharp teeth. Blood-red eyes blink slowly as it searches for us.

I point behind Eliana, instructing her to turn back and sneak away. We shuffle silently along the wall, keeping our heads low, and our weapons drawn.

Something heavy lands on the wall above our heads, raining loose stone and dust unto us. Eliana is struck by a large rock and falls to the ground, struggling to get back up.

An ear-splitting screech echoes through the ruins. The bird monster stares down at us with predatory eyes.

"Run," I scream at Eliana, helping her to stand and shoving her away, as the bird takes its first steps off the wall. It lands between Eliana and I.

It's focused on me, beady eyes watching me, unblinking. It chirps, clicking its beak together, and tilt its head as it inspects me. I stand very still, tightening my grip on my swords.

Its beak shoots out, stabbing at me, and I narrowly dodge the blow, trapped in the tight alley between homes. I strike my sword down on its beak with a satisfying crunch as the blade connects.

The monster shrieks and hisses, charging at me, mouth agape. I cross my blades and stand my ground, locking its jaws in the cross of my swords. It hisses again, spewing black blood and yellow pus onto my arms, chest, and face.

It continues to bear down on me, forcing me backward and down to the ground. I struggle against its weight, trying desperately to keep its serrated beak away from me.

The beast shrieks, releasing my swords, and pivots to face something behind it. Another rock flies at the bird's face, pelting it in the eye. It hisses, its eye weeping black blood, and swelling shut.

Eliana holds another chunk of stone in her hand, her sword resting against the wall next to her.

"Come get me," she taunts, goading the monster toward her. It hisses, bringing its head low to charge.

Another rock smashes against its face, sending it reeling backward toward me. I draw my swords up, spearing the bird as it stumbles into my blades.

It shrieks, the noise growing weaker as more blood runs over my blades and onto my hands. I kick its body to the ground, pulling my swords free.

Eliana runs up to me, her sword now strapped on her back.

"You owe me," she jokes, smiling triumphantly. "I could have let it eat you."

I roll my eyes. "Yeah, right."

She laughs.

The monster breathes shallowly. Its unswollen eye blinks slowly, rolling into the back of its head.

"I want to try to purge it," Eliana says, kneeling down next to the bird.

I place a hand on her shoulder, pulling her away. "No way."

"It's dying, Kai. Let me try. Please."

It's the 'please' and the desperation in her eyes that gets me. Eliana is struggling to keep it together. Her worry for our people, and the fate of Hevastia resting heavily on her shoulders.

"What are you going to do?"

"I'm going to draw my power and channel it. It's what I did for you and Naomi. Maybe stand back. Just to be safe." She laughs nervously to herself.

"There is Promise in the Light," she whispers, closing her eyes.

The faint aura that's surrounded her through the Shadow Realm glows brighter, and I block the blinding light from my eyes. Eliana is enveloped in the blazing light, and I'm shocked to realize that it's coming from inside her.

Her eyes are still closed as she places her glowing palms on the monster. The light spreads across its feathers, sinking beneath the surface.

The monster twitches ever so slightly, and my hand reflexively reaches for my dagger. It doesn't wake, and its breathing remains ragged.

Eliana pulses more light into the creature. Her hands sink into its black feathers, the light of her hands glowing faintly under the curtain of black.

The feathers begin to retreat from around her hands, falling off the bird's body and disappearing into a wisp of shadows before touching the ground.

Eliana's glow falters ever so slightly, but she sends more into the bird, sweat building on her brow.

The golden light ripples across the creature, and more feathers fall away, exposing not the body of a plucked bird, but of a young girl.

More of Eliana's light pulses through her, and as the feathers fade so does the beak, the wings, and the clawed feet. A young girl lies coiled in a ball at my feet.

A shriek pieces the air, and the mist whips around us. Rising from the body of the girl is a shadow dark as night with red, glowing eyes. It screams once more, plunging through the air. The *maligni* collides with Eliana before she can move. As it passes through her, it dissipates.

Eliana cries out, stumbling to the ground when she tries to stand. The aura that surrounds her pulses faintly, the light fading.

"Kai," her voice raspy. She coughs, and bright red splatters onto her hand.

"Eliana," I scoop her into my arms. "It's alright. I'm going to get you out of here."

"We can't leave her behind," she rasps out, pointing with a shaking hand to the girl unconscious on the ground.

"I can't carry you both. I'll come right back for her, but I need to get you out of here first."

She nods her head weakly, eyes fluttering shut. I hug her to me more tightly, rushing toward the hut where the entrance to the fold lies.

I step into the darkened hut, and panic floods my body. Where is the tear in the fold? The ominous red slit is no longer hovering in the corner. I spin in a circle, and find the hut void of any light.

Our exit is missing.

Eliana whimpers in my arms.

I run out of the hut, my boots skidding on the ground as I try to think of what to do. We can't be trapped here, there has to be a way to escape.

I retrace our steps back to the center of the town. The girl's body glows faintly as she lies lifeless on the ground.

I step up to the girl's body and nudge it gently with my boot. With my boot I roll her over onto her back. The tear in the fold floats over her chest, the illusion of a gaping wound.

I swallow, unsure of what to do. Eliana whimpers again, and I grit my teeth.

I reach out to the tear, hoping to move it away from the girl's body, but it won't budge.

I swallow down my repulsion and step onto the girl's body—except I don't land on the stone of the town center, but through the fold and back into the garden.

There's a sucking sound as the fold collapses in on itself, taking the girl with it.

Eliana stirs in my arms, and I rush her to the palace, barging into Noras's library.

He squeaks with surprise as I kick open the door, banging it loudly on the bookshelf and sending a stack of books clattering to the floor.

"Noras, help me." I pant. "It's Eliana. She's injured."

Noras sets down the book he was reading and floats to my side, his fingers gently hovering over Eliana's body.

"Sir, there's nothing I can do for her. She needs to return to the Light Realm." He pauses, looking into my fearful eyes with worry of his own. "Her light was stolen."

Zayne

A FAMILIAR FLASH OF iridescent feathers swoops down from the mast and lands on my shoulder as we board the Daughter of the Seas.

"Hello, girl," I whisper as I stroke her feathers.

Akiko coos, her head bumping mine.

She lifts her wing to expose her leg and the note attached to it.

She's alive.

My heart soars, pounding in my ears.

Ignoring Loith, I make a hasty retreat for my cabin. Loith grumbles about fixing us a meal before the door of the cabin shuts.

Akiko swoops into the cabin and lands on her perch with a satisfied chirp, delighted that I didn't disturb her nest or special items while she was away.

I have a small scar on my hand to remind me never to touch her things.

I collapse into my reading chair, my eyes eagerly devouring Eliana's every word.

The sketch of Akiko is magnificently rendered, nearly lifelike. I hold it up for Akiko. She stops preening herself to take in the sketch, chirping with approval before returning to her beauty routine.

"Loith," I shout.

Footsteps clomp up the stairs leading from the galley and across the deck, stopping at my door. My loyal first mate pops her head into the cabin, a greasy spoon clutched in her left hand.

"Yes, sir?"

"Call a meeting, I have the coordinates."

"So, your connection in the North finally responded," sneers the woman in the *laseron* mask.

Why couldn't it have been her on that platform?

It's not my finest thought, but I can't help it. This woman is the worst. She instigates every argument. Tensions are plenty high after the execution of seven of our members. Her disagreeable attitude is unnecessary and unproductive.

"Yes," I snarl through gritted teeth. "I propose we prepare everyone in the *Abskonditi* to leave Sandovell."

"Preposterous," bellows a man in a *rabbeon* mask.

More raise their voices in opposition.

The *laseron* mask silences everyone with a single raised hand and a sharp whistle. "It was an unfortunate loss of our members, but don't you think abandoning our homes so suddenly is a bit rash?"

Several on the outer edge of the room nod their heads–agreeing with her.

I straighten my spine, standing tall in my conviction, and clear my throat. "Is it rash to desire security? The deep sleep of a person unafraid to close their eyes?"

I step to the table, calmly placing my palms on the well-worn wood. "I for one would appreciate living without the need to look over my shoulder every time I enter the market or walk alone down an empty lane. I desire the chance to breathe easily, no longer whispering every conversation, holding my breath at the slightest glimpse of black hoods in a crowd," I slam my palm on the tabletop, "and practice my goddess-given talents freely."

A few nod in agreement with me.

"There are those in the camp that would benefit from proper training on how to control their magic—children especially." I smile, encouraged by the silence in the room as everyone hangs on my words. "They have those resources in the North."

"I'd rather fight here in my own home," interrupts a short man in a *crost* bird mask.

Cries of agreement rise in the room.

Loith places a reassuring hand on my arm, pulling me back from the table and the crowd of cowards.

She leans close. "Look," she points, "there are a few in the room who aren't cheering."

Scanning the crowd, there's a tall, clean-shaven, and well-dressed man in the corner, staring at me. I nod my head to him before turning to leave the room. He pretends not to notice.

Loith and I loiter outside the hidden entrance to the tavern basement where the *Abskonditi* meet. Several minutes pass with no sign of the other man.

"Let's go, Loith. We don't want to be caught loitering here."

I take her mask, tucking it alongside mine in the satchel draped over my shoulder. If we're stopped by the Haematitian guards I want to be sure to easily ditch these incriminating masks.

We leave the alley, sticking to the shadows of the lane, hoods up and eyes downcast. The docks are several blocks away, and the city is fairly dead at this time of night. Not many reasonable excuses to be out at this hour.

"Sir," a timid voice calls out behind us. My hand rests casually on the hilt of my sword as we turn back around.

The same well-dressed man from the tavern cellar stands before us, his mask now gone.

"So it's true. The famous captain of the Daughter of the Seas is one of us."

"How can I help you?" This kid appears barely older than sixteen.

"Ah, yes. You're a busy man. I won't take much of your time. Can I buy you and your friend a drink?"

"Yes," Loith answers for us, smiling. "We'd love a drink."

We follow him to a different tavern, fighting a crowd to slip into the last remaining booth in the darkened back corner.

Three tankards of mead are placed in front of us, courtesy of a young barmaid with several missing fingers. A reformed thief.

Loith eagerly sips hers, not having had a proper drink in many months.

"What can we do for you ...?" I draw the question out.

"Maesyn," he answers. "Seems only fair I share my name since I know who you are."

I nod my head.

Points to him for being polite.

"I want to accompany you."

He gets right to the point. I think I could like this kid.

"Is that so?" Loith asks between loud slurps of her second tankard of mead, stealing mine when I wasn't paying attention.

"Yes, and I know of several others who also want to," he lowers his voice and leans close to the table, "escape."

"Why?" I ask.

"I want to control my own fate. If the others want to wait around to be discovered and die for their stake in some shitty corner of this gods-forsaken city, by all means." He scoffs. "I, however, have nothing left to lose, and nothing left for me here. I'd rather take my chances."

I flash him a good natured smile, and Loith nods her head in appreciation.

Maesyn leans in close again, a sly smile on his lips. "So, when do we plan to leave?"

Loith glances up from her second mead, waiting for me to respond.

"Tomorrow night."

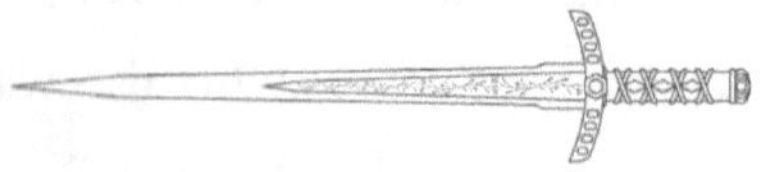

Eliana

TINY SHOCKS OF PAIN radiate from every inch of my body. I swallow and force my eyes open, crying out quietly from the pain.

The ceiling above me is a soft tan fabric, light shining on the other side–I'm in a tent, and definitely no longer in the Shadow Realm. My black shirt and pants from Hama have been replaced with a soft white nightgown. I grimace at the thought of being changed while unconscious.

I vaguely remember my face being pressed tightly to Kai's chest as he carried me from the shadow fold ... but after that it's all a dark fog.

What happened?

I grit my teeth, and hiss with the pained effort it takes to sit up and swing my legs over the side of the cot I've been lying on.

The tent is empty, save for me, a table full of herbs and tinctures in small glass vials of various bright colors, and a pot hanging over a fire.

The tent flap is pulled back, and the *solari's* light shines brightly in the sky–*so it's been at least half a day since Kai and I entered the Shadow Realm.*

From my limited view beyond the tent, I watch Raepheans in red cloaks and white shirts bustle around Isadora's settlement, carrying large grain sacks and a variety of other goods. I stand up, crying out from the pain. My legs buckle under me, and the dirt and gravel dig into my knees and palms as I catch myself before falling flat.

An anxious gasp comes from outside the tent, and a short, stocky woman with pale green skin, long white hair in braids, and large set, wide eyes of bright pink bustles into the tent. She finds me on the ground and gasps again, tutting under her breath as she kneels down in front of me, her pink eyes filled with worry.

"Princess, what are you doing on the floor?" Her voice is soft and melodic, not at all what I expected. "Here, let me help you."

She reaches out to grab my arm, and I flinch away, a spasm racking my body. I hiss in a shaky breath, and she brushes back my hair, her fingers so gentle against my cheek.

"It's okay your Highness. I'm a healer." She smiles.

"It's Eliana, not your Highness."

"My name is Joi."

"Joi, as in the Auror of Opulia?"

She flashes a proud smile and tips her head at me. "The one and only!"

"Am I in Opulia?" I ask, a little dumbstruck.

Joi laughs and shakes her head. "No, of course not. You're safely in Auror Isadora's camp. I heeded your summons. And just in time too, it seems."

She places a gentle hand under my elbow and helps me stand on weak legs, guiding me back to the cot. I scooch over to make room for her and she sits down next to me.

"What do you mean by just in time? Has something happened? Was the camp attacked again?"

I bolt to stand and Joi catches me, pulling me back down to the cot. Her hand rests on mine, trying to keep me planted in my spot.

"Everyone is fine. The settlement is doing well." She pauses. "I was referring to you, your Highness. When we arrived, your friend was clutching your unconscious body and pleading with Auror Isadora to help you."

"Did Kai mention what happened?"

"Kai?" Joi cocks her head. "Who is Kai? Your friend Naomi was the one pleading with Auror Isadora."

"What?"

That doesn't make any sense. Kai brought me back from the Shadow Realm. He wouldn't abandon me—would he? And if he's not here, then where is he?

"Your aura is dim. Something took a tremendous amount of your energy. I've never seen this kind of illness before—what happened to you?"

I swallow, trying to think of how much to explain. Luckily, Joi is easily distracted.

She hops up and rushes over to the table of herbs, dried flowers, and tinctures, and grabs an assortment of plants, plucking petals and leaves with practiced efficiency before dropping them into a mortar. The pestle scrapes against the stone bowl, grinding the selection to a crumbled mess. Joi adds a few drops of several different tinctures—green, light blue, and bright purple—and scoops a ladle of hot water over the mixture.

Steam rises from the bowl as she hands it to me, smiling. "Drink up. I promise this is helping."

I smile in thanks, tipping the hot brew to my lips. A fruity and floral liquid splashes over my tongue, the flavor so well balanced. It's the best tea I've ever tasted.

"Thank you, Joi."

"My pleasure, your High—"

"It's Eliana, please."

She nods her head, blushing. "Auror Eliana."

I laugh, sensing Joi is just as stubborn as I can be underneath her friendly, non-threatening appearance.

"I was trying to purge a shadow-cursed being of the darkness within them."

Joi gasps in shock. "A shadow-cursed creature? How frightful."

I wonder what it's like in Opulia, a land of healing. Does Joi know pain or suffering?

"Hevastia is a cursed, dark land. That's why I asked Isadora to summon the other aurors, I need your help."

Joi places her hands over mine, smiling sadly. "What you need right now is to heal. Your aura has been through a traumatic ordeal. Your gifts are not strong enough for whatever sort of magic you tried to engage in.

"Pardon my bluntness, but it was reckless and dangerous. Untrained gifts drain easily. You could have completely lost touch with your magic."

Tears well in my eyes, my worst fears now confirmed.

Kai was right. I was being headstrong and ignored the risks. All I could think of was myself and how I've felt so useless. I didn't think about the consequences, not really.

"I understand you recently discovered your heritage? It takes time and practice to harness and strengthen your gift. You are very lucky you have incredible potential. I can sense your magic is strong, but it's young and wild. It needs proper nourishment and discipline.

"It's a skill that takes time to hone, the same as sword fighting. You can't pick it up and expect to expertly wield it right away. You have to build the muscles and learn the movements."

"I didn't know," I whisper, my cheeks wet with tears.

"I know," Joi murmurs, taking the empty tea cup from hands and placing my hands in hers. "Do not blame yourself. Your friend told me what you did for her. It's unbelievable. You must train it."

"I don't have the time to train. Hevastia is dying as we speak. Vaiccar is corrupting everything he can get his claws into. I can't leave them unprotected and at his mercy."

"You don't have a choice, Eliana." Joi's voice is now firm. "If you don't properly train, then you'll be no help to them at all when you burn yourself out.

"You need to heal before you can train. Your body is too weak to handle the amount of magic you channeled. You nearly burned yourself out."

Joi pulls up my sleeves and I gasp. My arms are marred by burn marks, as if I stuck my arm into a roaring flame and held it there, the skin blistering and frying.

"Don't worry. I can fix the scarring. It won't be permanent. That part is easy, but cleansing your aura and strengthening it—that is trickier. I have several ideas on what we can do. Be patient with me. I've never healed this kind of injury, but I'm confident I can figure it out."

"Thank you," I whisper. "I really appreciate it."

"Of course. It's my gift, and my honor." Joi smiles. "Now, as my patient, I order you to get some rest. We can talk more when you've had a chance to let the tea you drank work its magic." She winks at me.

I lie down on the cot, closing my eyes.

Over the next several days, I tolerate Joi's constant humming around the tent, and feeding me more tea than I can count on my hands and toes. She's restricted anyone from visiting, insisting that quiet rest and solitude are essential to me regaining my strength.

After I pestered her for nearly three hours straight, she finally acquiesced and let Naomi bring me my sketchbook and charcoal. I tried to ask Naomi about Kai, but Joi ushered her out immediately.

The sketchbook sits open in my lap, and I trace a darker line over the rough outline of the flower I have been doodling absentmindedly while Joi hovers in the tent.

I noticed her peeking at my journal the other day and decided in her presence to keep my art simple, uninteresting.

I haven't told her about the Shadow Realm, Kai's abilities, or much about myself beyond the most pertinent information about my limited experience as Hevastia's auror.

When Joi leaves, I flip my journal to a different page—my ramblings about Kai, the Shadow Realm, and my connection to it staring back up at me. I'm no closer to unraveling any of these mysteries, and without Kai's help, I worry it will be too late by the time I do.

I sigh with frustration and collapse onto the cot, bored and annoyed. Soft bootsteps pad across the tent and I peek my right eye open, expecting Joi to be buzzing around the pot over the fire. Naomi smiles and winks, extending her hand to me.

"I figured you desperately need a break from all this?"

I bolt upright and pull her into a crushing embrace.

"I've been going crazy without you," I murmur into her shoulder as she holds me and pats my back in soothing circles.

"Let's go, before Joi gets back." Naomi makes a face when she says Joi's name, perfectly capturing how I feel in this moment about my overly kind jailer.

We dart from the tent and into the woods outside the settlement. In the small burst I'm winded, my cheeks flushed from the effort.

"Please tell me we're here to train. I'm itching to hit something with my blade." I groan. "Give me a moment to catch my breath."

Naomi laughs. "This may be the first time I'm able to beat you."

I roll my eyes and smirk. "Not likely."

We wander deeper into the forest, out of sight from the settlement where I'm sure Joi has already discovered me missing. Naomi bends down under a large tree, its roots raised above the ground–a makeshift cage. She brushes away the fallen leaves to reveal a long, wrapped package.

Naomi flips it open and I sigh in relief as my polished blade gleams in the *solari's* light that breaks through the dead canopy.

I snatch Fate's Guardian, its weight right in my palm. A part of myself is finally back, something no amount of tea or tinctures could ever supply.

"Ready?" Naomi stands, holding a familiar-styled falchion. She notices me staring at her blade and smiles. "Zayne won't miss this one, it was one of many in a pile in the hull of the ship. I fixed it when I got Isadora's forge working."

"Thief," I joke, lazily pointing my sword at her.

She blocks it easily, and I'm impressed by how much her form and technique have improved. She blushes.

"Kai's been giving me some lessons."

I smile, beckoning her to attack first. She whoops, a very Naomi-esque battle cry, and charges me, slashing her sword down toward my left shoulder. I bring Fate's Guardian up to easily block her blow. She recovers and swipes at my other shoulder.

"Naomi, where is Kai?"

My steps falter as I bring my sword up to block her. She hits me with too much force and sends me tumbling to the ground, my sword dropping from my hand.

Naomi rushes over and drops to her knees, helping me sit up. "Are you okay?"

A small bloom of red beads on my forehead and she wipes it off with the back of her hand. "I'm fine. Seriously, it's just a scratch."

Her breath hitches. "I don't know where Kai is." She swallows, tears brimming in her eyes. "When he stumbled into camp clutching you to his chest ... I feared the absolute worst. I screamed at him. I was so afraid—I thought you were dead.

"He laid you in my arms and apologized. There's been no sign of him in the area since. Maendril's convinced he's abandoned us."

"Naomi—"

"Don't. I already feel guilty about losing my cool with him ... I said some truly awful things. In that moment, all I could picture was your limp body and the black blood all over the both of you. I thought ... I blamed him for–"

I grab her hands and shake them, forcing her to look at me. "It was my choice. All my fault. I asked Kai to take me to the Shadow Realm. I thought perhaps I could learn something there. We entered a shadow fold, but different than the one you were in. It was dark, grim, and haunted by a hideous monster.

"We had to fight the monster, and when it was lying there taking its dying breaths, I tried to purge it of its dark shadows."

"Eliana, that was incredibly reckless–"

"You don't think I haven't realized that?" I snap back. Naomi flinches and I sigh. "I'm sorry. This isn't easy. I know I messed up, I just ... I hoped I could help them, the person trapped there."

"Did you help them?"

I whimper. "I'm not sure. Joi claims I overexerted myself, and that's why I fell unconscious. She's been feeding me so many different teas and keeping me hidden away ever since to try to reverse the damage I did to myself."

Naomi hugs me, and I hug her back. My shoulder grows wet with her tears, as my own cheeks dampen.

"I'm sorry I scared you. You must have been beside yourself. Kai will forgive you, Naomi. He's ... a good man. We'll find him."

"I'm so glad you're okay." She sniffles. "I couldn't bear the thought of losing you."

I wipe the tears from her cheeks. "Or I you. We'll get through this."

"Hug on it." Her arms open and I lean into them, folding my own around her shoulders.

Naomi stands, holding her hand out to me. "Do you want to hit more things, or should we go back to camp?"

I chuckle and take her hand. "We can probably hit a few more things before we go back."

We grab our weapons and square off. This time I take the first strike, dancing to her left and swiping my sword toward her knees. She squeals and jumps back, bringing her own weapon down on top of mine with a loud clang.

I slide back and pull my sword up, forcing her to quickly redouble and meet my sword before I slice her in half. Her arms strain to hold me back and I acquiesce, letting her attack next. She swipes in a wild arc toward my right shoulder and I easily block it, twisting my blade and knocking her back.

Naomi stands across from me, panting from the exertion. My own breath is ragged, but I feel more alive than I have since waking up in Joi's tent. Every part of my body is on fire with the mixed exhilaration and exhaustion of exercising muscles stiff from disuse.

I cry out, and Naomi startles, giving me an opportunity to slash my sword in a long arc toward her right shoulder. She brings up her sword, blocking it and I arc it over her head immediately targeting her left shoulder. Her sword glances uselessly off mine and I stop my blade within inches of her neck.

"I win," I announce, smiling broadly. "You've gotten a lot better, though."

She lowers her sword and rolls her eyes. "I'll keep that in mind for next time."

"Ready to head back? I'm sure Joi is probably beside herself in panic."

Naomi and I share a laugh, picking our way back through the forest. As the settlement comes into view it's impossible to miss the large crowd of people gathered at the center.

"What's going on?" Naomi asks from over my shoulder.

"I'm not sure, but I recognize those people."

"You do?"

The group clustered in the middle of the settlement wear black travel clothes and cloaks, their blue-white hair and grayish skin standing in stark contrast to their dark clothes.

"They're Keladonean. I think another auror has arrived."

"Well, let's go down and welcome them," Naomi says, flashing a smile over her shoulder as she walks down the hill and into the settlement ahead of me.

I follow her down the hill, scattering loose stones and dried twigs as I hustle to catch up to her.

A group of Raephean women have congregated in front of the Keladoneans, a sea of red and orange capes. Naomi and I pass through them, apologizing as we bump shoulders and accidentally step on a few toes.

At the front of the Raephean clan stands Isadora and her sister, Iamara, who is leaning on a cane, still recovering from her injuries in the Blud Revel Clan's attack.

"Welcome to Raephe," Isadora announces, tipping her head in greeting to a tall man with sharp features and cold blue eyes. His hair is loose on his shoulders, falling in soft waves, and his mouth is drawn in a thin line.

I swallow down a bout of nerves and step forward to stand on Isadora's other side. His sharp gaze lands directly on me and I resist flinching under the severity. Anger boils in my gut knowing his magic is responsible for Kai's memory loss and countless other victims of Vaiccar's cruel torture.

"I am Emmerrett, the Keladonean Auror. We have answered your summons."

There's a soft squeal of surprise from behind me, and already I know Joi's spotted Emmerrett in the crowd. Her eyes grow wide with shock as she takes in Emmerrett for the first time, her mouth forming a small 'o'.

I flick my hand, beckoning her to come stand at my side and introduce herself. She straightens her apron, tucking loose strands of hair behind her ears and pinching her cheeks to bring a soft rosy color to them. I laugh under my breath.

"It's been nearly one hundred years since the Auror of Keladone visited Raephe. I believe your predecessor's name was Emerys?"

Emmerrett frowns. "Yes ... I go by Emmerrett now."

"It's nice to meet you. I'm Isadora, the Raephean Auror." Isadora extends her hand out to Emmerrett who takes it, his hand swallowing hers in its massive grip. "I summoned you, in aide of Eliana," Isadora tips her head in my direction, "the Hevastian Auror."

"The Hevastian Auror?" Emmerrett's eyebrow quirks up and he smirks. "I didn't realize one had finally been found."

"Aren't your people seers?" I blurt out, clapping a hand over my big, fat mouth.

Emmerrett's laugh is surprisingly soft. "We are, yes. But no one's future is set in stone. It's constantly shifting." He smiles at me. "It's also presumptuous to think we have been searching for you these last one hundred years."

I groan.

"I thought it was funny."

Joi is practically bouncing next to me, waiting for her turn to introduce herself. The perfect opportunity to take the attention off myself. "Emmerrett, it's my pleasure to introduce Joi, the Opulian Auror."

Joi steps forward, placing both of her small hands in Emmerrett's. She's barely half his height, and as she cranes her neck to gaze up into his face, her entire face glows pink with a blush.

"We've met before. Joi, it's a pleasure to meet you again after all this time," Emmerrett replies, an amused smile on his face. "I've heard a great many things about the Opulian Auror's gifts for healing and protection."

Joi practically faints with his compliment, and Isadora and I share a knowing glance.

"So, Eliana, why don't you tell me why you've summoned us."

Isadora steps forward, holding her hand up. "That can wait. It's meal time and you've traveled a very long distance to be here. Let's eat first. We can congregate after dinner," she announces loudly, and then more quietly so only Emmerrett, Joi, and I can hear, "there's one more auror I want you to meet after dinner."

"It would be our honor," Emmerrett calls out, and just like that all the Raephean women scatter, taking the Keladoneans with them, showing them where they will be staying within the settlement.

Kai

ANOTHER BOOK SAILS ACROSS the room, narrowly missing my head. The library is a mess of tossed books and loose paper scattered everywhere. Since Eliana and I left, Noras must have been frantically searching his books for answers.

"None of this is helping," a scared voice calls out from behind the turned over desk, scattered books and scrolls lying abandoned all over the floor. The very same books he now throws over his shoulder.

"What is going on? Noras, get out from behind the table and we can talk."

"I don't have time to talk. I need answers! There must be a way to reverse the reckless damage Vaiccar's done."

I sigh, running my hand down my face.

Noras's head pops up, his eyes wide with worry. "I swear, Lord Kai, I didn't know Miss Eliana would be hurt." His bottom lip trembles.

Three long strides carry me across the room and right in front of Noras, peering over the makeshift barricade of discarded books.

"Noras, if you truly want to protect the shades, then let me help you. I want to save the Shadow Realm from Vaiccar's malicious intentions."

"I told you everything I know, I swear it. Miss Eliana was right. Lord Vaiccar grew impatient. When the gate was destroyed, and he was freed, he forced me to begin summoning you. I tried to resist, but–"

I gently grab Noras's arm, a tiny shock racing up my hand and arm from the touch. I grit my teeth against the unpleasant sensation. Noras reluctantly follows me as I drag him to the oversized chair beside the glowing fire. He squirms in the chair, not accustomed to sitting on furniture.

"Is that why he stole my memories?"

Noras averts his eyes. "He did more than that, sir." He squirms in the chair, not used to sitting on furniture.

"I believe you were intended to be the first to join his legion. Vaiccar drained you of nearly all of your blood, brought you to the brink of death, and then he filled you with his own ... essence. You were of the same essence as the monster you fought in the dark shadow fold."

That bastard made me into a monster, destroying who I once was.

"Miss Eliana purged you of that darkness. That dark shadow no longer resides within you."

It means Eliana can purge the maligni from the other dark folds. The only problem is ... she's not strong enough. Just one almost killed her, to do the same thing over two thousand times more? Impossible.

Something akin to hope blooms in my chest, and in the same breath the lightness becomes weighed down with the realization that the odds are stacked against us.

"Are you sure?"

Noras makes another phlegmy noise, scoffing at me. "I'm Keeper of the shades, of course I'm sure." His smile falters. "It's just that ... there's nothing there, sir."

"Nothing?"

His nod is almost imperceptible.

"What does that mean?"

"I'm not sure, sir. I don't usually interact with the living."

The pit reforms in my stomach, sucking the hope away.

"I need to go."

"Sir, are you okay?"

"I'm fine, Noras." I stride from the room, and Noras follows.

"If it is not too much trouble, can you bring me a copy of Miss Eliana's prophecy and the notes she's taken? I want to study them—to be helpful."

"I'll see what I can do." My promise brings Noras a lot of joy, his face twisting into the creepy smile he usually greets me with.

Noras hovers in place for a moment before darting back into his library, our discussion forgotten in favor of being among his treasured books.

I slip outside to the balcony overlooking the grounds, now almost entirely filled with shadow folds. Most of the folds are the same sinister red as the one Eliana and I recently ventured into. Their ominous glow surrounds the palace, and leaves me with a large knot in my stomach.

"Lady Hevastia, save us," I pray quietly in fear-stricken awe.

How are Eliana and I supposed to solve this?

Eliana isn't strong enough to purge all of these. I scream into the darkness of the Shadow Realm, letting out all of my rage, fears, and sorrow. I yell until my throat is raw, and I'm out of breath.

How is one monster supposed to stop an entire brigade of them?

"Lord Kai?" Noras rushes out to the balcony, scanning the palace grounds for any hidden threats. "Are you alright?"

Noras holds a laughably large book over his shoulder, prepared to swing. I burst out laughing, and Noras brings down the large tome. He sets the tome on the balcony's railing, hovering next to me.

"Noras, do you know what Vaiccar's next move is?"

"I don't, sir."

"I don't either, but I'm going to find out." My fingers clench into a tight fist that I pound against the dark granite railing. "I need to leave, Noras. I'll bring you back the prophecy as soon as I can."

"Goodbye, sir."

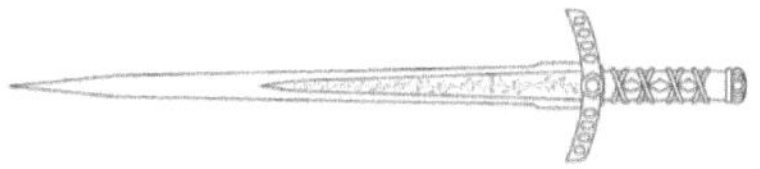

Eliana

NAOMI AND I SIT on the side of the great hall, empty plates resting on our knees. It's quite an interesting mix of individuals mingling around the fire, all of them too nervous to truly engage in conversation with someone from another land.

All except for Joi that is. She's been following Emmerrett, the tall, unreadable auror from Keladone, around all evening. They make a hilarious pairing, but even more surprising is that Emmerrett doesn't mind Joi's buzzing around him, chattering non-stop. On several occasions a soft, amused smile has lit up his face as Joi was explaining something to him.

Naomi's shoulder brushes mine as she leans in closely and whispers, "Joi wants to climb Emmerrett like a tree."

I burst out laughing, unable to contain it. I cover my mouth with my hand to muffle the sound, curling in on myself. The heat of everyones' stares burn on the top of my head.

I peer over at Naomi and hiss, "thanks for that."

She giggles conspiratorially and winks at me. "Anytime, El."

Naomi hops down from the table we're sitting on top of and strides across the room. Everyone stands back as she easily parts the crowd.

I haven't been able to discern whether Naomi is aware of the wariness and air of otherness the Raepheans have been treating her with since Kai's explosive use of shadow power in the *Venaripa's* camp, or if she simply doesn't care. The Opulians and Keladoneans also watch her with a degree of concern–word sure travels fast in this village.

My fist clenches.

This is Kai's doing. Everyone knows he favors her, so they're afraid of sweet, generous Naomi because of him. Some of the Raephean women treat Naomi like she is capable of the same dark, unfamiliar power Kai possesses and she'll use it against them if they dare cross her path.

Worse yet, Kai still hasn't shown his face back in the settlement since he dropped me near-death in Naomi's arms. I grit my teeth.

He owes her an apology, and both of us a damn good explanation.

Naomi returns carrying a plate heaped with steamed buns drizzled in a sweet sauce–Joi's speciality.

An added benefit of the Keladoneans arrival is that Joi's forgotten about me. My earlier transgression for sneaking out of the tent to spar with Naomi is forgiven.

"Steam bun?" Naomi offers, her fingers already sticky from the syrup as she holds one out to me.

I smile and open my mouth for her to pop the delicious treat into my mouth. This familiar scene plays out in my mind from the hundreds of times where Naomi, Brynne, and I would trade treats and desserts, feeding one another under a cloudless sky, *solari* warming us as we laid in the wildflower field that surrounded Bellamere.

I swallow the bun alongside the lump forming in my throat.

Naomi grows quiet, both of us lost in a bygone time that will never be again.

"Eliana," Isadora calls for me from across the room. She waves.

I hop down from the table, squeezing Naomi's fingers. She flashes me a sad smile before stuffing another bun in her mouth. I laugh quietly and smile back at her.

Gliding across the room, all eyes fall on me. The rumor I've lost touch with my goddess-touched gifts has undoubtedly spread like wildfire through the settlement. My unwavering gaze is met with a mixture of pity, anger, and worry.

"Isadora," I nod my head in acknowledgement, ignoring the weight of stares on the back of my neck.

"I plan to bring Joi and Emmerrett to meet Birvat. Would you be willing to accompany me?" She pitches her voice lower. "Neither of them have ever met a Leomarisian, and it can be terrifying the first time."

I take her hands in mine. "Of course."

She smiles with relief. "Thank you."

"I still have questions for Birvat, about the soul stones and their magic. Do you think they would be willing to answer them?"

"I don't speak for Birvat, but I believe they would. You'll have to ask them."

"You're a good match." My words bring a soft smile to Isadora's face.

"Would you answer something for me?" Isadora's voice quakes. "Something's been nagging at me since we last saw Birvat. If we're such a good match, why am I so afraid to share them with my people?"

"It's not an easy decision," I pause, chewing over my words. "You'll never know whether your people will embrace or reject the two of you until you try. Why would you want to be allied with folks who are stuck in their own prejudice?"

Her amber eyes gaze up into mine. "I never thought of it that way."

"It's difficult to forgive your enemy, to accept how they've hurt you ... I would know. You have to be willing to acknowledge that they may be just as victimized by circumstances beyond their control as you were by their actions. It's not an excuse for their actions, but it helps you to approach the person underneath it all with empathy."

"So it's true that you and Kai were once enemies?"

"Yes." I swallow. "He led the regiment that destroyed my village and murdered my mother and best friend. It was his order that executed them."

Isadora gasps. "And you forgave him?"

"Kai was blinded by the Haematitian Council's influence–what was ultimately Vaiccar's twisted scheming. I didn't know that when I forgave him, but I knew that if he was willing to turn his back on those principles, on the one constant in his life, and live to his values, then he was someone I would be willing to trust to have my back.

"His Morei partner, Cire, is the one who found me. Without him taking the first steps to defy the Haematitian Council and their doctrine, I wouldn't be standing here before you. I would have perished alongside my family in the siege of my village."

"Stars," Isadora exclaims under her breath. "And you're only eighteen?" Her face falls, tears brimming in her eyes. "That's so young to be burdened with so much."

A throat clears behind me, and I'm suddenly cast in the shadow of Emmerrett's towering form. His thin lipped smile dips when he sees Isadora's puffy red eyes.

"I hope I'm not interrupting something?" His eyebrow quirks up.

"No," Isadora replies, swiping away the last of her tears. "Are you ready?"

Emmerrett nods at the same time I say, "yes."

"I am as well," a small voice pipes up from behind Emmerrett, and Joi peeks around his legs.

I snort, unable to stifle my laugh at how Joi follows Emmerrett around so closely. Naomi's joke floats to the forefront of my mind and I cover my mouth to hide the snicker. Emmerrett growls low under his breath, and I suck in a breath, cutting my laughter short.

"Follow me," Isadora orders.

She leads us through a different door off the main hall. The kitchen is bustling with Raephean men in white clothes stained with food and grease as they prepare the next course. Isadora nods her head in acknowledgement of them before escorting us out of the kitchen and to the cellar. At the far end of the room is a door, and behind it a staircase. We wind down the stairs for several minutes before stopping at a rotting door I recognize.

I cover my nose with my sleeve and motion for Emmerrett and Joi to do the same. This time, I am prepared for the stench of stale air that attacks my senses with the force of the door opening into the dank, dingy basement.

Isadora and I step into the filthy room. Emmerrett and Joi remain rooted to the doorway, hands covering their noses.

"We're not going to kill you, if that's what you're thinking."

Isadora chuckles at me making the same joke.

Our boots squish on the thick, black mucus that sticks to the floor in disgusting globs. Emmerrett makes a sound of disgust as he shakes a rather large blob off his nicely polished boots. Joi squeaks as it lands near her feet, splashing some of the foul smelling liquid onto her aproned skirt.

She scowls at Emmerrett in the dark, and he laughs quietly under his breath.

We stop at a stone wall at the far end of the basement. I stand next to Isadora and together we push away the wall, revealing the moss-covered tunnel.

Isadora leads the way through the tunnel and out into the dead forest.

"What happened here?" Joi's voice is anxious and quiet.

"Greed," I spit out the word, sparing Isadora from answering. She sighs in relief and flashes me a grateful smile.

We walk deeper into the trees and across the slow moving stream with clear blue water.

"This way," Isadora announces, pointing to a thick copse of dried bushes. "It's just beyond here."

Emmerrett's hand rests casually on the hilt of his sword, and his eyes squint with distrust at the thick brush blocking out path.

"Emmerrett, there's no need for that." I point to his sword. "Trust us, please."

"Not likely."

I scoff. "Then why are you here if you don't plan to answer our call for aid?"

His mouth is set in a tight line, piercing eyes glaring down at me. "It remains to be seen."

"Ridiculous," I mutter to myself.

Joi steps up beside me and smiles apologetically. "Ignore Emmerrett. He's all bark, no bite." She smiles more genuinely and pushes through the bramble behind Isadora.

I follow Joi, leaving Emmerrett to forge his own path through the bramble.

That will teach him to be rude.

I can't shake my unease at realizing Emmerrett is not fully brought into our cause. I don't blame him for having reservations, and I imagine he has his own agenda–but it's unsettling nevertheless knowing what Isadora and I are about to do.

On the other side of the thicket lies the small wooden cottage, smoke curling from its chimney. I wonder how Birvat knew we would be coming tonight.

Isadora holds out her hand for us to wait and she opens the door. Joi steps toward the cottage, and I grab her wrist to hold her back.

"Wait, Joi. Birvat is shy."

"Who?"

"You'll see." I slip her hand into mine. "Try to keep an open mind, okay?"

She gazes at me with wide, fearful eyes and nods her head in agreement. I wait next to her for Isadora and Birvat to emerge from the cottage. Isadora steps out first, and then Birvat's large form ducks through the low doorway, towering over even Emmerrett.

"Hi Birvat," I say, dropping Joi's hand before walking up to my friend and offering a handshake.

My hand is tiny in their large, rough palm, but they accept my handshake gently, flashing me their garbled smile.

"The Leomarisian Auror," Emmerrett announces. "It's an honor to meet you."

All jaws drop. Neither Isadora or I expected Emmerrett to be first to approach.

"And you are?" Birvat asks, their voice rocky, words tumbling over one another.

"I am Auror Emmerrett of Keladone." He pulls Joi forward, his palm flat against her back as he ushers her closer. "This is Auror Joi of Opulia."

Joi gives a small, nervous wave. "Hello, pleasure to meet you."

"Thank you for coming," Birvat glanced nervously at Isadora. "Issa, I hope I have enough pillows for my ... guests."

"We'll make do."

Birvat smiles at that and leads us into the small cottage.

Joi and I sit close to the fire, sharing a blanket and two of the pillows. Emmerrett stands in the corner by the entrance, leaning against the wall. Isadora takes her usual spot in Birvat's lap.

When I glance at Joi, she's staring at Isadora and blushing. I laugh in my head, amused by Joi's innocence and sweet antics.

"I think explanations are in order." Emmerrett's voice emerges from the dark corner. "Eliana, since this is all for your *benefit*, I think it's only fair you go first."

The hair on the back of my neck bristles, his words getting under my skin.

"It's for all of our people's sake, not just mine. You might be in immediate danger, but Vaiccar won't stop at Hevastia's borders. He's already infiltrated Raephe and Leomaris."

I turn to address Emmerrett directly. "Your people were the ones that traveled to Hevastia one hundred years ago and promised my people a chosen savior. Spouting prose about the next goddess-touched daughter of Lady Hevastia.

"Well, here I am." I throw up my arms. "The evil darkness in your prophecy, it's real and it's destroying Hevastia from the inside out. It goes by the name Vaiccar. He sealed away Lady Hevastia's magic for one hundred years. I broke the seal, and now magic is slowly trickling back into the land, and a few of my people have reconnected with their gifts, however weakly."

Joi places her hand on mine, comforting me. "When I released magic, I also set Vaiccar free from his shadow prison. Now, he has a foothold here, in this realm, and he's not going to stop once he's conquered Hevastia. He wants to destroy us all."

Emmerrett's face is blank, unreadable. It makes my blood boil that he could be so cold to our plight.

"He stole Raephe's most sacred gift and corrupted it. For nearly one hundred years my people were murdered for his gain, bled for his power. He misused the soul stones of Leomaris as well. With them, he trapped Lady Hevastia's magic and warped it in his dark image.

"What's to stop him from coming for your gifts as well? And, if he can't use them, he won't just destroy them?"

Joi's frightened eyes search Emmerrett's face. In such a short time she's grown to trust him tremendously, and I worry if he walks away that Joi will, too.

"Let's say that is all true, what are you asking of us, Eliana? That we go to war for you? Why would I risk dying on your soil when I could return to Keladone and fortify our borders in the off chance Vaiccar comes to our shores?"

"Don't be dense," Isadora snaps at Emmerrett. "Fighting Vaiccar while he's at his weakest grants us all the greatest chance of defeating him. Playing the odds of fighting him as he picks us off one by one is arrogant and you know it."

My lip curls under my teeth, and I bite down. "Emmerrett, Vaiccar has a Keladonean prisoner. Her name–"

"Naevys." Emmerrett's voice falls, a deep sorrow draping over his face.

"You know her?"

"She's my twin sister." He steps into the firelight from the shadowy corner. His sharp eyes stare into my very soul. "Do not use her to try to deceive me."

"I'm not trying to deceive you, I saw her with my own eyes. Vaiccar is holding her prisoner in the Haematitian Temple.

"Don't you see? He is already abusing your magic. He's been forcing her to destroy the minds and memories of other prisoners in order to create a shadow army. Vaiccar is searching for you to replace her."

Emmerrett scoffs, "I'm no use to him."

Dread settles into my gut. "Why would you say that? You're the Auror of Keladone."

"My power holds no claim over memory. That's a very complex magic–an incredibly rare gift."

No.

"That can't be true–"

"Why is that so important to you?" He crouches down so we're eye to eye. "What do you really want with any of us?"

He's got me there.

"Kai, our friend, was under a sort of dark influence placed by Vaiccar, after Naevys removed his memories."

"And, you're hoping I can snap my fingers and bring them all back?" He scoffs and stands.

I flinch under his pressing stare, shrinking back. But, then I remember Naomi's wild, passionate hope of saving Kai, and my resolve hardens.

"I was hoping to receive help in restoring his memories. I was able to purge the darkness from him, but now he's a completely different person."

Emmerrett nods. Out of the corner of my eye, Birvat and Isadora share a look of deep sadness. Joi's small hand finds mine, intertwining our fingers. Somehow everyone in the room knows something I don't.

"Without memory, we are nothing. We exist as an ever-shifting reflection of our lived experiences. They create the person." Emmerrett's words reverberate through me, shaking me to my core.

I reach for Emmerrett, and he pulls away, but I grip his wrist harder. I'm not above begging if that's what it takes. I promised Alana and Hama I would save Kai, and I can't face Naomi with nothing.

"Please, there must be something you can do."

Emmerrett frowns. "I'm sorry Eliana, but there's not. The only one capable of helping your friend is Naevys. However, if his memories were stolen ... then they may not have been properly stored."

"I don't understand."

"Stolen memories need to go somewhere. If Naevys did not record them properly, then they're gone forever."

No. How will I ever tell Naomi this? I grit my teeth. *I won't–not until I'm certain that all hope is lost. I can't hurt her in this way.*

"How many times has she used her gift?"

"I-I don't know. I couldn't say for sure. Why?"

"Strong magic comes with a dire cost. To alter someone's memories she would have to lose some of her own. If she's erasing the minds of those subjected to her magic ... then there is nothing left of my darling sister."

"You can't give up on her that easily–"

"I never said I was giving up," he snaps. "Naevys is a talented time-weaver and memory-shaper. I am the auror and her brother. If Vaiccar's been abusing her magic, he will pay by my own hands."

"He will be made to pay for his transgressions by all of our hands," I reply evenly. "I won't ask you to risk the lives of your people. I only ask for your *mendott*."

Emmerrett towers over me as I remain seated on the pillow next to Joi, his piercing eyes bearing down into my very soul.

"I know it's a lot, if there was any other way–"

Emmerrett holds up his hand, cutting me short.

"You can have my *mendott*, and my aid in your war on one condition."

I swallow the lump forming in my throat. At this moment I would promise anything to secure my people's freedom.

"Anything."

"Deliver my sister–alive–to me, and I will stand at your side on the battlefield. If your friend's memories are stored, Naevys will be the one to decide whether to return them. I will not bargain my sister's magic away."

I nod, my teeth biting into my inner cheek. It's a fair deal, but not an easy one. Just not impossible–I hope.

Please be alive, Naevys.

"Do we have a deal?" Emmerrett offers his hand.

I rise from the floor on my own and stand in front of him. His hand still hangs in the air between us. I grasp his hand, shaking twice.

"I accept your terms."

The fierceness in Emmerrett's eyes softens, giving way to a deep sadness. It's the pained expression of someone at the brink of giving up hope–it's my own face staring back at me.

"Why have you never searched for your sister, Emmerrett?" Isadora's voice pulls his attention, and the moment of vulnerability is gone.

Joi gasps at the boldness of the question. Birvat whispers a warning to Isadora in a deep, timbery whisper.

"Keladone would have never permitted it. Everything must unfold as Destiny intends.

"Naevys and I are twins, an anomaly and a great blessing. But, also a burden. Only one of us would be chosen as the auror. The other would be gifted with great power. Yet, power comes at a steep cost."

"All magic has a price," Joi whispers reverently.

"Keladone gifted Naevys with the ability to manipulate memory. On the day of our calling, Keladone foretold of Naevys's separation from her people. In exchange for the gift of foresight, I would lose that which I loved the most.

"When Naevys was lost during our mission in Hevastia, Keladone visited me once more and forbid me from interfering. He told me all was unfolding as Destiny willed it."

"You were the one to tell my ancestor's the prophecy?"

Just how old is Emmerrett?

"I was the one to divine it."

Gasps echo through the small cabin.

"How–?"

"We age much slower than you. I was young when the vision of Hevastia's last auror appeared to me. I'm one hundred and ten years old."

"If you knew the prophecy, why were you so vague on the details?"

This time Birvat warns me to be polite in a low whisper.

"Divining is an art, not law–Free Will always has its way with Destiny. Any one of your ancestors could have made a different choice along their path–Fate is not written in stone.

"Losing my sister is my greatest sorrow. She's suffered these one hundred years. I wish her not to suffer another day more than absolutely necessary. My god may have commanded me to step aside once, but I will not abandon her any longer."

Emotions build in my gut and rise up my throat, choking me.

"I lost my mother, my best friend and many of my people in the siege against my village. My life went up in flames that day, and with it everything as I'd known it. That loss fulfilled your prophecy, forging my fate in the fire that burned my previous life to ash."

"We've all lost and suffered for this prophecy," Isadora replies solemnly.

The fire is warm on my back as I face my new friends. "I swear to you all, I won't let the suffering be in vain. I intend to win and avenge all of us."

"If Destiny wills it," Emmerrett declares, resting his hand on his chest, "and Fate fares you well," he finishes the decree with a flourishing bow.

"My *mendott* is yours to use when the time arises, Eliana. I've always known I was destined to bring peace to the world, as my Lady Opulia would desire it." Joi smiles warmly at me.

I open my arms to Joi, and she folds herself into them as I hug her deeply. "Thank you, Joi."

"Thank you. I am proud to stand beside you in the coming war."

"Issa, it is time," Birvat states, tipping her chin up toward their rocky face. "We must tell your clan."

"No, that could be disastrous–"

"And if they catch sight of me on the battlefield in Hevastia, what then? They would tear me apart, ignoring the true enemy." They gently swipe a rogue tear from Isadora's cheek. "You cannot face Vaiccar alone."

"Eliana, my mendott is yours. So is my strength, once I obtain it." Birvat's all-white eyes meet mine with a sort of reserved acceptance.

I want to thank them, but the fear is obvious on Isadora's face, and I close my mouth.

"You don't mean?" Isadora's voice falls. She clenches her fist, her face twisting into a mixed expression of anger and fear. "You can't possibly face him, Birvat, he will kill you."

"Issa–"

"No," Isadora shouts, scrambling out of Birvat's lap. "I won't let you."

"You can't stop me."

Tears are falling freely down Isadora's cheeks. She gazes worriedly into my eyes, pleading with me. 'Please,' she mouths to me, unable to speak as sobs rock her entire body.

"Auror Birvat, why is Auror Isadora so distressed?" Emmerrett steps closer, his hand once again resting on the hilt of his sword.

Joi grabs Isadora's hand, guiding her down to the floor and onto the oversized pillow we share. She finds a clean spot on her apron and begins gently dabbing Isadora's cheeks, wiping off the tears as she murmurs soft, calming sounds to her.

"My grandfather." Birvat's hand curls into a fist. "The King of Leomaris. He is responsible for the desolation of both our lands, and for the destruction of Hevastia's magic these past one hundred years.

"He is nearly four hundred years old, and very powerful."

"You're the auror, surely he is no match for you?" Joi looks up from comforting Isadora with hopeful eyes. She glances back down to Isadora, who clings to her, Isadora's grief having overtaken her completely.

"It is not as simple as that. All descendents of Leomaris have the potential to become the auror. It's not limited to one a generation as it is for other god-touched children. My grandfather is the first auror with the power of the soul stone. He discovered it as a young prince."

"You're connected to all the stones as well, right?"

My gut clenches. Birvat's milky white eyes look away. The cabin shudders as Birvat sighs heavily, the sound of rocks tumbling over one another shaking the rafters.

Emmerrett's hand rests fully on the hilt of his sword now. His sharp eyes pierce Birvat. The entire room is holding its breath.

"I was not entirely honest with you about the circumstances surrounding my banishment from Leomaris and the royal court.

"As the decades rolled by, and my grandfather spent more time connected to the soul stones, he became obsessed with them, with power. He murdered my parents, worried my mother, his own daughter, would connect to the stone and rend power from his grasp.

"He would have killed me too, if not for my mother's faithful handmaiden, who spirited me out of the castle and hid me away in a remote corner of the country. She raised me as her own."

"You don't have the power of the auror yet either," Emmerrett snarls, piercing eyes bearing down on Birvat, who does not flinch.

I flinch.

"Emmerrett, back off," I snap, placing my own hand on the hilt of my sword.

Birvat stands and steps up to Emmerrett, who despite his unnaturally tall stature, is nothing compared to the hulking mass of Birvat.

"Not all of us have lived comfortable lives of leisure. That's not to dismiss the tragedy of a life without your sister, but perhaps you should recognize we've all suffered some loss." Birvat's words are the thunderous rumble before a storm, powerful.

Emmerrett's jaw sets in a thin line, but eventually he gives the smallest nod of acknowledgement and steps back from Birvat.

"The King of Leomaris is the most powerful auror in our history. With the soul stone, he harnesses our people's essence and effectively renders them under his thrall."

A shiver runs down my spine.

"Birvat ... what must you do to harness the power of the Leomarisian Auror?" I fear I already know the answer.

"I must kill the king." Their voice shakes with a determined finality. "If he lives, the Leomarisian people will continue their destruction against Raephe, and I will be unable to bestow the power of the *mendott* to you, Eliana.

"I'm only ashamed I haven't stepped forward sooner."

"Birvat, no. Please," Isadora begs. "There has to be another way."

"Issa, I cannot continue on the sidelines hidden away any longer. I must wrest the power from my grandfather's hands and put an end to this war."

Kai

"WHAT ARE YOU DOING?" A familiar voice asks from over my shoulder. I flinch under the tone of the question. It was silly of me to expect Naomi wouldn't be angry with me for disappearing.

"Reading Eliana's notes on the prophecy. Noras thinks he might be able to use them to decipher Vaiccar's intentions."

"Where have you been?"

I set Eliana's journal aside and stand, taking a deep breath as I face Naomi. Her arms are crossed, disappointment pulling down her face.

"I needed to go back to the Shadow Realm, to get answers."

"Did you find what you were searching for?"

"Not entirely." I run my fingers through my dark curls. "Is Eliana alright?"

"She's with the other aurors. The Keladoneans and Opulians arrived while you were gone. It was lucky too. Without the Opulian Auror's assistance, Eliana would most likely be dead."

"I didn't–"

"She told me what happened, I know it's not your fault. You left—"

"I know. I shouldn't have run off."

I stride across the room, stopping right in front of Naomi. She peers up at me with tear-rimmed blue eyes. I cup her face in my hands and swipe a stray tear with my thumb.

"I'm sorry."

"I was so worried." Her words are a whisper.

"I know." I tuck a stray hair behind her ear. "Can you forgive me?"

She pulls my hands from her face and holds them between us. "Kai."

Her voice is so sad. My arms slip over her small frame, pulling her tightly to my chest. "Tell me what I can do to fix this pain I've caused you. Whatever it is, I swear to do it. I won't rest until this hurt is gone." I tip her chin up, staring into her deep blue eyes. "How can I fix this?"

She laughs and sniffles. "Stay, please."

"Naomi, I can't guarantee I won't need to visit the Shadow Realm again. There's still so much about the shades and Vaiccar's plans for them that we don't know."

"I'm not asking you to never return. Maybe wait a few days."

I kiss her forehead. "Of course."

Her eyebrow raises.

I exhale, a laugh escaping. "I promise."

"That's better." She smiles, standing on tiptoe to peck a quick kiss on my lips.

Naomi folds herself onto the settee, pulling a worn blanket over her shoulders. Warmed by the fire, she quickly falls asleep.

Eliana's journal is right where I left it, still open to the page. I continue tracing the strange symbols onto a piece of loose parchment. As I scratch my quill across the page one final time, completing the last verse of the prophecy, I stare down the symbols and words, satisfied.

"Forgive me, Naomi," I whisper. The door groans as I open it and I freeze, checking Naomi's sleeping form on the settee. She didn't stir, and I let out the breath I was holding.

Once in the hallway, I retreat quickly to the main staircase, taking them two at a time. I slip into the cover of darkness and out of the settlement into the dead forest.

I stumble upon a familiar gnarled tree with exposed roots. The perfect, protected hiding spot. The world goes dark as I focus on centering myself to travel back to the Shadow Realm.

The dark marble hall forms around me, and I stride into the unfinished corner, to the spot where the small library door will soon appear. As I reach out, the handle materializes in my hand, and I push the door open.

"Noras, I brought what you asked for."

The library's been cleaned, the overturned desk and bookshelves righted. Noras glides around from the desk he was hovering behind.

"Lord Kai." Noras's face spreads wide in the haunting smile he always wears.

"Noras–"

Noras straightens himself, his posture taking that of a well-practiced scholar. It's the same stance Cire used to take when he was explaining some historical fact he discovered.

Cire.

"I've discovered how Vaiccar was able to influence the Light Realm in the centuries he was trapped here. Vaiccar is the seed of evil. He's present at every nefarious event in our history, every blight on our land's legacy—on Lady Hevastia's legacy. The Great War is one example."

Noras, annoyed by my obvious lack of comprehension, grumbles to himself, "stupid memory, so fragile."

I roll my eyes, as if forgetting historical facts from a bygone era, a symptom of my memories being stolen, is my fault.

"The war was a feud between the Mad King Hayyel, and the Legion, an army led by the feudal lords of Hevastia who stood in opposition of King Hayyel's decision to unite the entire country under the rule of the royal family—essentially cutting the lords' share of profits and taxes in half to fill the King's coffers.

"Vaiccar was at the center of the dispute, his influence whispering in the ears of both sides until he drove them each mad with greed, and plummeted the entire land into the Great War. The tremendous death toll weakened the gate for a very brief time, and Vaiccar escaped."

"What? How?"

"With the messenger shades. A solution so simple I completely ignored it, at first. He was using them to spy on the Light Realm. He exploited the weaknesses of others, corrupting them. Through them he puppeteered countless tragedies. Each catastrophic event caused a rift to form in Lady Hevastia's strength, in the people's confidence in her, and their own faith."

I stagger back and fall into the oversized armchair beside the fireplace. The fire burns low, casting eerie shadows over Noras as he continues his explanation, his voice growing more manic with every breath.

"It was not the first time in the millennia that Vaiccar found weaknesses in Lady Hevastia's stronghold against him. But it was the last until now. He came close with Princess Atrya, but she outsmarted him and he had to wait for the next auror.

"When he returned from his time in the Light Realm, Vaiccar boasted for nearly a decade of how he had laid in motion a hereditary line, that eventually the heirs would be born at the time of his ascension."

My blood runs cold.

"Vaiccar's been planning this for a very long time. Every piece had to be perfectly executed, well planned."

"It wasn't random," I whisper to myself.

"I swear to you, Lord Kai, I didn't know." Noras's voice quivers. "After you left, I researched everything I had in the library. I wanted to find the answer for you."

"Why now?"

"Vaiccar's spent centuries plotting his vengeance against Hevastia. He left nothing to chance. He knew Miss Eliana would be born this generation. I found confirmation of it in an old scroll. He needed to ensure the heir of the Shadow Realm and the auror were born in the same generation. Without the two of you, Vaiccar would not have the power to ascend."

I stand abruptly, nearly overturning the large armchair. "Thank you, Noras. I have to go. I need to tell Eliana."

The settlement is bustling with activity when I return, the *solari* beginning to peek over the horizon, their light breaking through the canopy.

The Raephean women in their blood-colored cloaks run carrying large bundles of cloth, dried flowers, and freshly dug moss from the live forest floor.

"What's going on?" I grab the arm of one of the younger acolytes in a tangerine cloak as she bumps into me in her haste.

She locks frightened eyes on me.

"There's been an attack, we're gathering supplies to heal the ... victim."

Zayne

BITTER WIND BEATS AGAINST us as we enter the narrow passage leading up into the heart of the Ventemere Mountains.

"Someone forgot to tell the mountains it's spring now," Loith mutters under her breath as she clutches a threadbare blanket like a second cloak around her shoulders.

Several others struggle against the blustering wind, shielding themselves with the wagon pulled by myself and Maesyn.

Loith carries a crossbow in her free hand, eyes never stopping as she slowly scans the cliffs above us for any sign of a dark beast. She's paranoid after the close encounter we had in the Thessimis Fields. Where one flanked us in the tall grass and nearly ate my head off before she got a clear shot and killed it.

We haven't spotted another since, but there are many convenient hiding places in the crevices of the mountain passage.

"Zayne, I need to rest," Maesyn says through strained breaths.

The eighteen-year-old apprentice hatter has never experienced manual labor such as this in his short life. Born into what remains of Hevastia's elite families, he's had many privileges in life. That is, until he blew a windstorm through his father's shop.

Maesyn is one of many who had a violent "great awakening" of long-dormant magic thanks to Eliana restoring the Heart. One of many with a large target on their back.

He was able to convince seven others to join us on this cross-country journey. Seven out of more than a hundred hidden in the *Abskonditi*.

A middle-aged woman named Iris and her two daughters, Joon and Johana, are huddled behind the wagon. Joon is an earth mage, Johana an air mage. They flee Iris's husband and the girls' adopted father–a good for nothing man who threatened to turn the girls over to the Haematitian guardians if they did not leave immediately.

Sitting in the wagon is an older blind man, Maxir, escorted by his young grandson, Ethan. We know very little about them. They keep mostly to themselves.

Standing with Iris and her daughters are two women, Talia and Ava, each water mages. Talia's taken an interest in Loith, who pretends not to notice.

After a short rest Maesyn and I take back up the yolk of the wagon, resting the heavy beam on our shoulders as we lead our small band of refugees into the mountains.

Several hours have passed in relative silence as the chilly air whips against our faces, carrying away with it all desire for discourse.

The passage mercifully opens to reveal a breath-taking valley of rolling, lush green grass. Beyond the dancing field is a large patch of scorched earth surrounded by tumbled rocks from a collapsed wall. The valley greenery has slowly begun to invade the burned wasteland, small green plants growing from the crevices of the rocks, purple blooms spread open to the *solari* above.

Bellamere.

"We made it," I announce with a deep sigh of disbelief and relief combined. My breath is stolen by this hidden paradise.

Eliana's home.

"This is it?" Loith whispers fiercely, having stomped up to me from her position beside the wagon.

"Not exactly." I scan the horizon for the trail into the forest on the far side of the ashen village.

Loith gives me a scathing glare as I smile widely at her. "But, we're close."

Everyone follows me into the valley, the tall grass tickling our faces. Loith grips the crossbow in both hands, hey eyes roaming the grassland for any dark beasts.

The forest looms over us as we enter its shadow.

"Spooky," Ava whispers. Joon and Johana nod their heads in agreement, eyes wide as they take in the ancient, towering trees.

Three rocks sit stacked atop one another beside a hollow tree.

"There." I point to the rocks. "This way."

"Rocks?" Talia mutters, "great."

"What about the wagon?" Maesyn asks.

I groan. The forest is full of fallen logs, bushes, and tightly-packed trees. There's no easy path for our wagon.

"We'll have to leave it behind and continue on foot."

"You mean carry all of our supplies?" Ava's voice rises to a whine.

Loith turns a nasty glare on the girl at the same time her older sister smacks her arm. "Stop complaining, Ava." Talia leans closer to her sister. "We're not rich anymore. We have to do things for ourselves now."

"I'll help Maxir and Ethan," Maesyn offers, his face glowing with pride.

"Thank you, Maesyn. Everyone else, please grab whatever you're comfortable carrying. Whatever is left behind can be retrieved once we find the Burroughs."

Maesyn holds Max's hand as he steps from the wagon, his frail body shaking with the effort.

"Sir, may I carry you?"

"Papa, please let the nice man help us. I will carry our things." It's the first time we've heard Ethan speak above a whisper. It's clear he loves his grandfather.

"Oh, alright," grumbles Maxir with an exasperated wave of his bony hand.

Ethan clambers into the wagon, pulling two packs onto his person—one across his chest and the other on his back.

I climb into the wagon after him. "Ethan, do you want to know a secret?"

Ethan bites his lip before nodding his head, eyes wide and eager. "I brought my best friend along with us. Her name is Akiko."

The velvet cover slips off of Akiko's cage in one dramatic swoosh, revealing an agitated Akiko curled up on her perch. Her seed and favorite fruit litter the bottom of her cage, and she is displeased.

"Akiko, this is Ethan."

She chirps a quiet hello, impatient to be released from the cage.

"Ethan, stand back," I instruct, tucking my arm around him to pull him behind me. "Akiko likes to be a bit dramatic when she stretches her wings."

The latch opens with a soft click, and Akiko bursts forth, her iridescent wings spreading wide as she emerges from the cage. With a shriek of joy she takes off into the trees, disappearing out of sight.

"Sir, your bird!" Ethan gasps.

"It's okay Ethan. She's not far from us."

I hop down from the wagon and lift Ethan out of it. He wobbles on his small legs under the weight of both packs, declining my offer to take one when I reach for the strap.

"Keep your eyes peeled for more cairns. They'll point us toward the Burroughs." I lead us into the forest, the wagon and the disregarded supplies left behind.

Annoyance and disbelief flit across the group, but I notice with some satisfaction that they all begin surveying the forest for the next stack. None of us have ever traveled this far inland, or into a forest. The shadow of the trees is similar to that of the tall buildings of the port city we've called home. It's the silence that sends a chill down my spine. I miss the loud chaos of the bustling city.

Slowly, we make our way through the dense forest. *Crost* birds call from the upper canopy, their song echoing through the trees.

A large shadow crosses our path some twenty feet away. I hold my hand up to stop the group. Loith raises her crossbow as I unsheathe my sword.

Stay, I mouth to everyone before ducking behind a bush. A branch snaps on my left, and I pivot too quickly, losing my balance as my boot snags on a raised root, and I fall to the ground.

A large burgundy head with a wet brown nose, and rotten breath snorts in my face. Soft black eyes peer down at me with keen interest.

The *rabbeon* snorts again.

"Vendeekta?"

The bear huffs.

"I'll take that as a yes."

I rifle through my satchel, finding the small bundled cloth I packed away. The rag opens to expose a handful of plump berries I picked from a bush two days ago.

Vendeekta huffs, her eyes glinting at the sight of the berries.

"A peace offering." I hold my palm open and her soft lips suck the berries down in a blink.

I chuckle, *incredible*. "Eliana wasn't joking when she said you love berries."

Vendeekta gently tugs my sleeve, pulling me to my feet. Without a second glance she lumbers off, leaving me standing next to the large bush.

"Wait, girl," I call after her.

A deep grunt emits from Vendeekta, but she stops.

"This way, everyone." I retrace my steps back to where I left the rest of the group, all cowering behind Loith and her crossbow.

"Are you sure about this?" Loith whispers to me as we follow Vendeekta through the forest.

I snort. "If I hadn't spent several days on a boat listening to Eliana talk about this *rabbeon*, I'd be skeptical. She trusts this bear implicitly, and I trust Eliana."

Loith rolls her eyes. "You've got it bad, Captain." She snickers.

"I don't know what you mean," I shoot back, pulling my collar to cover the blush rising in my cheeks.

Soon, the forest gives way to stout bushes and loose stone. Nestled among the rocks above us is a single lit torch.

"See? The *rabbeon* is smart."

Vendeekta rumbles with pleasure as I scratch her behind her ears in appreciation.

Loith and I hike up to the torch, slipping into the well-hidden entrance. The tunnel is narrow, and we have to move slowly to slip through.

There's a soft click, and Loith shoves me to the ground as a large log comes careening down, swinging through the tight space like an oversized pendulum.

"Eliana could have mentioned a trip wire," Loith mutters. I chuckle.

I pull myself and Loith back up, ducking to avoid the log as it continues to sway above us. We keep our eyes peeled for more hidden traps. As we turn the corner, the tunnel opens to a vast antechamber with tents lining the walls, a makeshift *tehendra* in the center of the cavern, and raised garden beds dotting the lower floor.

People bustle back and forth, carrying out a myriad of menial, everyday chores. So far, no one's paid us a second glance.

We stay rooted in place by the entrance, both starstruck over the ingenuity of this hidden community concealed within the mountain.

A woman with deep skin and curly black hair notices us. A baby, with a fairer complexion and her mothers same dark curls, is strapped securely to the woman's chest.

She motions to a tall, barrel-chested man tending a garden bed, and he turns to face us. This man is armed to the teeth, a dagger on his belt, trowel in his hand, and an ax strapped across his back.

He sets the trowel down, dusting his hands off on his pants as he walks toward us.

Loith slowly raises her crossbow and I shove it down. "No, wait."

"He's heavily armed, Captain," she hisses in my ear.

"We're not going to shoot Eliana's people," I hiss back.

"Hello," the man says with a tight-lipped smile. "What brings you to the Ventemere Mountains?" He doesn't ask how we got past their trap.

"We're looking for Mythica."

The man turns to the woman, his hands moving quickly as he signs something to her. She eyes us warily and walks back down the path, disappearing into an adjoining tunnel.

"Where did you hear of us?"

Time to play all our cards.

"From Eliana."

His shoulders relax and he smiles. "So, she's alive then?"

I smile. "Yes, she sent us here."

"Wait here for Mythica. She will decide what to do." He holds up his hand, indicating we are to stay close to the entrance. Behind him, the rest of the residents continue their normal activities, very few have glanced our way.

"We have several companions–" I began to tell the man.

"Of course, they're welcome as well," he responds with a good-natured smile. He glances behind us and chuckles. "Sorry about the trip wire, glad no one was hurt."

"I tore my favorite pants," Loith mutters so only I can hear.

"Loith, go and gather the others. I'll wait here."

She hesitates, her eyes glued to the man, particularly to the hand resting on his hip, suspiciously close to his dagger.

"That's an order, Loith."

She grits her teeth. "Yes, Captain." She turns on her heel and marches back to the tunnel that brought us here.

"Captain?" The man asks with a hearty chuckle. "From Sandovell then?"

I laugh, quietly. "Yes, I'm Zayne." My hand hangs in the air, extended between us.

He grips my hand firmly within his own, shaking it twice. "Tyr," he replies. "My wife, Tenya, is fetching Mythica."

We stand in a comfortable silence, awaiting Mythica's arrival. While we wait my group arrives, clutching their few belongings to their chests as they take in the large cavern.

Soon after, a white-haired woman with a wrinkled, kind face strides arm in arm with Tenya.

"Hello, welcome to the Burroughs."

"Hello Mythica. I am Zayne of Sandovell. My crew escorted Princess Eliana, and her friends, Maendril and Naomi, on their journey." I leave out the part about leaving them on Raephe. I will tell her everything when the time is right. "She told us of this sanctuary in the mountains."

Mythica's eyes widen in surprise. "Refugees from Sandovell? My stars, how did you escape?"

Loith laughs. "You don't want to know."

My nose curls at the memory of the horrid stench of the sewers.

"Come rest," Mythica beckons us to a fire beside a small tent. "Warm yourselves."

Our first night in the Burroughs passed without much fanfare. After Mythica fed us a hearty meal around the fire, she escorted us to a corner of the cavern so we could make ourselves comfortable.

It's been two days since we arrived, and I have yet to speak to Mythica alone. We are sharing another meal with her and several others of Eliana's inner circle.

When the flames begin to die down I approach Mythica.

"Could we speak?" I interrupt her conversation with Alana who does not smile at me. Her partner, Hama, smiles warmly and gently takes Alana's hand, leading her to a different log around the fire.

"What can I help you with, Captain?"

"Zayne is fine. No need for unnecessary formalities."

Mythica flashes me a smile, her eyes twinkling. "You remind me of her, I see now why she took a liking to you."

Heat creeps up my neck.

"She gave me this letter with a note for you." I retrieve the letter from my coat pocket and hand it to Mythica.

"I fear my eyes are not what they used to be. Could you please read it for me?"

I nod, taking back the well-worn letter and note. I must have read the note a hundred times, and I still don't understand it all.

"Mythica," I clear my throat, "the god-touched powers united, must find the *Imortei Novemendott,* could be key to defeating Vaiccar. What is the ninth *mendott?*"

I refold the note. "That's all it says. Do you know what it means?"

She chuckles, shaking her head no. "Not one bit, but that's to be expected. Eliana is always thinking several steps ahead of everyone else. She forgets to catch us up."

"I suppose that means you did not come from being with her wherever she is?"

I swallow. "No, I did not. She sent me this letter courtesy of my bird."

If Mythica is curious what that means, she hides it well. "I suppose knowing she is alive is enough for me. Oh how I've missed her."

"She's seeking the aid of the other aurors. What does this *Imortei Novemendott* have to do with it?"

Mythica shrugs, "I'm not sure, but I will review our texts in case there is any mention of such a thing." She pats my hand in a tender, grandmotherly way.

"You've had a long journey to come to us, is it true that Sandovell is under occupation?"

"Yes, the Haematites have locked down the entire city."

"That's a shame. It was the one place we weren't able to visit."

"Eliana mentioned you were recruiting other mages."

Mythica's face turns down into a frown. "Not recruiting, per say, we wanted to help those who were threatened in their homes. Of those we've helped, none have been required to train their magic for the ensuing battle ... but many have chosen to.

"You and your crew are welcome to join the training classes tomorrow. Alana, Tenya, and Tyr are effective instructors. Learning to control your gifts could prove useful in protecting yourself, regardless of whether you choose to fight alongside the auror."

"I've already pledged my loyalty to Eliana."

Mythica smiles. "Why am I not surprised by that?"

I chuckle. "Thank you for the offer, Mythica. I am sure we will take you up on it."

"We'll speak more tomorrow."

I retire from the fire, leaving Mythica and her friends behind. Loith, Maesyn, and Iris sit around our own fire in the corner we've made a home in. I wave to them before retiring for the night.

Hama donated two brightly colored tents to us, each decorated with animal prints they hand-painted. The remaining tent is one I managed to retrieve from our wagon yesterday.

Akiko sits nestled in the corner of mine and Loith's tent on a makeshift perch. I carried the cage back to the cave for her, but she refuses to use it, not yet forgiving me for the time she spent in it on our cross-country journey.

I attach a small note to Akiko's leg. She chirps sleepily from her perch.

"Tomorrow morning, girl, I need you to bring this to Eliana."

I stroke her neck, and she hums deep in her throat, her beak nuzzling my hand.

"We need to let Eliana know we made it safely to the Burroughs."

Eliana

M Y HEART CONSTRICTS AS Birvat collapses to the ground, the sound erupting from them unlike anything I've ever heard. It's a gut-wrenching, animalistic wail of despair. Isadora lies on the ground, her eyes closed and motionless.

Emmerrett restrains the *Venaripa*, his hands growing slick with her blood as she struggles to rip free and resume her onslaught against her sister.

It all happened so quickly—we were returning from Birvat's hidden cabin in the woods. The plan was for Emmerrett and Joi to go ahead and gather everyone in the center of the settlement. Isadora and I were going to wait and escort Birvat into the settlement to officially announce his allegiance to her and the Raephean's cause. Birvat's slow pace kept them from keeping up, and they fell behind.

Iamara must have spotted us and misunderstood the situation. She attacked Birvat, seeing a Leomarisian stalking her sister and the other aurors through the forest. Just as the burst of malicious magic intended for Birvat was about to strike, Isadora dove into its path, absorbing it herself.

"I need *lunarian lucidums*, not *noctisia lucidums*, are you trying to poison her?" Joi snaps to a shaking Raephean acolyte. "In her state just one of these would surely kill her." She tosses the fungi back at the girl, the small black bulbs falling to the ground.

"Joi, what can I do?"

"Help Birvat, they'll listen to you." A shriek of rage pierces the air, and Joi grimaces against the noise. "On second thought, Emmerrett could use your help with Isadora's sister."

"Your Highness, stand down *now*," Emmerrett growls at Iamara as she fights against him. Her eyes are wild. I follow where her gaze lands, to her sister's lover weeping over her still body.

"Fix this." I wave my hand at Isadora, trying to keep the bile from rising higher in my throat.

"Fix it?" Iamara sneers. "Why would I help a traitor?"

I grab a fistful of her dress and pull her face directly in front of mine. "Your sister's not a traitor. Don't you care about her at all?"

Iamara throws herself against Emmerrett, and I let her go. Huffing, she smiles with all her teeth at me. "Raephe chose wrong. I'm the stronger sister. I'll be the one to deliver my goddess's land to glorious rebirth. They'll see that now. My people won't follow a traitorous whore."

I punch Iamara in the face. She reels back from the blow, blood dripping from her nose and down her face. She licks it off her lips with a satisfied smack.

"Eliana," Emmerrett chides me as he struggles to maintain control of her. But I see the smallest smirk on his face.

I draw my sword, my patience worn thin. I hold the blade to Iamara's neck, and she stiffens. "Iamara, pull yourself together. Don't force your people to grieve your loss as well. She loves Birvat. The Leomarisian Auror came in peace, as an ally."

"I won't accept that," she snarls, renewing her losing battle against Emmerrett, ignoring how my blade slices into her neck. "She is a traitor to her kin, and a disgrace to the One Mother."

I withdraw my blade, and groan with frustration. "This is for your own good." I slam my hilt into the back of Iamara's head, knocking her unconscious.

"Have one of the Raephean acolytes bandage her wounds so she can't use her magic and then restrain her," I order Emmerrett. He frowns. "Please," I add with a smirk.

His mouth is in a thin line, clearly not pleased to take orders from me, but he nods his head. Iamara dangles over his shoulder, her blood running down his back as he carts her off.

More Raephean women in red and orange cloaks flock to Birvat and Isadora, holding an assortment of materials and tinctures from Joi's tent. She's calling out ingredients and the women quickly shuffle in their tightly packed group, handing her each item in record time.

I walk the edge of the group searching for an opening to get to Isadora.

"Eliana?"

I turn at the sound of my name. Kai stands ten feet away, his face mixed with relief and confusion. "Naomi said you nearly died, when I heard there was an attack I feared the worst."

"I'm okay. It's Isadora—Iamara attacked her."

"Her own sister?" Kai shakes his head. "I need to tell you something Noras found."

"Not right now. Can it wait?" My thoughts are consumed by my friend's grief. Birvat's wails still ring in my ears. I breathe out heavily and run my hand through my hair, not believing what I'm about to ask. "The *Venaripa* knows you, do you think you could try to convince her that Birvat is on our side? And to tell us how to wake her sister back up?"

He scoffs, "I barely know her. She tried to use me to win a *duel to the death*."

I scowl and the argument dies on his lips.

"I'll try," he mumbles. "But, I really need to talk to you."

"It will have to wait," I reply, already scanning the sea of red for Birvat's hulking form.

I abandon my conversation with Kai and shove my way through the group of Raephean women, garnering rude glares and huffs of annoyance with everybody I push aside. When I finally reach Isadora, I sink to my knees next to her. Birvat doesn't tear their gaze away from her. Their large knuckles have a death-grip on Isadora's hand.

"She's going to be okay, Birvat."

Slowly, I reach for her arms to pull them from Birvat's hand. The woman closest to me is holding a dirty rag, and her lip curls in distaste at the state of Isadora. My blood boils at her blatant blasphemy and bigotry. The women at the back of the crowd of acolytes clearly are only there to save face, and not because they truly care for the fate of their auror.

Already support for Iamara grows alongside the unease at Birvat's unexplained presence in the settlement. The tension is an unlit match next to a barrel of oil. One word from Iamara and the match would be lit, and chaos would consume this village.

"Joi, we need to move Isadora to your tent." More quietly I add, "and, hide Birvat from prying eyes."

She nods her head, barely looking up from the assortment of herbs pilfered from her supplies and brought to the edge of the settlement, where Isadora sacrificed herself for Birvat.

"Birvat, I'm going to pick up Isadora."

Milky white eyes meet mine. No tears fall down Birvat's face, but a deep sadness radiates from them. "I can carry her."

"Absolutely not," Joi intercedes. "Isadora is in an incredibly fragile state. No offense, but you're much more likely to cause harm if you attempt to lift her." She places a gentle hand on Birvat's rough forearm. "I know you want what's best for Isadora. Let us help her."

Rocks shifting over one another is the only sound as Birvat nods their head.

I hoist Isadora into my arms, supporting her head on my shoulder. Birvat stands up beside me, casting me in their imposing shadow. Several of the acolytes who refused to help earlier scatter under Birvat's gaze.

Joi flicks her wrist and I follow, careful not to jostle Isadora as we part the crowd. She leads me to her medicinal tent and I lay Isadora on the cot that was previously mine.

Birvat moans with despair to see Isadora's lifeless form. It's a deep, ground quaking hum that scatters the loose pebbles around Isadora's body.

I gently grab Birvat's hands, and pull their arms toward me. "You can't hide away."

Joi is already mixing a poultice from herbs on her table. She pours a small amount of water from the pot over the fire onto the ground mix and kneads it into a paste.

I spoon several ladles of hot water into a bowl, dipping a cloth into the warm water and dabbing Isadora's wounds. Initially, it wasn't clear that Isadora was wounded. She just fell to the ground in a heap. Now, her red sleeves are soaked in blood. I clean all of the blood from her arms to see the extent of her wounds.

"Isadora, what were you thinking," I murmur.

The water dripping from the cloth runs red as I wring it out, before dipping it back into the bowl and dabbing it on her forehead.

Joi waves her hands to shoo me out of her way as she presses the poultice into Isadora's wounds. I step aside, but stay close in case Joi needs me.

Birvat watches everything, milky white eyes staring unblinking at Joi as she works to heal Isadora's physical injuries.

"Joi–" I want to ask what needs to be done, how Isadora can be healed.

"She needs to rest now. Let's go." Joi won't meet my gaze, and she averts her eyes from Birvat. My gut clenches. Joi curls her arm around me and gently ushers me out of the tent, closing the flap behind us.

"Thank you, Eliana."

"You're welcome," I breathe out, not realizing I had been holding my breath since seeing the rivulets of red blood running down Isadora's arms.

With Isadora being cared for, and Kai in charge of speaking to Iamara, I'm left with nothing to do. I walk across the settlement, the crowd of red cloaks from moments ago dissipated to only a few who rush to execute Joi's orders.

"Birvat, follow me. We need to speak to Wren, Isadora's first in command."

I duck into the great hall, the smell of roasted meat greeting me. Birvat hesitates, their foot on the bottom step that leads to the door of the great hall.

"I'll wait out here … I'm not welcome there."

I open my mouth to offer to bring Birvat a plate of food, my mouth already watering over the smell, but quickly snap it shut. I almost forgot Birvat doesn't eat.

Dinner passes in silence. The settlement is torn—a clear line of division has been drawn in the great hall between those who support Isadora and those who do not. Wren, Isadora's right hand, sits among the smaller group—those still loyal to their auror. I finish my meal with hundreds of eyes, and a few open glares, watching me before following Wren out of the hall.

"Wren," I call out her name.

She turns slowly on her heel. Birvat's shadow falls over both of us as they stride from the shadows of the hall and out into the center of the settlement.

"Can we talk?"

"You're still here." Disbelief pulls her eyebrow up. Her words are directed behind me, at Birvat. "I would have thought you had left already."

"I would never abandon Issa." Birvat's voice is a low grumble.

Wren's boot shifts slightly back, jarred by the timber carrying Birvat's words. She nods her head and beckons us to follow her to Joi's tent.

I pull back the flap expecting Isadora to be sitting up on the cot, miraculously healed. I try to hide my disappointment when she's lying there still. The candlelight wavers with the breeze of the flap falling shut.

"How is she?" Wren's voice is thick with emotion.

"Joi thinks she'll recover, but it's going to take time." I sniffle. "Time I worry we don't have. You saw the tension in the great hall. We need your help. Birvat came here to announce their allegiance to your people."

"So it's true, Isadora really did fall in love with a Leomarisian?" Wren's eyes search Birvat's expressionless face for clues.

"Yes. Her love is reciprocated. I would do anything for Issa."

"Are you sure?"

"Absolutely."

"I love Isadora. I've fought faithfully by her side." Wren swallows, clearly nervous. "If this was her choice ... then I'll honor her wishes, and help you win over the other Raepheans."

Kai

I STALK ACROSS THE settlement, searching for Iamara. Most of the Raephean women are busy helping Isadora and Eliana. Among them is a short, stout woman with pale green skin and bright eyes ordering the Raepheans around.

She must be the Opulian Auror Naomi mentioned.

A strange man with gray hued skin and blue hair with white tips leaves a partially collapsed building at the far end of the settlement. Recognition burns in the deep recess of my mind.

The Keladonean Auror.

I march across the settlement, stopping short of the Keladonean man's path. His steps slowed as he watched my deliberate course with vague curiosity.

"Can I help you?" He doesn't even try to hide his disinterest, staring down at me with mild annoyance.

"I wanted to introduce myself. I'm a friend of Eliana's."

He flashes me a thin-lipped smile. "Emmerrett, it's a pleasure."

"Kai." I take his hand in mine, shaking it once. "Thank you for answering Eliana's summons. We could really use your help."

His eyebrow quirks up with amusement. "You're welcome."

I point to the shed he recently exited. "Eliana asked me to speak with the *Venaripa*, is she in there?"

"Auror Isadora's sister?" The amusement fades from his face, his lip turning up with disgust. "Yes, she's in there."

Without so much as a goodbye, Emmerrett turns and walks away.

The shed is dark, none of the *solari's* waning light penetrating the small, cramped interior.

"Come back to spew more insults?" a familiar voice snarls from the dark.

"Venaripa?"

"My champion," she coos. "Come to rescue your queen?"

"I pledged fealty to Eliana, your Highness. And we both know you're not truly royalty."

She scoffs, "why does everyone care so much about that talentless girl?"

"She sent me to find you."

Iamara sits wedged between a fallen beam and the corner. Her arms are tied in front of her, wrists bound to her ankles. Bandages wrap both her wrists and her neck.

"What happened to you?"

"Your precious auror didn't tell you?" She fakes a yawn. "I valiantly defended my half-wit of a sister from a Leomarisian, and she got herself injured. Your auror made the Keladonean Auror tie me up and leave me here."

"Why did you attack Birvat?"

"They're a Leomarisian, our sworn enemy." She makes no effort to elaborate, and I can hear the exasperation thick in her throat. She gives me a withering glare. "They're dangerous. Leomarisians are constructs of their god's immature imagination. Leomaris was the youngest of Odora's children. While his siblings were crafting beautiful, intelligent, and truly whole beings in their image–Leomaris was unsuccessful."

"Unsuccessful how?"

"It is the reason the Leomarisians devour everything within their grasp, they're unwhole. They lack purpose, a soul. They have to continuously consume in order to survive, otherwise they fall into a deep, unending stasis."

"Is that what you were trying to do to Birvat–steal their lifeforce?"

"Yes." She smiles. "I would have drained them of all the life-energy they had consumed from our land. Emptied them out in the same way you gut an animal." Her smile widens. "My sister had to be *noble*," she spits the word, "and got in the way."

She smiles deviously at me. "Don't bother asking your next question. I don't know whether it can be undone. And if I did, I wouldn't say."

"She's your sister, your own flesh and blood." A cold chill spreads through me.

"She's a traitor and a whore. Not even the One Mother would claim her after she chose to bed our enemy." She sticks her nose up. "I certainly won't claim her as kin."

I turn and leave the hut, ignoring Iamara's angry screams and curses for not untying her.

Eliana

I LEAVE THE TENT, crossing the open square at the center of the settlement. A familiar figure stalks across the square, heading to the main building.

"Kai," I call out.

He stops and turns, eyes drawn down with sadness. He strides toward me, and I stop walking, worry building in my gut.

"What's wrong?"

"Is there somewhere we can go to talk in private?" he asks, leaning close.

We walk side by side into the forest outside the settlement, the memory of the other night and journeying to the Shadow Realm coming to mind immediately.

"I won't go back there," I blurt out, catching Kai off guard.

"Go back–"

"To the Shadow Realm. I'm not ready."

He shakes his head. "I wasn't going to ask you to. Naomi would probably have my head if that idea popped into my head."

"Then, what is it?"

"The *Venaripa* told me everything. She drained all of Isadora's life energy from her body."

I gasp. "How is that possible?"

"Apparently the spell she used was intended for Birvat. Leomarisians are vessels for energy. They don't possess a lifeforce of their own."

"Right. They channel a crystal, like the one's in Hevastia's Heart." A look of puzzlement crosses over Kai's face. "Nevermind. That's not really important. If it's a Raephean spell, perhaps another Raephean can help Joi revive Isadora."

"There's more, Eliana ... I'm not sure it can be undone. I didn't want to say anything in front of the others in case I'm wrong."

"You're wrong, Joi will figure out what to do." I shake my head, not willing to accept anything else. "You're not honestly suggesting they should give up trying?"

Kai swallows, not meeting my gaze. "There's something else, Eliana."

Kai's voice takes on a fearful tone and a chill spreads down my back.

"Noras said Vaiccar needs us as part of his Grand Design. Not just alive, but for our power. He's been plotting this for a very long time, probably since he was first trapped in the Shadow Realm. He's going to come for us."

"Then, we'll be ready." I stand tall, trying to hide the quiver in my lip and the way my words wavered with fear. "We have the support of four of the other aurors. With them, Hevastia stands a chance."

The rising *solari* illuminate the tent, warming the back of my neck. I sit up, blinking slowly and wipe a smattering of dust off of my face. It's been two days since Isadora fell into a sleep-like trance from Iamara's attack. I've been holding back from telling Birvat and Wren about what Kai told me of Iamara's magic and our friend's grisly fate.

That changes today. I decided last night to tell them, and a fitful night of sleep has not done much to bolster my courage.

Birvat sits across from me, holding Isadora's hand. Wren is sitting beside Birvat with Isadora lying on the cot in front of them, pale and unmoving.

"How is she?" My eyes roam Isadora's still form. There's no change from yesterday. It's difficult to swallow the lump in my throat. I don't know if I can tell Birvat that, though.

"Her color is improving. It's warmer now." Birvat smiles. "Whatever Joi's been doing is helping."

It's now or never. I worry if I don't say this soon, I may never have the courage to speak up. I just can't bear to hurt them in this way.

"Is now a good time? I need to talk to you about something."

"You're about to follow up with bad news." Birvat's milky-white, unblinking eyes stare intently at me. "Out with it."

I glare down at my hands, fighting to hold back the tears welling in my eyes. I suck in a shuddering breath and try to calm my racing nerves.

"Kai told me that Iamara managed to drain all of Isadora's lifeforce." The words fall out of me in a rush, tumbling over one another.

Wren gasps. Birvat curses something under their breath. I can't meet either of their gazes. Several heartbeats pass in weighted silence before Birvat's heavy hand rests on my shoulder. One ... two

... three deep breaths. I breathe out slowly and lift my gaze to match theirs.

"Where is she?" Wren's eyes flare with barely-contained rage.

"No, don't. I can tell what you're thinking, but she's not worth it. Hurting her will won't win over those in this very camp that believe her lies. They're already drawing sides. Your people need a leader. They need you, Wren."

"They all need to pay for what's been done to Isadora." Wren pounds her knee with a clenched fist.

"Isadora wouldn't want that." I take Wren's hand in my own. "I know how much this hurts. Trust me."

"But–" Wren begins to argue.

Birvat interrupts her. "Issa chose to step into the path of the spell, and save me. I was too slow–"

I take Birvat's massive hand, now holding both of their hands. "You can't blame yourself, please. This hopelessness, it leads to desperation. Don't give in, and don't listen to it." I peer into Wren's burning gaze. "Isadora believed in your people's ability to overcome their prejudice. Only you, Wren, can convince the other Raepheans to trust Birvat."

She sighs, resigned. "You're right. I can't let petty vengeance cloud my better thinking. Even if the *Venaripa* deserves every moment of misery I wish to inflict on her."

"Vengeance isn't the way forward. Trust me ... I would know." I peer down at my hands in shame. I gaze directly into her red-rimmed eyes, tears still glistening in the corners. "Set aside the anger, for now, and think of your people and their needs. They're scared and confused. They need you to set the example. Birvat is here to help you, but they can't do that alone."

Her eyes gaze over my shoulder and beyond the tent to where her people are milling about the settlement, carrying out chores.

"Don't worry about us. I'll get it under control. You have my word," Wren says with some mustered courage. Birvat nods their head in agreement.

I step outside, tilting my face toward the *lunei* glowing high in the sky. A single tear glistens on my cheek before sliding down to splash against my collar.

Iridescent wings flash overhead as a familiar, beautiful bird descends from the canopy of the large tree that looms over the great hall to land on my shoulder. I stroke Akiko's chest feathers, offering her the crust of my bread dipped in the gravy. Akiko gobbles it down, chirping with delight.

Attached to her ankle is a small scroll. She preens her feathers, uninterested in me now that my plate is clean, and there is no more food being offered. Gently, I untie the note from her ankle.

I unroll the torn parchment, recognizing the looping calligraphy as Zayne's immediately.

Mythica sends her love and regards.

I laugh quietly to myself. He didn't even bother to sign it this time. My heart lifts to know Zayne will be waiting for us when we return to Hevastia. Now that I've confessed the bad news about Isadora to Birvat and Wren, I feel in my gut that it's time for my friends and I to return home. We've been gone too long, and there's more work to be done.

"Go home, Akiko. I'll see you soon, girl." The *cantowauksi* affectionately pecks my cheek one final time before taking flight and soaring from the great hall into the night.

I find Emmerrett and Joi sitting together around the fire in the main hall. Kai, Naomi, and Maendril sit across from them—a roaring fire between them.

Naomi gives me a small wave as I step into the inner circle of the fire's warm light.

"Emmerrett, Joi, could I have a word?"

"Eliana," Joi says my name with a kind smile on her lips. Emmerrett nods.

They get up from the log they're sharing and follow me to the small room adjacent to the great hall. As I open the door, I nearly expect Noras to be standing surrounded by his books, the memory of opening a similar door to his library in the Shadow Realm fresh in my mind.

Beyond the heavy wooden door sits the large table, a map of Raephe and Leomaris still spread out on the table. The memory of my first meeting with Isadora brings a sad smile to my lips.

Funny how, in such a short amount of time, we've gone from enemies to allies, and now friends.

"I've received word from Hevastia. It's time to return home. There's been no word from the other three aurors, and I'm losing hope. I can't sit idly. I need to find the *Imortei Novemendott*, and perhaps then I can convince the other aurors. I haven't forgotten my deal with you, Emmerrett."

Emmerrett nods.

I take both of Joi's hands in my own. "Joi–"

"Your friend Kai already filled me in on the sinister magic used against Isadora. I don't know how to help her yet, but I'll figure it out. I need to refer to my people's books on medicine."

I nod, a lump in my throat. "I was going to start by saying thank you for being such a wonderful friend." I laugh. "And, then I was going to tell you the bad news about Isadora."

Joi laughs, the sound melodic despite the dark mood that's fallen over all of us. "It's not bad news, not yet. There's still hope. Now, off you go. We will take care of everything here."

"There's only one thing I need before we go. Emmerrett, I need a favor."

Displeasure at being asked for a favor pulls Emmerrett's face into a deep frown. Joi nudges him, and he nods for me to continue.

"I know about traveler's stones, and I know they're of Keladonean origin. I was hoping I could have one of yours."

"Time magic is not a toy, Eliana," Emmerrett chides.

I don't fail to notice he never addresses me as 'Auror Eliana.' I grit my teeth at the slight.

"I very much doubt you understand what you're requesting."

"Enlighten me," I growl out.

"There's always a price—using a *traveler's stone*," he says with mild disdain, "costs time. It's not free. You wouldn't notice a difference in short distance travel. A matter of seconds would pass. To travel back to Hevastia, what would be mere minutes for you could be the difference of weeks to the rest of us."

Emmerrett peers down at me, his tall stature casting me in shadow. "Are you willing to sacrifice that?"

I straighten my spine, giving Emmerrett a saccharine smile. "I would lose more time if I waited for a ship to deliver us back to Hevastia's shores."

He smirks. "A valid point. I wanted to make sure you were aware of the price."

"I understand." My eyes match his gaze. With more confidence than I feel, I declare, "I'll pay whatever price is necessary to ensure my people's safety and the security of Hevastia from Vaiccar's dark influence."

"Very well."

Emmerrett steps close and hands me a smooth green stone. The same swirled pattern is etched into its surface.

"Remember our deal–Naevys's safe return."

"I won't forget."

I take Joi's hand. "Thank you, Joi. Hevastia will be in debt to Opulia," I glance at Emmerrett, "and to Keladone."

She smiles and pulls me into a deep hug. "It's my honor, Eliana."

"Can you please tell Birvat and Wren for me?"

Emmerrett nods his head.

"Thank you."

Emmerrett and Joi leave the small council room and return to the large fire. Wren sits gathered with her closest warriors around the fire. As I pass by, I overhear her explaining Isadora's relationship with Birvat.

I find Maendril, Naomi, and Kai around the fire, balancing plates heaped with food on their laps.

"Let's go home." I exclaim with a big smile, excitement coursing through me.

Hama

A LOW GROWL WAKES me from a deep sleep. Orfuhno stands at attention at the front of our tent, hackles raised at something on the other side of the tent flap.

A shadow passes in front of the torch that sits outside our tent. Nails scrape against stone in a slow shuffle.

I nudge Alana awake, pressing a finger to her lips. I point to the shadow outside our door. It stopped directly in front of our tent, and I hold my breath.

Alana slowly climbs over me, reaching for her blade which rests beside our bed. Orfuhno continues to guard us, growling low in his throat.

A gray, sickly, and boney hand grabs the tent flap, pulling it back.

My stomach drops—a dark beast has wandered into the Burroughs.

I lock frightened eyes with Alana, and she presses a palm to my cheek.

Be brave, she mouths to me and I nod.

Without fail, I reply.

A scream echoes from a different corner of the Burroughs. The dark beast pauses, its head turning toward the sound.

Alana takes the opportunity to drive her sword through the beast, its black blood oozing out over the blade as it drops. She slides her blade out of its chest, wiping the black blood on her pant leg.

"Orfuhno, come." Alana commands our pup to her side and he obeys, still on high alert–hackles raised and teeth barred.

"Alana, what if there are more–"

Another scream pierces the silence as chaos breaks in the Burroughs. Alana rushes from our tent with Orfuhno at her side. I scramble to my feet, grabbing her spare sword. In the dim light of the torches that line the main path, I see several of our neighbors engaged in fights with dark beasts, others screaming in panic as they're pulled from their homes by the monsters.

Alana rushes to the closest dark beast as it attacks Daneth, woken up after resting from his most recent trip across Hevastia. He screams as he summons rocks to throw at the monster. They strike it in the head, but it's unphased.

I watch Alana bring her sword down on its neck, disconnecting its head. The head drops into Daneth's lap, spraying them both in the putrid black blood.

She's already running ahead, Daneth and the dead monster forgotten before its body hits the cavern floor. There are several more monsters swarming a tent shared by several of our younger mages.

Flashes of fire and bursts of air carrying large stones assault the monsters, but they don't back down. Tyr joins Alana and they fight alongside the children, pushing the dark beasts back.

Orfuhno blindsides a smaller beast, tackling it to the ground and tearing its throat to shreds.

Wet, heavy breathing reaches my ears, accented by the squelch of raw meat macerated between teeth. Bile rises in my throat. A dark beast gorges itself on a limp body–our poor neighbor that was unable to defend themself before succumbing to the monster's claws.

I throw up a little in my mouth as I raise my sword, shuffling slowly toward the beast. It turns, its head cocked at an unnatural angle as it stares at me with sickly, yellow eyes oozing pus.

Red blood drips down its maw and chest as it stands fully to face me. I swallow my fear, taking in its massive form–two heads taller than me.

"Hama!" Alana screams, having spotted me from afar. She won't make it to me in time.

I raise my sword and strike at the beast, my blade narrowly missing its left shoulder.

Its right arm swings wildly at me, claws raking across my chest.

I scream in pain, almost dropping my sword.

A white blur flies past me, knocking the dark beast back. Orfuhno stands between me and the monster, growling and snarling.

The beast roars, yellow pus flying from its disgusting mouth.

Orfuhno attacks it again, driving it toward the entrance to the Burroughs. A loud roar echoes through the cavern, and at the front of the cave stands a *rabbeon* on two feet, swatting down several other dark beasts pinned between it and Orfuhno.

Eliana once mentioned having a rabbeon companion. Could this be Vendeekta?

As Orfuhno drives the monster back, it swipes at him, but my agile pup dodges the blow, landing a hard bite on the monster's flank. It screeches in pain, arm raised to swipe again–but it never gets the opportunity. Vendeekta bites its head clean off, spitting it out onto the ground.

More dark beasts succumb to the onslaught of the Burroughs' residents as we fight back, killing them off one by one. The screams and screeches fade from the cavern, followed up slowly by the wails of our people as they discover the dead.

I stand rooted in place, my chest heaving with each excruciating breath.

"Hama, what were you thinking?" Alana scolds as she crushes me into her chest, tears streaming down her cheeks.

"I couldn't bear it if I did nothing," I whisper, relief flooding my body.

I could have been that monster's next victim.

The family of our slain neighbor crowd around their mother's body, young children wailing. We walk up to offer our condolences, and that's when I realize it's Abigael's shocked face staring up at us, eyes blank and dead.

I push away from Alana and throw up several feet away, unable to hold it back.

Lady Hevastia, save us.

Orfuhno's wet nose bumps my cheek as he checks on me, and I stroke his ears.

Above the quiet weeping of our neighbors, Tyr's voice calls for everyone to come to the *tehendra*.

Alana supports me as we walk slowly to the center of the Burroughs, picking our way past the dead bodies of dark beasts and our neighbors.

Mythica stands at the front of the assembled group, blood staining her robes. Her face is paler than usual.

"This attack was not random." Her voice wavers, shallow and breathy.

Oh stars, she's injured.

Pyria pushes through the crowd, rushing to Mythica's aid, but Mythica simply pats her on the head and sends her off.

"My time on this side is coming to an end. Our Chieftess, Eliana, remains beyond our borders seeking aid in the coming war." She wheezes. "Until her return, you will turn to Tenya and Tyr for guidance. Treat them with the same loyalty and respect you have all shown me."

They both step forward, covered in black blood. Tenya's young baby girl, Nyneve, lies asleep, securely strapped to her chest.

"We must move with haste, destroying the dark beasts' remains and sending our brave, lost loved ones to their final rest in the Beyond in a pyre." Tyr announces, his face drawn.

"I wish I could grant them all a traditional burial, but these are harrowing times, and we cannot risk another attack."

Many among the group nod their heads, all have wet eyes and tear-stained cheeks.

It will be a long night.

Zayne

TYR APPROACHES ME AND Loith after he and his wife, Tenya, finish giving the residents of the Burroughs instructions.

The mood is somber as the crowd disperses to begin the back-breaking work of clearing victims and monsters' bodies alike from the blood-stained floor of their home.

My heart clenches. These were good people that fell to these monsters.

"I'm sorry for your loss," Tyr offers.

Maxir and dear, sweet Ethan did not make it through the attack.

It's all my fault for not protecting them.

I grit my teeth. "We're sorry for yours."

"Thank you," Loith answers for us both. "How can we be of assistance?"

"Are there any healers among you?"

Tali and Ava approach us, cheeks wet with tears.

"I am," Talia announces with a bit of trepidation. "My sister can assist me."

Tyr nods his head with appreciation. "Follow Pyria, she will need your help."

He points to a woman with the same dark skin and black hair as his wife. When she looks at us, her gaze carries past us, so lost in haunted, all-consuming grief.

These poor people.

Tali and Ava give us a small wave before walking off to join Pyria.

A throat clears, and Tyr coughs.

"Are you sure you don't want to join them?" His gaze falls on my ripped, blood-soaked shirt sleeve.

"Zayne," Loith gasps.

She snatches my arm faster than I can move away. I try to pull away–a feeble attempt–and she yanks my sleeve up to reveal my shredded skin peeling off the exposed bone.

Loith's gasp is a hiss through clenched teeth. Tyr whistles.

"Captain, you need a healer."

"It's not–" my argument dies on my tongue as I stare down at my mangled arm. The skin is a dull gray with yellow pus oozing from the deep claw marks. It's *rotting.*

"I promise you, Loith," I sigh, "I will–just not yet."

She opens her mouth to object but I follow up with a firm, "that's an order."

She swallows. "Yes, Captain."

Tyr's uncomfortable standing in the middle of our disagreement. He clears his throat once more, drawing our attention back to him.

"You can help recover–" he chokes, "the bodies," he says more quietly.

"We'll treat them with the utmost care," I respond, placing a comforting hand on Tyr's shoulder.

He nods and walks away, his head hung low with grief. Already the other villagers have begun to gather the mutilated dead, piling them with the same monsters who murdered their loved ones.

"Where should we start?" Loith cannot tear her gaze away from the villager's gruesome work. I place a comforting hand on her shoulder.

"Let's check on the other refugees from Sandovell," my voice thick with emotion.

Loith's eyes brim with unshed tears. "Maxir and Ethan didn't make it."

"I know," I wrap a protective arm around her shoulders. "I'm sorry, Loith."

So many lost.

Maesyn's form towers over the rest of our group as they huddle close to one another. A threadbare blanket is draped over two forms lying on the ground near the fire.

Joon's tear-stained cheeks are being wiped by Johana's dirty sleeve as she murmurs kind words to calm her sister.

"Sir," Maesyn's voice deep with relief, "thank the goddess you're alright."

I grimace. "Does anyone need the attention of a healer?"

Johana tentatively raises her hand, eyes wet with fresh tears that threaten to spill over. Joon sniffles next to her. "It's our mother, something's wrong with her injury."

They step aside to reveal Iris, her still form laid out on a pile of bloody blankets. She's too pale, her breathing shallow. Glassy eyes gaze past us, unfocused. Red blood weeps from several deep gashes along her toros.

Loith steps forward, head bowed.

There is nothing a healer can do for Iris now.

Our silence is the only confirmation the two girls need before they burst into tears and collapse into Loith's arms. The group is quiet except for the sound of sniffling noses and congested throats thick with phlegm and choked by grief.

"What do we do?" Maesyn asks quietly.

"For now, keep her comfortable." I swallow. "When you're ready, do everything you can to help the citizens of the Burroughs, and look after one another."

Everyone nods, heads hung low.

"I need to speak to Mythica. I'll be back soon."

I duck away from the group, leaving behind our shared grief. The survivors of the Burroughs are busy at work gathering the bodies of those they lost and starting a large pyre. I stop in front of a modest tent near the center of the main antechamber. The fire we sat around not too long ago is now dead embers.

"Please come inside. I won't bite," a weak voice jokes, her laugh ending in a coughing fit.

As I duck inside, Mythica sits up from her cot.

"Captain," she says my title with a knowing smile, a shared joke between us now that she knows—like Eliana—I don't prefer the formalities.

"I'm sorry to—"

She waves her hand, cutting me off. "I'm afraid we don't have much time," she interrupts me. "Come. Sit." She makes space for me beside her on the cot. "I've thought of something."

"About the note?"

"I have never heard of such a weapon, if that's what it is, but perhaps the answer is within one of the old texts I have yet to read."

She motions weakly to a large wooden chest piled high with books and scrolls.

"I've been researching every record of the Hevastian Auror," she sighs, "sadly we don't know much. The most useful texts were probably in the palace library in Eternis. Goddess knows those Haematitian rats pilfered all of those texts long ago."

I chuckle under my breath.

Kneeling down in front of the trunk I remove the haphazardly stacked books and set them in neat piles on the floor.

Mythica breathes in deeply with a wheeze as she moves to the chair and makeshift desk that take up the rest of her tent.

"Anything in particular I should look for?"

"Ignore the records of Oeseth, they're mostly old trade logs." She says his name with apparent distaste, as if the name itself is poison.

"I thought Bellamere burned down, how do you have these records in your possession?" I ask without thinking.

"When you become my age, you've experienced a lot. I hid these records in this cave decades ago, fearing an attack from the Haematites. My best friend, Sarlaine, begged me."

She smiles, and it holds just a hint of mischief. "Who am I to deny an old woman's dying wish?"

I smile back at her. "I see where Eliana gets her preparedness from."

"Mmmm," Mythica hums in agreement. "That was her mother's doing, Chieftess Bellaema was an incredible woman."

A piercing, blood-chilling shriek pierces the air.

The hairs on my arm rise, and my stomach drops to the floor.

"Mythica, stay hidden," I bark at her as I rush out of the tent, stepping into absolute chaos.

It's a bloodbath.

Several dark beasts have once again found their way into the Burroughs, catching the grief-stricken citizens by surprise, and unarmed.

I reach instinctively for my sword and curse under my breath when I realize I left it in my tent. I wanted to cleanse it of the black, tar-like blood.

Screams of terror echo in the antechamber, a nightmarish thunder, adding to the sheer brutality of this second onslaught.

A crude staff is shoved into my hands, snapping me out of my fear-induced daze.

"Help them," Mythica pleads.

I run to confront the closest dark beast, whacking it on the back of its exposed skull with the staff. There's a loud crack and the staff splits into two pieces.

I growl with frustration. The monster was completely unphased by my strike, and it continues to rip into its poor victim as they shriek in agony.

"Captain," Loith shouts.

I redirect my gaze in time to catch my blade. Agonizing pain shoots through my injured arm. I switch grips, silently thanking my mentor for insisting I learn how to fight with both hands.

"Goddess save us," I whisper as I thrust my blade into the dark beast.

The onslaught continues, and I yell a war cry. I withdraw my blade from the monster's side and swing it down and through the dark beast's neck, decapitating it.

Black blood spurts everywhere, coating me and its victim.

I refuse to look down at the mutilated body. I know what I'll see and I can't stomach it.

The beasts roar and rally, bringing down villager after villager.

Water, fire, and earth strike the monsters, holding them at bay while Tyr, Tenya, and other sword-wielding villagers slice into the monsters. There's too many.

Tyr cuts down a diseased laseron, and it screeches before dropping dead.

I engage with a giant *rabbeon* dark beast, its side rotting, rib bones exposed. Red eyes stare down at me from rotting flesh and exposed bone as it roars, blood and pus splattering my face and chest.

I slash at the beast, and it swats at me with its large claws. Rolling, I narrowly dodge being raked across the chest.

The monster stands on two feet, towering over me. I roll again and it drops its massive paws where I stood a moment before, trying to crush me. It rears back up and I roll under it, thrusting my blade into its exposed stomach.

It groans, sagging against my blade. The sheer weight of the beast is too much for me as I struggle to hold it up. My knees buckle and I find myself pinned under the dead monster, my sword still stuck in its gut.

And that's where I find myself trapped, unable to save Mythica, as a smaller dark beast overtakes her. Its sharp fangs sink into her arm as she tries to block it from biting her neck.

It drags her down. My scream is feral as I'm hopeless to help in her futile fight against the dark beast. It lets go of her arm to slash her face.

A bolt whistles through the air and pierces the dark beast's heart. The dark beast drops dead on Mythica's bloody body.

Mythica's serene eyes lock onto mine. "Watch over my girl for me." Her eyes fall closed as she breathes out one final time.

Who am I to deny an old woman's dying wish?

Kai

MAENDRIL PASSES ME A carafe of alcohol, the smell attacking my senses. I shake my head, passing it to the Raephean woman who sits on the next bench. Naomi sits between me and Maendril, quiet. We haven't spoken much since I broke my promise and went back to the Shadow Realm, and now as we prepare to return home, she's subdued. Eliana stands, beckoning us to join her away from the fire. She holds a random green rock in her hand.

"Let's go home." Eliana is grinning ear to ear, eager joy spreading through her entire body at the anticipation of returning home.

The air in front of Eliana wavers and changes. What was once the wall of the hut is now a cavern of glittering crystals and calm water shines through the portal's window.

It's beautiful.

"Maendril, will you do the honors?"

"It would be my pleasure, princess." He gives her a quick wink before stepping through the portal, disappearing to the other side.

Naomi and I follow quickly behind, Eliana stepping through last.

The portal closes behind her and we find ourselves back in Hevastia.

Wooden staffs, swords and crudely-made weapons lay discarded around the perimeter of the cavern we stepped into.

"Let's go find everyone," Eliana exclaims, her excitement at returning barely contained.

Naomi loops her arm through her best friend's, and they lead the way, side by side. There's a lightness to their steps, they're both clearly overjoyed to be home once more.

My gut pinches. I wish to join in this happiness, but I feel no connection to this place, or to any of the people they are rushing to return to. My tether is Naomi, my light, and my lifeline.

The tunnel out of the cavern is wide, torches lighting the way.

Eliana stops short at the mouth of the tunnel, reaching instinctively for her sword, while shoving Naomi back behind her. Frightened eyes and a grim-set mouth are all I need from Eliana to know something isn't right. Maendril and I both draw our own weapons. Naomi shifts closer to me, a cutlass clutched in both hands. Her arms shake with nerves. Eliana steps cautiously into a large antechamber, the main cavern of the Burroughs.

Immediately I spot what's set her on edge, several dried bloodstains lay near the mouth of the tunnel. The reddish brown color is mixed with a darker stain–the black blood of an infected beast. The monster of the dark shadow fold comes to mind, and I shudder at the memory.

We edge forward, cautious. The smell of burnt flesh attacks our nostrils before we reach the remnants of a great pyre in the center of the *tehendra*.

The sound of something being drug against the stone echoes soberly through the cavern. A man in blood-stained clothes pulls behind him a mutilated corpse hastily wrapped in a cloth soaked through with blood.

"Daneth?" Eliana' voice is so quiet, but it still draws the old man's attention.

He drops the cord he was pulling and rushes to our group.

"Have you truly returned?" His eyes are moist with tears of relief. His eyes widen with surprise to find me lurking behind Naomi. "And you found Kai."

"What happened here? Where is everyone?" Eliana ignores Daneth's remark about me, her focus solely on her people.

He wraps an arm around Eliana, leading us away from the smoldering pyre, and to a tent further away. "Please, come sit."

None of us sit. Eliana nervously twirls her hair, Naomi is biting one of her nails, and Maendril looks as though he may rip in half whatever poor creature crosses his path next. I stand here, unsure what to do.

"We were ambushed by dark beasts. They descended on the Burroughs in the night, ripping victims from their homes. It was awful."

His lip quivers, tears running down his blood stained face.

"And as we were tending to the injured and the dead, they struck a second time and decimated the camp entirely."

"How many?" Eliana's voice is a thin, desperate plea.

"We've counted twenty—so far." Daneth sniffles. "Several of them had arrived a few nights prior, they were unprotected and fell quickly during the onslaught."

"And the monsters?"

"Twelve dead. Some escaped."

"How can we help?" Maendril interrupts. His drawn face barely conceals the fear and regret churning under the surface.

"Those of us with the stomach for it have been working to gather the fallen, and dispose of their bodies." Daneth sighs. "It is gut-wrenching work. Others are tending to the injured. The rest have been escorted further into the cave network to wait out the worst of the clean up."

We all rise, leaving the tent, but Daneth grabs Eliana's arm.

"Eliana, there's something else. Follow me?"

Eliana nods, dismissing the rest of us to begin aiding the survivors in recovering the bodies of the beasts and their victims alike. Two boys, no older than thirteen rush toward us, wrapping grubby arms around Maendril.

"Raen, Clyn—thank the stars you're alright."

"We did as you asked us. We fought," the tallest one states through sobs.

The other is crying as well. "We failed you, sir."

Maendril kneels down, looking both boys square in the face. "You did not fail me, or our people. Those that survived were given that chance because of your valor and selfless bravery. I am so proud of you, boys."

Maendril pulls them both in for a hug. Naomi steps forward and hugs them each in turn. They peer behind Naomi, clearly expecting someone else.

"Eliana is with Daneth," Naomi offers, her words directed at the boys.

The tallest one spots me hovering behind Maendril's large form, and his hand reaches for a dagger strapped to his belt.

"Who's this?" He points to me.

"Kai, the man we tried to rescue from the Aceolevia. We found him in Raephe," Maendril states with obvious indifference.

"You went to the land of the *ruffiras* like *him*?" The second boy stares at me with wide, frightened eyes.

"Not intentionally–" Maendril begins to explain.

"It's a story for another time," Naomi interrupts. "Clyn, where can we find Alana and Hama?"

"They're with the sick in Pyria's tent, over there." They both point to a tent at the very far edge of the main antechamber, several smaller tents encircling it.

"Let's go," Naomi says, taking my hand in hers. A small hand reaches out to stop her and Naomi squats down. "What is it, Clyn?" Clyn watches me fearfully, whispering something in Naomi's ear.

Tear-rimmed blue eyes meet mine as she stands. I meet her gaze evenly, unsure what news she received. My heart plummets to see her so sad.

"What is it, my light?"

The tear cascades down her cheek. She swipes it away, sucking in a deep breath. "I don't know what to say." She sniffles.

I take her hand in mine, drawing it up to my chest. "Everything's going to be okay. There's no need for tears."

"It's Hama. They're hurt."

The name tugs at the back of my mind, but I don't feel any special attachment to them. "Hama ... were you close with them?"

Naomi shakes her head no. "Not me, Kai. They're your family."

Family. I have a family? From everything I've learned of the 'old Kai,' it didn't seem possible for someone so dark to be loved. Naomi felt like a miracle, not simply one person in a wider net that was somehow caught and held in the 'old Kai's' heart. What would I even say to them? I don't know them, there's no comfort I can provide.

"Follow me." Naomi reaches for my hand and holds it tightly, tears already spilling from her brilliant eyes.

I'm dragging a forgotten lifetime's worth of worries on each ankle as I near the tent where a stoic form is sitting next to another person lying on a cot in the center of the tent. Maendril is gone, he must have stayed behind with the boys. Honestly, I don't know or care. My hand shakes as I reach for the tent flap, my fingers curling around the soft fabric.

Naomi places a comforting hand on my back, rubbing it back and forth gently.

"I'll be right here with you the whole time."

I pull back the tent flap and step inside, my large form taking up all of the limited space.

Hama lies with their eyes closed, large leaves from *pamu* grass lying across their chest. The skin of their arms, neck, and face is a sickly gray and my stomach dry heaves.

"Are you really here?" The stoic woman whispers—*Alana.* Her name whispers across my mind, too faint to catch the whole memory.

"Yes." My mouth turns up in a sad smile. I cannot help these people. My foot slides back, edging toward the tent flap. I want to escape this, spare them the pain of realizing I am a stranger in their loved one's body.

Hama stirs ever so slightly at the sound of my voice, their eyes barely opening.

"Son."

That single word breaks me, and without my consent my knees slam into the hard stone floor beside the cot. My hands reach for Hama's, gently holding onto them like a lifeline.

"I'm here Hama. I came back."

They open their mouth, a soft wheeze escaping their lips. Tears fall down Alana's face.

"Shh, shh, don't speak," I whisper to Hama, wiping her wet cheeks. "I'm sorry I didn't come home sooner. I should have been here. Stars, if I had—"

The words tumble out of me from some locked, previously inaccessible well of emotion. I cannot recall a single memory of my former life with Hama, but I feel it all. Love, sadness—the kind only someone who's raised you can stir in your gut. But, most of all, a deep, unrelenting anguish at their fate.

Alana's hand rests on mine. "You're here now. That is all that matters to us, son."

Son. They're the closest things to parents my former-self ever had, and he took it all for granted.

Naomi wraps her arms around my shoulders, resting her head against my neck. She gently rubs my back, whispering soothing sounds into my ear.

Hama's grip on my hand tightens for a brief second. Their eyes open wider, peering at me intently.

I bend my ear closer to their mouth, and they whisper, "I will see you ... in the next life ... I am so ... proud of you ... in this life."

Hama sighs out, a long, sad sound. Their hand falls limp in mine, the strong grip from a second ago now gone.

"Hama?" I whisper, sniffling. "No. No, you can't leave."

I grab their shoulders and gently shake them, but they don't open their eyes.

"No, Hama," I cry out, shaking more roughly.

"Kai." My name from Naomi's mouth does nothing to deter me, her hands grip my arm trying to pull me away.

"No, no. I didn't get to say good—"

"Kai." Alana places her worn hands on top of mine. "We have to let them go."

I look up from Hama's peaceful face to Alana's anguish. She pulls my hands from Hama's shoulder, and I slump against Naomi.

Whatever fight I had left in me leaves me body, and I sit in disbelief.

Alana weeps silently as she folds Hama's hands over their chest before bowing her head and reciting the warrior's rite for Hama.

"Lady Hevastia I humbly ask that you welcome this warrior into your service. They fought valiantly for your Light and your love. Send them to the Beyond for their hard-earned rest that they may revisit our world, once again reborn in your evershining Light."

Naomi joins Alana in prayer, ending with, "there is Promise in the Light."

Hama rests, so peaceful and out of place from the deep sadness shrouding everything in the tent and throughout all of the Burroughs. Two thoughts consume my mind.

How could this have happened? And, how can I make Vaiccar pay?

Eliana

DANETH LEADS ME TOWARD the entrance of the Burroughs, the path littered with debris and bloodstains–red and black. As we walk, passing the pyre and piles of discarded objects, I'm sickened to see my people's sanctuary reduced to this. Those who are toiling to clean up the damage do not even glance up as Daneth leads me by.

The still air of the cave is thick with the acrid burn of charred bodies and the metallic zing of fresh-spilled blood. The smoke stings my eyes, but I cry for our losses, and for their suffering.

The *solari* are high in the sky as we leave the cavern and step into the brisk mountainside. Fresh air assaults my senses. It's tainted with guilt as I gulp down the clean breeze, aware of how my people fester in the stench of death.

"I didn't want to tell you in front of the others." He coughs, his handkerchief spotted with liquid. He quickly folds it and tucks it away in a pocket. He motions for me to sit on a large rock.

I shake my head, refusing the offer. "I'm okay."

"I would feel better if you sat. This is going to come as a bit of a shock."

I want to make a sharp remark, the sass on the tip of my tongue, but I swallow it down. I lower myself slowly, anxiety creeping in, churning in my gut and clenching my heart. "Daneth, what is it?"

He swallows, face sagging with grief. "It's Mythica. She's gone."

"How?" My voice is so quiet, barely a whisper.

"In the second siege, as we were burning those we lost, more dark beasts descended on us—caught us completely unaware. Chaos broke loose, and Mythica fought to defend the newest members of the Burroughs.

"She was overcome by a small, vicious beast. Tenya shot it dead, but it was too late. She succumbed to her injuries yesterday morning."

"No." I sob into my hands. "I was too late."

Daneth pats my back, trying to comfort me. "I know she meant a lot to you."

"She did—does." My breath shudders out of me. "She was our last elder, the keeper of our history and traditions." My voice chokes. "How will we rebuild without her?"

Daneth pats my back again. "We will rebuild, Princess. I promise you that. I don't mean to add more to your burden, but there's something else you should know."

My vision is blurred by the tears that will not stop falling.

"Your friend, Hama, is also gravely injured."

"Where?"

"Pyria is tending to them."

I bolt from the rock, rushing past Daneth into the Burroughs. The cavern blurs around me as I sprint to Pyria's tent.

I yank back the flap, Kai, Naomi, and Alana's tear-stained faces greeting me.

Hama lies on the cot between them, eyes closed, and pale.

My knees collapse, and I hit the stone floor with a sickening thud, unable to catch myself.

"Do something, Eliana," Kai pleads, voice strained.

"I–I can't."

Powerlessness attacks me, suffocating me. I don't know what to do. I don't think there is anything I can do. And I've never hated my magic more than in this moment. Never felt more useless.

"I'm so sorry, Alana." Fresh tears flow down my cheeks.

"It's okay, dear. Hama is at peace now. I know they will watch over us."

Naomi guides me toward her, laying my head in her lap as sobs rack my body. She gently strokes my head, her fingers running through my tangled hair, soothing me.

"Eliana." Tyr's voice cuts through the silence.

Tyr sees Hama's still body and he lets out a ragged sigh.

Stepping fully into the tent, he kneels by Alana. His voice is thick with emotion as he says, "Alana, I am so sorry for your loss." He pulls her into his embrace and hugs her tightly.

Mythica, Hama–both gone.

My body is numb.

Tyr clears his throat. "I hate to do this, but Eliana you're needed."

"I'll be right there."

Alana stands and hugs me close. "They loved you, sweet girl. They wouldn't want you to fall apart on their account." She squeezes me once. "I'll be alright. Go."

"I love you, Alana," I whisper, crushing her to me.

Tyr waits, his hands fidgeting in front of him. As the tent flap falls from my hand he turns, beckoning me to follow him down the path. I grab his arm, stopping him.

"And Tenya? Is she alright?"

Tyr nods. "Yes, she and Nyneve are fine. They are waiting for us by the pyre."

Relief floods my body. "She had the baby?"

"Beautiful, and healthy. We are very fortunate." The words relay good news, but from Tyr's broken spirit, and exhausted body, they come out flat.

I wonder if he's been asking Lady Hevastia why his family was spared tragedy as he digs out the remains of his neighbors from the wreckage.

"Congratulations," I hug him and his arms wrap around me. "I'm so happy for you." My own voice is numb.

"Nyneve is a wild spirit. We are hopeful she was born with a gift." He flashes me a small smile, the first glimpse that the usually jovial Tyr is still there, deeply buried under our shared grief.

I squeeze his shoulders, sharing his hopeful joy. "Lady Hevastia will surely bless such a strong birth." I smile mischievously. "I can put in a good word for you." The joke lands flat.

Tyr's laugh is hollow. It's hard to overcome the horror of what he and the rest of my people have endured these past days.

I spot Tenya standing among a crowd of men, faces and clothes stained in soot. In her hand is a list of instructions, she's pointing to them as she disperses the group to do her bidding.

Tenya glances up from her instructions and spots us. She splits the crowd easily, running toward us. Strapped to her chest is a small baby with dark curls. She stops short of plowing me over, wrapping her strong arms around me, sandwiching Nyneve between us.

Nyneve coos softly, disturbed from her peaceful nap against her mother's chest.

Eliana. Thank the stars, you're home.

It's good to be back, Tenya. I've missed you.

She pats my cheek, smearing a bit of soot under my eye as she wipes away a lone tear.

And Hama? I saw you coming from my sister's makeshift triage.

I shake my head ever so slightly, not able to voice it outloud.

Tenya sucks in a breath and hugs me to her, petting my head.

She pulls away, wiping her cheeks with the back of her hand and then mine.

"We've been gathering the bodies of the fallen dark beasts and burning them. We sent off our dead immediately." Tyr leads me past Tenya and toward the smoking pile in the center of the *tehendra*.

"Vaiccar is behind this. There's no way so many found their way into the burrows at once." The words are hissed. Fiery rage burns beneath my skin's surface. It claws at me, begging for release.

"We've never seen more than one or two at the same time. But more than ten? You're probably right." He runs a hand down his face. "I'll be honest, Chieftess, I'm not sure what to do."

My heart pinches at the casual use of my mother's title. In my heart I know it will never truly belong to me. I don't deserve it.

"I'm not sure either, Tyr, but one thing is for certain—Vaiccar will be made to pay for their deaths. You have my word."

The crystal cavern is quiet except for the soft echo of my hiccups from crying deeply. I stormed away from the pyre after speaking with Tyr and Tenya, my vision already blurring with unconsolable tears. I've been alone in the cavern ever since, not yet ready to go back.

I know what awaits me when I leave this bubble of solitude. My people will expect me to lead them.

What kind of leader leaves her people defenseless?

A shiver runs down my spine.

Worse yet, what kind of leader hides from her people when they need her most?

I sniffle.

Pathetic.

The crushing weight of unspoken expectations and responsibilities piles onto me, suffocating me. I want to be a strong leader, and yet I've failed my people again.

I toss another loose pebble into the crystalline waters resting peacefully under my dangling legs. The pebble disrupts the surface, sending small ripples that grow and then fade.

Vaiccar is the pebble—more like a massive boulder. My people are the peaceful water—always disrupted by his force.

Just once I wish he was caught unaware.

I pinch a small clump of dirt between my thumb and forefinger, crushing it to dust.

"Eliana," a tentative male voice calls out to me from the entrance to the cavern.

I shrink away from my name, trying to ignore whoever is searching for me. Bootsteps echo against the crystals, stopping behind me.

After some grunts of frustration and annoyed mutters, a familiar form sits next to me on my right. His sea-washed boots dangle over the ledge, bumping gently into mine.

"I'm sorry about Hama, and Mythica," Zayne says solemnly. "I heard from Tyr of Hama's passing."

"Thank you," I quietly reply. An anger rises within me, and before I can contain it I snarl, "I hate saying that."

"I do, too."

His strong arm wraps around my shoulders and I fold into his embrace with closed eyes. His salt water, and aged book smell has been replaced by the smokey stench of the pyres.

I pull away. "I can't," I whisper.

He clears his throat. "Would you prefer to be alone?"

I begin to nod my head, but suddenly find myself uninterested in hiding away alone. I shake my head no.

Zayne sits in comfortable silence next to me for several deep breaths. His hand sits rested on the small gap of stone between us. I place my hand on his. He wraps my fingers in his and gives them a little squeeze. My heart constricts with the onslaught of emotions bubbling up from where they've churned in my gut.

"How can I support you?" His voice is gruff, his own grief coating his throat.

I swallow.

We're two people shrouded in so much grief. How can we comfort one another?

At this moment, I know what I should say, what's expected of me. But, all there is is the red-hot fire that burns within me, painting my worldview the color of spilled blood–my people's blood.

I set aside vengeance once, let my mother's and my people's deaths go unavenged for too long. That ends now.

"Vaiccar must be made to pay." My voice is low, and it echoes through the cavern ominously.

"Eliana–"

"You asked how you can help me. This is how."

I shift to face Zayne, and for the first time I observe how he has changed since we departed. His right arm is gone, cut off right below the shoulder. A large bandage, dried blood flaking off the crude knots, peeks out from his loose shirt sleeve.

I swallow, and the rage dissipates momentarily. "Your arm ... how did it happen?" My voice is a hoarse whisper.

Zayne runs his left hand through his hair–a motion all at once familiar and foreign.

"The dark beast attacks–the first. One of them got a hold of my arm and shredded it. The wound turned necrotic, spreading." He swallows. "Pyria amputated my arm to save my life."

"But sailing ..."

"I'll adjust." His voice is thick with emotion. "I won't let this slow me down. Loith thinks she can manufacture some sort of replacement for me. And, if not, I'll learn how to do things a little differently." He shrugs.

I nod my head, all at once grateful for Zayne and his positive demeanor and terrified over the circumstances of his injury.

These new dark monsters are able to spread death. Yet another one of Vaiccar's vile tricks, I think to myself, unwilling to voice the disturbing thought.

I count down from three in my head, making peace with what I must do next. I stand up, scattering loose pebbles into the calm water below.

"Keep them safe for me, please. There's something I must do."

He scowls. "I can't let you do that. I know you believe there's no other choice—"

"There is always a choice," I snarl. "Every choice I've made has been the wrong one for my people. I have been *weak*." I spit out the word. "I will no longer hide from Vaiccar, from Destiny. He will kneel at my feet, beg for his life, for mercy, and I will not grant it to him."

"Eliana—" Zayne pleads with me. He scrambles to his feet, reaching for me. His hand closes around my wrist, stopping me from bolting away.

I touch his face tenderly, and his eyes and lips soften under my touch. My heart pinches. "Protect them for me, please."

Here stands a man who respects me, listens to me, and not once doubted my ability to handle myself. He's unlike any other man I've ever met. He doesn't think of me as a sheltered mountain girl, but a fighter. Even better, he's willing to fight alongside me.

I smile, my eyes landing on his lips, and for the first time in my life I wonder what it would feel like to be kissed.

His hand cups my jaw and cheek, pulling my face closer to his and I lean in, nervous energy coursing through me. My lips are mere inches from his and when I gaze into his eyes, they crease with a smile. When I feel as though I can't wait another second, he brings his lips down to mine, kissing me gently, with a deep, urgent need. I bring my own hands to his face and meet his urgency with my own, experiencing all at once our shared joy, and sorrow, and the brief promise of something more.

I break off the kiss and turn on my heel, striding away as quickly as I can, unwilling to let Zayne see the rogue tear sliding down my cheek.

"Eliana, don't!" He calls after me, "I promised Mythica to watch over you."

I disappear down the tunnel, leaving a small piece of my heart behind.

Kai

"**H**AVE YOU SEEN ELIANA?**"** Naomi asks me, her voice pulling me from my quiet contemplation as I've stared at Hama's pyre.

Her touch is gentle and reassuring on my shoulder, and my hand finds hers.

I redirect my gaze to Naomi. Her eyes are red and puffy, shoulders weighed down by the grief-stricken work of helping Pyria to tend to the dying.

It's not lost on me that she's experiencing all of this for the second time. The first pyres after Bellamere's siege were built by her own hands.

My mouth opens to offer some comfort, but no words slip out.

"No, I have not." At least not comforting words. I haven't seen Eliana since she rushed out of Hama's triage tent. Perhaps she needed time alone, too.

Soft lips press against my forehead in a gentle kiss before Naomi's hand slips from mine, and she leaves me once more to sit alone.

Beyond the pyre, the residents of the Burroughs continue to sort through the wreckage of the dark beast attacks.

The man I've learned is called Tyr stands beside his wife, Tenya, who is signing something to him. As Naomi approaches them, Tenya opens her arms to Naomi and she collapses into them, fresh tears springing from her eyes.

They stand holding one another for several heartbeats before breaking apart. Naomi signs to Tenya something I don't know how to decipher, and just as quickly she disappears out of my sight.

I make no move to follow her.

Alana won't leave the tent she shared with Hama. Her silhouette and that of her new companion, Orfuhno, sit bent over in the candlelight shining from behind the mosaic fabric.

My hands hang down in front of me, elbows rested on my thighs as I stare into the flames and silently wish they would consume me as well.

I am thoroughly hollowed out.

I grieve doubly—for Alana's despair that I don't feel, and because I don't know how to comfort her in it. Admitting to her at this moment that I have not regained my memories would only cause her more pain. I grimace, slamming my fist into the log I've been perched on.

A man I don't recognize sits down next to me on my left without a word. I don't give him much thought.

"She's gone to confront Vaiccar," he announces the statement void of all emotion as he stares glass-eyed into the flames of the pyre.

I pause, unsure whether he's speaking to me. His face wears the same lost, broken expression as my own.

"I tried to stop her," he says more quietly.

"Are you okay?" I ask.

He slowly turns to face me, his eyes widening in surprise—as if he's only just noticed me sitting next to him. His throat clears with a deep rumble, thick with emotion.

"Not really." He looks up to meet my gaze. "You?"

I chuckle halfheartedly, and shake my head, no.

"Zayne." He sticks his left arm across his body and out to me.

"Kai." We shake hands, falling back into an uncomfortable silence.

"Eliana told me about you. Glad to see they found you." He laughs under his breath. "You seem yourself."

The captain that abandoned them.

"Ah, she didn't mention me." He redirects his gaze to the pyre, left hand rubbing the back of his neck.

"Naomi mentioned how you left them on Raephe to fend for themselves."

"Captain." A tall woman with a fierce expression addresses Zayne, and he flinches at the title.

"Loith, meet Kai." Zayne gestures to me, and I stare at her.

She barely glances at me, clearly not interested in conversation.

The feeling is mutual. I didn't even want to talk to Zayne.

"Pleasure," she replies with a dry expression.

"Likewise," I nod my head.

"Captain, they've agreed to allow us Iris, Ethan, and Maxir's ashes for a sea burial ceremony."

"Right." He slaps his knee and stands, dusting his hand off.

"Would you want to join us?"

His question catches me off guard, and suddenly sitting alone isn't as desirable as before.

"Sure, let me find Naomi."

Zayne nods, while Loith just watches me as I walk away.

I find Naomi standing once more with Tyr and Tenya, a small wiggling baby bouncing in her arms.

"Hello," I offer with as much warmth as I can muster. My hand extends to Tyr and Tenya. "We never had the chance to meet."

They smile, sadness—or is it wariness—rimming their eyes.

"Nice to meet you, too," Tyr answers quietly, not taking my outstretched hand.

My hand falls back to my side with a soft thud.

Naomi smiles at me, the corners not quite upturned as they usually are. The baby coos in her arms, and she flashes a bright, genuine smile to the baby.

I clear my throat. "Naomi, would you want to accompany me to Zayne's sea burial ceremony?"

Naomi's eyes widen in shock. "Zayne's dead?" She sucks in a deep breath. "Does Eliana know?"

My hand reflexively reaches up to Naomi's face, pulling her eyes to meet mine.

"Everything is okay. Zayne's alive. He's hosting a ceremony for someone else. He invited me. I thought you might want to join me."

"Oh, yes."

I plant a kiss on her forehead and she relaxes under my touch with a deep sigh. She hands Tenya the baby who snuggles back into her mother without fuss.

"I'll find you both later," Naomi promises over her shoulder as I turn her away from the couple. "Kai, we should find Eliana. I'm sure she would want to be there to support Zayne."

Suddenly I recall what Zayne said, *she's gone to confront Vaiccar.* In the span of a slow heartbeat I wage a mental war within myself.

In the end, I grit my teeth and decide to lie to Naomi. "Eliana wants to be alone right now. Zayne already spoke to her."

It's not a complete lie.

Naomi nods, trusting my lie. My heart constricts.

If I tell her Eliana's gone, she'll want to follow her without hesitation. Selfishly, I'm not ready to face Vaiccar, to return to the Aceolevia.

The mere thought of returning sends an icy chill down my spine.

I will not risk Naomi being caught and tortured.

Naomi hugs my arm. "Are you okay, Kai?"

I swallow and then kiss her forehead, my lips brushing over her skin as I answer. "I'm okay. Come on, Eliana will show up when she's ready. Let's go find Zayne."

Naomi takes my hand and follows me down the tunnel Zayne and Loith disappeared down earlier.

She'll forgive me ... eventually.

I tell myself this lie, and I don't even believe it.

Zayne

LOITH AND I FIND Maesyn, Joon, Johana, Tali, and Ava waiting for us in the crystal lake cavern.

The very same place I last saw Eliana.

My hand clenches into a fist.

I should have never let her go.

I want nothing more than to go after her, but once more, my duty is here and not with her. She asked for my help protecting her family, and I owe it to Mythica to uncover the truth of the supposed weapon on her behalf.

"Captain," Maesyn addresses me. "Thank you for arranging this."

"It's only right they be laid to rest before their journey to the Beyond."

"I hope we're not interrupting?" A sweet, familiar voice asks from behind me.

Turning, I find Naomi escorted by Kai and two young men no older than thirteen.

"Hi, Naomi."

She smiles. "Hi, Zayne. I'm glad to see you're alright." Naomi turns to the boys who flank either side of her like small body guards. "This is Raen and Clyn. They wanted to participate. If that's okay, that is."

"Of course, all are welcome. Thank you for coming."

The four of them move to stand beside Loith.

"Gather together," I instruct. I join hands with Loith and Johana stands on my other side, all of us in a circle facing one another.

My throat constricts at the memory of the last time Loith and I recited this prayer together. Her and I stood on the deck of the Daughter of the Seas overlooking the bay of Sandovell. We prayed for my best friend, Pilo, and her love, Nita.

I clear my throat.

"Oshia, goddess of sailor's hearts, great water of Odora, your humble servant calls out to you. Cleanse these souls within your divine waters. Wash away their mortal trappings, and let your soft waves carry them safely to the golden shores of the Beyond."

I break away from the group to pick up the seashell Loith and I brought with us—a gift from Nita. With the shell I scoop the calm water of the cavern lake and hand the shell to Loith. She holds it while I dip my fingers into the shell.

I stop in front of Joon, her eyes downcast, as I draw the rune for water on her forehead.

"May Oshia guide you to safe shores," I murmur.

"All waters lead to her embrace," Joon echoes in response.

I repeat this for everyone, ending with Loith. She repeats the blessing. When all have been blessed I sprinkle the remaining water on the three canisters at our feet.

As one, we repeat the blessing one final time. "May Oshia guide you to safe shores."

Maesyn, Joon, Johana, Talia, and Ava each light a small candle with a matchstick. I bend down, ready to pick up the canisters, but with one hand my grip is clumsy and I end up dropping two of them. With a disgusted, frustrated growl, I set the last one down. Loith gathers the three canisters and joins them at the water's edge. They place each candle in the sand in a semi circle around the canisters.

"May these light the way to the Beyond and its golden shores," I pray solemnly. "All waters lead to Oshia," everyone echoes.

Joon begins to weep quietly, and Johana goes to comfort her sister.

I break away from the group on the beach, rejoining Naomi, Kai, and the boys.

"That was a beautiful ceremony," Naomi says, small tears gathered in the corner of her eyes. "Tyr told me of your injury. I'm sorry for your loss."

"It's alright, if anything I think it makes me look more roguish." I smirk, and give Naomi a charming wink. Kai stiffens next to her.

Joon and Johana bury their mother's ashes in the sand, dumping the contents of the canister into a small hole carved by their own hands. Maesyn and Loith bury Maxir and Ethan's.

"I'm sorry Eliana couldn't make it, she's taking the loss of Mythica and Hama really hard."

I glance over at Kai who wears an obvious guilty expression. I don't know him well, but if he hasn't told her best friend she's gone … I want to trust he has his reasons.

"I saw her earlier. She was really beating herself up over everything."

"Do you know where I can find her?"

I swallow and lie. "I don't. I'm sorry."

"She may have gone for a walk to find Vendeekta," Kai offers, wrapping a protective arm around Naomi's shoulders.

"You're probably right." Naomi relaxes into his touch.

Kai escorts Naomi, Raen, and Clyn back to the main antechamber, leaving me and the remaining Sandovell refugees to mourn in peace.

I sit on the same ledge overlooking the beach where just a few short hours ago Eliana sat next to me.

Wherever you are Eliana, I hope you're okay.

Eliana

THE BITTER WIND BLOWING down from the high peaks of the mountains sends a chill down my spine. I bundle my cloak more tightly around my shoulders, the cold wind's not the only thing chilling my bones.

Guilt creeps along my body over leaving the Burroughs without so much as a brief goodbye to my beloved friends. I know if I had stopped I would have lost the will to leave. To do what must be done.

Halfway down the mountain, concealed by the shade of the forest, my grief sucks me down, calling me home to my family. I won't turn back. If I can't be the leader my people deserve, I can be their avenging blade.

A twig snaps, pulling me from my thoughts.

Gratitude washes over me for having Fate's Guardian strapped to my back, and my favorite dagger tucked securely in my boot. I unsheathe my sword, rolling onto the balls of my feet—prepared to strike.

A large shadow breaks between two trees to my right before disappearing behind a large bush. I hold my breath in an effort to calm my racing heart. The shadow rises once more above the brush, saplings and small plants crushed underfoot. It lumbers into the light, breaking through the forest's canopy. A familiar fuzzy head with soft eyes and a wet brown nose rams into me, knocking me over.

"Vendeekta," I gasp, grabbing onto her burgundy scruff and burying my face in its plush comfort.

She snuffles my hair, face, and hands. Soft black lips and a wet brown nose leave damp trails all over my face.

I giggle. "Vendeekta, settle down." I hug her head tightly. "I missed you."

She snorts. I'm choosing to interpret that as her missing me, too. Standing up, I take in all of Vendeekta and my heart constricts. Her once glossy coat and healthy spines are now dull and chipped.

She's sick.

The thought rocks me with the force of a punch to the gut. I stagger back and fall. Twigs and stones bite into my butt and palms.

Vendeekta settles down next to me and I lean against her. Her warmth has dimmed with the sickness overtaking her.

She's a dark beast, the traitorous thought whispers in my mind.

I stare up at Vendeekta, and it's true. There are subtle similarities between my beloved companion—my *animtah*—and a dark beast.

One ... two ... three deep breaths. Warm rivers flow down both of my cheeks.

I burrow my hands deep within her fur and close my eyes, sucking in a shuddering breath. My vision goes dark as I close my eyes and center myself, calling to the golden light that lies dormant within me. Pleading with it to show itself.

"There is Promise in the Light," I whisper to myself, calling out to Lady Hevastia for her help.

Grief-laden tears spill down my cheeks. Nothing happens, no light–nothing.

I squeeze my eyes shut and command the light to heed my call. I picture it pooling in my hands and spreading into Vendeekta. A faint warmth spreads down my body and the golden power courses through me. I smile to myself. Vendeekta's fur glows faintly as my golden power flows from my fingers.

Thank you.

The golden light fades, taking its warmth with it. When I open my eyes, Vendeekta stares back at me, her coat once more healthy and glossy.

"Unbelievable. You're using your gift." A mystified voice announces from behind me.

I whirl around, knees cutting into the stones, Fate's Guardian clutched in my fist.

Atrya strides from the flames that always accompany her, beaming with pride.

"It's truly something to finally witness the auror's gift."

I scoff. "Some good it is. I still wasn't able to save my friends."

"I know, and I am deeply saddened by their loss. I wish to comfort you, but that is not why I am here." Atrya replies, her voice nearly devoid of all emotion.

"Then, why are you here?"

Atrya kneels beside me. She reaches out to touch me, then hesitates. "You found the other aurors?"

"Well, not all of them," I correct her.

She nods, a small smile on her face. "They will come to you in their own time."

"We don't–"

She interrupts me. "I know you think there's no time and no other choices, but that's simply not true."

I groan, exasperated. "I was going to say we don't know if the other aurors will join us." I scowl. "And, you're wrong, we are running out of time. My people are *suffering*. I can't stand by and allow it to continue. I need to do something–"

"Eliana, be rational. This is exactly what Lord Vaiccar expects. He wants you to deliver yourself to him."

"Lord Vaiccar? Deliver myself to him? How did you–"

"It didn't take much to assume you had reverted to your original plan to march to the Aceolevia. You seem to always find yourself there when something happens. Taking drastic, reckless measures." Atrya scolds me, "and, you were going to do what, exactly?" She gives me a withering glare. "You have to think of what's best for everyone else."

The memory of my words to Wren and Birvat whispers across my mind.

You must set aside the anger, for now, and think of your people and their needs. They're scared and confused.

While that was weeks ago to Wren and Birvat, I said that to them just yesterday. Portal travel is confusing–Emmerrett was right. I sigh, all the fight leaving my body.

Why can't I take my own advice?

Internally, I scream in anguish and anger over my own carelessness. So blinded by rage and grief, I almost hand-delivered myself to Vaiccar.

"I came to warn you, Eliana." Atrya's voice draws me back to her, and the forest around us. There is no noise, not even the heavy breath of Vendeekta. It's as if the world is holding a collective breath in anticipation of her next words.

"The gods are drawing sides. They have been following Vaiccar's infiltration of Hevastia with depraved interest. There are those among them that would enjoy nothing more than watching Lady Hevastia, and this land, destroyed as vengeance for the death of their brother, Soran. There are also those among them who desire a return to harmony, and the eradication of Vaiccar and his dark influence.

"When you face Vaiccar on the battlefield, you will have the might of gods and their fickle alliances to contend with. You have until the first sign of fall, three months. The war against Vaiccar will wage on your nineteenth birthday."

"How do you know any of this?"

A cold chill courses through me as Atrya's words sink into my very being. An all-consuming fear of this new threat washes over me, cooling my fiery rage.

Less than three months to prepare. It's impossible.

I squeeze my eyes shut, and focus on forcing the onslaught of anxious, self-loathing thoughts from my mind. I shiver against the overwhelming helplessness that's frozen me in fear.

The memory of Hama's still body, hands resting on their chest, and my best friend, surrogate aunt, and a confused Kai all sitting on either side of their body, flutters through my mind. I think of Brynne, my mother, all of the brave villagers who sacrificed themselves to give the rest of us a chance at survival. Only for those survivors to be attacked by a different monster of Vaiccar's making. All of this resets my blood on fire, stoking the rage that burns through me, threatening to burn the world down and take Vaiccar and everything with it.

The vengeful rage which has long burned under my skin sears through me, lighting every fiber of my being on fire. I am an avenging inferno sent to engulf Vaiccar and reduce him to ash. I scream in anger for the pain my people have borne for his machinations, and for the pain yet to be endured to ensure our freedom from his dark grasp.

I am the living fire that will burn through Hevastia, purging it of Vaiccar's darkness. Golden flames travel across my body, setting me alight in a blazing glory.

There is Promise in my Light. I am Eliana Bellaema, the Auror of Hevastia, and I dare the gods themselves to step down from the stars and burn in the inferno of my righteous fury.

Epilogue

THE *SOLARI'S* LIGHT FILTERS into my dank, dark cell–barely penetrating the grime encrusted bars that make a 'window.'

I shift on my 'bed,' a nest of blankets bundled together on the cold stone floor.

The sliver of rock clutched in my fist digs into my fingers as I use it to etch another line into the corner of my cell. Eighty three in total.

My eyes drift closed, and I settle back into the black emptiness that is my existence.

You are nothing, I've taken everything you were. Everything you could be–made it all mine.

My sole memory is the threat I received from the blonde man with cold, dead, green eyes.

He was right about one thing–I have no memory beyond this tiny cell.

The one thing to look forward to is the disgusting meals brought to me by the young acolyte who feeds me and the other prisoner with deep purple skin and white hair.

She is pulled from her cell several times a day. Screaming always pursues–not her screaming–but that of her victims.

Harsh whispers carry over from her cell ... she is speaking to herself, again. The whispers started recently, maybe five screaming sessions ago. It's the simplest way to measure the passing of time.

I place my hands over my ears to block out the noise. I have no interest in what she's doing. I want to rot away in peace and solitude.

Even with my ears covered, I still hear the tell-tale click of a cell door unlocking.

A feminine voice now whispers outside my cell, and I ignore it.

"Hello?" she calls out.

This is a delusion, I've finally lost it.

She whispers something else, but I ignore it.

The door of the dungeon groans open, and the imaginary woman disappears.

The light footsteps of the boy tap down the hall. He always goes to the white-haired girl's cell first.

The food tray clatters to the floor.

"You're not supposed to be free."

"Larsus!" echoes through the dungeon and I flinch. The High Priest.

There are harsh, angry whispers I can't make out, so I shift closer. Eventually, standing on weak, shaky legs from disuse, I manage to shuffle to the bars of my cell.

The white-haired girl brandishes a thin dagger against the startled boy.

"Please," she whispers fervently.

Snap.

My eyes darted to the boy's hand as his fingers pinch to snap again.

That's odd, why is he–

Sparks light in the boy's palm. The white-haired girl jumps back from him.

"Please." The word is now a whimpered plea.

"Follow me," the boy whispers, beckoning her forward and out of the dark cell.

She takes a step and falters, gripping the bars desperately to stand back up.

"It's my foot, I can't walk alone."

Her foot is a mangled stump, unable to bear any weight on its own. No doubt the cruel work of the man with dead, green eyes .

The boy's conflicted. He cannot wield his strange magic and help her walk.

"Take me." My voice is hoarse, barely comprehensible.

Both of them pivot frightened eyes to me, all but forgetting about me until now.

"Please, I'll help her walk."

"He can't be trusted," the boy hisses. "He's one of them. I saw what Lord Vaiccar and High Priest Marius did to him."

The girl shakes her head. "No, he's not. He's a prisoner and a victim, like me."

The boy eyes me warily one more time before turning back to the white-haired girl. "Are you sure?"

She smiles at me. "Yes, Cire can be trusted."

Acknowledgements

To my husband, Brandon, thank you for always cheering me on, and for allowing me to spoil the entire series so that I could have someone to bounce ideas off of. You listen to my rants, hold me when I need a hug, and support me in all the ways I need. Thank you for doing my share of the chores when deadlines were tight. I love you.

To my parents, Bryan and Tricia, thank you for your support. I love you. To my momma, thank you for being a beta reader and the best hype woman. I don't know of anyone else who can sell their daughter's book to a stranger at an airport. To my dad, as soon as the movie for *Prophecy of Blood and Flames* happens, I'll be sure to start on this one!

To my beta readers, Becca, Holly, Jennifer, Kelly, Megan, Morgan, Phoebe, and Stephany, it's been one of the greatest honors of my writing career to connect with each of you as readers and friends. Thank you for the critical feedback, the unending support, and your friendship. Your questions challenged me to see my book from different perspectives. *Children of Gods and Monsters* would not be the book it is today without your feedback.

To father-in-law, Gary, thank you for honoring me by finding a love for reading through my work. I'm so humbled that reading *Prophecy of Blood and Flames* led you to find adventure and enjoyment in literature. Brandon and I have so many recommendations for you, don't worry!

To my mother-in-law, Brenda, we miss you and love you. Thank you for your love and support, I feel it from afar.

To my readers, thank you from the bottom of my heart for reading *Children of Gods and Monsters*. Thank you for supporting an indie author's dreams. It's my sincere hope that you enjoy the story, and that you see at least a little of yourself in my characters.

About the Author

Author Lacie M. Lou is the author of *Prophecy of Blood and Flames*, book one in the *Aurorian Trilogy.* She lives in Madison, Wisconsin with her husband and their two cats. In her free time she enjoys hiking, playing board games, cuddling her cats, and new adventures.

Children of Gods and Monsters drew inspiration from the author's own experiences with self doubt, anxiety, grief over the loss of loved ones, and assault. Additionally, this book is inspired by the authors desire for more diverse representation and normalization of identities in the fantasy genre.

You can follow Lacie on her social media accounts.

Instagram: author_laciemlou

TikTok: author_laciemlou

Facebook: Lacie M. Lou